D1436099

95800000185462

The Piano Room

CLIO VELENTZA

Fairlight Books

First published by Fairlight Books 2021

Fairlight Books
Summertown Pavilion, 18–24 Middle Way, Oxford, OX2 7LG

A CIP catalogue record for this book is available from the British
Library

1 2 3 4 5 6 7 8 9 10

ISBN 978-1-912054-89-3

www.fairlightbooks.com

Printed and bound in Great Britain

Designed by Leo Nickolls

To my parents

Prologue

There was nothing before the snow.

There was nothing before the snow that he cared to remember. Even this was fading.

His feet were bare, and the coldness crunched under them. Sharp aches darted through him, needling into his hands and feet. He couldn't tell yet if the pain was a positive or negative sensation; he had nothing to compare it to.

An inkblot moved through the dazzling whiteness towards him, melting into a familiar shape. He retreated away from it. Its face was a blur. The shape caught hold of him and pulled him forward, and he dug his heels in because this was the one place he knew that he did not want to be.

Heavy presences swept past them, their voices twisted by the wind. He couldn't see anything but he knew they were there, that they had always been there. They, like so many other things he used to know, were fading from his memory.

He couldn't tell if the blizzard was something or nothing. He decided it was Something; because he could still remember Nothing, even if only faintly now, and it hadn't been like this.

Mist escaped his panting mouth. Being dragged through the coldness did not matter; it mattered that the shape that pulled him filled him with dread. It mattered that despite how hard he fought, he couldn't escape its grip. It was solidifying with every step, becoming less abstract, more terrifying. He stumbled and fell and still it hauled him up and dragged him forward.

The towering form of a building emerged in the snow, a blunt thing with blind eyes. He gaped at it. His fear amplified, crushing him. Behind them were those things, those horrible things.

Something moved within the shadows inside the building. There was a person in the window of the building, looking out.

The shape that was pulling him stopped. It smelled the air and glanced around until it focused on the person in the window. It waved at the distant figure, a confident, challenging gesture. The person in the window disappeared.

Still being dragged on by the shape, he stumbled through the last steps.

Then he was left alone outside the building, wet, shivering, lost.

He knocked on the glass.

And then there was the warmth.

And then there was the shame.

And then...

PART I

1990

The entrance to the bar resembled a dark wooden panel pasted arbitrarily on the side of the alley. The light of the menu display was broken and the iron handle regularly stuck. People often thought it was closed until the door opened, and music and tobacco spilled out. Stairs covered in moth-eaten carpet led down to the dining area, a room of low arches and chipped brick, and a narrow stage where a rickety piano hid under faded cloth. The owner was Mrs Soltesz, a religious widow of eclectic taste in wine and questionable taste in food. Portions were large and cheap, and the place was an establishment where grizzled figures in drab raincoats and woollen hats could drink, eat, read the newspaper and smoke for hours on end.

On mornings like this, where clouds hung low above Budapest and a thin wet mist floated, the only commotion came from the routine deliveries of meat and groceries. The grocery boy was hauling crates of produce down the service door steps leading into the kitchen, while a gangly young man with a grave face was following the boy's muddy trail, mopping the tiled floor. His thick black hair, short and unruly, stuck to his temples, and the hands that clutched the mop were rough and clever. A thin gleaming scar traced the length of his cheekbone like a kiss, illuminating the side of his face and giving him an uneven, curious expression. He put the mop aside and set about unloading and putting the groceries away, handling each vegetable with care. Every now and then he would glance up at the piano through the open kitchen door.

The grocery boy caught his gaze. 'No good,' he smiled, gesturing at the instrument while piling up the empty crates. 'They never tune it.'

The man didn't reply, and dragged a sack of potatoes out of the way. The boy shrugged and disappeared through the service entrance. The man pulled out a large basin, filled it with water and sat by the sink. He picked up a knife, twirled it pensively between his fingers, and started to peel. Slowly his eyes became vacant, his mouth relaxed and his mind went quiet.

'Ferdi Molnar!'

Ferdi jumped out of his reverie. A woman appeared in the doorway, still in her overcoat. The strands of hair sticking out from under her hat were damp.

'Ferdi, the meat is sitting on the counter! Why haven't you put it in the fridge?' He hurried to put the meat away, while the woman shook her head at him. 'You'd never hear the end of it if she was here before me.'

Ferdi resumed his seat and picked up another potato. 'Thanks, Erzsi.'

She sighed. He watched as she took off her coat and hat and put on an apron. She rubbed the numbness off her cheeks, leaving them scarlet and warm. 'Did you mop up?'

'Yes.'

She went back into the dining room and he heard her switch on the radio, then the knocking of chairs being turned upright. She started humming the words to the popular song currently being played.

'Erzsi?' he called.

There came a faint 'Yes?' through the scraping wood of the chairs.

'Is the band really not playing here anymore?'

'No. Emilian told me they found a better job.'

'So who is playing these days?'

There was an exasperated sigh. 'I don't know, Ferdi. Nobody.'

'What about the piano?'

'What about it?'

He bit his lip. 'Nobody has played it since I came here.'

'Well, so?' The knocking of the chairs paused. 'Ferdi, spit it out already.'

'It's out of tune,' he said at last.

'What do you know about pianos?'

He shrugged, and kept peeling. 'It's a waste, that's all.'

*

By the evening the bar was full, and the air thick with the scent of food and clothes steaming as the rain dried off them in the warmth. Ferdi's sweat dripped into the hot dishwater and his shirt clung to his back. The crew were dancing round the ovens, ladles and sizzling pans in hand, and above the din Erzsi's voice could be heard dispensing orders from the doorway. When at last it was time for a break Ferdi wrapped himself in his coat and climbed out into the alley. The service door, being further away from the street than the main entrance, opened to a quiet, sheltered spot. There he collapsed on a pile of wet crates.

The abrupt silence calmed him. It had rained in the afternoon, and the evening was fresh and cold. His breath fogged the air. The street was gleaming, peaceful and dim. From somewhere came the roar of cars. Two women with identically brushed hair walked past him, their heels echoing. The strip of sky between the apartment buildings was pink and gold.

Ferdi rubbed his hands and examined them. The palms were hardened; the skin around his knuckles was cracked and spattered with small scars. His nails were cut painfully short, and his fingertips were flat and square. He flexed them a few times. He couldn't remember the last time he had played the piano. It could have been a decade.

He saw his reflection on the dark window of the sporting goods store across the alley: ghostlike, floating, his face lost in a blur. He moved and the ghost moved too. The feeling was familiar. There was a sharp pain in his left wrist, and he pressed it until the pain subsided.

The service door creaked open, and light and steam trickled out. The new head cook, a stocky blonde man, walked out balancing a pack of cigarettes on a cup of coffee. He nodded at Ferdi, put the cup on the crates and lit a cigarette with a mint-green windproof lighter. He offered him one and Ferdi took it, noticing a faded tattoo between the man's thumb and index finger. The cigarette paper was warm from the coffee vapours. It tasted very new, almost green.

The cook stubbed out the rest of his cigarette and sipped his coffee. 'Not really my break,' he sighed. 'I just needed a smoke. All that tobacco coming from the dining room, it makes a man weak. One thing I hate about kitchen jobs, you can't smoke.'

Ferdi nodded. The cook waved a fly away with his thick arm, releasing the smell of fried oil. 'What's your name again?'

'Molnar. Ferdi Molnar.'

The cook sized him up. 'I'm Dieter.'

'A German name?'

'Yes.'

'You speak Hungarian well.'

'My grandmother was from around here. Made the best walnut cream cake you'd ever tasted.' Dieter drank again, his face crimson from the scalding beverage.

Ferdi smoked with no particular pleasure. He liked the cook well enough from the couple of words they'd exchanged in the kitchen, and his cheery disposition was pleasant. Dieter chatted on, his sandy hair illuminating them both like a street lamp.

'It's like hell in there. Hot and cramped and it stinks.'

Ferdi took one last uncertain puff, filling his lungs until they prickled and burned, and threw the butt on the wet ground. 'It's not too bad.'

'I'm glad I'm here, don't get me wrong. But I've had my share of odd jobs and kitchens is still the one I hate the most. Ask me where I learned how to cook.'

Ferdi almost smiled. 'Where?'

Dieter winked. 'If I told you I'd have to kill you.'

They heard chatter, and a group of laughing young men and women appeared further down the alleyway. The group took no notice of them and stepped into the bar. One of the boys was wearing a crisp suit and a bowtie.

'Music students. This city is filled with them. My neighbour is learning the bassoon, so I might kill him one day.' Dieter chuckled, and his whole body shook. 'Do you play? No, you're the bookish type. I know them when I see them. You like to read, don't you?'

'I do. I also play the piano,' Ferdi said, rubbing his wrist again.

'Really? You don't look like a music student.'

'I'm not.'

'What are you then? A teacher? An artist? No dishwasher is ever just a dishwasher.'

Ferdi glanced at the ghostly reflection floating in the dark window of the sporting goods store again. He shrugged and didn't reply. Dieter downed his coffee.

'Well, good talking to you, Molnar, whatever you are.' He turned to leave, and paused at the door. 'Do you know Erzsi? The head waitress? I've seen you two talk.'

'Not much. We just work the same shift.'

Dieter's face fell for a moment. He took his cook's cap from his pocket and put it on: it was too small for him and made him look childlike. He grinned. 'All right. See you in hell, Molnar.'

Then he laughed, pleased with his joke, and disappeared.

Ferdi walked home a little drunk that night, pressing his chest to smother the hiccups. He had left right when the revelry was reaching its peak, and Mrs Soltesz had grabbed him and sat him down next to her. She had poured him wine and refilled his glass until his eyes swam and all he saw was the swirling violet smoke. He wasn't used to alcohol, and now and then he stumbled on the wet pavement. He kept hearing Dieter's words, circling around his head like birds looking to perch. *See you in hell. See you in hell. See you in hell.*

He made a detour and headed towards the Danube to clear his head. The black river was bloated with rain, curving and ready to burst. He collapsed on a bench, inhaling air scented with gasoline. Sky and water were flecked with the amber of street lamps and stars. A boat restaurant was anchored close by, and from its bright deck came a cheerful din. The water swelled gently. He watched it until his eyelids drooped.

He woke up with a start. A heavy hand was on his shoulder.

'Hey, you. You can't sleep here.'

Ferdi rubbed his eyes. The hand retreated. 'I was on my way home,' he mumbled. He turned to look but there was nobody. Ferdi shuddered, wrapped his coat tighter around himself and sneezed. His hair and neck were wet: it must have drizzled while he was asleep. The music from the boat restaurant had died down. A waitress passed him while taking out the rubbish, and glanced at him with curiosity. When Ferdi met her gaze she hurried to look away.

See you in hell, Molnar.

Ferdi scratched his scar, picked himself up and walked along the embankment, taking his time. His mind was rejuvenated with sleep and he relished the river air against his clammy skin, the comfort of the shoddy shoes on his tired feet. It was a beautiful night, soft, as if it could be moulded by a skilful hand into pleasant shapes. He trapped gusts of wind in his mouth and sucked at them. They had the vague alcoholic taste of rotting fruit.

He thought of Sandor at that moment, with a tightening of the stomach and a sinking of the heart.

He thought of the perpetual darkness of the gun room at the Esterhazy manor, the damp walls, the rough towel drenched in icy water. The thirst, the hunger, the silence. Skulking against the wall of the house, jumping through the window into the warm piano room. The glossy piano lid, the crisp hiss of the music sheets. The taste of milk.

Sandor towering above him, his knuckles dusted with blood.

Dragging an impossibly heavy body through the forest, with twigs stabbing at his sides.

The images dissolved. Ferdi focused on the reflections dancing on the wet ground, following the ripples of the blues and the oranges. He began to translate the lights into a melody, adding or shedding a note here and there, until his stroll became a distracted lullaby. He was hungry, and he needed to shower. The melody kept playing in his mind, and his fingers danced inside the pockets of his coat.

He dreamt of the Esterhazy mansion that night. It was crumbling, silent. Books were rotting on shelves. Cupboards sat agape, their contents caked with dust. Unmade beds, windows dark with dirt, peeling wallpaper streaked with mould. The piano's innards showing, its chords silent like tendons. And the keys broken and immobilised with dirt, sticking out and abandoned mid-song, still pressing down a note into infinity.

*

It was blissful to have a routine: the creaking of the water pipes in the morning, the sound of water boiling in the pot, the slice of bread and jam washed down with instant coffee. Finding the communal lavatory down the corridor from his room clean, misty with the eye-watering smell of bleach. He was off just as the city was beginning to stir, and he could glance at the wilting magazines at the newspaper stands, dodge the sweepers' brooms and peek into the bread-laden trucks.

A tram line stopped close to the bar, but he only took it when there was rain or snow: Ferdi preferred walking. He liked to watch people go about their morning while the crisp air stung his skin, and the blood thumped reassuringly in his limbs. He would open the bar alone before the deliveries began and Erzsi arrived, enjoying the feel of this darkness that was saturated with alcohol and tobacco. As Ferdi would then set about his chores, he would be accompanied by the silent reflections of himself on the floor and the varnished counters.

On that day the butcher's assistant was one Ferdi had never seen before: a densely built teenager, nineteen or twenty perhaps, with close-cropped hair and a thin moustache. A flimsy Orthodox cross slipped out from his collar when he leaned in to let the parcel fall from his shoulder. Ferdi watched both boy and meat with fascination. There was something horribly alive about the animal leg, still intact to the hoof, and as the boy turned it over it seemed about to kick. The tip of the boy's left ear was stained with blood.

The boy's hands moved fast, separating and counting the cuts. The skin of the pig, lined with white fat, was the same hue as the arm that had handled it. The fingers left deep prints on its flesh and Ferdi had the same sensation of being prodded. He imagined his mind bearing the same marks, and within the round indentations a residue of human contact left, like the oils of a fingertip. The boy wiped his hands on his apron, saw Ferdi watching and grinned, revealing a row of sharp pearly teeth. Ferdi wrapped the meat again and carried it to the fridge, careful not to touch any part of the animal.

There was still an hour of solitude left. Ferdi stepped into the dining room. On the stage, the cloth draped over the piano seemed to be billowing softly. He walked up to it, paused and then pulled it off. The wood was lustrous and amplified the low light, sending reddish puddles of it around the brick walls. Ferdi was relieved: he had half expected the piano to be derelict and useless like the instrument in his dream. He opened the lid. The hinges were stiff with rust, and the keys were covered with a strip of green felt older than the piano itself. On it the words *Dieu vous garde* were stitched in yellow thread, with the faint unevenness of something handmade.

Ferdi touched the keys and felt their stiffness. He pressed down a chord, and the echo jumbled around the room. There was a grainy quality to it, as if someone had brushed their nail through the teeth of a comb. As his fingers traced the keys he felt the same erratic indentations forming in him by this touch, just as he had when the butcher's boy had been poking the fresh meat.

He played a short tune. The sound was coarse. He flexed his hand once more and contemplated it, then tried a different tune: a swirling piece from a folk song. The twang of the lax chords enriched the melody with a strange vivacity. Ferdi smiled, repeated the tune and filled it up with gusto, until the cacophony worsened and reduced the music to a rattle. He straightened his back and gave the piano a satisfied look. A chuckle escaped him.

'I'll be damned! You've never laughed before.'

Erzsi was standing at the doorway, dripping with rain. She applauded.

Ferdi drew back. 'I didn't hear you come in.'

'I didn't know you could play. That's what all this was about yesterday?'

Ferdi replaced the cloth on the keys, shut the lid and pulled the cover into place. He felt Erzsi step closer. The bar's garlicky smell had seeped into her clothes. 'Don't be embarrassed, Ferdi,' she said.

'Please don't tell anyone about it,' he replied and fled into the kitchen, re-emerging with his apron on.

*

Dieter seemed to have decided in the meantime that now he and Ferdi were perfect friends. Whenever their eyes met he gave him a grin or a wink. Once he slapped his shoulder to congratulate him on the fast removal of a brimming pot, and the blow made Ferdi's bones clatter. The tall, sandy-haired cook was more heavyset than excessively muscular, but seemed to have no control over his strength. Glasses broke, towels ripped and toes were crushed in his wake, but his goulash was the finest that had ever been served in that questionable establishment.

When Ferdi stepped out for his break he found Dieter already there.

'I heard you met Petar today,' the cook said, while the coffee worked its way into their system. 'I went over to take a look at their meat and met him. Looks clueless, doesn't he? But he gives us the best cuts, and Holy Mother has never been happier.'

'The boy from the butcher?'

'Yes, he's Yugoslavian. Have you seen his cross? Apparently they drink wine with their communion. If I'd known that I'd have become an Orthodox years ago! Good kid. I took him out since he's new here, and he ate, drank and bled me dry. Then I took him to one of those nice places full of university girls and he clammed up like a schoolboy.'

The service door creaked open and Erzsi's sweaty head appeared, reflecting the copper light of the street lamps. 'Ferdi, can you spare a minute? I need to fill the carafes and everyone's busy.'

Ferdi glanced at Dieter, who was contemplating his coffee dregs. 'Sure.'

She disappeared. Ferdi finished his coffee and got up, stretched his legs, and was met with Dieter's sheepish grin.

*

When work was finished and Ferdi returned home, the caretaker had closed up and retired to his radio, so Ferdi had to push the heavy door with his shoulder to slip into the reception corridor and through to the open courtyard of his apartment building. This small rectangular atrium got little sunlight and the ground was perpetually green and slimy, with a puddle of stale rainwater. As Ferdi crossed it and climbed the open stairway a couple of cockroaches darted away from him, and the smell of old cooking oil clung to the back of his throat.

He took out his keys and heard a familiar cough in the darkness. A sliver of light fell on him and widened as someone opened a door into the hallway.

'Good evening, Miss Ilona,' he said.

She peered back at him. Her long grey hair was side-plaited and fell over her flannel dressing gown. From her apartment came the smell of roasted peppers. 'Mr Molnar! I thought you might be a thief. It's late.'

'It's only half past eight. Did you have a nice day?' She shot him a suspicious look and nodded. 'Well, goodnight then.'

He was about to close the door when he saw her step out. She put two nicotine-stained fingers in the pocket of her dressing gown and took out an envelope. 'This came for you. Your box in the front hall is unmarked, so the postman threw it in mine. You should fix that.'

She handed it to him and he took it with the tips of his fingers. He glanced at it and then at Miss Ilona's amused face.

'What do I do with it?'

The corner of her mouth twitched. 'Open it, I hope. Goodnight, Mr Molnar.'

She shuffled back inside. Ferdi placed the envelope on the table that took up most of his little room. There was no return address. He hung his coat behind the door and put on water to boil for tea. The kitchen consisted only of the small stove, a tiny sink, a cabinet and a stumpy fridge, along with a green stain on the ceiling from the lack of ventilation. The rest of the furniture was just as sparse: a single bed in the far corner, a wooden table with mismatched chairs and a wardrobe. A deep window with double panels over-looked the atrium.

Ferdi sat at the table, poured his tea and opened the letter. There was only one page, written in a steady, upright hand:

Dear Mr Molnar,

    I have been informed that you reside peacefully and unob-trusively at this address, to my great pleasure and surprise after Sandor's vanishing, and you having disappeared from my sight for so many years. I am very curious to hear from you. What would you say to us meeting and exchanging stories over a pleasant cup of coffee? On the evening of the 30th of October I will be waiting for you at the café across the street from the Opera House, at 9pm.

    Do come.

Until then, I remain,
Your oldest friend.

There was no signature. Ferdi's first thought was that he would have to get a calendar. His left hand began to shake uncontrollably. He clenched his fist and clutched the hot mug until the tremors subsided.

*

Petar was the first person he met the next day. When Ferdi asked him about the date the boy told him it was the twentieth. In his bloody butcher's coat and that moustache he looked like a horror film poster.

'Did you miss your girlfriend's birthday?' he grinned.

Ferdi shook his head and put the parcels away. He calculated the time he had left until the meeting at the café, and realised he would be working; he would have to switch his day off with someone. Behind him Petar was washing his hands, humming a pop song. On his right forearm was the tattoo of a ram skull. When he saw Ferdi looking he flexed his muscles.

'Fearless,' he bragged.

Ferdi paused. 'Can I ask you a question?'

'Fire away.'

'What would you do if you only had ten days left to live?'

Petar blushed to the roots of his bristly hair. He dried his hands on his coat, avoiding Ferdi's eyes, and stood silent for a while. 'I'd forget about the consequences,' he said at last. He walked out and slammed the door behind him.

Ferdi thought the shock of the letter would numb him, but he went on with his work with newfound alertness. He couldn't understand why he wasn't simply quitting, packing his few possessions and leaving the city. It struck him that he didn't fear much for his life: surely it was too unimportant for anyone to hold it hostage.

Shuddering despite the heat from the stoves, he allowed the fragmented memories of the snowstorm to pass through his mind undisturbed, like some dangerous animal. The memory was blurred, but still so potent that he could forget to breathe.

'Hey, Molnar, where's your mind?'

Someone walked into him and Ferdi huddled at his post. He sank his hands into the dirty water where the pots soaked. The sheen of filth and grease on the water had a soothing, grounding effect, and the rough wire brush diverted his focus to his fingers. As he squinted through wafts of steam he was aware of his scar, stretching the skin under his eye.

And where had Sandor disappeared to, all those years? They hadn't lain eyes on each other for such a long time. At times Ferdi felt an inexplicable pang of incompleteness without him around. He dreamt about him occasionally, about the two of them young and sitting in the piano room as they used to. In those dreams Sandor was kind and friendly, and he watched Ferdi with pride from the side of the piano. But the guilty sweetness the dreams would bring made waking up to the harsh reality of Sandor's cruelty even worse. On those mornings Ferdi's loneliness was so pervasive it made his bones ache.

The scar was smarting again, and his throat had closed. Ferdi breathed deep and counted each scrub until all the pots were clean.

Dieter came over. 'You get off work around seven, don't you, Molnar?'

'Usually.'

'Let's go for a beer tomorrow. It's my day off.'

'All right.'

'I'll pick you up after your shift. Do you have a car?'

'No, I don't drive.'

'Somewhere close, then. By the way...' Dieter glanced nervously at the door leading to the dining room.

Ferdi caught his look. 'You can ask Erzsi yourself,' he said.

Dieter deflated a little. The sight amused Ferdi. 'You know her better,' Dieter complained. 'Ask her. You'd be there too, I mean. Like friends.'

Ferdi shook his head. 'Incredible.'

'What?'

'That someone so big can hide behind me.'

Dieter turned pink. He began to laugh, leaned in and gave Ferdi one of his fearsome slaps on the back. 'You're right, Molnar! I'm sorry. Let's just go the two of us. I'll figure something out.'

Ferdi rubbed his aching shoulder. He liked Erzsi, and he liked Dieter. And it was unprecedented being involved in other people's lives.

'I'll ask her, if you're decent about it.'

'I'm not half as decent as you're turning out to be.'

Ferdi found Erzsi in the dining room, piling plates on her arms with the apparent improbability of a magician's act. Her freckled face was glistening. She didn't notice him until he spoke.

'Do you have any plans tomorrow night?'

She glanced up in alarm. 'No, why?' One of the plates teetered on her wrist.

'Dieter and I are going out after work, if you'd like to come along.'

She exhaled. 'Oh, all right. Sounds nice.'

Ferdi returned to his post, and caught Dieter watching him before hurrying back to his frying pan.

Later that night Ferdi watched the cars pass on the far bank of the river, their headlights blinking like fireflies. Bicycles sped past him. A group of girls dressed for a night out were sitting on the ledge and laughing, and as Ferdi passed they paused and stared. Ferdi was conscious of the cooking smells clinging onto him, of his old coat and messy hair. He tried to slow down his breathing. It was a busy night, perhaps a Friday or a Saturday. He could only remember that it was the twentieth, and that he had ten days left.

What was it that Petar had said?

I'd forget about the consequences.

*

The next day, there wasn't much Ferdi could do to look presentable: he combed his hair, put a sweater over his stained T-shirt and brushed his jeans with a wet towel. Last of all, he took off the signet ring that hung round his neck and put it back on his finger. It was made for a bigger man, and sat a little loose on him. He dusted its green bloodstone on his sleeve and the crimson flecks gleamed cheerily. The cold weight of it on his hand gave him confidence.

Stepping out he saw Erzsi in the ladies' bathroom, applying her brown lipstick with care. Her hair, usually tied up for work, fell thick and wavy round her neck. She glanced at him through a frizzy strand and smiled. Dieter was waiting for them by the service door, wrapped in a blue pea coat that solidified him into the shape of a wardrobe. He had left his hat behind to preserve his neatly combed hair, which shone. He flashed them both a wide smile and they set out together.

'You look pretty,' Dieter blurted out at Erzsi.

She smiled, tying her scarf. 'Not as pretty as Ferdi. Did you see the ring he's wearing?'

As he turned his back to her to look, Erzsi yawned and rubbed her eyes. When she saw Ferdi looking her way, she brought her finger to her lips.

'Molnar, what's that about a ring?'

'Nothing.'

'Oh, boy. Did you find that at the flea market?'

Ferdi held up his hand into the light and the bloodstone shone. 'It's a family heirloom,' he said.

'Is that a crest?'

Ferdi glanced at the Esterhazy coat of arms and gave the ring a couple of nervous turns.

'I've seen you make that gesture many times,' said Erzsi. 'I don't think you know you're doing it. My grandmother used to turn her wedding ring just like that.'

Dieter laughed. 'I know, there's something about Molnar that smacks of old folks.'

They reached a shiny new bar. Boys and girls danced lazily and gathered in clusters, where hands glided casually to rest on secret spots. Dieter guided them to a table and they sat under a blue light that made their faces seem two-dimensional. On the wall above Erzsi's head was a mural of flying fish. The three of them ordered beer, and Ferdi sat so that he could look at the dancers. The music was deafening. He didn't notice anyone talking to him until he felt Erzsi's hand on his own.

'It's a bit much,' she shouted, and he nodded. They watched for a while, as young men and women collided drunkenly like boats in the harbour. Several couples were kissing where they stood; a group of boys were shouting and making obscene gestures; a girl was dancing alone to the pop song; another girl slapped a man who had put his hand where he shouldn't.

Ferdi turned towards Dieter and Erzsi. They were discussing something inaudible, absorbed in one another. Their beers sat almost untouched. He sipped his own and, having little else to do, it went down fast. He got up and sat against the counter, feeling no hurry to return to the table. He looked up and for a moment terror rushed though him before he realised that he was standing across from a mirror. He turned his back to it and drank. Dieter and Erzsi were still talking, sitting so close that their shoulders touched. Ferdi finished his third or fourth bottle.

Across the room someone was watching him. Ferdi thought he recognised the familiar face through the shifting lights. Could it be? How long had Ferdi been sitting there drinking, being watched? The face disappeared in the crowd. Someone close to him blew out cigarette smoke and his vision blurred. He slipped down from his stool and tried to cross the dance floor, while elbows hit him from all sides and warm bodies pressed against his. He pushed through, stumbled towards the other tables and fell against one where two young women were sitting. One of them reached out and caught him. She asked if he was feeling all right and he nodded, trying to regain his balance.

'I thought I saw someone,' he said, but his voice was drowned in the noise.

The woman eased Ferdi onto a chair while her friend laughed. His rescuer put her glass of water in front of him. The familiar face appeared once more across the room, among the people watching the dancers. Ferdi tried to focus on it, but it was proving difficult. The face smiled and vanished again. He leaned towards his hosts. 'Did you see it? Did you see the man watching me?'

The woman who was laughing ruffled her permed hair. 'Sure, darling.'

A shadow fell on the table and Ferdi twitched. Dieter's sandy head glowed above them. He put a hand on Ferdi's shoulder. 'Has he been bothering you, ladies?'

The girls laughed. Dieter pulled Ferdi to his feet. 'Sorry, Molnar. We abandoned you.'

Erzsi appeared, carrying his coat. 'Why don't we go somewhere else?'

Ferdi rubbed his eyes, and followed them outside. The cold cleared the fog from his brain. As they walked away he glanced back, but the only people outside the bar were a young girl crying in her friend's arms.

Erzsi turned back at him and said, 'See you in hell, Ferdi.'

He stumbled. 'What?'

'I said, you look like hell. Do you need to vomit?'

'I'm okay.'

'Should we take the tram?'

Erzsi put a hand on Dieter's arm. 'It may be better for him if we walk. Not too far though.'

Dieter agreed. His flustered manner was gone, and Ferdi wondered at this newfound intimacy.

Eventually Ferdi vomited, and it made him feel better. His body shook with alertness, hollow and strong. He felt aware of the entirety of his skin. *Let him come*, he thought. *If it was really Sandor just now, then let him come and try what he wants. I'll fight. I'll fight until I'm dead.*

His eyes were burning. He counted with his fingers. Nine days left. He hadn't seen the man in the tuxedo since he had dragged Ferdi through the blizzard all the way to the Esterhazy manor, all those years ago. And now he was hallucinating visions of Sandor. The wind brought the scents of Erzsi and Dieter as they walked quietly ahead of him, touching elbows. Onions, cigarette smoke, hairspray, green soap. He could disappear right now. They would never know. He could turn into that alley and never look back, and that would be that.

You're a monster, Ferdi.

He turned his ring, one, two, three, four times. A fine, elegant signet ring bound in silver, bearing the same coat of arms imprinted on the custom-made music notebook he carried round.

He kept turning – one, two, three, four; one, two, three, four – but Sandor's voice kept returning.

I wish you never existed.

I know, thought Ferdi.

He was terrified that Dieter and Erzsi would glance back and see the tears in his eyes. One, two, three, four turns.

It had been a beautiful spring morning when he had taken the ring, when he had woken up in Sandor's bedroom. Even though the night had been spent digging with his hands he had hardly slept, because the bed had been so much softer than what he was used to. So he had sat, wrapped in a blanket. He had watched the sun peek between the treetops, a bloody, shapeless chunk of light. He had been consumed with the desire to keep a memento of that morning, a reminder that it had been real, but he hadn't dared take anything from Sandor's room. When the noises down the corridor had died down, he had tiptoed to the master bedroom. Salomon and Karolina's bed was still unmade and warm. He had found the ring with the green bloodstone in a writing desk drawer. He had put it in his pocket and only then noticed the filthy state of his fingers. The nails were chipped, lined with dirt and blood.

'This looks nice. Look, Ferdi, they have a band!'

'Molnar?'

Ferdi looked up from his hands, where he could still see the blood. He glanced round, recognising the street. They were close to his home. The place Erzsi was talking about was an open door down a flight of stairs, from where the din of a cheerful violin floated out into the wet night. He heard himself reply that yes, it looked nice, and he followed them down the stairs.

This time they sat him between them, but there was no danger of anyone disappearing in here: the room was wide, low and softly lit, with only a few patrons. Onstage a middle-aged woman was playing the violin, next to a man at the cimbalom. They had that vaguely similar look of people married to each other a long time. Behind them was a covered piano. Ferdi let his body relax. On the violinist's long dress a snake made of green sequins circled her legs, and when she saw him looking at it, she winked. The wine was a light red, and Ferdi finished a glass without noticing. Erzsi and Dieter were getting silly telling work stories, and soon he too was sharing his own in a low, even voice that betrayed intoxication only with its long pauses.

The music ended and everyone applauded. Dieter was unable to keep the volume of his voice under control, and his words echoed round the stone arches of the room. The glasses rattled. Erzsi was laughing until her eyes streamed, and Ferdi let himself be swept along in the merriment. A full bottle of wine magically substituted the empty one, and a cheese-and-sausage plate manifested in front of them.

The lights were lowered, more patrons arrived and then somehow the violinist and the grizzled cimbalom player were sitting with them and partaking of their wine. He was a former professor of musicology and she a retired biologist, now touring the country at her leisure. They later returned to the stage and by the third bottle the three of them were giving standing ovations. The owner sent over some complimentary cherry brandy, which ate away at the last of their inhibitions, and soon Dieter had met everybody in the bar and people were bringing in chairs. Now everyone was one rowdy company, and Erzsi's hair was beyond salvation.

Eventually the performers retired and joined the assembly, and people started arguing about what music to put on. Some complained that they wanted to hear more live music, and the argument was taken up. Then Erzsi rose from her nook under Dieter's arm and nominated Ferdi. All eyes turned to him.

Ferdi's mind was gone in a reckless, wine-induced euphoria. He barely offered a half-hearted protest before standing up. He took a moment to steady himself while everyone laughed, and then walked onto the stage. He pulled off the cover of the piano in one tug, like a magician. There was a burst of applause and some more laughter as there was no piano stool and he had to bring a chair. He opened the lid, threw away the red felt covering the keys and sat.

And then, Ferdi's mind went utterly silent.

The tip of his finger landed on the cold ivory key and muted the world. There was nobody else in the room. The first note wormed itself into the base of his spine. His reflection in the varnish of the piano blinked, no longer terrifying. He fished from his memory a piece he was putting together during his walks. It was unfinished, but this quiet, still world wasn't urgent. Time did not matter.

Ferdi straightened his back and started playing. He was climbing up a steep mountainside while the air thinned and icy blades of grass collapsed under his heels, and he was reaching ever higher spots while grasslands unfolded far beneath. Then he was sitting by the shore of a still lake, wetting his toes while mist rippled on the surface. He didn't know how he could feel these things; he had never been to a mountain or a lake.

Gradually, the world began to exist again. The room behind him was eerily peaceful. There were a few whispers. He couldn't see what was happening, and didn't care. His hands were moving on their own. Sweat stung his eyes.

Images and sensations burst through. The cold glass against his outstretched palm as he pushed open a window. The mirror with the two identical faces. The dark woods. Dragging a warm mass through the undergrowth, thorns stabbing at him, nettles stinging his fingers – and the man's body weighing Ferdi down, its head lolling forward, exposing the crushed skull...

The melody disappeared, Ferdi's hands floundered and the sound was destroyed. He jumped to his feet, pushing the chair back, and it rolled off the stage with a crash.

There was a moment of silence, and then everyone started applauding. Ferdi looked at them without seeing. Astonishment sank in as the low ceiling reverberated with cheers. Erzsi's eyes were red, and Dieter sat unusually quiet. Hands led Ferdi back to his seat, patting him on the back, filling his glass. Now that the rush was leaving him, drunkenness flooded back. In an instant his head was throbbing again.

'Molnar, you sly bastard!' Dieter's hand fell on Ferdi's shoulder like a breezeblock. 'You never said you were bloody Mozart! What are you doing peeling potatoes and washing Holy Mother's greasy pots?'

Ferdi rubbed his eyes. The green snake uncoiled as the violinist appeared next to him, and took his hand.

'What was that piece you just played?'

He tried to think. 'I'm not sure.' The memory of the crushed head resurfaced and he tried to take deep breaths. The cimbalom player stared at him.

'Was it yours? What else can you play?'

Ferdi nodded absent-mindedly, without taking in his words. His body was too heavy. He shrank and shrank until he was curled up on the chair. People shifted around him. He smelled Erzsi's hairspray. 'We should be going,' she was telling them.

More murmurs and goodbyes, more hands patting him on the back. Erzsi helped him stand up and put his coat on, and Dieter hauled him up the stairs. It was pitch black outside, and he had no idea where he was. Someone tied his scarf for him.

'Come on, Mozart. Time for bed.'

*

The sunlight woke him up. It sent an instinctive jolt of dread through his body and he groped for the alarm clock. He was late for work.

Ferdi sat up with a groan. Something heavy was rolling round inside his head, knocking against his skull whenever he moved. He waited for the room to stop swaying and got up. He saw that he was still in last night's clothes, reeking of wine and cigarette smoke. His shoes were placed neatly by the bed. There was a note on the table, written on a paper napkin.

Good morning, Mozart!

Don't worry about work. Erzsi will open up and you can make it up to her sometime. Drink lots of water. It was fun tonight! You'll probably regret it in the morning.

Dieter

Ferdi yawned, and tried to piece together last night's events. There was a bar with blue lights. There was a girl holding him up. There was a restaurant, there was wine, the jingle of a cimbalom. A snake woman. Then? He rubbed his unshaven face, drank some water, put some more on to boil for coffee. Then it struck him. He had been exposed. He had walked up on a stage in front of people, and he had played the piano. One of his own pieces, no less. Embarrassment rose in him and for a crazy moment he considered running away instead of having to hear Dieter calling him 'Mozart' again.

When he stepped out into the hallway on his way to the bathroom he came face to face with Miss Ilona, who hovered by her front door, smoking a cigarette. In the daylight she was almost mellow. She smirked at him.

'Someone had a late night.'

'Good morning, Miss Ilona.'

'Your friends woke me up when they were carrying you upstairs.'

'I'm sorry about that.'

'It's all right. The big German fellow offered me a smoke.'

He realised that she wanted to tell him something more and waited, shivering in his T-shirt, his towel slung over his shoulder.

'You didn't fix your mailbox, Mr Molnar.' She dug round her pocket and his heart jumped, but she only took out a handkerchief and wiped her nose with it.

'I'll get on it. Nothing else came for me?'

'No. But someone rang for you.'

'Rang?'

'At the caretaker's desk, this morning. You should get a phone line, if you can.'

'What did they say?'

'Oh, Mr Polyak said they asked for you, but he thought you were out. It was this morning.'

'Did they leave a name?'

She extinguished her cigarette in a plastic cup on the floor and shook her head.

*

He arrived at work just as Petar was parking the truck. Erzsi was setting up the dining room. The boy threw him a strange look but said nothing. Ferdi held the door open and Petar lingered, undecided, then walked past him with a scowl. Ferdi waited until the boy climbed out again.

'Did I upset you the other day?'

Petar scoffed and threw a pack of wrapped pork over his shoulder. This time, his left ear and the hair on his temple were both lightly coated with dried animal blood. Ferdi remained standing by the entrance so Petar had to walk round him.

'You're a funny one,' he muttered.

That night as he walked home, exhausted, lights caught his eye – light beams from the glass loft of an abandoned art-nouveau building by the riverside, flashing in arbitrary motions and drawing whirling patterns in the night fog. Ferdi stood and watched, yawning. His mind slowly emptied. Time relaxed and swashed against his feet like water. When he blinked and resurfaced, he had no idea how long he had been there. The lights had disappeared. There was a strange echo in his ears, as if someone had called his name, and he peered into the night. A shadow stood across the street, merging against a wall. Ferdi couldn't see but sensed that he was being watched. He shifted a little, and the figure moved too.

They stared at each other. Ferdi stood up slowly, and the figure stepped back. He moved forward to cross the street but a couple of cars passed, and when he looked again the figure had disappeared.

He tightened his scarf and headed home, keeping his gaze straight ahead. People passed him, taking no interest. The fog made his eyes smart. Through the night hum he could make out the sound of the footsteps around him: of high heels, of worn rubber soles and crisp new shoes; purposeful or lazy, aimless, shuffling, scraping, hurried, uneven, limping. And among them the slow, long paces of quiet soles, whose rhythm matched his own.

He slowed down. The footsteps slowed too. He turned, pretending to check the name of the street, and something in the corner of his eye darted away. He kept walking. When he finally arrived home and frantically unlocked the front door, the street behind him was empty.

1979

Sandor, about to turn eighteen, only child and heir to the Esterhazy name and fortune, was lying on his back on the frozen grass thinking about his family.

The musical Esterhazys had emerged from anonymity a few generations back with the sheer force of their talent. And even before that, Sandor guessed, before the concert halls and the operas and the newspaper clippings, his ancestors had still made their way through the world with music. He had vivid images of them: grizzled gentlemen performing at fairs and feasts, malnourished sons delivering violin masterpieces on wet street corners, broad-hipped daughters singing for neighbours' dances. A long line of musicians, dating, for all he knew, back to Roman times.

His father, Salomon, was the quintessence of the family name: a small man with an egg-shaped skull and kindly dark eyes with a downward slant reminiscent of an elderly dog. His thinning hair was always carefully combed round a shiny bald patch, and a pair of slim, gold-rimmed glasses gave him the appearance of a shopkeeper or bank manager. As a child Sandor harboured suspicions that his father would sneak off at night to work a distinguished desk job. The shiny tuxedos, the white silk scarves, the soft leather gloves and the fur-trimmed coats he donned as battle gear before a concert looked odd on him. Still, Salomon Esterhazy always pulled off the splendid outfits and the civil exchanges, and had the skill of making a glass of wine last the night. A modest, laconic man who, sitting in front of a piano, would transform into a god.

Sandor picked up a blade of grass and stretched it in the space between his joined thumbs. It was sticky and coarse like a cat's tongue. He brought it to his lips and whistled. The sound escaped into the shadows, bounced off the tree trunks and vanished. An unseen bird caught it and trilled a response. He whistled again and the bird replied with a few more notes to its song. He attempted to imitate it, but the sound was stumbling, awkward. There was a flapping of wings followed by silence. Sandor put the grass blade between his teeth and crushed it, savouring its bitterness. He closed his eyes, and inhaled deeply. The weather matched his mood: a heavy autumnal breathlessness underlined with bursts of unseasonable warmth.

The image of his father's embroidered slippers floated into Sandor's mind. Burgundy and shiny with decades of use, they sat in the hallway next to his own. Sandor's slippers were perpetually stiff and new to fit his growing feet, and the contrast would give him the uncomfortable feeling of being a guest in the house. He had to wear the slippers as soon as he returned home, leaving his muddy shoes back to be cleaned, and as everyone else in the household floated by him in a soft rustle of old soles he had to self-consciously clomp round. One could always tell if a family member was in or out of the house by glancing at the neat row of slippers. There was only one exception to this rule, and that was when Salomon was in the piano room.

At those times, Salomon would take off his slippers and laboriously put on freshly brushed shoes, his face reddening as he bent over. Then he would walk to the piano room and the sound of his heels on the hardwood floor would echo round the mansion, warning everyone to carry on in respectful silence. The ritual inspired awe in little Sandor, who, if he saw his father's slippers in the hallway but his coat and hat still on their peg, would shudder with excitement. Something particularly magical and secret always seemed to be happening in the piano room, when the doors were shut and nobody was allowed inside.

His first piano lessons: a younger Salomon, of a slightly fuller head of hair, and a toddler Sandor sharing the same seat. Pudgy fingers and a frown of concentration. Child Sandor, with sagging socks, bony knees and black hair peaking to a maximum of messiness, allowed to wear slippers as his feet still couldn't reach the pedals. Swaying his legs and trying hard, with the old stool now starting to creak ominously. Then on his ninth birthday two seats side by side, brand new and cushioned, with knobs to adjust the height: gifts from a piano maker friend. Sandor had highly mistrusted these and refused to sit on them, until the old piano seat had to be thrown away.

And what about Karolina? Sandor scowled at the sky as drifting clouds made the brief winter sunlight disappear. He loved his mother, more easily now that he had taken off into the garden alone. A tall, powerful, good-humoured woman, her back straight as a bowstring; wide shoulders, dark blonde hair and a square face all freckles and mouth. Her mezzo soprano voice made the ground quiver, and in her opera gown she seemed vast and omnipotent. They were great friends when Sandor was a child. She was always indulgent of him, and liked to read to him every night before sleep. But their characters had proved too much alike to get on well as he had grown into a short-tempered adolescent. It was impossible now for them to carry on a conversation without fighting – and especially since Karolina was resolute that her son should enrol in the Academy of Music immediately after graduation.

Blood rose to his face. The *Academy*. He was not good enough for it. He knew they were aware of it, and yet they still hoped. But Sandor was talentless. There was no spirit to his music: instead of rising into the air with warmth and spice, the melody clambered out of the instrument and lay on the floor like a lifeless thing, wheezing and grey, begging to be put to death. He wondered miserably if he was the first one, or if there had been other kindred souls, shunned and erased from history, black sheep sacrificed to the family name. Or perhaps they had studied and played their way to mediocrity, and then gave into an early decomposition of the soul. He saw them float along with the passing clouds, a procession of ghosts that shook their insubstantial heads at him.

There he was. Every household has one unmentionable secret, and in this particular one it was Salomon and Karolina's denial of the fact that their son, whom they had lovingly groomed for the life of a famous artist, and in whose veins ran the blood of countless extraordinary musicians, possessed in fact no talent whatsoever.

He clenched his teeth to prevent tears from spilling out. His muscles stiffened and he took a deep breath, then sat up and exhaled until the familiar sensation burned through him and was gone. He put his face between his knees, wrapped his long arms round his legs. They had been through this over countless breakfasts on either side of Salomon's newspaper. What had changed, other than the erosion of his hope? He was still expected to show up every day, do his homework and put in hours upon hours of practice. And still nothing changed.

The sky was now completely overcast. The chill made him alert to the fact that the hairs on his arms were raised, and that thick raindrops would soon be falling. There was a gust of wind and the birds stopped singing. Sandor got up and shook the brown leaves off his clothes. He put his hands in his pockets and walked back home.

*

Snow was falling on that day in December, melting on the soil with sorrowful gentleness as Sandor was making his way home from school. He slowed down, lifted his face and let the snowflakes land on his mouth. He held out a hand. The intricate geometric details of the flakes shone for a moment against the black glove before dissolving, and he felt a wave of tenderness for them.

Instead of taking the path to the front entrance he entered the garden from the side, where a rusty gate led to the south-eastern side of the building. There was a basement there that had fallen into disuse, its narrow stairs secluded behind the rose bushes and its entrance hidden from the windows above by tree boughs. He kicked at the weeds, climbed down the cracked steps and took out a key. It turned with effort. He shoved the door with his shoulder and it opened, releasing a mouldy stench. Something small darted out between his shoes and scurried away. He waited until the smell dissipated and stepped in. He felt for the light switch and turned it.

A single bulb sputtered into life. It was a small room, shrouded in cobwebs and empty except for a heavy wooden table with peeling varnish. The walls had long rectangular niches and cabinets, and nails stuck out from some of the beams. It must have been the old gun room. He swept the table clean, dropped his school pack on it and looked for the small volume hiding between his school books. The shabby little black book had uneven, stained pages and a leather cover falling apart at the spine. He leafed through it carefully and set it on the table, then threw the bag over his shoulder, turned off the light and locked the door behind him. He had to pause and take a few breaths of clear air before he could go on.

In the hallway hung two unfamiliar coats. He followed the sound of voices into the small sitting room, a cosy room with thick carpeting on its red brick floor and narrow, soft armchairs. The slim stove was blazing and the air smelled of coffee. Karolina sat next to a middle-aged woman in an elegant outfit that was too light for the season. The two of them were absorbed in hushed conversation. Karolina's hand was on the woman's shoulder.

'Hello, Mrs Storm,' said Sandor.

The woman looked up and gave him a weak smile. She opened her mouth to greet him, but an exclamation interrupted her. A brown-haired girl Sandor's age rushed into the room behind him.

'Sandor!'

'Maggie, dear—'

The girl ignored her mother and leapt at him, trapping Sandor in a powerful hug. Her glasses lightly grazed his cheek. She released him, and suddenly he hoped the cellar smell hadn't clung to him.

'Did you hear?'

'No.' He paused, and made a painful effort to switch to his broken English. 'What happened?'

'Father is being transferred again. We're going home!'

'Home? Oh.' His jaw clenched. 'Washington.'

'We're sad to leave you so very suddenly,' sighed Mrs Storm. Karolina gave her hand a squeeze.

Maggie tugged his sleeve and nodded. 'Let's go talk.'

They retreated to the sun room, a narrow glass dome protruding from the eastern side of the building. It was lined with a faded window seat and they took off their shoes to sit their usual way, across each other and their legs resting on the opposite seat. Maggie's socks next to him had a bright holly pattern.

'Your socks,' he said. 'What is the word?'

'Silly?'

He laughed. 'No!'

'Festive?'

'Yes.'

She blushed, and crossed her ankles. 'I only just found out this morning, you know.'

'When are you coming back?'

She made a face. He jerked forward. 'Never?' he asked.

'Maybe. I don't know! Nobody tells me anything.'

'Are you leaving soon?'

'The house is ready. I imagine we'll spend New Year's there.'

His throat was burning with indignation. He groped for the right words. 'You said you hate that house. It's not home. You *said*!'

'But my home *is* the States. You know I hate being dragged around, changing schools all the time!'

'I thought you liked it here!'

'I do!'

'I thought we were best friends!'

'We are!'

They slumped back in their seats. Maggie looked up. Snowflakes swirled and piled briefly on the glass above them. The trees were ablaze with a silver glow, and a web of ice was forming on the greenery. The light reflected off Maggie's glasses, hiding her red eyes. She *should* be upset, Sandor caught himself thinking. She should have convinced them to stay until they graduated.

She glanced at him, and Sandor felt a rush of guilt. He wanted her to be happy, but not at the other side of the world.

'If you leave, I will be alone.'

She sighed. 'I wish we could stay here. But what can I do? We *will* write to each other. You can practise your English. I could practise my, um, five words.'

'Letters!' he scoffed. 'You will leave and forget me.'

'I won't! I promise! But you *have* to write. Keep the books I gave you, you need them to practise. We can go walking this weekend like always, can't we? I'll still be here, I think...'

The thought of spending the weekend apart made Sandor's throat clench. She *could* stay. She could make them.

'Maggie...'

'What?'

'Nothing.'

She pinched his toe again. '*What?*'

'Very well, Saturday morning, let's go.'

*

Saturday came, and Sandor was hiking alone through the pines. His skin was flushed and steaming and his boots crushed the snow with vicious satisfaction. He kicked at the bushes and climbed on, took his gloves off and clutched at rough branches to pull himself forward. The previous day Maggie and her little sister had been sent abruptly ahead to their grandparents in England. Then the ambassador and his family would fly together to Washington, and get settled by Christmas Day. There had been no apologies for Maggie's rushed departure. No goodbyes.

Sandor came to a halt, leaned against a tree and closed his eyes, inhaling the scent of resin. His hands were shaking. A thorn stuck out of his left palm but he was so numb he hadn't noticed. He pulled it out and pressed the spot until bright red drops trickled out, and he licked them off. The taste of warm blood made him wild. He put the gloves back on, wrapped his scarf tighter and went on, muttering and cursing through the blue shadows.

He stopped suddenly and looked round, worried that he was lost. But then he recognised the spot: if he took a left turn he would find himself at the hillside, from where the fields stretched on in all their midwinter glory. If he took a right turn and walked downhill, he would find himself on the path to the back gardens of the ambassador's estate; Maggie's old home. The house would have been meticulously cleaned by now, and soon white sheets would be draped over the furniture. He peered into the trees and saw that there was a third path he had never seen before.

He toyed with the idea of sitting down on the soil right there, waiting for the frost to creep up on him and lull him to sleep until his lips were blue and his heartbeat slowed down, while people with flashlights combed the forest, and then Salomon and Karolina would be crying over his grave, and the newspapers would be telling of the ignoble end of the family...

Sandor shook the fantasy away. He had a plan. It was a desperate one, but he was determined to live through his triumph. Even if he was a failure he was still young, and he was still strong.

He started making his way back through the unfamiliar route and found himself at a small, quiet opening he had never seen before. He paused.

There was something in this place that set his teeth on edge. He looked round at the tranquil clearing, at the roof of intertwined branches sheltering the even ground, the pale green light slipping through, the quiet stream peeking from the cluster of rocks before disappearing again into the earth. And then the words returned to him; the words from the small shabby book he had discovered in a box stuffed with yellowed kindling papers, and had now left hidden in the gun room. The passage came clear and exact:

Therefore look for a place fitting and pure to draw a circle. Let the place be where no rooster's cry echoes; let it be clean and untrodden or near a river or by the fork of the road. Let it be where nobody looks upon it and no human voice sounds, lest by finding you they should stop you. Hold the knife wearing the aforementioned ring and carve this onto the earth...

Sandor's feet against the hard soil confirmed the inevitability of the action he had, until now, never considered. He consented to the idea of *here*, and stood for a while in the dimness with his mind blank. A breeze made the boughs above him quiver and shower him with snow. He mapped the route in his head, and then went on his way.

*

After dinner, Salomon and Karolina left Sandor to catch up with his practice and they began their concert rituals. Karolina's golden mane would be tamed into an elegant knot; Salomon would have an early shave; gowns and suits would be slipped into their garment bags while the car was waiting out front. December was a busy month and they were absent a lot, sometimes for days at a time. Sandor had a standing invitation to join them, but he always refused. He made up for it by performing something for them at home every once in a while, which seemed to make them happy.

Sandor finished with his practice and waited until the house was empty, put his coat and boots on and stole out towards the gun room. He placed on the table a pencil and a large roll of paper, and started leafing through the small black book. He had also brought a second hand Latin dictionary from the house library, re-bound and bearing his grandfather's initials on the spine, but the little black book itself had no title or markings. Its confusion of chapters were full of odd and upsetting etchings with cryptic descriptions. It had no title or author, and wasn't a book that would be looked upon with a kindly eye by anyone.

He found the page he was looking for: the text he had memorised, and the engraving that pictured a circle within another circle, both within an array of squares. From the inner circle a triangular gap formed nearly all the way to the outer square, and in that gap a knife had been drawn, with crude pentagrams around it. There was writing in the space between the two circles that he couldn't understand: it turned out not to be Latin and he thought it looked a lot like ancient Greek, but not quite. The description below the engraving simply stated: *Invocatio.*

Sandor paused, his pencil suspended above the page. Was he really about to try such a thing? And yet – why not? He was bright, clever, capable. Why would he succumb and let one flaw define him, drag him through a life of misery and humiliation?

But this is how it has always been, said a voice inside him. There used to be a hope that he'd get through it. Why now?

As if in answer, his thought strayed to a memory from last winter: walking into the house with Maggie after a hike through the snowy woods, and her large glasses instantly fogging up. It made her look ridiculous. He smiled at the thought, and instantly felt a stab of pain.

If you leave, I will be alone.

Just like that, he had been left behind.

He shook the doubts out of his head and began copying the engraving on the paper.

'*Animalis, vegetabilis, mineralis,*' he mumbled. He scribbled the symbols in their respective places. *Ignis, terra, aqua, aer. Is this sequence correct? Is this where they should be placed? Omnia ab uno, omnia ab unum, yes, yes. The circle and the point, the point within the circle, the circle is eternity – the point a moment, the moment within eternity. It is the symbol for the sun; the metal gold; the seed within the fruit - no, that's not suitable, it's useless to me. No. No theories! Right. Think. The practical approach: a ring. I must find a plain gold ring. And the knife.*

A blast of wind whistled through the cracks, making the door shake. A shiver ran down his spine and he looked up, but there was nobody there. He returned to his work, examined both images to make sure he hadn't missed anything, folded the paper and put it in his pocket. He wrapped the black book in a handkerchief and looked round for a hiding place. There was a bulky coat rack hanging on the wall. He tugged it forward and shoved the small package in the gap between wood and wall. He patted his breast pocket to feel the paper crunch, and left the basement.

He had a nightmare that night. The wind was blowing until every crevice of the house was screaming, the shutters were banging, unswept ashes were scattered over the living-room carpet. He was in the forest again but in that strange dream weather when, though daytime, the sky is dim as if under an eclipse. He was standing in the clearing except now weeds were growing everywhere and the ground was full of sharp rocks, and he was barefoot, with bleeding soles. There was a rustle of leaves in the darkness. Something large was closing in. His feet ached too much to run away. He was about to die, the creature was tearing through the bushes towards him, he could almost see it… But it was only a stag. It loped by him, hooves clicking. He could feel its hot breath on his skin. Then it slid back into the greenery and it was gone. He woke up drenched in sweat.

*

The advent wreath with its four unlit candles was on the breakfast table when he joined his parents. It was the only sign it was Christmas Eve. The sight made him feel oddly guilty. He wondered if there was any way to get out of the festive dinner tomorrow. It was only going to be the three of them this year; no more escaping to his room with Maggie and skulking back for pudding.

Salomon glanced at him over his coffee. The Sunday newspaper must have been already read.

'You didn't sleep well?'

Sandor shook his head, and poked at his food, trying to work up some appetite. Karolina leaned across the table and placed a cool hand on his forehead. He flinched and drew away.

'Mother!'

'You feel hot, darling. Your eyes are red. I'll have some soup prepared for you. It's a pity to spend your holiday with a fever.'

'I'm all right. I just couldn't sleep, that's all. Must have been the wind, it kept me up all night.'

'There was no wind, dear,' she replied, holding his wrist for a moment as if to check his pulse. He resisted the urge to pull away again. 'It was quiet, it's been snowing all night.'

'There wasn't? Oh. I must have dreamt it then.'

His mother gave him a peculiar look.

'Here, finish your egg. I'm sure there's some fruit left in the house. And why aren't you wearing a sweater? Go upstairs and put one on as soon as you've eaten.'

'I'm fine, I'm not a baby.'

'*Sandor.*' His father threw him a warning look. Sandor clamped his mouth shut.

'I'm only worried about you,' said Karolina.

He pushed his plate away. 'May I be excused? I have to practise.'

His parents glanced at one another. He took it as permission to leave, and pushed his chair back. As he was walking away he heard them whisper to each other.

Sandor reached the piano room, closed the door behind him and looked round. The snow outside was thick, casting a harsh glow through the window. He turned on the light. He shivered and thought he would warm up after playing a little, so he took out his notes and opened the lid. His fingers rested idly on the keyboard. He lacked any urge to play, any energy to make himself *want* to play. Instead of practising one of his father's pieces as he should, he played the 'Adeste Fideles' he had prepared to accompany his mother for her carol singing. It was a comforting sound: straightforward and familiar like music from a wind-up toy. He made a mistake that somehow made it more enjoyable, so he played again more carelessly, and now the music poured out with more ease. He forced himself to focus on his homework. Playing his father's compositions created in him a physical distaste for the music. The pieces always came out viscous and misassembled – crude, joyless little monsters.

He stopped. He turned and looked out of the window, where the grey sky was indistinguishable from the ground through the light curtains. Any other Sunday he would already be on his way to the ambassador's estate, meeting Maggie along the way. Any other Sunday they would take a long walk, have the odd snowball fight, and end up in front of the stove sipping hot cocoa together and listening to records.

He felt guilty and miserable. He turned back to the piano, his fingers limp. *I wish I wanted this.* He began playing again.

I have to do something. I'm a grown man. I have to take my fate into my own hands. I have to do something. I have to do something. I have to do something I have to do something I have to do something...

His thoughts spiralled as he pounded away at the keys.

1990

There was something Mrs Soltesz had said, and Ferdi struggled to remember it – Mrs Soltesz, never missing Sunday Mass and still filching from drunken tourists. 'All life is precious,' she had said, 'even that spider's.' So she had Erzsi scoop the creature up with a newspaper and toss it in the street, where it would find itself suddenly exposed and helpless. If all life was precious and good, perhaps then even Ferdi's could be.

Yet wasn't it wickedness when he had dragged that man's body into the forest, burying him in a shallow, unmarked grave? His salvation was beyond even Mrs Soltesz and her plastic vials of holy water, with which she liked to dab her skin jealously as if it were perfume. He knew that it was one evening when she touched Ferdi's hand and her fingers were still wet from it. Whether it had been an accidental blessing or exorcism, it hadn't worked.

Petar was still aloof with him, while Erzsi – embarrassed since she had exposed Ferdi's secret the other night – hovered about him sheepishly. When Dieter arrived she stepped out, and through the closing door Ferdi saw them steal a kiss.

Dieter kept watching Ferdi with unfeigned interest that made him uncomfortable. When Dieter followed him outside at break Ferdi sat sullen and avoided conversation, but this was impossible with Dieter. He was going on about his landlord and the lack of hot water in his building, when Ferdi interrupted him.

'You treat me differently,' he said.

Dieter raised his eyebrows.

Ferdi was crouched on the pile of wooden crates that smelled of cabbage, hugging his knees. 'You, and Erzsi,' he went on. 'Since Sunday.'

Dieter's expression softened. He toyed with his mint-green cigarette lighter. 'Well, Molnar, that's because you've changed too.'

Ferdi scowled.

'True, I barely know you. But that was quite a stunt you pulled last Sunday.'

'It was just a little music.' There was a knot in Ferdi's throat. What he believed – what he *really was* – this was irrelevant. It was vital that everyone knew there was nothing, truly nothing special or strange about him.

Dieter shook his head. 'I may know nothing about music, all right? But you didn't see the look on the old man's face. The cimbalom player – wasn't he a professor? And Erzsi was crying all over my shirt.'

'We were all drunk. Very drunk.'

'Yes, we were.' There was a long silence, while Dieter contemplated his lighter. 'It was the strangest thing,' he said at last. 'While I was listening, I thought my grandmother was holding my hand and telling me I would be all right, because there would always be someone out there making walnut cake like hers even after she was gone... It's crazy, I know. But I could taste the cake: the walnut, the meringue. For a bit, I didn't know where I was. Mother was still crying about the Wall and cousin Margareta. My dog was licking jam off my fingers. I was getting out of jail and the sun was on my face. When the music stopped, I had to find my way back.'

Ferdi sank back and rubbed his aching face. Despair welled up inside him, along with something else, shapeless and alien. Dieter was flicking his lighter, casting momentary flashes into the dusk. Suddenly he burst into laughter. The sound echoed round the quiet alley.

'Swear not to tell Holy Mother about the jail bit – she'd cut my pay in half.'

The service door banged open and the waiter, a cross young man with a pimply face, peeped out.

'Dieter!'

'I'll be right there.' The door banged shut again. Dieter winked at Ferdi. 'Want to go out tonight? No pianos, I promise.'

'Sure.'

'Great. I'll stop by your place around ten.'

Ferdi remained outside alone, watching the clouds shift. The air smelled of rain. He thought about it falling on the gravel by the Esterhazy mansion, knocking against the wall of the gun room. He thought about it bruising the flowers, darkening the barks of the pine trees, rotting the piles of foliage. Falling on the dirty bones of a man buried in the forest, limbs dug up by foxes.

Some feeble raindrops landed on his head. All of a sudden he recognised that alien feeling he had when Dieter was talking: it was pride.

*

'A woman rang for you again, Mr Molnar,' Miss Ilona informed him, manifesting as soon as he had the key out of his pocket and was about to step in.

'Did she leave a name? Or a number?'

'It should be with Mr Polyak.'

Ferdi went downstairs to the caretaker's apartment and rang the bell. The old man answered the door in pyjamas and a ratty cardigan. Inside, a radio was blasting a news bulletin.

'Sorry to disturb you. Was there a message left for me today?'

'Name?'

'Molnar.'

Mr Polyak shuffled back indoors, and Ferdi heard him mutter as he opened and closed stiff drawers. He returned with a piece of paper marked: *Gedeon, Gabriella. For Mr Molnar.*

There was a phone number scribbled underneath. Ferdi had no memory of that name. He set the note aside, casting nervous glances at it every now and then.

He was washing his dishes when the buzzer rang, making him almost break his only good plate – it was the first time he had ever heard it. He stood for a moment like a deer caught in the headlights. Not like this, he thought – Sandor wouldn't dare, he wouldn't... Then he remembered his plans with Dieter.

Tentatively he pushed the button with the figure of a key on it. There was a thunderous noise from the stairs, then someone knocked on his door with all the politeness of a battering ram. Ferdi hesitated, then opened the door.

'Hello, Dieter.'

'Hello, Molnar! Nice of you to be conscious this time.' Dieter stepped inside, paused and looked back into the corridor. Then he reached out a large hand and dragged inside a very displeased-looking Petar. 'Look who I found up past his bedtime!'

Petar looked even younger without his butcher's coat. He was wearing a cheap puffy bomber jacket and a faded hoodie underneath. He eyed Ferdi's room, pouting.

'Boys' night out tonight.' Dieter patted Petar's shoulder. 'Time to make up, you two.'

'Leave me alone.'

'Will you listen to that! And to think he was calling me "sir" a few weeks ago.'

Ferdi stepped aside. 'Let me put on my shoes. Sit, um, anywhere.'

Petar didn't move. He watched with his hands in his pockets while Ferdi hunted self-consciously for his shoes. Dieter flicked through the pile of books on the nightstand. He pulled out a stained, cloth-bound hardcover and leafed through it, pausing at the illustrations.

'*Old Fairy Tales*. Is this what you read before sleep?'

Ferdi tried to grab it, but Dieter pulled away. 'It's a collector's item.'

'Are you a collector, Molnar? This is a first edition.' He glanced at the first page. 'Who's *S. E.*?'

Ferdi snatched the book away and set it back on the pile. 'It's a loan.' He put his coat on. 'Let's go.'

They found a quiet, dark bar full of the amber glow of the liquor bottles. A few other patrons sat about, deep into the vague defeat of a late Tuesday night. The three of them sat at the bar's wooden counter. When Petar found out that they served his local plum brandy he insisted they all tried it, so soon they were sipping a pale golden liquor that tasted sharply of fruit.

A lesser man would have struggled to keep the conversation going between Petar and Ferdi, but not Dieter. His large body spilling from the high stool, sleeves rolled up to expose constellations of faded tattoos and muscles that demanded compliance, he regaled them with impossible anecdotes of his strange life. By the second round his stories became increasingly lewd, which made Petar dissolve into laughter. Dieter sat framed by the two young men who watched him spellbound, his light freckled skin and silvery hair wrapping him in a golden halo like a blurry god. The bartender hovered close by, refilling their glasses and chuckling at the obscene litany.

Ferdi watched Petar become consumed by the enchantment. The boy seemed barely at an age to be out of school, and yet in a sense much older than him. He had mastered the teenage art of scornful dismissal, which so reminded Ferdi of Sandor. The boy vibrated with unspent vitality in a way that Sandor in his suppressed malice never had; but perhaps Sandor had always been a lost cause. Unlike Ferdi, Petar's defiant presence was confident and assured. In the shadow of Dieter's brightness he occupied a steady, definite part of the world while Ferdi dissolved into the fringes, smudged and incomplete.

'No more for them,' Dieter's voice came, addressing the bartender. 'I've taken them under my wing tonight. If you're feeling generous, you can always pour me some more of that excellent brandy.'

Petar noticed Ferdi observing him and clutched his glass harder.

'And how about a nightcap to feel nostalgic?' Dieter went on. 'Maybe tonight we can all drink something that made our grandparents merry. Some apricot schnapps would do it for me. How about you, Molnar? What kind of spirit made the folks back at home sing?' His hand fell on Ferdi's back, almost knocking his spine loose. 'Was it wine? Or some bitter aperitif? You look like the boy given half a glass of watered-down red at dinner. Did you hide in the vines to read while the other kids played?'

'Some soda would do, thanks.'

'Ah, yes, the legendary soda brewers of the eastern valleys, I've heard of them...'

The bartender brought soda. Petar made a discreet signal to be served some of the schnapps too. He downed it all while Dieter wasn't paying attention, and had a refill. When Dieter slid off his seat and excused himself in less than elegant terms, Petar moved closer to Ferdi and looked steadily at him.

'How did you get that scar?'

Ferdi's hand prodded his cheek. 'Kitchen accident.'

'Makes you look like a gangster.'

'I guess.'

Petar leaned in. The cross slid through his jacket and dangled over the counter, casting specks of white light.

'If *I* had to guess, I'd swear it was a bullet graze.'

Ferdi stiffened. Petar closed in and pointed at the edge of the scar.

'The way it widens as it goes, and those pointy tips like flames.' He hovered his finger across the length of the scar, tracing the sharp points that flared round it. Ferdi shivered and drew back.

'How would you know?'

The boy shrugged. His breath smelled thickly of apricot schnapps. He winked. 'Don't worry, I know how to keep a secret.'

Ferdi stirred the ice in his glass. 'There's no secret to keep.'

Petar laughed and was about to say something, but then Dieter reappeared and he shifted his focus back to his drink. Dieter clapped their shoulders.

'Good to see you two making friends.'

His face was evenly red, and there was a faint sway to the way he was trying to hold himself upright. He looked for his glass and finished the drink off.

'Shall we call it a night?' Ferdi suggested. Petar's attitude had alarmed him, and he missed the safe predictability of the blunt morning light, the chores at the bar.

'Sure,' said Dieter. 'There's always better places to be.'

Petar swivelled to face him. 'I like it here.'

'No, I'm not thinking about a bar. I'm thinking about the most beautiful woman in whose arms I should have been tonight, instead of out here getting drunk with you two perfectly nice but – pardon me – not nearly as exciting gentlemen.' Dieter steadied himself by holding onto Ferdi. 'But no,' he sighed, 'today was simply *no good*.'

'The head waitress?' said Petar. 'You finally got together?'

Dieter smiled dreamily. 'Yes, at Molnar's recital. He's my good-luck charm.'

Petar turned to Ferdi. 'What recital?'

'Oh, he's bloody Mozart!'

'Have some water, Dieter,' said Ferdi.

'Sorry, sorry.'

Dieter sat heavily and lit a cigarette. Petar took one too and leaned in for Dieter to light it but he kept missing with the flame. They started giggling and Dieter nearly dropped his from his mouth. The lights around them lowered, and more of that horrid apricot schnapps appeared. Ferdi passed his to Dieter and had another plum brandy instead. The effect of alcohol now was different; perhaps brandy and schnapps mixed better than beer and wine. Tonight only a pleasant drowsiness settled in him, slowing down his mind. He watched Petar and Dieter joke around without listening. His gaze swept round the small space at the people talking, the bartender filling luminous glasses of beer. Ferdi's limbs relaxed as he sank lower against the counter.

The door banged open and a couple walked in, wrapped in identical scarves. Ferdi glanced up, and through the glass he saw Sandor pass by the bar.

There was a loud noise. Ferdi was on his feet and his seat had toppled over. Dieter and Petar were looking at him. Ferdi rushed to the door and out into the street.

It was deserted. Further down a person could be seen walking: a hunched figure in a large coat, its hands in its pockets. The figure was already far away. Ferdi struggled for a second but couldn't bring himself to utter the name.

'Wait!' he shouted.

The figure kept walking with unchanging pace, and he ran after it. Cold stung Ferdi's skin and his chest began to hurt as he gulped down the icy air. He couldn't remember the last time he had been forced to run. A stabbing pain burst through his left side, throwing him off.

The figure in the coat turned left into an alley and disappeared. There were a few people on the street now; someone slammed into him but Ferdi didn't pause to apologise and ran on. He turned blindly into the side street, collided with a dustbin and fell down.

The alley was empty.

He picked himself up from the wet pavement. His lungs struggled to work and he leaned against a wall, panting. His palms were scraped and bleeding. The pain under his rib returned with a vengeance, making him double over. He realised he was crying freely, and he clutched his stomach.

Footsteps closed in from the main street and Dieter appeared. Ferdi let himself slide down on the ground.

'What the hell, Molnar?' He lifted Ferdi up.

'He left,' whispered Ferdi, trying to stifle his sobs. 'He left!'
He let Dieter dust him off as if he were a small child.

'Who did?'

Ferdi wiped his eyes, and the tears stung the scratches on his hands. His face and throat were burning. 'He left me there to die.'

Dieter stared at him. Ferdi was trembling with hate and cold.

'Is someone after you?'

Ferdi nodded. And then, reconsidering, he shook his head.

Dieter grabbed his shoulders and shook him. 'Listen, if you're in trouble you can't go off like this.'

Ferdi pushed him away. 'It's all right.'

'Who left you to die?'

Ferdi turned and kicked the dustbin. The sound echoed round the alley. He stood glaring at it and blaming it for everything, for the nightmares, for all the times he cried himself to sleep, blaming it for the night of the blizzard, for the terror that refused to go away.

'I've had enough,' he said. And he knew that it was a lie, he knew that he could go on putting up with much more as long as he never had to go back to that locked room.

He felt a light touch on his shoulder. It seemed impossible that Dieter's spine-crushing hand could suddenly be so careful. Ferdi almost crumbled under the lightness. Dieter would be touched like this by Erzsi and she by him, like people did, going on touching each other in the place of words until the end.

One of the windows above them lit up, and instinctively they both drew away. They walked back towards the bar, saying nothing else.

*

Petar kept throwing them dirty looks, but didn't dare ask. None of them felt like talking, and Dieter had the courtesy to finish Ferdi's drink and order him another soda while he sat passive, brooding. They paid – Dieter somehow ended up paying for

55

Petar again – and left. Petar waved goodnight and walked away without another glance. Ferdi was uncomfortably reminded of his earlier wink.

'Come, Mozart. I think I'll walk you home tonight.'

Ferdi glanced up at the night sky, which glowed a muddy shade of red. 'Let's go by the river. I need some air.'

They walked in silence. The wind howled, Dieter began to hum a tune. Ferdi stopped abruptly.

'What is it?'

The abandoned art-nouveau building he had paused at recently loomed over them, with its intricate metalwork shining like curved blades. Up, through the glass loft again, beams of light were once again moving about frantically.

'There,' Ferdi whispered. Dieter looked up.

'What are we looking at?'

'I pass by this building every night, and these lights keep appearing. At first I thought someone had broken in.'

'Only an idiot would raid a glass house with a flashlight.' The beam danced around, slipped through the glass and then was gone.

They examined the entrance from afar. The ground floor had a large window like a shop, dimly lit with green. Dieter crossed the quiet street in large strides with Ferdi at his heels, and they put their faces against the glass. The interior was a wide space with upturned chairs and two metal staircases leading up to a dark mezzanine. An unnaturally large chandelier was hanging low, casting a monstrous shadow.

'Is this some kind of stage, or a fancy restaurant?' Dieter wondered. 'Maybe it's a ghost house. Maybe they left everything in, and there's jewel boxes gathering dust.' He moved towards the main entrance and gave it a decisive push. 'The door is ajar.' Dieter grinned. 'Let's go in.'

Ferdi's eyes opened wide. 'Go in?'

'What? It's abandoned. We could find something. Don't be a wimp.'

Ferdi glanced nervously round the empty street. A sudden horror gripped him. 'No, I don't like this. Let's go.'

Dieter ignored him. He put his shoulder against the door and it opened, scraping horribly against the marble doorstep. Silence fell. From the far side of the bridge came the rumbling of a passing tram.

'Dieter, come on. I don't want to spend the night in a holding cell.'

'You should. It's nicer than your place.' Dieter slipped in and pulled Ferdi after him. He pushed the door back in place, rubbed his shoulder and looked round.

Inside it smelled musty, as if river water had been trapped. From the far end of the hallway came the eerie green light, illuminating an entrance to the main room. Further ahead, hidden from view, was a narrow flight of marble stairs. There was a flash of headlights as a car passed outside.

Ferdi saw the gleam of Dieter's smile in the dark, and then of his white-blonde hair as he headed towards the stairs, and followed.

They went up three flights, passing apartment after apartment, groping at an iron rail worn smooth by generations of hands. At the top floor there was only one door with a blank nameplate by the bell. The door was high and elegant, with frosted glass and twisted iron bars. Ferdi expected a beam of light to appear from within and fall on them at any moment, but nothing stirred.

'Well?' whispered Dieter. 'After you.'

Ferdi reached for the handle. The door was unlocked. He opened it and had the fleeting impression that the handle was warm, and quickly withdrew his hand.

In the large bare loft was no smell of damp. It seemed in fact to have been recently ventilated; the air was crisp and faintly smelling of matches. Ferdi walked in, his steps echoing on the hardwood floor. The pink glow of the night was spilling in from the side overlooking the street, and even from where they stood they caught a glimpse of the Danube gliding towards the south.

The place seemed empty. Ferdi heard the click of Dieter's mint-green lighter. The small flame cast a shaky light around them.

'Now we're the strange lights,' Dieter whispered.

He took a couple of steps, admiring the view, and whistled. Ferdi turned and, in the patch of night behind Dieter, he saw a pair of eyes.

'Not alone,' said a voice in the dark.

Dieter went down fast. His knees hit the floor, with a thud that reverberated round the room. The stranger had an arm round Dieter's throat, a skinny arm in dirty rags that pressed until Dieter's face turned dark red.

Ferdi lunged, driving his fist up the stranger's nose, but the blow didn't land properly. The man wavered, and this was enough for Dieter – he took a large gulp of air and threw his head back, and his skull collided with the man's face with a terrible sound.

Dieter stood up like a bull, dragging the stranger along, and backed up into the nearest wall. The crushed man let out a pitiful cry. Dieter wrenched himself free and turned, landing two quick punches. Then he retreated, growling and rubbing his throat while the stranger squirmed and groaned on the floor.

'What the hell was that?' Dieter rasped, imitating Ferdi's weak punch. 'Don't you know how to hit?'

Ferdi leaned carefully over the fallen man. His hair was grey but the face was so dirty it was impossible to guess his age. The man sank back. His eyes shone like little church candles, their whites showing widely, and he stank. A matted beard covered his mouth.

'He said you would come alone,' the man whined, hugging himself.

'He's mad,' sighed Dieter. 'Maybe we should call someone.'

The man twitched, curling up against the wall. 'No police!'

'Yes police! You almost killed me!'

'But he said that he would come alone!'

'Who would come alone?'

The man pointed at Ferdi. Dieter threw him a puzzled look, but Ferdi shrugged.

'You know this man, Molnar?'

'No.' Ferdi's stomach sank. Suddenly he wanted to turn and run away. He leaned in and spoke quietly. 'Do you know me?'

The madman stared, then nodded, licking his cracked lips. 'You will never be real.'

Ferdi took a step back. Exhaustion swept through him. He wanted to sit there on the floor next to the madman, and give up.

Dieter tugged at his sleeve. 'Come on, let's go. There's nothing we can do.'

Another hand took hold of his other sleeve, pulling urgently. 'Stay,' the madman begged. 'He said, stay and wait.'

Dieter's gaze scanned Ferdi. 'Who said?'

'Him! *Him!*' The madman rubbed his filthy face. 'He said so! Oh...' He tugged at Ferdi again, making him stumble closer. 'Oh my brother, my brother...'

Ferdi was pulled to his knees next to the crouching man. The man's face was close enough to make out the honey-brown in his bloodshot eyes. His breath came spasmodic and hot to Ferdi's skin.

'We escaped, didn't we?' the man asked, searching Ferdi's face. 'We took our own path.'

'Yes,' Ferdi whispered.

Dieter's grip tightened and he drew Ferdi up, dragging him away. 'Let's go. Come on, come on.'

The madman scrambled after them, stopping at the doorway. Ferdi caught a last glimpse of his haggard face as Dieter was marching him down the corridor.

'But we are never free!' the madman shouted, and the echo of his sobbing followed them down the stairs.

1979

On Monday morning the snowfall subsided and the frost deepened, leaving a thin layer of solid ice. The walls radiated cold at the Esterhazy manor and the heating was panting away, working simultaneously with the stoves. Heavy curtains had been drawn in every empty room to keep the warmth in, and the house was echoing with the groaning of hot water pipes.

The Christmas table was set early, as Salomon and Karolina had work later. The candles on the advent wreath were lit and adorned with slim golden ribbons, and the meal consisted of his father's favourite dishes: spicy fisherman's soup, beef stew, sweet walnut bread; and, for dessert, plum dumplings and a box of chocolates. Plenty of food had been prepared to last the holidays, and the help had all been dismissed.

A record of Bach's oratorios was playing and the family hugged and kissed before sitting at the table. They ate in amiable silence. Sandor was usually allowed red wine on special occasions, and by the time the main course was served it had made him talkative. His nerves had been on edge all day; he would have finished the entire bottle given half the chance. He mumbled for permission to refill, and his parents, having had a few glasses themselves, were in too good spirits to refuse him. Their beaming, flushed faces made his stomach turn with shame.

Sandor picked up the plates and cleared the table himself, and they relocated to the piano room. He took his place at the instrument. Salomon brought chairs forward and lit a cigarette.

Karolina, still red-faced, clasped her hands, waited for Sandor to begin playing and delivered her confident 'Adeste Fideles'.

Sandor played the best he could, and made the same mistake as the previous day but perhaps nobody noticed it, though he thought he could feel his father's eyes land briefly on him at that moment. It seemed to him that the misplaced note gave a texture to the piece that it was previously lacking. He wondered if he had been playing it wrong all his life, and that that which he perceived as a mistake was actually the song in its truest form. Salomon applauded when they were done, extinguished his cigarette on the marble ashtray, stood up and joined Karolina with his gentle baritone in one last song. They applauded again for Sandor who, drunk with his misplaced note and two glasses of wine, stood up and bowed.

The mood dissolved and his parents went off to prepare for their performance. Salomon and Karolina disappeared upstairs and Sandor headed downstairs to the kitchen. The large tiled stoves were still giving off heat, and scents of food wafted in the air: paprika and cloves and singed sugar and dough. A nearly finished bottle of wine by the sink caught his eye and he took a big gulp from it. He put it back, rubbed his temples, changed his mind and drank the rest. He put it away, opened the cutlery drawer and selected a meat knife with a long, pointy blade and a bone hilt. He wrapped it in a towel and took it back to his room. A while later his parents knocked on the door to announce they were leaving. After hearing the front door close behind them he opened the window, listening for the car as it pulled through the snow and down the front drive.

Sandor stole into his parents' bedroom. It was a high, spacious room, the warmest and the best-lit on the floor. The dim wallpaper had never been changed since the house had been built in the previous century. Several items of furniture were just as old: the gilt framed mirror, the glossy chest of drawers, the small stove with its elegantly glazed tiles. There was also a slim mahogany desk lined with green baize, and a fragile chair with striped upholstery.

Sandor tried not to look at the mess of clothes on the bed that reminded him so much of his parents' presence. He rummaged through his mother's jewellery boxes. He was sure they had left their wedding rings behind. They never wore them when they performed, and perpetually seeing them take them off was one of the great perplexities of his childhood. He made his way to the writing desk, pulled out the slim drawers and there he found them: two plain gold bands engraved with their initials and wedding date. He couldn't tell which was which, so he took one at random and fled the room.

*

Night fell fast as he walked. Sandor turned back to look at the blunt shape of his home, almost invisible among the trees, aside from above the front entrance where a small light swayed morosely in the wind. The rest of it was no more than a patch of non-sky in the starry night, and everything inside him was urging him to turn back and hide in the coarse blankets of his childhood bed. It seemed the coldest night of the year. The snow had stopped but his teeth were chattering behind his scarf, and his muscles were stiff though layers of wool. And yet he peered into the forest and moved forward, clutching his flashlight and the strap of his schoolbag. At least, he reassured himself, he had the knife.

It took a long time to find the right path in the thick darkness. During the first section of his journey, his feet avoided the protruding roots and puddles of sludge mechanically, but from a certain point he had to examine everything with the beam of his flashlight, counting the signs he had memorised. Terrified of being lost in the woods, he had brought a piece of chalk with him, and every now and then drew an X on the tree trunks.

Don't follow the lights, a voice in his head whispered whenever he caught strange gleams in the dark. Reflections of stars on icicles, or animals' eyes, or maybe little lanterns held by spirits to lure wanderers away from their paths. Tonight all seemed possible. Anything could happen. The realisation made his heart beat wildly, and blood rise to his cheeks. This was what heroes did in the fairy tales, wasn't it? They set out on freezing winter nights to look for a lost love or a stolen sibling. They sought truth and knowledge. They walked into monsters' dens, they crossed mountains and valleys, glaciers and deserts, they starved, and they feasted with kings. What had happened to all of them? How had it all ended? All knowledge seemed to elude him at the moment. Had any died, or never came back? Wasn't there always a price to pay? An icy sensation spread through his chest as he felt around for answers.

He reached the clearing abruptly, tripping over the stream. The sudden lack of trees was unnerving. The boughs above hid all light from the night sky, and the only glow came from the halo of frozen snow. The temperature here was slightly warmer than the rest of the forest. He placed his bag on the ground, got the hurricane lamp out and lit it. The burst of light made his eyes water, and there was the flapping of wings through the leaves. Then silence fell again, and nothing could be heard but the creaking of laden trees.

Everything seemed entirely unreal. The warm, electrical glow of the lamp in the bluish dimness resembled a stage spotlight. It was absurd.

'Ah, yes,' he heard himself say. 'My greatest recital.'

He took his gloves off, fished the ring from his pocket and put it on his finger. It sat a little loose and he guessed it was his father's. The metal was icy against his skin. He blew on his hands to warm them up, knelt down and started unpacking: the paper, the knife, the black book, a glass bowl, and a dirty envelope filled with ash scooped up from the fireplace of the piano room. He unfolded the drawing and took the knife, washed the blade in the brook and started carving the shapes on the ground. The soil was hard and it took a lot of effort.

He began to arrange it all according to the symbols in the drawing. Here he emptied the handful of cool ash, there he placed a stone washed clean in the brook, over there the small glass bowl filled with water. In the place of air he unrolled a few of his father's expensive cigarettes, lit the pile of tobacco with a match and blew on it until it released a thin line of smoke like incense. The familiar smell was comforting, as if a warm hand had briefly touched his shoulder. He double-checked everything, and then placed the knife, point outwards, within the triangular gap in the carved shapes. He stood up, facing the tip of the blade.

He opened the book. It took forever to find the right page with the flashlight dancing in his shaking hand. He took off his hat. His throat was dry and sound refused to come from it. He ran his tongue over his lips.

It's just a poem, he told himself. He took a deep breath and went on to read it aloud.

The sound of his voice was jarring against the sombre landscape. Once he had finished reading he looked round, but nothing had changed. The words had dissolved into the night.

He waited. Nothing happened. Nothing, as the minutes trickled away, as his limbs slowly became rigid, his head heavy and the gurgle of the stream louder. Tiredness overcame him and he sat down. He grew angry and doubtful. Tears rose to his eyes. He hugged his knees and buried his face in his arms.

'Come on,' he whispered. 'Come on. Let's get this over with.'

His watch counted one hour, then two. His parents would be coming back soon. His stomach was growling. He realised he was alone in the woods, with nothing stirring around him except for the local wildlife.

It's over. I'm such an idiot. It was all a joke. It's all right. It's over. It's all right.

Relief washed over him. He gathered his things, buried the ash and the tobacco in the hard soil, and upturned the hard ground until none of the carved shapes remained. He tore the paper into little pieces and scattered them into the darkness. The flashlight kept flickering, setting him on edge. He threw everything back in his bag and returned home as fast as his feet could carry him, stumbling and tearing through the undergrowth.

The car was still missing from the driveway, and the house was empty. Its silence was reproachful. He returned the knife and the bowl to the kitchen and washed them, and gave his coat and trousers a vigorous brush. He cleaned his boots and left them in their place in the hallway. Then he dragged himself upstairs to his room, threw off his clothes, crawled into bed and sank into sleep.

*

Sandor dreamt of a single image that night: he was in the forest and the stag lunged towards him with eyes bulging and nostrils dilated, its grey neck bent down, its ridged antlers gradually piercing his chest. It pinned him against a tree, the antlers crushing his ribs and pushing them apart. Cold was sinking in; his hands clutched the animal's head and its eyelashes twitched against the skin of his palms. The stag retreated, Sandor's knees buckled and he slid down onto the mossy ground. Just that one moment, stretched across infinity.

When Sandor woke up he saw that he still had his father's wedding ring on. It was as if the awareness of the foreign object had shaken him awake. He jumped out of bed and hopped into a sweater, teeth chattering, but then he stopped with his hand on the door. He took off the ring and stared at it. He had tarnished it. How could he let his father wear such a thing? He felt the sudden urge to open the window and throw it away. Let his father believe he'd lost it. Salomon would get a new one, unspoiled by his son's profane tampering.

A door opened somewhere and he heard slippers shuffle through the hallway, then the screech of hot water pipes. He opened the curtains. It was late morning, and the grey light was weak, as if the sun had already set. He walked out just as his father was closing the bathroom door behind him, looking like a tired old man with his few dishevelled hairs and camel dressing gown. Salomon yawned and gave him a sleepy nod. Sandor forced himself to smile.

'Good morning! Did the concert go well?'

Salomon nodded and yawned again. Sandor held up the ring. His father slowly took it and looked at it.

'I was looking for this everywhere...'

'I found it on the floor,' said Sandor.

'Your mother was dazzling last night.' Salomon put it on his finger and gazed thoughtfully at his son. 'Your eighteenth birthday is coming up,' he said.

Sandor felt his stomach drop. He knew what was coming.

'You should have been there,' Salomon went on. 'Everyone was asking about you. You're not a child anymore, to be hiding at home like this all the time, and it's getting disrespectful.'

'I wasn't trying to be—'

'I know what you were trying to be, Sandor. In a few years you will be an Academy graduate and then it will be you on that stage. And then you'll want these people to know you. You should have been there last night.'

Sandor's ears burned. He thought of the knife, the book, the handful of ash. 'Next time. I'll be there next time.'

But Salomon wasn't listening. He turned and gestured at his son as he began to shuffle down the stairs. 'Come, we're setting the breakfast table. Let's make a nice surprise for your mother.'

The week that followed was unbearable. Sandor was either bristling with tension or completely lethargic, paying little attention to his homework and barely eating, moping round the house and jumping at sudden sounds. He wouldn't play for the world, and when at last Karolina forced him to try he was so relieved to rediscover his ineptitude that he burst into tears. He had fight upon fight with his mother, who never tolerated well her son rebelling against her plans. Sandor knew what she was struggling to avoid saying. *It's easier for everyone if you want it yourself.* And Salomon, who usually tried to keep the peace between them, now remained punishingly quiet and Sandor had to suffer his looks of cool disapproval.

The upcoming holiday of the New Year was a relief to all. Salomon and Karolina were busy again with rehearsals for a New Year's Eve gala. As for Sandor, he was glad to have some days to himself. He was discreetly pushed to accompany his parents for a change of environment, but he had flatly refused. When New Year's Eve arrived, the mood in the household was strained. No festive carol singing, no wine-induced merriment this time; instead it was Salomon and Karolina's turn to be tense as the rehearsals left them anxious and sleep-deprived. They departed early on the last day of the year, leaving their son alone in the big, empty house.

Sandor found the emptiness soothing. He ate in the kitchen in the half darkness, watching the snow fall silent and fast, in large, dry clumps. It was the perfect snow for a snowball fight: it would pack nicely without being too hard. He washed his plate and returned to his room, picked up one of Maggie's books and leafed through it. It proved impossible to focus, but it was relaxing to sit in the warmth while staring at the words, letting his mind wander through happy memories.

He recalled the notorious deer hunting incident, one of their adventures of another New Year's, which now seemed so very long ago. When they had heard that the ambassador was preparing a hunting expedition to go after the stag, Sandor had broken into the house and stolen all the bullets. Maggie had never told on him. She was furious, but mostly because he had left her out of the scheme. They always suspected that the ambassador had guessed the identity of the thief, although he had never mentioned it. Sandor had been uncomfortable in his presence ever since.

He didn't care enough to stay up until midnight so he turned in early, lulled by the hum of the snowfall. The idea that he ought to make a New Year's wish floated into his sluggish mind. *No more stupid decisions*, he decided as he drifted off into sleep.

*

He climbed out of bed noiselessly, walked to the window and drew the curtain aside. A blizzard raged on. There was movement in the vast whiteness of the back garden, but it was impossible to see through the screen of snow. Two figures were approaching the house, stumbling on the way. The first figure was larger, and pulled the other forward. The slighter figure, though just as distorted, made the hairs on the back of his neck rise. It seemed reluctant to follow its companion, breaking free and falling behind. The larger figure reached back each time and pulled it forward. He stood there, watching them. Then the first figure lifted its head and turned towards his window. A burning gaze met his own. He froze. The figure waved at him. There was the violent, jumbled sound of the piano, as if someone had savagely struck the keys.

*

Sandor woke up with a jolt. His heart was beating wildly, and he sat still, listening. Nothing but silence. He got up, put a sweater over his pyjamas and took his flashlight from the nightstand.

The corridors of the house were freezing, faintly lit by the hallway light downstairs. He made his way to the piano room in the dark. The double doors were closed. He paused and knocked. When no sound came he turned the handle and stepped in.

Dim rosy light stole in from the tall windows, but the room was empty. Letting out a breath he hadn't realised he was holding, he turned to depart.

'You aren't leaving already?'

Sandor jumped and dropped the flashlight. The male voice, light and amiable, had come from the shadowy corners of the room.

'Who's there?'

'Close the door, Sandor.'

He remained where he stood. His mind calculated fast the distance to the telephone in the hallway.

'Are you going to tell on me now? Don't be that way. I'm only here because *you* called.'

Sandor felt his knees go weak, and he leaned against the doorframe. 'Who is it? Who are you?'

The voice sighed. 'Let me draw the curtains a bit.'

'No, don't!'

'Don't be afraid. I'm not a monster.' A familiar shape of glowing white fabric hovered where the voice was coming from.

'Close the door, Sandor,' the voice repeated.

Sandor did as he was told and remained there, standing against the door. He picked up the flashlight and shone it. The beam was met with a raised hand. Sandor recognised the particular shape of white he'd glimpsed: the man was wearing a tuxedo.

'You're blinding me.'

'Sorry.'

On a chair close to him was a grey overcoat, dripping wet. A hat rested on the closed lid of the grand piano. The snow on it was slowly melting into little puddles on the varnish.

It's going to leave a stain, was the only thing Sandor could think of.

'Turn that thing off,' the man commanded, and before Sandor could object the man reached the window and pulled the heavy curtains open.

The person revealed was short and bulky, wearing a dinner jacket so matte black that it sucked the light in. His light brown hair was combed back with an old-fashioned curl, and the eyes were rather protruding and of a washed-out shade of green. He gave the impression of someone utterly unexceptional, someone you wouldn't look at twice if you passed them in the street. Sandor had the vague sensation they had already met, and realised his mind was going through past dinner parties, trying to place him.

'Who are you?' His mouth had gone dry. 'Are you…?'

'Well, yes. Why, what did you expect?'

Sandor didn't know what to say.

'You called.' The man brushed a speck of dust from his cuff. 'I've answered.'

Several moments passed before Sandor's thoughts became coherent enough for him to speak.

'But – last week – nothing happened! I didn't do anything, not tonight – you're mistaken.'

The man turned and looked at him, and Sandor was knocked back by that impassive, insect-like stare.

'I'm not *mistaken*,' drawled the man in the tuxedo. 'Despite your *clumsy* work. But I like you; I think you are interesting. So here I am.'

Sandor clutched the flashlight. 'Please leave.'

The man chuckled. 'You entered an agreement when you called me. My part was to show up, and now it's your turn. Come, at the very least we can have a little talk. Have a seat.'

Sandor sat at the chair closest to the door. The man sat at the piano stool with his back to the keys, crossed his legs and took out of his pocket a silver cigarette case. He put one between his teeth and offered Sandor another with a nod.

'No, thank you.'

The man shrugged, fished out a lighter of the same polished silver and lit his cigarette. The smell was the first hint to Sandor that all this wasn't a dream.

'Why tonight?' blurted Sandor. 'Why a week later?'

The man shrugged, exhaling a puff of smoke. The smell was so sweet it made Sandor gag.

'There is a charm about the night of a New Year's Eve. Seasonal changes carry a strange intensity, don't you find? People have always felt the need to celebrate them. There's a kind of *power*. Did you know animals can talk tonight?'

Sandor thought of the stag, and imagined a grey-skinned man with naked feet hiding in the forest, wearing a skull with massive antlers and dark eye sockets. A chill ran down his spine.

'And now it's my turn to ask: what made you seek my help? You're a bright young man. Not wise, perhaps, but intelligent enough. What made you walk into the forest alone and carve secret things on the ground, things you weren't supposed to know?'

Sandor groped for words. *Because Maggie was the last straw*, he thought. Her memory gave him strength, and he lifted his chin.

'Perhaps I shouldn't have done that,' he faltered. 'I don't – I don't want to be manipulated.'

'I'm hardly more manipulative than anybody else. Every conversation is a manipulation of sorts, really.'

Sandor remained silent. The man sighed and smoked. Ash floated onto the hardwood floor like snowflakes.

'Haven't you had enough, Sandor? Haven't you had enough of these days, of this room with its stench of parquet cleaner and mouldy velvet? Doesn't your stomach turn when you step in here? Aren't you tired of the crowd in your head always watching your hands, always listening, always waiting for you to make that one terrible mistake that will expose you?'

Sandor tensed, and tried to wave the words away with a stiff hand. The man smiled again.

'With my experience,' he went on, 'all one has to do is take one look at you and around this room and guess. I've been here for many people eager to unburden themselves of their troubles. I do not judge. There is little variety to human misery, but this has never made anyone feel comforted. Pain is pain, of any shape or size, and I respect that. Perhaps that's why they never cease turning to me.'

The man ran his palm over the perfect curl and patted it thoughtfully before continuing.

'Your thoughts are a dark, dark tunnel, Sandor. When you decided to call me, you allowed me to walk in your head freely. I found so much *unpleasantness* in there. I wandered all the way down, past the worst bits, and there I saw your future.'

Sandor looked up. His mouth opened, about to form the question.

He remained like this, lips parted, heart banging against his ribcage. He could not tell how much time passed; his head started spinning and he reached out a hand to steady himself. The rough tapestry of the chair with its gilt thread was an anchor into the present. Slowly, he shut his lips and sat up with back straight, much like his mother. The colour had drained from his face, and his messy black hair made him seem lifeless. He crossed his hands, his eyelids sank down and he remained still and glassy-eyed, like a little boy in church.

The man nodded in approval. He extinguished his cigarette on the floor, leaving a black spot on the varnish. His fingers rose to his mouth and he plucked a thread of tobacco from the gleaming point of his sharp, red tongue. He waited.

At last, Sandor spoke. His voice was flat.

'What are you offering, then?'

'Freedom. Absolute freedom.'

'At what cost?'

The man remained thoughtful for a while. His hand rose to meet the curl again in a composed gesture.

'Is—' Sandor tried to go on, but his voice broke and he looked away. 'Is damnation even possible if you don't believe in anything?'

'I'm afraid so.'

There was a pause. Sandor looked up. The man uncrossed his legs and leaned forward. His pale eyes focused on Sandor with such flattering intensity that his stomach fluttered and he shifted uncomfortably in his chair.

'What do you want? My soul?' He forgot himself and scoffed.

'Yes,' was the plain response.

Sandor's mouth went dry. They stared at each other. The feeble light that enveloped them, the bruised glow of the snowy night, shimmered. The rest of the room, the rest of the world, fell into darkness.

'You won't miss it, Sandor. You'll be dead by then.'

'Are you going to kill me when it's time?'

'No,' the man replied patiently, in the tone of an adult explaining something to a small child. 'This has nothing to do with your lifespan, or the manner of your death. It makes no difference to me. All I want from you is to stick to our deal. No more back and forth. No more drawing circles. Do you understand?'

Sandor tried to collect his thoughts. His hands twitched, and he trapped them between his knees.

'What does it mean,' he asked, 'to give up a soul?'

'Let me answer this with another question: do you believe in hell, Sandor?'

The expressionless eyes were fixed on him and Sandor felt them like shards of glass. He was reminded of the fairy tale about the boy who got a splinter of an evil mirror in his eye.

'...No,' he muttered. But his feeble reply faded into the quiet.

Amusement flickered in the pale eyes. 'Quite sure, then?'

'Well, what if I'm not?' He suddenly felt rebellious, as if this were another squabble at the breakfast table. 'Would it be any better if I believed everything? After all – believing makes no real difference, does it? Not to me! Isn't it better if I don't, then?'

Isn't it easier for everyone if I want it myself? He felt stupid, and suddenly very small. The man nodded in sympathy. Sandor clenched his teeth.

'So what would I gain from this... this exchange?'

'Everything will be taken care of. You will be free to lead the life you choose rather than the one laid out for you.'

Sandor clenched his fists. 'But you won't hurt anyone? Not my parents...?'

'I would never lay a finger on them. I only deal with you. I told you, everything will be taken care of.' His voice dropped to a whisper. 'Would you like that?'

There was a moment of silence.

'Yes,' Sandor said.

The man leaned back, exhaled and smiled. 'Get up.'

Sandor stood up. His chest felt constricted, his joints cold and stiff. He looked round, half expecting a clap of thunder and the smell of brimstone. The man got up too and smiled fully for the first time, a smile so devoid of any human element, all sharp teeth and gleaming eyes, that Sandor should have fled for his life then and there. But he didn't, and he thought he was being the bravest he had ever been.

'Now, my dear boy, now we must seal our deal.' The man reached out a hand.

It was then that Sandor froze. He tried to raise his right hand but nothing happened – it remained hanging by his side like dead game suspended from a hunter's belt. He couldn't make it move.

The man's hand hovered steadily, his expression unchanging. It was as if he had been expecting this reaction, as if he had all the time in the world. A muscle strained the fabric of the sleeve, but it didn't betray a single hint of tremor.

It was a paralysis, a statement of independence of Sandor's body resisting his decision. He started feeling scared, embarrassed and foolish. He didn't dare meet the man's eyes and fixed his gaze downwards, on the beautifully polished shoes. The reflections on them began to shift in a slow, hypnotising motion.

As if someone had snapped their fingers Sandor slipped out of his trance, met the man's eyes and then reached forward. They shook hands.

Then the man's other hand flew up and grabbed Sandor by the wrist. He jumped back with a yelp: the hand was burning. He struggled to free himself but the grip was too strong. Then abruptly the hands released him, and he stumbled backwards. Under his wrist where the man's thumb had pressed was a bright red mark, the size of a cigarette burn. Sandor put his cool palm on it to relieve the inflamed, throbbing flesh.

'You branded me,' he mumbled.

The man nodded. 'Thank you for your cooperation.'

Sandor took a wary step back, flexing his fingers.

'I don't feel any different.'

'I wouldn't expect you to.'

There was the sound of a knock on glass. Sandor glanced round. The man turned to the window with a grin of satisfaction. Someone was standing outside in the mist, knocking timidly.

'Just in time,' the man said.

In the half-light of the snow clouds and through the fogged glass nothing was visible but a dark silhouette. A wet palm pressed against the glass pane and tried to push it in. The man walked to the main window and started unlatching it. Sandor was seized with an incomprehensible terror.

'Don't let him in. Don't let him in!'

There was a screech and a clang as the window was dragged open, its metallic frame grating against the latches. A blast of freezing wind sneaked into the room, and in followed a young man. He was shuddering and stumbling in his thin, snow-covered clothes. His face, hair, hands and naked feet were plastered with a layer of white that gave him a distorted, monstrous appearance. As he climbed through the window and stumbled into the warm piano room, the snow began to dissolve and fell off him in clumps like melted wax.

Then his face came into view, and Sandor saw that he was looking at himself.

1990

Erzsi came to work early the next day. Outside a storm had extinguished all daylight, and beat madly against the front door. She helped Petar with the meat while Ferdi was cleaning the dining room, and Ferdi heard them talk about last night's outing. Then they lowered their voices and he had the fleeting suspicion that they were talking about him.

He had spared little thought to last night's encounter with the madman, but Ferdi could still see his brown eyes and the tangled beard, smell the ammoniac, musty odour of the man's clothes. The echoing sobs that had followed them down the stairs were now confused with Ferdi's own in the wet alley where he had chased Sandor, and the pity and disgust evoked in him disturbed Ferdi, as if directed at his own person too.

The butcher's truck drove off, and Erzsi walked in with a fresh cup of coffee. She tiptoed round the freshly mopped spots, turned a chair and sat close to him. Now and then the lights flickered, undecided if they would give up or not. Ferdi put the mop away and joined her. She put her feet against his chair and said nothing for a while, absorbed in the sound of the rain. Lightning flashed through the small frosted window.

'The storm keeps circling,' she said.

'How do you know?'

'I'm counting the seconds between light and sound.'

He waited with her until the next lightning, and counted along.

'So you were out with Dieter and Petar last night?'

He nodded. 'I like Dieter.'

She smiled into her mug. 'I like him too. And you've made an impression on the boy. You didn't end up playing again, did you? I'd be sorry to have missed that.'

'No, but there were other surprises.'

'Really? Do tell.'

'Dieter will fill you in.' He fiddled with the hem of his apron. 'You have the key to Mrs Soltesz's office, don't you? Where the phone is?'

Erzsi squinted and nodded.

'Would you let me in for a minute? I need to make a call but I have no line at home.'

'What am I getting in return?'

Ferdi was taken aback. He struggled to come up with something. 'Do you want money...?'

Erzsi kicked his chair. 'No, you dolt! You have no imagination. You want to use Holy Mother's phone? You have to earn it!'

'What do I have to do?'

She glanced at the covered piano and then back at him.

'Erzsi, come on...'

'It's just the two of us!'

His chest tingled. The thick piano cover seemed to be breathing softly.

'All right, but it's out of tune.'

He stepped up onto the small platform. Erzsi sat upright. He pulled the cover and it fell fluttering around him. The green felt protecting the keys was tossed aside.

Dieu vous garde.

He pulled out the piano stool, sat and placed his fingers on the icy keys. His body collected itself into a tight coil, alert to all the creaks coming from the wooden bulk. A familiar shadow sat by the corner of his eye, watching his hands. He did not resist it.

He played for what felt like a very short time. He wasn't sure about the piece; it must have sprung from the crispness of the autumn still clinging to his hair, the cinnamon-scented bakery he had passed earlier, the piles of mouldy leaves in street gutters. The twanging of the loosened chords joined the grumbling storm.

Erzsi applauded, biting her lip to hide a grin. Ferdi stood up and made a stiff bow. He covered the keys and the piano, and resumed his seat next to her.

'Do you have a cigarette?'

'No. Have some of my coffee.'

He took the cup with a shaky hand. Erzsi's gaze burned a hole in him.

'I'm just not used to playing, that's all,' he said.

'I think I've heard this piece before, it's a famous one.' She tilted her head. 'But it was very different today. You made it yours.'

'What do you mean?'

'I'm not sure. As if I was listening to your voice, I don't know. Thank you,' she said, and he gave her an awkward smile. She rummaged in her pocket and produced a set of keys. 'Don't mess anything up.'

The air inside Mrs Soltesz's tiny office was thick: a sticky mixture of tobacco, lemon cologne and hairspray. Photos of family members and icons of saints were stuck round the walls. On the desk was the account book, an ashtray full of stubs with lipstick marks, an empty bottle of holy water with a dried flower in it, and the phone. Ferdi closed the door behind him and put his finger on the dial.

Gedeon, Gabriella. Everyone he knew was here; anyone he didn't know was a threat. The straining dial tone waited while Ferdi frowned at the number.

He dialled; there was no answer. He put the receiver back and waited, then dialled again. A man picked up, and Ferdi asked for the name on the paper. He waited some more, then a woman picked up the phone.

'Hello?'

The calm, raspy voice was familiar. Ferdi struggled to place her.

'Hello, is this Mrs Gedeon? My name is Ferdi Molnar.'

'Of course! Mr Molnar. Do you remember me?'

'I'm afraid not.'

'We met the other night. You played the piano for us, I was playing the violin.'

Of course. The pythoness. The scientist with the glittering green snake and the violin. He stood blankly for a moment, not sure what to say.

'Mr Molnar? Are you there?'

'Yes. Yes, I remember you, Mrs Gedeon. How are you?'

'Gabriella, please.' Her voice was rough and pleasant, never fluctuating too much.

'Then I'm Ferdi.' There was a soft rustling sound and he imagined her smile, the wrinkles round her eyes deepening.

'Ferdi, excuse me for prying, but are you performing somewhere at the moment?'

'Performing?'

'Playing the piano.'

'Oh. No, I'm not.'

'Would you be interested in it?'

Ferdi glanced round at the faces of the saints, looking for a cue. 'I haven't thought about it.'

'I would like to talk to you about it, if it's all right. Over coffee, maybe. Would you like to meet this afternoon? Or in the evening?'

'...Sure. Of course.'

'What time works for you?'

'Half past seven would be good.'

He heard the scratch of pencil on paper. 'Good. Can you meet at V– Square?'

'Yes.'

'Then I'll see you there.'

'...Yes.'

'Have a nice day, Ferdi.'

'Thank you. You too.'

She hung up. He remained listening to the tone for a while, and put the handle in its place. He made sure that nothing on the desk had been moved and locked the door behind him. Erzsi was filling the salt and pepper shakers. She looked up, and took the key back.

'Work or play?' she asked.

Ferdi shrugged. He recalled what he could about Gabriella Gedeon: her fine wrinkles, her dark eyes when she winked at him, her silent laughter at Dieter's jokes, all framed by the undulating snake on her dress as it caught the light. Everything else faded into that night's drunkenness.

He and Erzsi finished their chores early and sat together in the dining room, listening to the downpour. Erzsi turned off the lights, poured strong coffee and lit a candle. Ferdi toasted some stale bread under the grill. They sat next to each other, savouring the mood. Ferdi sprinkled salt on his bread, while Erzsi dipped her own in her mug. There was something wonderfully special about toasted bread in the morning half-darkness, while the wind howled. Everything seemed faraway and unimportant. No threat was big enough to overpower the taste of the salt dissolving in Ferdi's mouth. Erzsi was smiling and he was smiling too, blissful through this sacramental exchange of warm food and drink. They spoke of many things he couldn't afterwards remember.

Ferdi told her about Gabriella Gedeon's phone call. Erzsi remembered Sunday night more clearly, and mused for a while over the mysterious woman.

'I liked her,' was her verdict, and he felt encouraged. 'Where did you study music, Ferdi?'

'I didn't. I had to make a living early.'

'What about school? Did you learn to play there?'

'No, I was home-schooled – but not terribly well,' he added, thoughtfully.

'No wonder you're stuck here.'

'Why are *you* here, then?'

'I had to make a living early, too. Did your parents teach you how to play?'

The candle flickered, making the shadows dance. Ferdi shaded it from the draught with his cupped palm. 'My father did.'

'And you're talented. Even I can see that. She must have seen it too, this Gabriella Gedeon. I wonder how she got your home number... Who knows what else was said that night?'

'Are you talking about Dieter?'

Through the candlelight he saw her cheeks redden. She passed her finger though the small flame a few times, then licked the soot off it.

'I don't know. Seems ridiculous at first sight, doesn't he? Fun, puppy-like. But then he's all quiet, contradictory. It can get confusing.'

A drop of wax landed on the polished wood and she scooped it up, pressed it into a flake and put it on her plate.

'I'm not sure about this life sometimes, Ferdi. I was never a city girl.' She caught more drops of wax, piling them together into a crumb, moulding it into the shape of a face. 'But it's too early to say. Careful – whatever happens, I'll have you to blame!' She laughed.

Ferdi rubbed the finger where the ring hanging round his neck usually sat. He put his hands in his pockets, opened his mouth to say something, and then changed his mind.

'What's wrong?'

The rainfall had stopped. His voice came low. 'I'm not sure about this life either. Maybe we shouldn't talk about these things.'

She began to scoop the crumbs with her hand. 'You always go around like this, Ferdi. Like you're embarrassed that you exist. It doesn't do anybody any good.'

The air seemed to become solid, pressing him down. 'What if there's nothing I can do about it?' He clutched the ring through the shirt. 'What if I was never supposed to exist?'

'Don't make fun of me...' She saw the expression on his face and frowned. 'Ferdi, you're a runaway, aren't you?'

He nodded and Erzsi drew her chair closer to him.

'What happened?' The same light touch as Dieter's. It was barely on his shoulder and then it was gone. 'Is it how you got this scar?'

He nodded again, very slowly, his eyes pinned on the floor. 'We saw a man last night, when we were out with Dieter. And he knew me. I'd never seen him before, but he knew me.' He was nodding as he talked, rocking back and forth and trying to assemble his scattered fears into something definite and whole, something that could make sense. 'And there's someone... following me.'

'Why are they following you?'

Ferdi looked up. Erzsi's eyes were watching him earnestly. He sought a truth in himself, something no longer a secret and untouched by the lie he had been forced to live by. He stopped moving.

'I don't know. I really don't.'

The sound of the service door made them jump. Someone walked into the kitchen and tossed a set of keys on the counter. Erzsi turned on the lights, blinding Ferdi for a moment. She threw him an anxious glance over her shoulder and left.

*

'Might get snow soon,' said Dieter later, looking up at the evening sky. Ferdi, too tired to enjoy his break, followed his gaze.

'I hate snow,' Ferdi said vehemently.

'Then you might consider heading south soon, along with the birds.'

Ferdi blew on his cigarette for the flame to catch. It had just stopped raining, and the alley was colder than usual. Frost was settling in, slow and deliberate, promising a clear night. Despite the threat of snow Ferdi found the air invigorating. It smelled of soot, and he was comforted by the idea that someone close by had a fire going in a stove or fireplace, and was inching closer to it as the night approached.

'You're all right, then, Molnar?'

Ferdi replied with a noncommittal sound. Dieter had come to work with a bruise on his neck and bloodshot eyes, and didn't appear to mind. Erzsi, upon hearing the story of the madman, had simply glanced at Ferdi and made no comment.

Dieter's bruise made Ferdi queasy. He had noticed enough scars on Dieter to guess that he must have seen worse, but this one deeply bothered him, as if he had inflicted the injury himself. He glanced at his own hands, cracked, roughened and yellowish, with countless tiny scars and burns, and wondered if they were capable of causing such damage. He recalled the fight with Sandor and how Dorika had then appeared, staring at them with terrified eyes, and his mind wandered to her: the first woman he had ever seen, the first human he ever laid eyes on that wasn't Sandor. Up to then he might have believed that the world was populated exclusively by people who looked like themselves. Dorika's appearance had ended that surreal idea.

And right after that had come the flood of new faces: Salomon and Karolina, the streets, the school.

That day shone in his memory: the cold sunny morning when he could be someone else, someone who went to school, who had parents. The first ray of sun on his face. The first kind touch, as Karolina inspected the bruises and cuts her son had left on Ferdi's skin. First feeling of warm water and fresh clothes. First mouthfuls of warm food and hot coffee and cherry jam. First walk out of the estate, under the shivering trees. Being greeted by girls and boys he didn't know, casually talked to and laughed at for his confused expression. Other languages, other concepts. The world expanding. People listening to him, asking him questions. Nobody minding that he spoke, nobody recoiling in terror or disgust.

And again the warmth of the sun through the foliage, while walking back to the Esterhazy manor. Seeing it again tower above him just like that first time through the blizzard, enormous with an obscene and seductive charm – glinting and certain, inviting and excluding at the same time. Ferdi had felt himself split for a moment then. Part of him wanted to burrow in his hole under that stone behemoth and lie there in the womb-like safety of the cruel life he had been used to, and another part was anxious to turn and run away. All he had wanted was to return to the vivid world he had just come to know, and would be forced to abandon.

In his short life, full of the hardship thrown at the dispossessed, Ferdi had been forced to make many hard decisions. But none had been as difficult and defining as the one he took that day, returning to Sandor. By the time he had been through the thorny forest path and appeared at the top of the stairs down to the gun room, he had forgiven him of many wrongs. It was no surprise then that his guilty dreams of a loving, friendly fantasy of Sandor persisted: it was the hope that such forgiveness would someday be reciprocated. For this impertinence he was left with this scar, and shadows populated the corners of his eyes.

Ferdi flexed his fingers. Dieter was no longer paying attention to him, and Ferdi followed his gaze as Dieter stood with a cigarette dangling between dry lips, hands on his waist. He was looking at the violet sky, streaked with fiery clouds and dotted with stars. A flock of birds was circling, their hoarse calls raising a din. The swarm fluctuated with each gust of air, casting mysterious shapes.

'I miss the sea sometimes,' sighed Dieter.

*

Gabriella Gedeon smoked thin cigarillos and watched Ferdi with curiosity from across the table. The snake was gone, leaving her oddly lonesome in her thick camel coat and pastel blue sweater. Her fingers looked thin and brittle, and it was shocking to remember the wiry strength they had employed on the violin.

'You look familiar,' she said, studying him while Ferdi ate his warm strudel. 'Are you sure we haven't met before?'

He shook his head. Gabriella sipped some coffee.

'It will come to me. My memory is a mess.'

'But you're a musician.'

'It's my hands that remember the music, not my head. Same goes for biology – unless my work was in a lab, I was terrible at it.' She tapped the cigarillo in the ashtray. 'Anyway, there was never any money in either. But at least we are enjoying ourselves in retirement.'

'Your husband?'

'Yes, Balint was playing the cimbalom, remember? *His* memory is excellent. He remembers everything he reads, and can write down music after listening to the tape just once. I've seen him take notes to the radio. Of course, he says it's nothing. Meanwhile, I'm counting my change twice like an old lady!'

She laughed. In the busy café someone was shouting to get the waiter's attention. The man at the next table turned the pages of his newspaper with disproportionately loud sounds. Wine glasses and pastries floated by on trays. Ferdi tried to make out people's faces through the smoke.

'Are you married, Ferdi? Any babies?'

'No.'

'I have a daughter, about your age. She's doing her postgraduate studies in America, too far away to be embarrassed by her parents, the wandering entertainers. I'm sorry, where are my manners! Smoke?'

Ferdi took a cigarillo out of politeness, and let her light it for him. The taste was thick, almost starchy.

'Balint prepared her well for academia,' she went on. 'He knows his stuff, he has an ear for it.'

'For what?'

'Everything related to music. He wanted Natalia to go into his field, but she switched to mathematics. Close enough, when you think about it. So, when Monday came he couldn't stop talking about your playing.'

Gabriella smiled. Ferdi let out an awkward puff of smoke.

'We all had plenty of wine that night,' he said.

'True, but your style is rather unique. It would be a pity not to share it.'

Ferdi poked the crumbs around his plate. 'You're too kind. But it's just a hobby.'

'What was your musical education?'

'I had a teacher at home.'

Ferdi saw her eyes pause at his worn cuffs and battered coat. 'What did your teacher think about your playing?'

'They never said.'

'They must have put decent work into you. Your technique is basic but well-ingrained. You can't miss an education in someone, even if your style was a little unorthodox. That's not a bad thing,' she added, seeing him shy away. 'It was this unorthodox streak that gave your piece its texture. Balint calls it "the artist's signature"; he loves this kind of thing, and he can always tell. Yet… Balint's world can be small.'

'What do you mean?'

'I mean that he wouldn't go out of his way to say this to a young artist! But I like you, Ferdi. I too saw something in your work: something marvellous. And we talked nicely, even if you don't remember most of it.'

Ferdi sat back. The sudden interest made him uncomfortable, but the bustling café gave an aura of informality to the whole thing. Gabriella probably believed that discussions like this were a regular occurrence to him. He couldn't exactly explain such things to himself, much less to a stranger.

'Is this why you called, then?'

'Yes. I would like to help, if I can.' Gabriella leaned in with a sly smile that gathered the wrinkles to her right eye. 'We oddballs should always help one another.'

Ferdi blushed. He sought refuge in the cigarillo but it was smoked through, and he extinguished it. She shook her head.

'Modesty is admirable, Ferdi, but don't get too lost in it. Listen, I didn't bring you here to lecture you, that's a flaw that comes with my age. I had a nice idea the other day. A friend of mine is putting together a recital for amateurs at the Academy of Music. The event is open to the public, a rather informal affair, no credentials required. A sort of open call, where emerging artists can share their work with people of the trade. I thought you might be interested in taking part. All you need is to register, no entry fee. It takes place on Sunday the twenty-eighth.'

'The twenty-eighth!'

'Is this a problem?'

Ferdi thought of the appointment waiting for him on the thirtieth, across from the Opera House, and his heart beat hard. It was just so – at least there would be one thing still before that day, one good thing...

'None at all.' He tried to avoid her gaze.

Gabriella sighed, lifted her handbag and started rummaging in it. 'You might not trust me, and Balint always says I'm coming on too strong.'

She produced a pen and an address book and started scribbling something on her paper napkin. She pushed it towards him.

'I have to rush now, but I don't want to pressure you. I was calling because the deadline for registration is tomorrow. This is the number of my friend. And that's my home number underneath; you can call me if you need me.'

Ferdi took the napkin while Gabriella put on her scarf and coat.

'Think about it. I will be there anyway. Mention my name, if you do call.'

She paid for both of them, cutting his protests midway.

'Good luck, Ferdi. I hope I'll see you there.'

She left, while he was still trying to digest her invitation. The smell of stale perfume and camel hair lingered until the man on the next table dispelled it with one turn of his newspaper.

Ferdi stepped out into the wet night, the napkin carefully folded in the inner pocket of his coat. In the tram, lulled by its gentle rocking, he went through melodies and tapped them out on his knee. The thought of performing was outrageous. And yet there he was, putting pieces together, connecting, smoothing out; he remembered the night lights dancing on the wet pavement and the music he had teased out of them, and he watched them again now out of the window, swirling away.

It was time to name them, he decided, all those fragments that filled his tattered burgundy notebook like bits of string. He liked to pair and shuffle them in his mind until something fit, and when last Sunday he found himself at a piano he had plucked the piece closest to the surface. Now there was a presence to that piece. The music had escaped him and snuck into other people's minds, so it was proper that it should have an identity, a name to go with it. As he was watching the city glide by, golden and mossy, he knew the names: there were names that had always been there for him to discover, orphan titles without songs. They had been waiting in the blue cloth-bound book of fairy tales, which contained a part of him. His purposeless music would be named just like he was named, to be defined and tamed and used, and to be called upon whenever needed.

Ferdi got off the tram and headed for the riverside, following an inexplicable feeling of obligation. At the sight of the abandoned art-nouveau building he stopped. He wished for Dieter like a little boy, for his overwhelming physical presence with that slow, wide-kneed strut and the precarious gentleness of a well-fed wild animal, for his booming laughter and the glow of his blonde head. He wished for Erzsi, with her unflinching gaze and the warmth that exuded from her dark skin. There was nobody to offer him comfort. Just the swelling river up ahead, sleepy and glittering, and the familiar building with its darkened glass loft.

The main entrance stood with its lock broken, just as they had left it last night. Ferdi gave it a push, glanced round to make sure nobody was watching, and slipped into the quiet building. The meeting with Gabriella had left him with a bizarre feeling of confidence. It was as if his existence, a shaky and uncertain thing, had been recently reconfirmed. He walked up the stairs.

The door at the topmost floor was wide open. Ferdi stepped in.

'You came alone today,' said a voice.

Ferdi recognised the voice as the madman's, and peered into the far corner.

'I knew you'd come,' wheezed the voice again. 'I knew you wouldn't forget me.'

The words dwindled in a gurgling cough, there was the sound of spitting and of something wet hitting the hardwood floor. Ferdi put his hand in his pocket and held onto his keys. He walked a little closer. He could faintly make out the shape of someone sitting on the floor, with his back against the wall and his legs sprawled.

'I'm not going to hurt you,' said Ferdi. 'I want to talk. I need some explanation.'

A blast of light blinded him. The madman chuckled. Ferdi shielded his eyes and the beam of light lowered. The man let the flashlight roll away from him, casting its shaky light at their feet. Ferdi saw his face, covered in bruises from Dieter's defence. Dark spittle was hanging from his lip.

The man gestured at the floor. 'Take a seat,' he grinned.

Ferdi hesitated for a moment, then sat down. 'How do you know me?'

'I know—' He coughed again, gasping for air. 'I know what you are. I can see it.'

Ferdi's insides went cold. 'See what?'

'I can see his mark on you.'

He pointed at Ferdi and for a split second his worst fears were true – Ferdi looked down at himself and clutched at his face, searching for that telltale sign that was obvious to everyone, the one thing setting him apart from people.

The madman let out a wheezing laugh. 'Others can't see it. I can. It's on your right wrist.'

Ferdi grasped his wrist. There was nothing out of the ordinary about it, just skin and veins and small dark hairs.

'The mark is small. It glows – how it glows! Like a beam of light.'

'What is it?'

'His seal, of course.'

Ferdi gave his ring a turn. 'Whose seal?'

The man gestured at Ferdi to move closer. 'Father's, of course,' he whispered.

'I don't have a father.'

'Oh, me neither.' The man picked at his filthy coat with trembling hands. 'You and I are brothers, because neither of us were born...'

He seemed to nod off. Ferdi shook his leg to rouse him.

'Tell me what you know. Tell me!'

The man coughed again, dribbling more black spit. 'Why should I tell you? All my life I've tried to forget what I am. All my life...'

He nodded off again. Ferdi grabbed the man by the coat, but his fingers sank in something warm and wet. He recoiled in disgust.

'All this time...' the man drawled. 'All this unbearable time circling upon itself, with no ending and no beginning, all this time in the darkness...'

Ferdi groped for the flashlight and turned it towards the man. The coat was covered in blood.

'Nothing else but nothing...'

His blood was all over Ferdi's hands. The flashlight slipped in his wet grip. 'I'm going to call for an ambulance, don't move—'

The man grabbed Ferdi's sleeve. Blood kept trickling from his mouth and into his beard. 'Too late – stay, stay and wait with me.'

'Wait for what?'

The hand crumpled Ferdi's coat.

'I want to see if I can die…'

Ferdi moved closer, taking the man's hands in his own. They were an old man's hands, gnarled and spotted, the rough skin fissured and stuffed with dirt. The wheezing was getting stronger.

'Who did this to you?'

'Someone came… I didn't see them. They didn't want me to talk anymore, they didn't want me to say all I remember, they had a knife… They came here for me, like you did…' The man turned his head to look at Ferdi. Suddenly the look on his drawn face was full of contempt. 'I'm nothing like you,' he said. His gaze wandered over Ferdi's shoulder, where the river glinted through the glass. 'I was… splendid.'

His hands relaxed in Ferdi's grip. The gaze remained. Ferdi began to shake him.

'Hey. Hey!'

But the man just slid down and his head lolled forward.

Ferdi retreated with a cry of horror and scrambled to his feet. His hands were shaking. He leaned in and wiped them as best as he could on the edge of the man's coat. His stomach gave a nasty turn. He staggered, leaned against the wall and took a breath.

He saw through the corner of his eye someone standing by the entrance, watching him.

Ferdi straightened up slowly and the person retreated into the dark stairwell, where he couldn't make them out. Ferdi stepped forward and they stepped back again with a squeak of rubber soles.

Ferdi sprang. He didn't pause to think that this could be the murderer, that he had nothing to protect himself with – he just ran headlong into the hallway, ready to fight. But the other slipped away unseen and ran down the stairs, lithe and fast, their shoes slipping against the marble steps. Ferdi followed three steps at a time, but when he reached the ground floor the door was open and the hallway empty, and only his own panting could be heard, echoing round the big empty building.

*

The young, pimply waiter was leaning against the wall of the alley, eating a sandwich. When he caught sight of Ferdi his face twisted into a grimace. Ferdi dug his hands deep in his pockets to hide his stained cuffs.

'Will you get Dieter for me?'

The boy swallowed his last bite. 'It's mad inside. Big party of business jerks.'

'I can wait.'

Ferdi nodded towards the door. The boy snorted, threw his napkin on the wet ground and stepped into the kitchen. Ferdi picked up the dirty napkin, wiped his hands once more and put it in his pocket. It was some time until Dieter managed to emerge, red-faced and sweaty. Before he even greeted Ferdi he lit a cigarette.

'We're about to run out of meat,' he gasped. Then he noticed Ferdi's strained expression, his hair standing in a mess, his twitching knee. 'What's wrong?'

Ferdi plucked Dieter's cigarette from his fingers and tried to smoke, but coughed and choked. Dieter snatched his cigarette back.

'I went back to the abandoned building,' said Ferdi.

'Why the hell would you do that?'

'Because I was curious.'

Dieter groaned. 'What happened?'

'The man was there...'

'And?'

'And someone had hurt him.'

Dieter swore.

'He was bleeding when I found him. He – he died, right there, in that room. In my hands. He just – he died.' Ferdi ran his fingers through his hair, tugging at the greasy black strands. He sat on the crates, tugging, until Dieter reached and pulled his hand away.

'You've never seen a man die before, have you?'

Ferdi shook his head.

'Molnar, be honest. Do you know him? Last night he spoke as if he knew you.'

'No. I'd never seen him before last night.'

'Why would someone kill him?'

'I don't know! I wanted to talk to him, find out why he said he knew me, so I went back and he was sitting on the floor, bleeding all the while, and I hadn't even noticed!'

Dieter offered him his cigarette, but Ferdi shook his head.

'And there was someone else there, in the dark... They ran away, I couldn't see them.' He stared at his reflection in the shop window across the alley. 'The man died.'

Dieter gave him a shake. 'Come on. There was nothing you could do. He was a luckless bastard in a big bad world, it could have been over anything. It could have been over a coat or a sleeping spot. Christ!'

'What?'

Dieter's voiced dropped into a whisper. 'Is that blood on your sleeves? Have you been walking round with blood on your sleeves?'

Ferdi tried to rub it away with the inside of his shirt.

'Stop, you're making it worse. Did you call the police?'

'No. Should I?'

'I don't know. Did you touch anything?'

'No – maybe? I don't remember! Nobody saw me go in, I think. Nobody saw me come out.'

'You *think*?' From inside the kitchen, someone shouted Dieter's name. 'Think faster!' he said.

Ferdi shrugged in despair.

'Look, Molnar, it may be all right. That old building is long abandoned. Maybe they won't find him for a while. And when they do, they'll take one look at him and I doubt they'll break a sweat. God rest his poor soul.'

'I doubt that,' said Ferdi without thinking.

'What?'

'About the police, I mean,' Ferdi added hastily.

'Well, human indifference knows no bounds. Anyway, you didn't do anything.' His hand tightened on Ferdi's shoulder. 'Right?'

Ferdi shrugged him off. 'I didn't kill him, Dieter.'

Dieter's grip relaxed. 'That's good to hear.' He stomped on his cigarette. 'Are you going to be all right?'

Ferdi rubbed his eyes. 'I think so. I'm exhausted.'

With a jolt, he remembered his meeting with Gabriella Gedeon earlier. He felt in his inner pocket for the napkin with the phone numbers. It was still there. Dieter patted his arm.

'Go home. Take a shower. Rinse your clothes in cold water. Read those fairy tales of yours and go to sleep. Tomorrow is your day off, isn't it?'

'Normally yes, but I swapped my shift. I need to take the day off next Tuesday.'

'What for?'

'...Personal reasons.'

'Fine.' Dieter sighed, and turned to go back inside. 'Please be careful, Molnar. Trouble seems to like you.'

1979

The *thing* didn't move. It looked back at Sandor with wide eyes – no, they were his own eyes: black, deep-set and with a faint upward slant. It stood meekly, and watched Sandor with the wariness of a dog that had been kicked around all its life, trembling from head to toe. When it noticed Sandor's gaze fixed on it, it blushed and lowered its head.

The world spun around him. There was a moment of absolute blackness when he must have momentarily fainted on his feet.

There, on this horrifying *thing*, was everything he saw in the bathroom mirror every morning, except grotesquely inverted: the uneven way his hair grew as if every tuft had its own purpose, except now they all seemed to curl differently. The small mole by his eyebrow, on the wrong side again. The bony toes, dripping in the puddle that formed around the creature's feet, had the familiar inward convergence. The thin, colourless lips ended in the same tiny hollows. Around the angular jaw, which protruded awkwardly in a body not grown into it yet, were the exact same signs of thin, patchy stubble.

'What is the meaning of this?'

But the man in the tuxedo was not there. While Sandor was studying the creature bearing his likeness in every conceivable detail, the man had disappeared. Even the coat and the hat were gone, and the only proof he had ever been there at all was the wet ring on the piano and the cigarette burn on the floor. The cigarette butt was nowhere to be seen, and there was no trace of ash.

However, there was still the burn on his own wrist. He wrapped his hand around it. The full realisation of what he had just done struck him, and he drew a long, painful breath.

'No,' he whispered.

The creature looked up at him and its lips parted in curiosity. It glanced around and raised its eyebrows as it too realised that the man had disappeared. But the knowledge didn't seem to bother it. Instead, its posture relaxed slightly, and it met Sandor's eyes with a little more confidence.

'Don't look at me,' said Sandor with repulsion, but for a second he felt pity for the miserable, shivering thing as it hurried to look down at its toes again. And then his disgust returned. He was consumed with nausea and thought he would gag. He bent over, leaned against a chair and tried to control his breathing.

Fighting every natural instinct, he stepped forward and grabbed the creature's arm. The limb twitched under the wet fabric as its slim muscles tensed at his touch. The creature – the young man – was very much real. It even exuded some feeble warmth and the sharp odour of fresh sweat. Its face contorted with shock at the contact and it drew back, but didn't dare resist. Sandor let go and it retreated back to a safe distance.

They stared at each other. He had to say something, anything, or time itself would end and he still wouldn't know what to do.

'Do you have a name?' he asked, and suddenly was frozen with panic. *Please let it be named anything other than my own name.*

It shook its head and immense relief washed over him. At least it understood what he was saying. The idea that he would have to name it himself was so strange that his mouth cracked into a smile. The *thing* saw the smile, and tried to imitate the expression with a forced movement of its muscles. Then it stopped, considering the process, and tried again. It managed the smallest grin, and at that moment it looked exactly like the picture standing on the bookshelf behind it, that of Sandor smiling between his parents on a summer day at the lake. Sandor felt his stomach convulse again.

For a single, crazy minute, he considered killing it.

him

Killing *him*.

Something wild inside Sandor desperately wanted this creature dead. He could do it right now, it looked unable to defend itself. There was the flashlight, it was heavy enough. There was the decorative brass paperweight on the bookcase. He could scar the face and the hands beyond recognition. He could drag the body out in the snow himself, and could hide it – where? He would find a way, if he needed to, he could—

Couldn't he?

But this seemed to be a person. *A human being.* Wasn't it? It had to be. No matter how twisted and evil its origin might be, there was no proof it was twisted and evil itself. Sandor was the reason for this creature's existence, and it had to be kept alive. He felt the responsibility tighten around his neck like a noose.

And he had just traded in his soul for its life.

He gestured briskly. 'Come here.'

The other boy took a hesitant step forward and stopped again. Sandor lowered his hand.

'Come here. I won't hurt you.'

It approached and raised its hand to touch his own, but when it moved closer Sandor stepped aside and nodded towards the piano stool.

'Sit.'

It did as it was told. Sandor lifted the lid. As the keys shone in the dimness it was like opening a coffin. The other stiffened, and looked at the piano with narrowed eyes.

'Play something.'

It didn't budge. Sandor's heart started racing and his muscles trembled. He moved abruptly, grabbed its hands and placed them forcefully on the keys, causing a cacophony that echoed around the empty room. He drew back and saw the creature's hands lying on the keys in two fists. Then hesitantly the fingers straightened, hovering over what was clearly perceived as a hostile object. Finally they withdrew to the safety of its lap.

Sandor's throat had gone dry.

'I said, *play.*'

It looked up, a pitiful thing. Drops of melting ice ran down its face from the clumps in its hair. Their eyes met again, and he saw the hopelessness and the utter ignorance in them.

It was all for nothing.

Tears started welling up and Sandor couldn't fight them any longer. He banged the piano with his fist.

'Play, PLAY!'

The young man cowered. Sandor punched him on the shoulder and he shrank away, rubbing his injury. Sandor hadn't meant to do it but his anger was brimming; he hit the piano again, picked up the flashlight and threw it away. It shattered against a corner of the room.

Then he looked around and was suddenly aware of every single object and living thing – and of the swelling frost and the heavy clouds outside, of his straining insides, of the burn on his wrist – and he sank onto the floor, put his face in his hands and cried for a long time, while his newfound twin watched sadly from the piano seat.

When at last he was all cried out and his chest was empty, he didn't know how much time had passed. He lifted his bloated face and saw that the *thing* was still there, waiting. Its nose was red, its cheeks flushed and the eyes bleary. The skin glistened with sweat, and its whole body vibrated with low fever. Its toes were curled against the bare soles, and it let out a powerful sneeze.

Sandor took off his slippers and handed them to the young man, who put them on after fumbling for a while. The sensation seemed to please him. Sandor rubbed his own cold feet through his socks and mused for a while. Some time passed before he could find some end to his thoughts.

This creature needed a name, one that reminded Sandor of nothing and nobody. His gaze swept around the room, and paused at the bookshelves for inspiration.

'Listen to me.'

The young man shrank and looked at him with a mixture of fear and hope.

'Your name will be Ferdi. Do you understand?'

It nodded slowly.

'And my name is Sandor.'

It nodded again.

'I am Sandor Esterhazy. This is my home,' he added, gesturing around them, and saw his gaze following the gesture with curiosity. 'So, what is your name?'

Sandor was trying to push words such as *creature*, *thing*, out of his mind; more to keep himself sane than out of civility. The young man frowned and mouthed the word a couple of times.

'*Ferdi...*' He spoke carefully, letting his mouth wrap around each sound with care.

The voice was identical to Sandor's, but used so differently that it sounded foreign. It was even, low and unexpectedly soft, oddly pleasing. Sandor was certain he had never spoken like this. The young man appeared surprised by the sound of his own voice, and fell silent again.

Sandor got up. The other followed his lead, stumbling a little in the slippers. His eyes shone with fever. 'You'll need to wear something warm,' muttered Sandor. 'Follow me, and be quiet.'

He opened the door and peered into the hallway. Everything still looked absurdly the same, and at the same time unfamiliar, as if replaced by doubles too. This was his home, and yet not anymore – it had been desecrated beyond repair. And perhaps nobody would ever find out. Perhaps when morning came people would go about their business and would be none the wiser.

The lights at the front entrance were still on. He couldn't guess the time, but his parents weren't home yet. He gestured at the silent figure behind him and, very quietly, he and his corporeal shadow went upstairs to his room. He locked the door behind them, and wasn't sure if he did it to keep someone out or in.

Sandor had the young man take off everything he was wearing, looking away as the other hopped awkwardly, trying to disentangle himself from the clothes. Once they had all been removed, Sandor threw them aside, making a mental note to burn or bury them as soon as possible. He dug in his wardrobe for clothes that wouldn't be missed. Thick socks, underwear, old jeans, a woollen sweater with elbow holes, an old shirt and childhood scarves, and on top of those some scratchy blankets and a pair of old slippers handed down from his father. The young man put each layer on with increasing gladness, until he seemed to have grown twice in size and stood there looking comical, revelling in the warmth of coarse fabric.

'Sit down.' Sandor gestured towards the bed, and drew his desk chair close so that he was sitting face to face with him. 'There are some things I need to make clear, and you should always keep them in mind. Do you understand me?'

The other nodded.

'The most important thing is that *you are not me*,' he began, and it struck him as a very ridiculous thing to say. 'You will *never* be me. We are two *separate beings*. Is that clear? You are Ferdi, I am Sandor.'

There was another obedient nod.

'You are not allowed to see anybody. If somebody sees you, you are forbidden to talk to them. Unless I tell you otherwise.'

The young man's face stiffened a bit, and he nodded again.

'However,' Sandor went on, 'if you are seen, you will act as me. If you are forced to speak, you will speak as me. As far as the rest of the world is concerned, you will *be* me. Nobody is to find out who you are and where you come from. *This*' – and here he indicated from one to another, mapping some secret route between them – 'is a secret. Is that clear?'

They stared at each other.

'Answer me.'

'Yes,' came the slow, deliberate reply.

'Good. You must never forget these rules.'

'Why?'

Sandor was taken aback. 'Why? Why do you think—?'

Then it struck him. Sandor got to his feet and opened the wardrobe again. Attached inside was a mirror. He gestured at the young man to approach. Sandor drew him close, uncomfortably close, and stood with his hands on the other boy's shoulders so that the narrow mirror could show both of them. They looked into the glass. They looked at themselves and at each other, and they saw the same face side by side.

The shoulders stiffened under Sandor's hands. He saw the eyes in the mirror widen, the jaw slacken with shock. The young man stood still. Then his expression cleared as he seemed to comprehend something beyond Sandor's grasp. A change came over him, a subtle, important change, one of severity and darkness. Something dim passed over his face.

'I understand,' he said.

He sat back on the bed and remained quiet, staring at his hands on his lap. Sandor had the horrible impression that he had trampled on something small and frail, crushing it to death. He felt the urge to apologise for what he had just done. But he lacked the right words and so said nothing.

He sat back on the chair.

'As for tonight—' he began again, but was interrupted by a thunderous stomach growl. The young man put a hand on his belly and raised his eyebrows in surprise.

'Of course,' Sandor mumbled, and didn't know whether to laugh or cry. 'Of course. Fantastic.' He got up. 'Stay here, and be quiet. I'll get you something to eat.'

He stepped out, leaned against the wall and closed his eyes for a while, wishing hard that he could vanish from the face of the earth. But nothing happened, so he pulled himself together and walked downstairs to the kitchen.

He returned with a plate of cold cuts and boiled potatoes left over from lunch, some bread and a glass of milk. The sight of food made his stomach growl as well. As he placed the plate on the desk he took a slice of bread and nibbled it. He nodded to let the other know he could eat and, behaving again like he would towards a spooked animal, he stepped away from the food and allowed the other to approach uncrowded. The young man sat with hesitation, poked the potatoes a couple of times and then fell on the food savagely, emptying the plate in seconds. Then, glancing guiltily back at Sandor, he downed the glass of milk and gave a loud burp.

Sandor chuckled. 'Good?'

The young man nodded, wiping his mouth with the back of his hand. 'Very good.'

They sat in awkward silence. Sandor despised himself for what he was about to say.

'You will stay in the old gun room. I'll look for a better place, but for now that's all there is. It will be cold, and dirty.'

And locked, he added inwardly. The young man's expression didn't change.

'Come on.' Sandor got up. 'While my parents are still away.'

At the thought of the freezing gun room he picked up a spare pair of gloves and some more socks, a knit cap and an old school sweater. He threw everything into a blanket and gave the bundle to the young man to carry.

'It's going to be very cold,' he repeated, avoiding his eyes.

On their way they stopped by the kitchen again, and there Sandor wrapped some bread and cheese into a towel, along with more leftovers and dried fruit. He handed this too to the young man, who watched him with hunger and curiosity.

'Don't eat these yet,' he warned him. 'Make it last as long as possible. I don't know when I'll be able to bring you food again.'

In the hallway he put on his coat and changed into his snow boots, and they stepped outside. The cold wind knocked the breath out of them. The young man behind him shivered violently and nearly dropped what he was holding.

'It's just around the side of the house,' Sandor said, and led him carefully. The entrance was packed with snow, and he had to dig it with his bare hands while the other stood shuddering in his damp slippers. By the time Sandor was done he could hardly hold the key. When they finally stumbled in, teeth chattering, the stillness of the basement felt warm and welcoming in comparison.

Sandor flipped the light switch, and helped the other boy put everything on the long wooden table.

'Better if you sleep on the table,' he said. 'It's sturdy enough. Less cold, and no mice will trouble you that way. There are also facilities here.'

He indicated the tiny bathroom in the far corner, with a small lavatory and a cracked sink; things once used by the hunters before they set out, at a time when this room was kept clean and lined with comfortable chairs, when the polished cabinets held shotguns and gleaming knives and the wooden table was crowded with bloody game and warm ashtrays.

'You can drink water from the tap here. Everything works. Oh, have this too.' He handed him a roll of toilet paper. 'You'll be absolutely quiet, do you hear? Don't push the table around, don't bang on the door or start shouting. I'll return as soon as I can with more food, but that may be a day, or longer.'

Sandor turned to leave, and as he did he heard Ferdi call him.

'Don't leave,' the young man pleaded. He was clutching the woollen cap, wringing it pathetically between his twig-like fingers. 'Don't leave me here alone.'

Sandor looked at him. The boy's face was twisted with fear and agitation, and he was leaning forward as if about to dash through the door as soon as it opened. Would he disobey? Sandor clenched his fists, ready to fight if he had to.

'Goodnight.'

With one last look at the grim room, and with a shiver he couldn't suppress, he walked out and locked the door behind him.

Sandor plodded through the snow going back to the house, dragging his thoughts behind him like a felled tree. When at last he found himself in the warm silence of the hallway, he stood for a while to gaze at the high ceilings and the fine woodwork of the narrow staircase, the elegant coats and hats on their intricate hangers, the thick wine-red carpet. He contemplated the row of slippers by the umbrella stand. His home life could no longer include him, and from now on he would be a stranger haunting the thick-walled rooms. There was a sense of farewell as he walked up the stairs and traced the smooth lustre of the banister, and when he stepped into his room he knew that the boy who had grown up here was forever lost.

His thoughts went to Maggie, to her wide smile and fogged-up glasses: already she had been packed into a small memory-box in the attic of his mind. He saw that his pyjamas were dirty and wet, so he put on fresh ones and crawled into bed. As soon as he closed his eyes his mind flooded with chaos and he wondered if he would ever manage to rest, but soon he drifted off into uneasy sleep.

In the middle of the night he stirred awake. Slivers of purple light stole in. Sandor had the image of his double lying curled up and shaking with fever in that freezing room, experiencing sleep for the first time in his short, miserable life. Lying there warm and drowsy, Sandor wondered if that *thing* was capable of dreaming.

It was the coldest hour, and the gun room would be unbearable. Not even insects would dare crawl out. One blanket would never be enough, and he should at least find him a pillow...

As sleep crept back to Sandor, it seemed that his mattress was becoming flat, creaking wood, his feet were sticking out from the covers of bedding too high up, and he thought he could hear the patter of small brown mice – and that the world was wrapped in snow and cold, and a horrible, horrible sense of shame... He was slowly consumed by that sensation until nothing else remained.

1990

Ferdi woke up long before the alarm went off. The building was dark and quiet around him, with the occasional rumbling of the water pipes. He turned on the light and sat at the table with his notebook.

The burgundy cover was shiny with age, its edges soft. It was bulging with the various paraphernalia he had written on through the years: napkins, pamphlets, newspaper pages and magazine covers, ticket stubs and receipts, all thick with his small, cramped handwriting. He found the two pieces he had played last Sunday, and set out to make a clean copy. There were only a few blank pages left. Ferdi leafed through the earliest pages and felt pity for all the unrealised music, all the pieces that had been left in this dubious state of half-existence. He picked up the book of fairy tales and leafed through it, looking for a name for the new arrangement, and finally decided on the title 'White Lizard'.

On his way to work he stopped at a public phone and called the number Gabriella had written on the napkin, giving his name, address, and a rough description of what he would be performing. When he mentioned Gabriella's name the woman on the phone chuckled and told Ferdi not to worry.

'There is no rehearsal for this,' she added, 'so participants are asked to rehearse in their own space. Is that all right?'

Ferdi said 'yes', and 'thank you'. She said he was required to show up on time, play and not much else. There was no money or scholarships offered, the woman pointed out. Ferdi agreed to the terms and hung up. The matter of money hadn't crossed his mind, but now he found it a little disappointing. He went on his way, sneezing in the morning chill. Nothing in his life had prepared him for this, and the small glint of joy was a strange sensation. There seemed to be a heady quality to the air he breathed today, as if he had been climbing up a mountain.

Petar arrived early that day as Mrs Soltesz had put in a big order to replenish the stock, so that morning he hurried up and down the steps without idle chatter. When he was done he sat on the doorstep, and Ferdi brought him a glass of water.

'Don't you have anything stronger?'

Ferdi passed him the cup of coffee he had poured for himself. Petar took a sip and grimaced.

'I'll have to show you how to make coffee someday,' he said. 'Proper, Turkish coffee like back at home, good for your heart. Not this tar.' He immediately blushed, as if he had surprised himself. 'I mean – thanks.'

'No problem.'

The boy rubbed his close-cropped hair and side-eyed Ferdi. 'Do you think I should shave?' He ran his finger across his moustache. 'Nobody wears these anymore.'

Ferdi examined him. By the look of him Petar was on the far side of a late adolescent growth spurt. Though shorter than Ferdi, his upper body was wider, stronger and more developed. Ferdi's own strength, after years of odd jobs and malnourishment, was concentrated in the core and his long limbs betrayed none of it.

'I don't believe you need it to look older, if that's what you're going for,' he replied.

'It's not!' Petar protested and sank back, fingering his upper lip and clenching his jaw. He opened his mouth to speak again, but changed his mind. He sprang up, put his cup down on the step and left.

Ferdi picked up the cup, baffled. This was certainly preferable to Tuesday night, but these mood swings made him uncomfortable. He waited until he heard the truck turn into the main street, then returned to the dining room.

The piano lay uncovered, its lid open. The burgundy notebook was propped open above the keys. He hid the notebook in his coat, closed the lid and threw the heavy velvet cloth over the piano. Rehearsal had gone better than he hoped.

While he was peeling potatoes Ferdi told Erzsi about the meeting with Gabriella. She was setting up the tables and did not say much, but it was clear that she was trying to hold back a smug smile, which amused him. She disappeared into the dining room to hide, and Ferdi felt a wave of tenderness towards his friend. He went on peeling thoughtfully for a while, and then called her back.

'I called the number on my way here today,' he said when she reappeared. 'The performance is this Sunday.'

Her face lit up. 'May I come?'

He paused. 'Of course. I'd like that.'

He stuck his knife into the muddy potato and watched it slide jaggedly. His hand was shaking again. He put the knife down and stretched his fingers. The smell of detergent crept into the kitchen as Erzsi resumed her work.

'Erzsi, when I finish I'd like to practise with the piano here.'

There was no answer.

'Would you tell anybody if I did?'

Her shoes echoed as she approached the doorway. She stood there for a moment, watching him. When he looked up at her, she laughed.

'Go ahead and give that relic a purpose, Ferdi.'

*

Dieter arrived earlier than usual and to Ferdi's embarrassment he and Erzsi disappeared together in the bathroom for a while, and he tried not to notice how her hair had come undone when she stepped out. Dieter flashed a grin at him as he entered the kitchen, tying his apron. Some of the staff were already there.

'Any news?' Dieter asked in a low voice.

'None,' said Ferdi.

'Good. Did you check the papers?'

Ferdi shook his head.

'I did. Nothing there.'

Ferdi braced himself and let Dieter land an encouraging pat on his shoulder.

'Don't worry, Molnar,' he whispered, and nodded towards the dining room where Erzsi had disappeared. 'There's someone out there for you too.'

It was raining heavily by the time Ferdi got off work. The city was subdued and the clouds hung low. Ferdi avoided the river bank and took a quiet detour. The plaid umbrella Mrs Soltesz had loaned him filtered the light into greens and reds. People passed him by, shapeless and obscure. It was some time before he noticed that he had passed his tram stop, and so carried on walking despite the cold water seeping into his shoes. Trams whooshed by, filled with thawing city dwellers.

He noticed the shadow move behind him as soon as he turned the corner of his quiet street. Ferdi's heart clenched, but he didn't react. He reached his doorway, closed the umbrella and fidgeted for his keys while rain fell through his collar and ran down his back. The darkness shifted, and Ferdi's well-trained ear caught a dissonance in the sound of the rain as someone moved through it. He fumbled for the lock, but the rain blinded him. He wiped his eyes.

Ferdi glimpsed the stranger behind him moving towards the shadowy shelter of a building's entrance but made no move to go in. Ferdi turned and splashed towards them.

Just before Ferdi reached them they darted away, but he was faster – he grabbed hold of a jacket in the dark and pulled, waving his keys blindly with the other hand. They fought him off, but Ferdi kept stabbing in the dark, until a fist landed on his face and he staggered and fell, dragging the stranger along.

The glow of a faraway street lamp fell on them. Ferdi saw the flashing teeth, the wild dark eyes and coal-black eyebrows.

'Petar?'

The boy tried to push him away, but Ferdi wouldn't let go. He shook Petar violently until he stopped thrashing, and stared at the boy, whose face was distorted by the rain. The hood of his jacket fell low over his stark face. The moustache was gone.

'You shaved!' Ferdi exclaimed indignantly, as if that was the worst of Petar's offences.

Petar tried to wiggle free. 'Let me go!'

Ferdi's grip tightened around the boy's arm and Petar flinched. 'Why are you following me?'

'I'm not! I just saw you and—'

'Don't lie to me!' Ferdi dragged him closer. 'This is why Dieter found you around here the other night, isn't it?'

Petar clenched his fists and said nothing. Two long scratches were bleeding on his left cheek where Ferdi's keys had hit. The rainfall diluted the blood, spreading it down his neck.

'Who sent you?'

'Nobody!' Petar tried to grin. 'Why, are you in trouble?'

Ferdi let him go, feeling sick. The rain was falling so heavily that his skull was aching. He was soaked to the bone and shivering.

'You idiot! You *idiot*!' he gasped. 'What do you want from me?'

Petar hardly seemed to move in the darkness, and Ferdi felt something soft and wet land awkward on his mouth.

Petar was pressing his whole face against his, in a clumsy, determined kiss. For a moment Petar grabbed Ferdi's sleeves to pull him close, then let go and took a step back. He glanced around the empty street.

Ferdi stood frozen. He could still taste Petar's blood. Ferdi rubbed his mouth and looked at his hand, half expecting to see the kiss printed there. Petar watched, bursting with tension, and raised a fist, ready to defend himself. But he just kept staring at this strange, aggressive young man who had so rashly claimed Ferdi's first kiss.

A car honked somewhere and they both jumped. Ferdi turned towards the entrance, and waved at Petar to follow him. He did, keeping his distance.

They sat in Ferdi's room, their coats steaming over the radiator, while Petar watched him like an alley cat. Under the strong electric bulb half of his face was grotesquely red. Ferdi took from under the sink a plastic bottle of vodka Miss Ilona had given him, which he used for chest rubs and toothaches, and a box of Band-Aids. Petar was shaking, so Ferdi offered him the bottle first. Petar sniffed it, took a swig and gave it back.

Ferdi wet a napkin with vodka and awkwardly began to clean Petar's face. The boy jumped back, then let him. He winced when the alcohol came in contact with his cuts.

'I'll kill you if these leave scars,' Petar growled.

Ferdi put several Band-Aids on him. The result was a little comical.

'Where and when did you follow me? I won't get angry. I need to know.'

'Just Tuesday and tonight.'

'What about Monday night and last night? Were you at the river bank? At the abandoned building?'

'Last night I was out with a friend. You can ask him!'

Ferdi got up and wiped the blood from the boy's mouth with a harsh motion. Petar rubbed his sore lips.

'Sounds to me like you're a busy man, Mr Kitchen Accident Scar,' Petar said.

'Swear you're not lying.'

'On my mother's grave,' Petar said, and looked down at his dirty nails. 'I swear, all right? I'm telling the truth. Now you swear.'

'About what?'

'That you won't tell anyone. Come on.'

'I swear. Don't worry. I don't – I don't mind.'

Petar's ears turned scarlet. The side of his mouth drew up into a shy half-smile. Without getting up from his seat he hooked his finger through the waist of Ferdi's jeans and pulled him closer. Ferdi didn't resist. Petar buried his bandaged face in Ferdi's stomach.

Ferdi could feel warm breath through his damp T-shirt. It made the hairs on the back of his neck stand up. He put a hand on Petar's shoulder and the muscles there were taut, as if against some great restraint. Petar undid the button of Ferdi's jeans, and put his mouth on the small patch of bare skin under his navel. Fear swept suddenly through Ferdi's insides, obliterating all other sensations.

'Stop.'

Petar looked up at him. His fingers found Ferdi's zipper.

'I can't – I'm sorry. I don't know what may happen.'

Petar's knees pressed the sides of Ferdi's legs. 'I do.'

'No.' Ferdi tried to disentangle himself. He pulled away, buttoning up his jeans.

Petar's face fell. 'I thought...'

'I'm sorry,' repeated Ferdi, at a loss.

Petar got up unsteadily, glared at him in disbelief, grabbed his jacket and rushed out. Ferdi saw him from the window as he crossed the atrium, ripping the Band-Aids off his face.

*

Petar did not show up on Friday morning. Ferdi's practising was improving, despite the state of the piano. While he played his thoughts were absent, but when he was going about his chores they wandered back to the boy, and the feeling of his breath against his stomach.

He had hardly slept last night. It seemed to him that he had said the wrong things from start to finish, and he caught himself regretting having stepped back – and he cursed his fear, wishing that Petar had somehow persisted, that…

There his thoughts would come to an abrupt stop. Petar's hands then would transform into Sandor's, with fists curling over his face, hitting, shoving; Petar's confused face would turn into Sandor's, twisted in disgust. There was no way to explain this to Petar. There was no way to explain how he had been shunned and robbed of all trace of affection until it was too late – even now, after so much time, when it was so freely offered to him.

There were no strange shadows or unexpected apparitions when Ferdi walked home that night. He almost expected to see Petar hovering by his front door, but there was nobody there and he realised he was disappointed. Again he felt that warmth on his stomach, as if the boy's face was resting against it. He put a hand on it over his coat.

Later, when he stepped out of the shower, Ferdi examined his body in the foggy mirror. The sallow skin covering his abdomen was lined with slim long scars, stretching in rows. They were old, and thin bluish skin had grown over them. He put his fingers against them. They matched his fingernails perfectly.

He wanted to be free, to be his own person. He wanted to tell the truth, to be believed and comforted for it. And above all he wanted to play the piano, with a need that exceeded thought or emotion. Ferdi counted the scars. If Gabriella Gedeon and her friends were his only chance to play, then he would take it.

That Saturday the bar was full from early on. In the kitchen, swear words echoed more than the usual amount – and Dieter's sweeping hands, laden with hot pans and knives, had cleared a circle around him that nobody dared step into. Ferdi kept to the sinks while Dieter tossed sizzling crockery in them, singeing Ferdi's arm hair until he learned to stay out of the way. Only when Ferdi finally took off his apron did he realise that he hadn't practised the piano at all. His feet were aching and he reeked of rank butter and dish soap. He stumbled into the golden-and-blue evening thinking of nothing besides his pillow.

He took the tram, and even climbing into the car was too much work. He slid into an empty seat and rested his head against the glass. It was stained with the oily imprint of a previous occupant's hair, someone who must have sought the same rest on the cool surface. Ferdi followed the marks on the glass as the tram glided through the busy streets, while headlights danced out of focus and dissolved into scarlet fog in hypnotising swirls. Slowly his eyes grew heavy.

When he opened them again he saw that he was several stops past his own. He jumped up and stumbled out, rubbing his eyes. He looked around at the quiet neighbourhood, all closed shops and dimly lit windows. Dark shapes passed behind the curtains. Nobody seemed to notice him standing there, alone in the empty street under the sputtering street lamp, in a pool of reflections on the wet pavement.

The shapes around the windows lingered, watched him and then disappeared. Ferdi moved closer to see, thinking he recognised some, but he couldn't place them. The world beyond became muffled; the cold had disappeared. The echo of his rubber soles was the only sound. Somewhere on his body he ached imperceptibly, and the sensation was elusive, subliminal.

A different echo joined his own and approached steadily. He glanced around. The footsteps were coming from the darkness. Their reverberations surrounded him until he didn't know where to look, and then suddenly stopped.

Someone was standing just out of the spotlight. The ground trembled slightly as if the tram had just passed, though there was no sight or sound of it. Their hair seemed to glow in the electric light. A smooth forehead and a nose showed, but the rest of the face was lost in shadow. The shape was thin and youthful, dressed primly but with no coat on. It stood on the elevated platform of the tram stop, watching him back.

'It's on your hand,' the stranger said in a familiar voice. 'Lift your sleeve.'

Ferdi drew up his right sleeve and found the source of that low, throbbing pain. It was a small oval mark on the inside of his wrist, a bit of taut brown skin glistening like a burn.

'Same as myself,' the stranger said.

Ferdi touched the mark with the tip of his tongue. It tasted metallic and raw.

'Did you kill him?' Ferdi asked. 'Did you kill the man in the abandoned building?'

The figure made no reply and descended from the platform. Ferdi retreated.

'I was looking for you everywhere,' the stranger said, and stepped into the light.

Ferdi saw that it was himself.

He backed away until he pressed against the wall of a building – a wall that should have been wet and freezing, but instead was warm as if alive.

No – it wasn't himself. It was Sandor, closing in on him – young Sandor, in school clothes, eighteen and smiling in a way that sucked the light in.

Ferdi reached out and touched Sandor's shoulder. Wool and skin and bones. He drew back his hand.

'I'm here,' the boy said. 'I'm always with you.'

'Go away,' Ferdi whispered.

'I see what you see when you toss around in your bed at night. I'm always with you.' He advanced. 'I'll never let go.'

'Leave me alone!'

The boy stepped back, smiling. 'Hush. I'm here to say: beware. Liars lie.'

Ferdi peered at him. 'You can't be real. It's been years. You should have grown.'

'Hush.'

'No! I hate you!'

'I know.'

Before Ferdi could resist, the boy leaned in and put his arms around him. Ferdi's whole body convulsed. For a moment he struggled to free himself, but the grip on him was strong, and Ferdi gave in. He clutched at the boy's sweater. Ferdi's eyes burned, and a sob rose in him.

The body began to shrink under Ferdi's touch. He tightened his hold, but Sandor kept dwindling. Ferdi noticed the absence of any human scent.

'This is a dream,' said Ferdi.

But the boy was already gone, and he was grasping at handfuls of air.

His inner compass woke Ferdi up right before his stop. He gasped and glanced around, trying to orient himself. The tram throbbed under his feet. He stepped out, blinking stupidly at the cold wind that pinched his face. Here was the familiar corner shop, here was the closed newspaper stand and the half-blind lamp post, and the air smelled of citrus peels and anise. He made his way back home.

*

Sunday dawned under a silvery sky. Ferdi lay tired in his bed, watching the light shift around the room. Somewhere in the building a radio was turned on, and the bathroom down the hall creaked. There was the faint thud of the front door being propped open by Mr Polyak. A gust of air made the window above him shake. He crawled back under his warm blanket.

Lies. It was all lies. Nobody was watching. Nobody was there but himself, groping around in the dark, with shame and the stench of frying oil clinging onto him. Perhaps he would stay under the blankets today, job and concert be damned. Perhaps he would lock himself in this little room and wait for someone to bring him stale food and drag him out into the cold.

Last night's vision of Sandor with that unlikely smile floated into his mind. Ferdi's memories of young Sandor were those of a haunted boy with an exhausted, suspicious look in his eyes. The vision was only another one of those recurring dreams of tenderness, which left Ferdi empty and desolate.

Feeble snow fell on him as he walked to work, turning his ears a vivid red. That morning Petar was on time, grim and scarlet-cheeked. He spoke no more than necessary, and kept his eyes glued to the floor. Ferdi sank into a gloom as the truck revved away, and kept at his chores with half a heart. Sunday was Dieter's day off and it was quiet. Ferdi was too nervous for practice so he turned on the radio and he and Erzsi went on with their work.

As soon as his shift was over he rushed home, showered and changed into his most presentable clothes. He braved a look in the mirror and tried earnestly to pat his hair into submission but with little success. Then he grabbed his notebook, put his coat on, and headed out for the performance.

In front of the Academy he stopped for a moment to catch his breath, feeling dwarfed by the solemn, grey building, which seemed to frown at him. He climbed the front steps, his heart pounding. There was no event at the main stage tonight and the main hall with its dark marble and low gilt ceilings was muted and dark.

Ferdi took in the dim surroundings as he walked upstairs. Was this what Sandor was so terrified of? The place sent a chill up his spine. If it weren't for the perceived threat of this place, he would never have come to life. As his footsteps echoed, a second thought struck him: if all had gone according to plan, then by now Ferdi would have already spent years here and graduated under Sandor's name, and Ferdi Molnar would have never existed.

And yet, here he was.

A door to what seemed like a conference room was ajar, releasing the hum of activity. He pushed it open and peeked inside. It was a

modestly sized auditorium, lined with rows of chairs facing a platform framed by heavy curtains. A woman walked out from behind
the curtains carrying more chairs, and gestured at Ferdi to go over
and help her. When they had arranged them Gabriella appeared,
stepped onto the platform, sat on a chair and patted the one next to
her. He sat too, gazing at the room from his elevated post.

'Good to see you here, Ferdi. First time on a stage?' she asked,
watching him.

'Yes.' He pressed his hands between his knees, squeezing
his notebook.

'Better if you've seen the view before the audience gets here,
then.' She pointed at the end of the curtains. 'That's where you'll
come in from. There will be a piano here waiting for you, we'll
roll it in during intermission: you'll be performing last. I'll be
introducing everyone from the sidelines. We have the string quartet
first, then a tenor, a violin, a jazz trio, intermission, solo piano,
piano with drums and bass, a soprano, and then you. You'll do
great. There should have been a rehearsal, really, but what can you
do. Do you have your sheet music?'

'Yes.'

'You aren't going to read from this notebook, are you?'

Ferdi looked at the shiny cover and put it away. He had never
imagined it would be embarrassing. 'No. I know the piece.'

'Don't worry if you have to, this isn't too formal. Something we
like to do for the community. You'll be fine.'

Gabriella called someone to show him backstage and hurried
to greet three students who had appeared by the door, nervously
clutching their instrument cases.

Soon the small room was crowded with people. From his
hideout behind the curtain Ferdi watched some greet each other
like friends, introducing their companions and chatting on while
glancing around. They were casually but elegantly dressed.
When he saw someone notice him, Ferdi retreated and stepped

back into the dressing room to wait by a woman engrossed in a spy novel.

He heard Gabriella give her introductory speech, then music filled the room; slow, spicy, and unexpected. People clapped heartily. Ferdi could not put one thought after the next. His fingers had left deep imprints on the cover of his notebook. The soprano next to him put her novel down, tucked her hair and was gone. He tried to follow her sorrowful song, but kept missing the melody.

When he walked towards his mark behind the curtains, Gabriella was speaking again – he caught words like 'fresh' and 'emerging', and then his own name, sounding wooden and strange being spoken so loud. He walked onstage.

He saw Erzsi sitting in the front row. She smiled, trying to catch his eye, but Ferdi could not focus. He was glad that the piano was slightly angled so that he faced away from the audience. He sat. The stool creaked deafeningly in the silent room. His last thought was, *I hope nobody notices me.* The signet ring on his finger gleamed, and he began to play.

*

Ferdi's eyes were misty when he stood up and took an awkward bow towards the blurry crowd. A familiar voice in the back shouted 'Bravo!' He squinted – for a moment he thought that this bespectacled gentleman was Salomon Esterhazy, but the fleeting impression disappeared. Erzsi was leaning forward, as if trying to kiss him from afar. Gabriella was in the audience, whispering to a man sitting next to her.

The rest of the artists appeared; they flanked Ferdi and guided him in a group bow. He was underdressed and graceless and his smile stiff, but his eyes were blazing. His throat was dry, his chest swollen with exhilaration, the music clung to his hands and teeth and people were smiling at him.

They dispersed: the other musicians disappeared in the embraces of family and friends, and Gabriella and Erzsi appeared next to him. Erzsi looked older with her hair sleek and side-parted, dressed in ill-fitting shades of black. Her eyes were red and she smiled continuously while speaking, and Gabriella nodded with grave assent at Erzsi's words. Ferdi was light, surprised to find his feet on the earth whenever he looked down.

Balint Gedeon appeared and shook his hand.

'Very well done, very well,' Balint muttered distractedly. 'Excellent piece, excellent...' He drifted off and he was gone again.

Ferdi felt Erzsi's touch on his shoulder.

'Your hand is shaking,' she whispered.

Ferdi put it in his pocket and nodded as thanks. On his sweat-covered neck, he could feel the draught of people rushing past him.

Gabriella pulled him away towards a group of strangers. Ferdi couldn't hold on to the names she recited: there were musicians and professors, raining polite questions on him. Dazed, he lied as he was used to: about his home, his education, his life.

'Gigi's always right,' one of them said. 'You gave us a wonderful finale.'

Gabriella laughed. 'I'm just glad I could persuade him.'

'Thank you for considering me.'

'So formal, Ferdi! But you made Balint take off his glasses to listen better, and that's not nothing.'

'Easy, Gigi, beware of overindulging the artistic ego.'

'There's no fear of that,' Erzsi piped in, 'he has none.' The others glanced curiously at her, but she didn't notice. 'Oh, Ferdi, look.'

She pointed at the door where the large shape of Dieter hovered, looking at his shoes. Ferdi felt a rush of affection for them both.

'It was his day off,' Erzsi said by way of an apology, but Ferdi didn't care. 'He sat in the back. He said he didn't want you to see him since you didn't invite him, and more or less was a big baby.'

When Dieter noticed them looking he approached with the sly look of a dog that knows it's getting away with mischief. His thin sandy hair had been combed with gel to the point of nonexistence, and he was overflowing from a buttoned-down shirt. Ferdi was so glad to see him he forgot to brace himself for the shoulder pat, and was surprised to receive only a hesitant, self-conscious tap.

'Bloody Mozart,' Dieter mumbled.

*

The three of them sauntered down the quiet streets feeling celebratory – Erzsi and Dieter hand in hand and Ferdi lagging behind them, conscious of everything: the exhaust fumes, the northern breeze, the weight of the wet mist in his hair. There was the scent of the approaching rain, and he felt his mouth sticky and shut forever to the uselessness of speech in a world of music, his hands were sore, and he must have never noticed these certain stars before – because they were particularly beautiful tonight, assured, committed to the firmament, just like that spring night in the forest forever ago...

Ferdi didn't notice Erzsi's approach until she had an arm around his shoulders. She planted a kiss on his cheek. 'See you tomorrow.'

'I thought it was your day off.'

'No, that's Tuesday, but you'll be off then too, right?'

'Right, yes. The thirtieth.'

Dieter patted him, properly this time. 'Cheer up, Molnar. Treat yourself today, get a bottle of wine, sleep in.'

Ferdi made a face.

'I know, I know,' said Dieter, 'you were terrified. We'll tell nobody.'

'Ignore him!' said Erzsi. 'It was wonderful. I hope we'll hear you play again soon, and not just on Holy Mother's relic.'

They left him and walked on, waving at him from afar.

As soon as he turned the corner Ferdi saw someone waiting for him, sat on the doorstep. He paused. His instinct to run away was immediately countered by the awareness that he had nowhere to go.

Petar stood up and stretched. 'Did I scare you?' he grinned.

'I thought you weren't speaking to me.'

'I wasn't. Where were you?'

'Out.' Ferdi took out his keys and noticed with a pang of guilt the marks on Petar's face from last Thursday. 'What do you want?'

'Let me in, we can't talk here.'

Ferdi's hand tightened on the doorknob.

'I'll behave,' said Petar. 'I promise.'

Once inside the room, Petar didn't remove his jacket but sat there by Ferdi's decrepit table, looking dangerous and out of place. Ferdi took off his coat and put on some water to boil. He offered Petar a cup of sweet coffee, and sat. The boy stared into his drink for a while, as Ferdi sipped from his own scalding cup.

'I lied,' Petar said. 'About Wednesday night, I mean.' He paused, but Ferdi didn't speak. They watched each other in silence and Petar frowned at him. 'You chased me down the stairs,' he added.

Ferdi set the cup on the table and rubbed his forehead. 'Oh, you idiot,' he said at last.

Petar sprang to his feet but Ferdi just chuckled, and then buried his face in his hands to stifle an uncontrollable burst of laughter.

'You're crazy!' said Petar.

Ferdi kept laughing. Petar slowly returned to his seat while Ferdi wiped his eyes and took some deep breaths.

'What do you want, then?' he asked.

The boy clenched his fists. 'Was he giving you trouble? Is that why you killed him?'

Ferdi sobered up. He blinked. 'If you were there, then you saw it wasn't me.'

'When I arrived he was dead. You chased me. Do you think I'm stupid?'

'You can't believe that!' Ferdi held the edge of the table with white knuckles. 'It wasn't me, of course it wasn't!'

'I saw you! I saw you wipe the blood off your hands,' Petar went on mercilessly. 'Who was he? Was it the one who gave you this scar?'

'I didn't know the man!'

'Why did you go into that building, then?'

Ferdi shook his head and shrugged. Petar stared at him, then sprang up again and kicked the table. Hot coffee spilled on the chipped varnish.

'You're a liar!' He paced around the small room. 'I knew something was off about you! I knew it!'

'Calm down, please.'

'I should turn you in!'

'No, you don't understand…'

'What?' Petar stopped and turned to him. 'What is it that I don't understand?'

But when he saw Ferdi shut his mouth tight again he flew into a fresh rage and banged his fist onto the old wardrobe. Ferdi flinched.

'I am not what you think I am,' Ferdi said when the echo died down.

'Then what? Come on, it's always something – drugs, money, what?'

Ferdi shook his head again. 'I didn't kill him.' He saw Petar tense. 'I didn't kill him, and the rest is none of your business. Why are you here?'

Petar bit his lip. He reached into the inner pocket of his jacket, drew out a piece of paper and tossed it on the table. It was a page torn from a newspaper. Ferdi hesitated, then unfolded it. A short paragraph reported the discovery of the body of a homeless man in an abandoned building on B— Embankment. There were no further details.

Ferdi was aware of Petar's agitated breathing as the boy stood over him. He folded back the clipping and tried to return it to him, but Petar made no move to take it, so he put it down.

'You're in danger,' said Petar.

'Not from this.' Ferdi drank the rest of his coffee, still very hot. He got up and rinsed the cup. He picked up Petar's cup too. 'Are you going to finish this?'

There was no reply. Ferdi emptied and washed it, dried the cups and put them back in the cupboard under the sink. He felt Petar's eyes on him.

'This doesn't concern you,' said Ferdi.

Petar followed his movements as he wiped the spilled coffee from the table with a towel.

'I'm a witness,' Petar said.

'A witness to what?'

'Murder.'

'No, you just saw me finding an injured man. How do I know that *you* are not the murderer?'

Petar bristled. 'What? Listen, you bastard—'

Ferdi put up a hand. 'See? Why do you think I chased you? I thought you were the one who killed him. But best forget it now. Forget all about Wednesday night and leave it alone.'

'Are you threatening me?'

Ferdi sighed. 'I'm not.' He sat back on the chair and put his head in his hands. 'I'm actually relieved it was you, instead of something worse.'

'Like what?'

Ferdi looked up: the dark eyes were searching him. The memory of what had taken place the last time they were here alone together made his temperature rise.

'Fine, then.' Petar got up, fists clenched. 'Now you know. Let them lock you up then, see if I care.'

He rushed past Ferdi, who felt a sudden panic seeing Petar go, and grabbed the edge of his jacket to stop him.

'Thanks. For warning me.'

Petar's eyes widened for a moment, then the familiar scowl settled in. He disentangled himself from Ferdi's grip and walked out, leaving the door open. Ferdi could hear the echo of his heavy tread long after he was gone.

*

'Molnar, gut the fish for the soup!'

Ferdi had to dodge two large carp as they were tossed, paper and all, into his empty sink. He rinsed his hands and grabbed one of the filleting knives. The fish still smelled of earthy river water. Their glossy eyes watched him as he sliced their bellies open and deftly tugged their innards out, then chopped off the heads and set them aside. Dieter's large hands scooped the fish up and cut it in chunks, his cap begrimed with sweat. Ferdi was still cleaning up when the cook's hand descended again for the fish heads and disappeared back by the stoves. Ferdi was prodding round in the guts for roe when his finger nudged something hard.

'There's something in here.'

'These bastards eat all kinds of rubbish. Just don't look closely and throw it away. Is there any roe? Are the onions chopped?'

'One moment.'

Ferdi dug deep, finding and feeling round the brittle roe. He extracted it with the tip of the knife, and with it came a small metallic object, tangled in bloody strings of intestines. He rinsed the roe and set it on the board for Dieter, then washed the little piece of river treasure.

It was a ring: plain, thin and gleaming. He glanced around but nobody had noticed. He rubbed it against his apron and slipped it into his pocket, and forgot about it for the rest of the day.

He remembered it on the way home as he was strolling along the river bank, while fragrant breezes blew against his hot skin. He took it out and turned it around, slipping it on and off, making it clink against the bloodstone of the signet ring on his finger. It appeared to be made of some kind of cheap, low-carat gold that refused to humour the light. Its humility warmed him. He noticed an inscription on the inside of the band, but it was too dark to read. He waited until his path brought him under a street lamp again and he paused to squint at it. It read:

Abel and Dorika – Until Death

The ring fell from his hand and landed on the pavement. It rolled about and he stumbled away from it, watching it settle with a musical tinkle. Some passersby turned to look and he felt forced to pick it up again. He looked up and down the street, but nothing appeared out of the ordinary.

Abel. So that had been his name. Abel, with his soft brown curls tangled with nettles and grass. Abel, with his half open eyes glossy like the fish, head caved in with darkness, blood pooling around the eyelids. Abel who had smelled like bedsheets and green soap, while Ferdi had hauled him from the armpits and seen his coat fall open and his powder-blue pyjamas glow in the forest night.

The Danube behind him was making gentle sucking sounds against the tethered riverboats. He wanted to toss the ring in the water, but then he imagined it arriving at his hands again through another gluttonous fish, and he had to stop himself. He put it back in his pocket and walked home.

He recovered the letter from the depths of his cupboard and read it again and again, trying to decipher some hidden message he had missed, something to shed light on the appearance of the ring. But it yielded nothing.

I remain, your oldest friend.

The thick, decisive strokes of someone who knows perfectly all they need to say, someone who is familiar with, and even a little superior to, the sender. The handwriting of a king to his subject, of a father to his son. Ferdi grimaced at every knife-sharp intonation. He folded back the letter, put the ring in the envelope with it and hid it away.

1980

Sandor woke up with a start, gasping as if breath had failed him. Dawn was breaking. He wondered groggily if it was time to get ready for school, then remembered it was the morning of New Year's Day.

Did you know animals can talk tonight?

His heart kicked and he sat upright, looking around frantically. The room was empty, the old house mute. The snow-quiet day was peaceful. He rubbed his eyes. It was nothing but a dream, a horrible dream. Sandor lay down, his eyelids heavy, and as he drifted off again he recalled something from a Russian book. *Good men live without lies, and they never have doubles...*

He snapped awake. The *thing* – such a *thing* couldn't have been real. It was impossible. It was a nightmare, nothing more. He began to feel hot suddenly, the room was stifling. He got up and opened a window, taking long draughts of cold air that smarted against his clammy skin. He unbuttoned his pyjama shirt and drew up his sleeves.

And then he saw it: a small circular burn mark on the inside of his right wrist, still angry and raw.

'No,' he said.

It all came back to him: the man, the handshake, a stranger's hand pressing against the window of the piano room.

It couldn't be.

No; if he walked into the gun room now he would find nobody. No food crumbs, no slept-in rags. That burn on his wrist could be a sleepwalking accident. Yes, he thought, as he turned and darted about the room, getting dressed – all this was only a nightmare. He knew he was being childish, but he would go down there right now and make sure. He rummaged for the key, not pausing to think why the gun room key would be in his room, or why his stomach clenched as his fingers closed around the cool, grainy cast iron.

Sandor stepped out into the dark hallway and ran quietly downstairs to the front door, pausing only to put his boots and coat on. He saw his parents' coats: they had come home while he was asleep. Outside the snowfall had stopped. All was covered in ice. He reached the little basement in quick, precarious strides and tried several times to get the key to work, but the lock seemed to have frozen. Tears of frustration blinded him and he began to bang his fist on the door. The sound reverberated for a moment, then was swallowed up by the trees.

He stopped, afraid to wake his parents. He clutched his throat to ease the painful throbbing of his blood, and listened. Nothing. Mad joy swelled in him, and he brought his cold hands to his face.

Then a sound interrupted the sweeping silence. Someone was standing on the other side of the door, knocking back.

Sandor stumbled backwards, slipped and almost fell, then turned and fled back to his room. He crawled into bed and lay there curled up, shivering.

When he came to, it was almost noon. He heard the door to his parents' bathroom down the hall, and then the creaking pipes. Karolina's firm tread resounded down the steps, and after a little while the smell of coffee wafted upstairs.

There was something in the gun room, waiting for him. What a fool he was.

Sandor got up, moving as if through water, and put on a sweater. He opened the door and then he stumbled across something small and hard he hadn't noticed earlier. It was a slim blue box with a golden ribbon on it: his parents' customary New Year's surprise. Any other year he would have opened his door with childlike anticipation, but now he looked at it strangely. He sat on the bed with the box in his lap and untied the ribbon. Inside the box he found a glossy resin fountain pen, and a leather-bound notebook wrapped in fabric.

There was a tightness in his chest. Sandor brought his hand to it, but it refused to go away. He tugged his sleeve down to hide the burn mark, and forced himself to go to breakfast.

When he stepped into the small dining room a record was playing quietly, and empty brandy glasses had been left overnight. Salomon and Karolina hadn't bothered to dress, and looked unglamorous and frail; Karolina was in her dressing gown, her hair falling about freely, Salomon in his grey flannel pyjamas. The stove was radiating heat that clung to the corners like spider webs. They smiled when they saw him, their hearts still bright and open.

Sandor had the momentary urge to turn and run. He sat reluctantly, smiled with effort and clutched his butter knife while his parents chatted on. He thought of that *thing* trapped in the basement, knocking back at him.

With a jolt, he remembered the piano room and half rose to leave. 'May I be excused?'

'This is a family holiday, Sandor!' Karolina protested, but he wouldn't be stopped. Before Salomon could speak too he escaped into the hallway. Looking over his shoulder, he quietly slipped into the room and closed the door behind him.

Pieces of broken flashlight were scattered everywhere. Water stains tarnished the piano and chairs were strewn about haphazardly. Only then Sandor realised that he had been still clinging to one last hope – one desperate hope that this could all be a trick of his imagination. He sat at the piano stool and put his head in his hands, staring at the small burn mark on the floor between his feet.

A change came over him, then: the gradual, gloomy acceptance of the inevitability of his circumstance and its obscure consequences. Sandor's jaw clenched, thin muscles stuck out from his neck. There was a shift in the centre of gravity of his mind as it prepared to lift heavier weights.

He got up, picked every shard of glass he could find and threw them out, and polished the piano with his sleeve. He opened the lid and tentatively pressed a chord. He had hoped it would stay silent, that its power to speak would have been spirited away along with his old life, but the cruel sound reverberated through him. He saw brown smudges on the white keys – there was a cut on his finger from the glass he had picked up. He wiped the bloodstains until the keys shone again.

He had to go face it, that *thing*, that boy. It was his responsibility now. While his parents settled in for a peaceful snow day, Sandor returned to his room, his mood tense and savage, and waited for the swift nightfall.

*

The lock still hadn't thawed. Sandor fought until the mechanism finally gave in, grinding and snapping, dragging against the frame. Nothing could be heard now from the gun room or the house, apart from the creaking of frozen twigs.

He kicked the door open and stumbled inside. A voice came from the darkness.

'Is it you?'

The tone faltered, as soft as he remembered it, and a little low. Sandor did not want to answer. But he turned the light switch, and there was the young man. The resemblance shocked Sandor afresh. The boy sat crouched inside a nest of clothes and blankets at the far corner of the room, blinking against the light.

Sandor closed the door to stop the draught. It didn't make any difference; the room was still just as cold.

'I can't stay long.'

He stepped closer. Again came that savage urge, same as the night before. *Kill it, kill it.*

Could he? Who was to say that maybe it wasn't the right thing to do, the only mercy, the only way to regain his life, his freedom? He should do it – here, now, while he was still brave—

'Do you have any more milk?' the young man asked hoarsely.

'Milk?'

The other put his hand on his throat. 'Thirsty.'

He hesitated. 'I showed you how to drink from the tap.'

Sandor strode into the bathroom and turned the knob, but no water came through. He turned it all the way, and the tap rattled and spat. It had frozen overnight. He looked back at the dishevelled figure sitting on the floor with its arms around its legs, and it dawned on him that the boy had had nothing to drink all day.

There was a final loud crack and water came gushing out, spraying him. He turned the tap down until only a thin stream of water fell into the dirty sink.

'If you keep the tap always running a little, then it won't freeze again. Come, drink. I'm going to get you something to eat.'

So much for freedom, Sandor thought, and was momentarily disgusted at his own hesitation, his pathetic weakness. He watched as the boy stood up stiffly and hurried to drink, hands and face twitching at the contact with the icy water.

Sandor left and walked back to the house. In the linen cupboard he found an old lumpy pillow, then went back to the kitchen and set aside a mug, some poppy-seed bread, cold cuts and hard-boiled eggs. He wrapped them in napkins and stuffed them in his pockets.

Back in the gun room the young man had satisfied his thirst, and fell on the food like a wild animal. He ignored Sandor's warnings, until he had to be forced to stop.

'I told you, go easy!' said Sandor. 'Save some for later, you can live with less. You must behave if you ever want to get out of here.'

With a sinking feeling he saw the young man's face light up with delight. 'Which will only happen if you obey.'

There was a vigorous nod.

'Shall I...' he started, and hesitated, feeling a bit ridiculous. 'Shall I bring you something to read next time?'

The young man's face assumed an inquisitive expression.

'Can you even read?'

There was some hesitation. 'I don't know. Can I?'

'I'll bring you something and we'll find out. I have to go now.'

Ferdi stepped forward and grabbed Sandor's sleeve. 'Can you stay a little longer? Please?'

Sandor looked at the hand tugging at him, and twisted himself free. He struggled to contain the swelling disgust in his stomach.

'Do *not* touch me.'

The hand withdrew and they stepped away from each other. The air around them became heavier. The other boy wore an unhappy expression, and pinned his timid gaze to the floor. Sandor tried to speak calmly.

'I can't stay. My parents are upstairs, and may be looking for me. From tomorrow there will be more people around the house. This is why I need you to be quiet. Understood?'

'Yes.'

'I'll return as soon as I can.'

Sandor locked up behind him and stepped into the garden. He let his head fall back and took a deep breath. There were no clouds and a feast of clear stars shone with rare brilliance, cooled down into gem-like stillness. He could have plucked them from the sky.

Help, he thought.

A mad idea flashed through Sandor's mind like a meteorite. He paused, weighing it. He considered the piano room with its thick walls and insulated, locking double doors, and everything fell into place. He would have smiled if he weren't feeling so miserable.

He looked around. The snow-capped trees surrounded the grounds like a battlement, and the porch lamp cast an island of light on the gravel path. The silence was magnificent. He let it seep through his body.

Something moved from the far side of the yard. Sandor's heart gave a kick. Where the edge of the forest brushed against the eastern side of the gardens, the bushes shook. A large, dark shape stepped through, stark against the blue haze. It was the stag.

He immediately relaxed. The stag, its coat sparkling with snow, paused and smelled the air. It turned its head towards him and stared. Sandor put his hands in his pockets and stared back. Only once before had it been hungry enough to approach the house, on a midwinter night just like this. Sandor and Maggie had discovered its fresh prints during one of their rambles. It was as large and powerful as ever, a compact force of nature. Sandor took a step forward.

'Off with you!'

Instead of fleeing, the beast moved a little closer. It sniffed and snorted clouds of steam. Sandor could see its muscles rippling with shivers, the wet eyes following his movements. He stepped forward, and wondered if it was about to attack him. A wild rush came over him and he took one more step. The beast shook its beautiful head, stomped and snorted – but then seemed to decide he wasn't worth the trouble and stepped back. It turned and vanished into the darkness. Sandor exhaled. His head was light. With a strange mixture of relief and disappointment he walked back into the house.

*

The next day Sandor sat at the breakfast table with grim determination. Faced with his father's newspaper erected like a fortress between them, he nearly gave in.

'I was thinking...' he began, and had to force himself to go on. 'We should talk about our time in the piano room.'

The newspaper lowered.

'We could assign time slots. Homework is piling up, and setting a precise schedule would be a big help, so I know when I can use the piano.'

Salomon and Karolina glanced at each other. 'Certainly,' said Salomon. 'You know how little I need it these days. I'm glad to hear you're dedicating more time to practice.'

'Does this mean...' Karolina said, and stopped to exchange another look with Salomon. It made Sandor feel excluded. 'Does this mean that the Academy...?'

'I'm reconsidering.'

'Reconsidering, as if—!' Karolina blurted, but her husband looked at her and she stopped.

'Thank you,' Sandor said quickly, his ears burning as he tried to steer the conversation clear from the familiar row. 'I'll do my best – I promise.'

His heart was beating erratically and he struggled to focus on buttering his bread. Perhaps his mad idea could work. For all he knew, that was what the man in the tuxedo expected him to do. Or perhaps he was going insane: thinking of sneaking that boy – his double, a monster, an abomination – into this house, and teaching him how to play the piano. He bit his lip, terrified that he might burst out laughing.

He would not visit the gun room that day, afraid that he would falter if he did; that he might kill that boy on sight – or worse, pity it and set it free. This was the only chance he had to gain something from this nightmare he had got himself into. He would see it through.

At school the following day he was listless and agitated, counting the hours until he was able to leave. It was a clear, windy day and the snow had solidified into an uneven, muddy layer of ice. By the time he arrived back home, evening was falling and his legs were sore. He was starving; unable to predict when he would be able to steal food again, he had saved his school lunch for the one waiting for him anxiously like a dog tied and forgotten at its kennel.

During dinner that evening Sandor and Salomon set a schedule for the piano room: Sandor would have it to himself late in the evenings, long after it was cleaned and when the household was more subdued. It was odd watching the innocent domestic rituals unfold at home, while being aware of someone locked up just under their feet. It made Sandor feel powerful, superior to the others who walked unsuspecting so close to such a creature. He pictured his home like a doll's house, with people moving about as foggy miniatures of themselves and all the rooms exposed: from the warm kitchen below, the ground floor busy with the piano room and the study, and the dining room and the living room shining darkly in their baroque glory, to upstairs where the bedrooms were being aired, and to the low attic above. And under all that a bare room where a small, crouching shape was sitting, its skinny arms wrapped around its shins.

*

Night had fallen when Sandor went through his bookshelves and selected a tattered book of fairy tales his mother used to read him, along with music sheets of some folk dances simplified for children, which were among the first pieces he had been taught to play. He folded the sheets and put them in his pocket. Sandor stepped into the piano room, locked the door behind him and climbed out of the window into the yard. The piano room overlooked the back of the house towards the southern side, close to the gun room, which was located in the south-eastern corner. It was a short distance and he was protected under the evergreens growing close to the house, but still Sandor hurried and kept close to the walls, tripping and slipping until he reached the stairs.

The figure sat crouched in its nest, so tired it barely looked up when he stepped in. When he caught a glimpse of its face his stomach turned. Sandor paused, wondering what this creature standing in front of him was. The gun room was suddenly inhospitable and unreal – the world around him felt alien, the young man before him a grotesque apparition. It talked – and it thought – it acted unpredictably, and produced desires of its own accord.

'Is something wrong?'

The boy's voice had come from a place far away. Sandor snapped back into reality.

'No, why?'

The young man only looked at him in silence, and Sandor stared back.

'Are there any more of you?' Sandor asked.

'More?'

'Do you have a... a...' He frantically felt around for words. '...A family? Are there more like you?'

He was met with a blank stare.

'Parents?' he persisted.

'Parents?'

'Yes – I have a mother, see...'

'Will she be my mother too?'

'No – of course not! Don't you know...? Where did you come from, then?'

The stare darkened and the boy averted his eyes. Sandor's mouth was dry. He realised that he didn't want to know, that he shouldn't have asked; that the answers may or may not exist but perhaps he shouldn't know them, perhaps he wasn't supposed to. Vertigo swept through him and he shut his eyes for a moment, trying to suppress the feeling.

He forced himself to smile and held up the small parcel. 'I brought food,' he said.

Ferdi sprang up and grabbed it from his hand, ripped the paper open and fell on the bread and cheese. Sandor produced some small apples from his pocket and put them on the table. 'Save these for later,' he added, mechanically.

When the young man had finished eating he stepped back and stared at him, waiting for Sandor to disappear again. His eyes widened with surprise when Sandor ordered him to put something warm on. He hurried to put on the worn sweater that was a little small on him, and stood there so expectant and dishevelled that Sandor started having misgivings.

'You will follow me into the house,' he ordered, watching the other's face – his own face – brighten with excitement. 'We'll be quiet now, and very careful.'

He experienced a moment of panic watching Ferdi step out and blink at the night glow, afraid suddenly that he might bolt, but the young man waited for him to close the door and take the lead. They ducked to avoid being seen from any window and made their way towards the pool of light falling on the snow from the open piano room window.

Sandor climbed in first and reached out to help Ferdi, but was met with a horrified expression. The young man was trembling. His eyes were searching the room behind Sandor with such intensity that Sandor turned in alarm, expecting to find someone there. But the room was empty.

'Come!' He leaned out to grab Ferdi, but the other took a step back and shook his head.

'I don't want to.'

Sandor started climbing out again, and Ferdi lunged forward and grabbed him by the arm.

'Don't let him take me! Please! I don't want to go back!'

Sandor slowly freed himself from the grip and tried to catch his frantic gaze. 'He isn't here. Don't be afraid, he won't come again. You belong to me now.' Carefully, he backed into the room and guided him inside. 'See?' he whispered. 'We are alone. Now, be quiet.'

He closed the window, went to the back of the room and brought a second seat to the piano.

'Sit.'

The young man approached with caution, hesitated and then obeyed. The memory of what had happened last time they were here together hovered between them. Sandor sat on the right side of him, and pushed the soft pedal down to muffle the sound. He took the small book of fairy tales from his pocket and opened it.

'Can you read this?'

The young man squinted and took the book in his hands. He bent down over it until his nose was almost touching the page, then slowly held it at arm's length until he seemed satisfied. He blinked a few times.

'*Once upon a time, long, very long ago, in the midst of Fairyland, there stood an extensive forest, so large that it would take many, many days to walk across it; in fact, it was an enchanted forest, for all night it was the haunt of all the little fairies in the neighbourhood...*'

His beautiful voice, low and hesitant, had a mysterious effect on Sandor. When he stopped reading it echoed gently around the room like an extinguished stove still giving off heat.

'You *can* read. Good.' Sandor reached to take the book but Ferdi made no move to give it back.

'May I keep it to read the rest?'

Sandor was taken aback. 'Yes, all right. It will be good for you.'

He stared at the young man, trying to gauge his thoughts and abilities. He looked human, every bit of him – but who was to say what one would find if they cut him open? Sandor was seized by the sudden desire to dissect the scrawny body sitting next to him. Would he find flesh and bone, or sawdust and straw? Or perhaps something more sinister? He shook the thought away.

Ferdi set the book down next to him with reverence. Sandor opened the piano lid and saw the young man tense.

'Look,' he began and then stopped again. The words weren't coming easily. 'I'm sorry for hitting you the other day. Don't be scared. I won't hit you again, I promise.'

Ferdi relaxed, and leaned a little closer. Sandor took out the music sheets and set them up. He showed him the notes one by one on the keys, and how they corresponded to the sheet. Then he positioned Ferdi's fingers for a simple chord. He nodded at Ferdi to follow his lead. Sandor pressed down, and the muffled notes throbbed through their bodies. Ferdi blinked in surprise and straightened up, focused, and Sandor almost smiled.

When the lesson was over, Sandor noticed a strange glow about Ferdi's face. His brow was relaxed and the mouth was half open dreamily.

'You're picking it up fast,' he said, with a pang of jealousy. It had taken him months to learn the simple piece that Ferdi was already playing – he recalled his father's thinly masked frustration at those early signs of ineptitude, and his own dread at disappointing him.

The young man blushed, and stroked the keys with the tips of his fingers. 'It wasn't hard.'

'No, it wasn't hard,' Sandor snapped, unable to restrain himself. There was a long pause.

Ferdi looked down. 'I liked it.'

'I'll find something harder next time, then.' Sandor glanced at the ornate clock across the room. 'Time to go back.'

Ferdi looked up. A hint of panic flitted across his face while Sandor folded away the music sheets. The young man pulled his fingers away reluctantly, and Sandor closed the lid.

'I'll come for you tomorrow around the same time, and we'll resume the lessons.'

Ferdi picked up the book and held it with both hands. 'Promise?'

'Promise.'

They climbed out of the window once more, and back at the gun room Ferdi meekly let himself be locked in. Sandor returned to the piano room to tidy up then stepped out into the hallway, suppressing a wave of bleak enthusiasm. He nearly collided with Karolina.

'Darling, were you playing soft pedal all this time?'

'Yes. Not listening to myself play sometimes helps.'

'Sandor!'

'Sorry.'

'There's a letter for you, I forgot about it earlier. It's from Maggie, look.'

Sandor took the envelope from her hand, flooded with that day's peculiar mixture of emotions. He went to his room, opened it and read the letter over and over, though it was riddled with strange words. *I miss our walks in the woods.* While he read he forgot all about New Year's Eve, all about the boy in the gun room, and almost got up and rushed out to meet her. *I hope you're not going to give in easily.*

He understood the last word she'd written before the familiar sight of her name, bright as a call to arms: *Fight!*

*

In the days that followed Sandor began drawing a strange satisfaction from the lessons. It was a surprise to see how he could affect someone – how his words could alter another person's mind – and he took to planning the lessons during school hours, mentally outlining work and calculating Ferdi's abilities. But the fatigue and anxiety of the secret increased his bursts of anger; he grew mean with his parents, which was followed by bouts of guilt that drove him further into himself. Though he wrote Maggie back, he felt she was now greatly removed from what his life had become. And it wasn't long until he finally withdrew from his few school friends, until the only person he spent time with was Ferdi.

It seemed to him that slowly Ferdi *grew.* The hollows of his cheeks were starting to even out despite his meagre diet, and stringy muscles began to fill his skin. He looked more substantial, a creature getting accustomed to its own existence. He seemed fond of his name; Sandor had often noticed him mouthing the word, rolling it around with his tongue. The things the young man took pleasure in were plain on his open face: the book of fairy tales, the feeling of music, the sting of the air outside, the plucking of the sleek piano keys. Any other thoughts he had, he carried in him reluctantly: they manifested in his red-rimmed eyes, and the way the corner of his mouth gave the odd involuntary twitch. Sandor asked Ferdi once if he could remember anything from before his arrival, or anything about the man who brought him, but Ferdi's only reply was 'He was like being in a room with no doors,' after which he set his jaw and refused to say more.

Sandor couldn't help gazing at Ferdi's hands during lessons. They moved over the keys weightlessly, landing here and there like moths; he wondered how sound was produced when they seemed to scarcely touch the yellowing ivory. Sandor had only ever seen his father play like this. He increased the difficulty of the lessons but, as Ferdi responded exceptionally, Sandor couldn't suppress a quiet streak of malice. He grew impatient at his pupil's mistakes and his wrath exploded erratically, until Ferdi learned to fear his hard sideways glances.

Yet all that only accelerated Ferdi's flourishing. The young man soaked up information as if his mind was a vast empty space. His memory proved remarkable, and he was able to reproduce a whole piece not long after first learning to play it. In a matter of weeks he had advanced to a level of ease that Sandor knew, even if his own technical knowledge was still greater, he would never be able to match.

Sandor would watch the boy while he was playing: Ferdi's chest would relax and his breathing became shallow and soft, his eyelids drooping into a dreamlike state contrasting with the feverish energy of his fingers. When it was time to learn something new Ferdi would jolt awake and, forgetting his place, return keenly to the present and flood Sandor with questions that he was ill-equipped to answer. He never begged to be let out of his prison again, and Sandor was finding it harder to lock the door on him every night.

It was abundantly clear to him that Ferdi was closer to being the son that Salomon and Karolina had always wished for – and he knew it was a petty obsession, an idea he should have been above, but there he was. *Well then*, he thought – *in good time they can have him.*

*

And once, only once in all this time that followed, Sandor went back to that clearing in the forest.

He saw no reason why it wouldn't work: he was careful to do everything exactly as he had on Christmas Day. And, same as it had happened, he waited in vain in the frozen woods, shivering while night creatures hunted about him.

Seven days later, he listened out for the sound of footsteps, for the piano, of anything – and when it didn't come, he climbed down into the piano room himself while the house was asleep and peered into the dimness with breath held.

But there was nothing. Even though he waited and waited until dawn broke, no man came, no wind howled. Only when he began his weary ascent to his room did he hear something. Perhaps it was his imagination, a trick of his exhaustion or something of his strange, desperate state – yet he was sure he heard, low but distinct, the distant echo of someone laughing at him.

1990

In the metro, tossed about in the dinky carriage, Ferdi tried in vain to piece together the day that had just passed. It had taken a while to wash, brush his unruly hair and dress in his best, and then wait – wait for longer than he could bear. He got off at the Opera House, which was lit up and banner-decked, and he looked for the café. Though early to his appointment, the idea of what might wait for him inside made his body stop dead on the pavement. He forced his legs to move.

He walked into the café past tourists studying the pastry display and found a table in the ornate back room, quiet and dim at this hour. He ordered a cake, but when it arrived his throat had closed up so he poked round the hard dried apricots while he waited, as his eyes nervously darted about and the antique clock dragged on.

And then he saw his guest arrive.

The man was not wearing a tuxedo this time but an unremarkable grey business suit, wrinkled under a boxy trench coat. He strode into the back room and settled in the creaky chair opposite Ferdi, with a hiss of cheap clothes. Only his tie seemed expensive and new, deeply black along his chest like a gash. Ferdi glanced at it once and felt his head swim.

The man in grey ordered drinks for both of them, and exchanged pleasantries with the waitress with a drowsy half smile. His bulging, watery eyes followed her as she served them and walked away. He sniffed his glass but did not taste it. Then he began talking in a flat tone and Ferdi, frozen to his seat and his mind blank with shock, heard nothing until the man rapped the little table with his knuckle.

'You're not paying attention, boy,' he complained.

'I'm sorry.'

'Did you like my present?' Ferdi looked up at him. 'The ring.'

Ferdi nodded slowly.

'Only for safekeeping. Don't go giving it away.'

Ferdi's heart was thumping. 'Where is Sandor?'

The man stared at him for a while, then shrugged. 'I can't tell.'

'Liar!'

He had shouted. The waitress peeked around the doorway but the man waved her off. The room was empty apart from themselves.

'Calm down,' said the man quietly, and Ferdi felt his knees weaken.

'If you want to kill me then get on with it,' Ferdi whispered. But the man smiled and nodded towards the table. Ferdi followed his gaze and saw that his own hand was clutching the fork. He tried to let it go but his fingers refused to open.

'You are not mine to kill, boy.'

'I am nobody's!' Ferdi was hoarse, sweating and clutching desperately at the fork. 'I belong to myself – I made it all this time on my own, after he abandoned me – I starved and I froze and I worked and I have nothing to do with either of you! You can't just order me to come here, you can't *make* me do things anymore!'

The man shook his head and knitted his fingers against his stomach. 'Don't be dramatic. It was only an invitation to a drink, I'm not here to take anything away from you.' He gestured at the café, the city beyond it. 'Not worth fretting over, if you ask me.'

Ferdi sat still, clenching his jaw. 'You stole my life, Sandor's life. He was only a child, and you – you deceived him. You're a thief, a common thief.'

'A thief? Don't belittle my work, you foolish make-believe boy. Would it have been better if you never existed?'

'I didn't mean that!' He stopped, red-faced against the man's stare. 'I – I like being here.'

'Might want to thank me, then.'

'There's nothing I ought to thank you for. Look – this is all I know, this is all I am. Just like everyone else.'

'My boy, you are nothing like everyone else.'

'Don't say that! Cut me, and I bleed – I shave – I'm hungry, thirsty – see, I have scars! I'm even a little short-sighted, and I get nightmares – I wake up in the middle of the night because I can't breathe, because I need air like everyone else; I need warmth and rest, and to cut my fingernails every once in a while…'

'…And to play the piano…'

They stared at each other. The waitress crossed the room carrying empty plates, and disappeared into the kitchen.

'I'm right, aren't I? Every once in a while you have to play or you'll go mad. Every once in a while you have to play or you'll start clawing at walls, at yourself. You have to play, or else you'll have to pluck out your eyes and break your fingers one by one, so that maybe the desire will go away, and you—'

'Enough! Enough. I know.'

'That, boy, is not "like everyone else".'

'Stop calling me boy – I have a name!'

The man's face twisted with scorn. 'A name *he* gave you?'

'Such as it is, yes!'

He scoffed. 'I knew you before you existed here. You want trivialities? Names? You are fitting in well, *Ferdi*.'

'Enough – what do you want from me?'

The man glanced at his watch and sighed. He nodded in the direction of the Opera House. 'When do you think the performance will be over tonight? Are Tuesdays the usual times?' He waved to the waitress and asked her, then turned back to Ferdi. 'What have you been up to all this time, then?'

'Don't you know?'

'I'm not omniscient,' he said with a trace of annoyance. 'I'm a very busy man. When I last saw you, you were in school.' He smirked and Ferdi's face darkened.

'But you knew where to find me.'

'Well, I have my tricks. Come, give me some stories. How did you make it this far?'

'Hardly far.'

'You have a job, you pay bills. I'm surprised you even kept yourself alive. But then again you were always a fast learner.'

'It helps when you have no choice.'

'Then how did you crawl out of that basement?'

Silence fell. Ferdi bit his lip.

'Do you know what happened the last time I saw him?'

'He shot you,' the man in grey replied, so impassively that Ferdi winced. His fingers flew up to touch the scar on his cheek.

'Yes,' Ferdi said. 'He meant to kill me.'

'But he didn't. Always weak, that boy. It was pathetic.'

'Maybe he really was weak. Or maybe he didn't kill me because he'd done enough murder. Or perhaps he thought I was going to bleed out or die from the concussion, I don't know. He left me for dead and that was the last I knew of him. I was in too much pain. When I woke up I was alone, lying in my own piss, and my face was covered in blood.'

Ferdi paused. He wanted to add that he had lain there and cried while his head throbbed with bone-crushing pain, that his chest had ached with sadness until he became feverish and delirious, calling for Sandor to come back even if just to kill him, to come back and stay with him like he used to. But he was ashamed and he kept those memories to himself.

'I remained there until I ran out of food. I thought I would simply go on reading my books and wait for death, but hunger drove me out. So I packed everything I could carry and left.'

Again he did not include the details: the rat he killed with the shards of glass, and tried to eat raw but failed and vomited up.

The countless hours haunting an abandoned house, looking for traces of people. How he had walked around blindly in the dark countryside, taking any road that led away, sleeping rough and avoiding populated areas until he had no choice – a starving bum with a bundle of books, until he sold all of them but the collection of fairy tales for food and a bus ticket. And then being confronted with the staggering sight of a big city for the very first time.

The man quietly sipped his drink, watching and guessing.

'I slept in the streets for a long time. I asked others who did the same how to do things: how to look for work, where I could find food. Most did not care to help, but some responded. I think... I think I wouldn't be alive without these people. I knew nothing. They guided me. And when summer came I saw them die in the heat, by the same bottle that kept them living through the cold.'

Their faces came to him now, wrinkled and stiff, hanging jowls and messy nicotine-stained beards, tired eyes and swollen noses. Some of them hadn't even told him their names, never asked for his. He was a child among them, sheltered by those who had, in one way or another, lost their own.

'I expect you paid for your papers.'

Ferdi blinked. 'Yes. It cost all I had, and then I had to start afresh. But at least I had a name. I existed.'

'Let me see them.'

Ferdi took out his identity card and handed it over. The man examined it with a look of amusement. 'I see the birth date is New Year's Eve.' He smiled and gave it back. 'You look older than twenty-nine.'

Ferdi glanced at his photo, at the surprised, boyish face with the uneven jaw and the flame-like scar.

'I'd been waiting for you to turn up, all these years,' Ferdi went on. 'You, or Sandor. I expected you to appear out of nowhere and drag me back through the snow. I thought you'd throw me again into the piano room, and he would be waiting for me there, angry, sitting by the keys and looking at his watch.'

Ferdi paused and wrapped his fingers around his glass, staring at the pale wine within. The man seemed able to simply erase the sense of his presence when Ferdi looked away from him. Ferdi had been speaking to the walls, to the small rosy lamps, to the heavy furniture cramped in the corners of the room. Now he glanced back at his companion. He stole a look at the tie: a thin sliver of abyss in the middle of the café, until the man's pudgy fingers descended and ran over it to straighten the strange fabric, breaking the spell.

'And yet neither of you came. Neither of you looked for me.'

'But you didn't want to be found,' said the man in grey.

'I didn't; but I expected – I thought – I would imagine some sense of responsibility over something – someone you brought to this world.'

'Would you hold a farmer responsible for a lamb they sold to the slaughterhouse?'

Ferdi banged his fist on the table, causing the little plastic menu to topple over. The man simply picked it up again, and took no more notice. He remained silent and cool, waiting for Ferdi to speak.

'So you abandoned Sandor the same way he abandoned me?' said Ferdi. 'Like you took away everything and left him with nothing?'

The man ignored him. 'I must say, Ferdi. You haven't moved around much, but you have blossomed in unexpected ways. It is a pleasant surprise.'

'Really?' Ferdi leaned forward. 'A *pleasant surprise*? That I latched on to the only thing that made sense anymore, the urge to stay alive? A *pleasant surprise* that despite the fact that I was deprived of sunlight or kindness from the first day of my life, I could still speak to a human without cowering in fear? That despite being wrong – being *monstrous* – I could still—'

He stopped; the word *love* lodged itself in his throat like an angular thing and refused to budge. Ferdi's eyes brimmed with tears but he fought them away. He jumped to his feet but didn't dare leave without the man's permission, so he lingered there, shivering with emotion, until his body relaxed enough to let him sit again.

He was done fighting. He had said all that he needed to say, things that had been lurking in him and now had shoved their way out of his mouth. There was only one thing left, something he carried inside the safest place of his heart like someone in an interrogation room would do. He let go of it with great reluctance.

'I met a man who knew you,' Ferdi said, and watched.

The man in grey shifted in his seat. He ran his fingers again over the tie, which shivered like living skin.

'I know many people,' he snapped. 'What did this man say? Was he specific?'

'No.'

'Then how did you know?'

'I just did. All this time, I've never met anyone who felt so true.'

'You mean you've met others who claimed to know me?'

'Yes, but they were drunk or delirious. They were speaking about their own fears and fantasies, nothing like what I know...'

'And this man, was he sane? Calm, collected?'

'Well, no...'

'Did he have a name? Did he provide any proof?'

'He said he saw a mark on my hand. A seal.'

The man raised his eyebrows. 'But there is nothing on your hand.'

'I know, but—'

'But you believe any madman now? Anyone who pays you the least bit of attention?'

Ferdi pressed his lips shut. The feeling was tainted now. The night when the madman had died in his arms, the glass walls with the soft reflections of the night light, all had now shrunk and dried up under the man's scornful dismissal. He was suddenly exhausted.

'May I go now?'

The man started in mock offence. 'You haven't even finished your drink! No, please, stay a little longer. I'd like you to meet a friend.'

'I want nothing to do with any friends of yours.'

'All right, perhaps not a friend – in fact we've never met, so hold on.'

Ferdi clenched his fists. 'What are you doing?'

'Oh, my boy. My boy, I am horribly bored.'

'What?'

'It's true. Sometimes there are dry spells, and it kills me.' He sighed. 'I have to be everywhere, take care of everything, and there comes a season when the spark is gone and it's all mechanical, do you understand? No, how could you? So I have to push things sometimes. People are only hitchhiking towards their fate, and occasionally I pick them up and drive them for a while. It's the merciful thing to do.'

Ferdi realised he was very hot. Sweat was pooling over his lip. He rose to go, but the man lifted a reassuring hand.

'Please, stay. The show across the street must be over by now. Look!'

Ferdi sat back. Worldly noises were picking up in the café. Well-dressed couples peeked into the back room, some walking in and settling not far from them, looking handsome in their pressed suits and dresses. A group of students brought a few tables together and squeezed into the rest of the room, their shoulders and legs squeezed together, lighting cigarettes with one another's lighters and chatting, some of them in a foreign language that Ferdi couldn't place. He didn't recognise anybody. He rubbed the tension from the back of his neck.

'Well, that was all,' said the man. 'Don't be a stranger, now.'

Ferdi blinked and looked at him. The man carefully counted some change for the bill, then straightened his tie once more and stood up. On his own at the table Ferdi felt suddenly exposed.

He nearly grabbed the man's coat as he was putting it on.

'Is that all, then? Are you going to leave me alone?'

The man smiled.

'My boy, you are always alone.'

The waitress came to pick up the glasses. The man gave her an absent-minded smile, nodded at Ferdi once, and left. A couple of heads turned to see, but quickly lost interest.

Ferdi got up and numbly began to gather his things. The letter and the gold ring were still in his pocket. He crumpled the letter and put it in the ashtray, but didn't know what to do with the ring. The idea of wearing it made him sick. He rose to leave, but the scraping of a chair behind him made him glance over.

A young woman who sat among the students was watching him, her eyes widening behind a pair of large glasses. She was sitting upright, ignoring the man talking to her from across the table. Ferdi turned instinctively to avoid her attention, but she pushed her chair back and called to him.

'Sandor!'

His blood froze. For a second he almost turned but he forced his stiff limbs to move, and he began to make his way through the confusion of little tables. He felt sluggish, trapped. She was trying to move now as well, apologising to strangers and stepping over handbags.

'Sandor!'

He still didn't turn, pushing on, his mouth open and dry. A hand landed on his arm. He gasped and tried to tear himself away but the hand clung to him, demanding to be acknowledged. He surrendered.

She had the square face and prim collar of a schoolgirl. She was examining him expectantly, her straight brown hair dull with ciga-rette smoke and parted in the middle with old-fashioned care. Nothing about her looked like it had been put on especially for a night out. She smiled a toothy grin, and began to talk to him in a foreign language. He looked at her blankly until she switched to broken Hungarian.

'It's me, Maggie! How are you?'

She searched his face. Her eyes stopped at the scar and the drawn skin around the eyes, and whatever she saw in him must have displeased her, because her grip relaxed and her eyebrows gathered over the rims of her glasses.

'I'm sorry,' he said. 'I don't think we've met.'

'Come on!' she teased. 'I haven't heard from you in years! I was worried! My letters started coming back, with no explanation at all—'

She stopped. Her face fell when she saw no sign of recognition.

'Sandor, do you really not remember me?'

Another young woman from the group approached them, curly-haired and with a serious expression that felt familiar to Ferdi. She exchanged a few quick words in the foreign language with the woman in glasses, who was glancing at Ferdi and was now evidently upset. The curly-haired woman turned to him and translated.

'Aren't you Sandor Esterhazy?' she asked.

He shook his head, avoiding the gaze of the woman in the glasses. 'You must have me confused with someone else.'

He left, not waiting to hear more. When he stepped out into the night he glanced behind him and saw the woman in the glasses standing at the entrance, watching him, a deep crease on her brow. When their eyes met she tilted her head and mouthed something unintelligible to him, but he made no reaction, and she disappeared back into the café.

PART II

1990

The following morning Ferdi peeled the potatoes with the zeal of someone who had earned a reprieve at the foot of the gallows.

'Make-believe boy, make-believe boy,' he kept muttering to himself. He had woken up furious. As if his being could be held together by sheer force of belief! Belief required a subject as well as an object. It required a believer, and nobody who knew about his true nature ever believed in Ferdi. People were merely fooled into considering him real, and if his existence had been founded on this illusion then he would have crumbled the moment it dissolved. *Make-believe* – not even Sandor, the one human who knew the real him, could properly believe: he could only grudgingly accept Ferdi as an inescapable horror, the way people dealt with natural disasters.

But the words of the man in grey had wormed their way under his skin, and the knife strokes on the potatoes couldn't vent his anger. Peels thick with wet flesh dropped into the filling bucket, and Mrs Soltesz would have smacked him if she had seen the waste.

Erzsi poked her head around the kitchen door.

'No practice today?'

'No.'

He buried his face in the potatoes and did not insist. He heard her turn the radio on and get to work, humming. He stabbed a potato and rubbed his eyes with the back of his mud-stained hands. The earthy smell was comforting.

The woman in glasses haunted him. The joy of her smile when she mistook him for Sandor was a painful sight. He tried to imagine what kind of relationship the two of them had had: were they friends? Lovers? And had she known him before or after Ferdi's time? At the same time it was baffling to know that someone could have liked Sandor, despite… despite everything Ferdi knew about him. It was tempting to imagine the boy who was once able to elicit such emotions, but Ferdi steered his thoughts clear of that direction. He placed himself in the moment when her pleasure owed itself to the sight of confused, skittish, ambiguously real Ferdi. But then had come the collapse of that fleeting bliss. The thought of walking into her again filled him with terror. He had never imagined the city like this, full of the potential danger of stumbling into someone who knew Sandor.

I must leave, came the gut reaction again, but there was no safe place.

Petar banging on the door brought him to his senses. He jumped, wiped his hands on his apron and hurried to open it for him. Petar rushed in, hidden behind a giant package of meat. He grumbled something, and put it on the counter.

'We have a big reservation tonight,' was the only thing Ferdi could say. The boy glanced at him with suspicion.

'Fully booked,' Ferdi went on, usually so laconic but now, caught off guard by everything, he found himself chattering. 'A wedding, or a birthday. I almost couldn't come today, but they'd never make it short-handed…'

'Why?'

Ferdi held his tongue.

'How come you weren't coming to work?'

'I thought I couldn't make it.'

'Why?'

Petar moved closer. Ferdi retreated until he was pressed against the sinks. The humming in the dining room had stopped and he knew Erzsi was listening. The radio kept blasting music.

'You thought I'd tell on you?' said Petar. 'You think I'm a snitch?'

'No, it had nothing to do with that.'

Petar's voice dropped to a whisper. 'You were going to run away? You don't trust me? You think I'm a snitch? I'm not a snitch.'

'I believe you.'

Ferdi impulsively raised a hand between them to hold him off, but Petar advanced until Ferdi's palm was pushing against his chest. A stringy muscle twitched under Ferdi's fingers and he quickly withdrew his hand. It left a faint trace of mud on the bloody apron.

There was a clatter from the dining room and Petar jumped back. Ferdi remained where he was. There was no further noise and he hoped Erzsi had deliberately created the distraction for his sake. Petar glared at him, rubbing his lip where the moustache used to be.

'You don't need to worry about me,' said Ferdi. 'I have a lot on my mind as it is.'

'Yes, you're all secrets, aren't you?'

'Not all of them are mine.'

Petar paused and clenched his fists. 'You swore,' he whispered.

Suddenly Ferdi didn't care. 'So did you! You swore that you weren't there last Wednesday, and you lied. What good is your word now?'

Petar made no reply. Ferdi stepped forward and spoke in a low voice.

'How can I trust you? Tell me! You come to my door like a ghost – or you growl at me like a dog. You want secrets? A secret is only as good as the man who keeps it, and you're still just a boy.'

Petar's frown melted off. He blinked and looked away. Ferdi wished the ground would swallow him.

'Look – don't run off,' he muttered. 'You always run off.'

It was no use. Petar was already moving away, and the door swung open and shut again. Ferdi lingered for a moment, then followed him outside.

'I'm sorry.'

Petar locked the back of the refrigerated truck. His face was expressionless.

'No,' he said. 'You're right. You're the big man, so you should know.'

He climbed into the front seat and drove away. Ferdi watched him leave, and returned to his potatoes until Erzsi joined him in the kitchen. They made coffee and they drank it standing up, in silence, as if it had already been a long day.

'I miss your playing,' she eventually said.

He glared at his cup. 'What's the point of it?'

'What does that mean?'

'It's no use to anyone. I did it because I couldn't *not* do it. The fact that it was noticed was just coincidence. So what's the point?'

Erzsi considered it. 'The point,' she slowly said, 'must be that I miss it.'

*

If there was anything worse than Petar being angry with him, it was Petar being perfectly polite to him. Ferdi did his best to follow his example, but the emotional strain of the past few days was beginning to show. In the days that followed he began to unravel out of pure weariness. After work he would remain for a goodnight glass of wine at Mrs Soltesz's table, sometimes lingering long enough to walk home with Erzsi or Dieter. Once he even invited them up for a nightcap, which was simply the plastic bottle of bad vodka – at its sight Dieter almost turned and left – and a pack of biscuits. They got drunk on the combination of these and the comfortable pleasure of sitting around together, and Erzsi sang in her low voice until Ferdi's eyelids drooped. Dieter, stinking of raw onions and pickled peppers, fell asleep on the bed, which was too narrow for his frame, while Erzsi and Ferdi gossiped, curled up on a blanket spread on the cold hardwood floor while the rain outside drummed on.

Little by little daily life was beginning to settle again, when Gabriella Gedeon called once more. Ferdi, roused from his sleep by Mr Polyak, took the call at the reception desk by the entrance while shivering in the frosty November stillness.

'Do you know that everyone loved you the other night?'

'No,' he mumbled, slow to comprehend.

'You impressed them. Ferdi, are you awake? This is big. There is to be a concert at the Opera House in January, and they're going to pick a series of new composers to showcase. I'm not on the committee of course – you know I'm supposed to be retired – but I know these people. We've collaborated, I know what they're looking for. I can send them your work. It is brilliant work, and my word will go a long way. But you'll have to commit, Ferdi. This won't be as casual as last time. Do you want to do it?'

'A concert? At the Opera House?' He recalled the elegant building he'd glimpsed the other day. Horror dawned on him, and with it a new thrill tugged at his insides. Ferdi nodded vigorously.

'Ferdi?'

'Yes. I'm nodding yes.'

'Great! The concert will take place on Sunday, January the twentieth. I'll let you know of course, but it's as sure as done. You'll have to apply and register after I give you word, but the fee isn't big. Arrange to practise at a piano there, they'll have everything you need. I'm giving you the number now, are you writing?'

He grabbed the ballpoint from the desk and scribbled on the empty envelope of an old electricity bill.

Gabriella's rough voice dropped conspiratorially. 'I'm very happy for you, Ferdi.'

'All thanks to you.'

'Nonsense. This is your work.'

'No, if you hadn't—'

'Oh, we can settle this peacefully. Will you come to dinner tonight? Natalia is home for a while, and Balint is cooking special every day.'

'I'm working tonight. But tomorrow is my day off, if...'

'Tomorrow it is, then. We're not working until the weekend anyway. Do you like Italian food?'

'I've never had it.'

'First time for everything.'

She gave him the address and told him how to get there. The torn envelope was filling up. She hung up and he stood there in the cold half-darkness, trying to decide if he was dreaming.

Dieter of course needed no excuse to celebrate. He took no notice of Ferdi's weak protests, and didn't stop until Erzsi pointed out that he was jinxing him. But the fire was in him, and he had a reason to convince them to go out. Erzsi, who held a fondness for Mrs Soltesz, wanted to stay at the bar with her until Dieter's shift was over, but it was already busy in the dining room so the two of them headed to Ferdi's place to wait there.

'Let's trick him into staying in,' said Erzsi, so they stopped on their way and bought red wine, bread, salami and potato chips.

They made an impromptu picnic on Ferdi's creaky bed. Erzsi lamented the absence of hard-boiled eggs, and opened the wine with no trace of guilt.

'I'll toast,' she said, holding her chipped tumbler high. Ferdi followed suit with a solemn face and wine in a coffee mug.

'To music. To luck. To violinists everywhere. May you never get stage fright again!' They drank, and Erzsi tore a handful of bread from the loaf. 'Dieter will be lucky to find anything left to eat. More wine, please.'

Ferdi poured some for both of them. The buzzer sounded, and Ferdi got up and pressed the button. They waited, but there was no sound of footsteps. They looked at each other.

Ferdi grabbed the keys. 'It must be broken. I'll go let him in.'

The corridors were dark and silent, but the atrium was illuminated with the silver glow of the laden clouds. Ferdi smelled the crispness of oncoming snow and winced.

When he heaved the front door open there was nobody to see. He peered out into the night.

'Don't be alarmed,' came Dieter's voice. 'But I'm bleeding.'

'Dieter!' Ferdi rushed forward, then stopped, glancing left and right.

'It's safe. He's gone. *Fuck!*'

Ferdi stumbled towards him, feeling about.

'Is it bad?'

'Well, Molnar, it's not good! But I'll live. I've been stabbed before. Help me up.'

'No, don't move! I'll call an ambulance.'

Dieter groaned as if he found ambulances too much of a hassle, but Ferdi ran back to the communal phone at the desk. The silence of the building was ghostly. He returned and sat on the doorstep, helping Dieter lean against his knees.

'Who did this? Did they mug you?'

'No.' Dieter's voice came slower. It was suddenly that of a tired, older man. 'And I had half my pay with me, but he didn't take it. He just...' He made a weak gesture of dismissal. 'Grabbed me. Jumped out of nowhere while I was looking for the doorbell. Put a knife to my throat from behind. I could have taken him if he hadn't, I could have – he wasn't big – tall but scrawny chap, like you.'

'Maybe you shouldn't be talking.'

'An amateur. Didn't know that a good stab has to be pointing upwards.'

'Dieter.'

He sighed. He was very heavy against Ferdi's leg. 'I can protect myself, you know. If he'd wanted to kill me he'd have gone for the throat right away. I struggled so he got me on the shoulder, right on the bone.'

Ferdi looked behind into the stillness of the atrium. Erzsi would be looking for them soon. He could sense movement in the patch of light coming from his window.

'He said something,' Dieter mused thickly, and yawned. 'He asked me... what was it? Oh, yes. He kept asking, "What did he tell you? What did he tell you?" Over and over. I was so angry by then, I elbowed him right in the chest so he stabbed and ran.'

Ferdi's heart was beating heavily.

'What did he look like?'

Dieter scoffed. 'Who knows? The idiot clearly had the wrong man.'

There was the sound of footsteps from behind. Erzsi was approaching carefully, looking for them through the darkness.

*

Mrs Soltesz was apparently furious: finding a replacement for Dieter would prove a *nightmare*, and she would have to take several dishes off the menu. Ferdi didn't witness the phone call, but Dieter's colourful language painted a strong picture.

Dieter was only in need of a few stitches, hydration and plenty of rest. The three of them walked out of the hospital in the small hours of the morning, exhausted. Dieter had his arm in a sling and was almost sleeping on his feet. Ferdi clutched an armful of flowers from the hospital shop to offer Gabriella at dinner, and Erzsi had wrapped her arm around Dieter's, her face pale and vacant. Ferdi could sense the storm brewing in her. They dropped Ferdi off with a taxi and carried on to Dieter's home. Ferdi watched them disappear with a gnawing feeling of guilt.

It couldn't be an accident that Dieter had been attacked at Ferdi's own front step. And then there were the stranger's words. Ferdi had the nagging suspicion that Dieter had been stabbed by the same blade that had taken the life of the madman.

He remained standing on the doorstep for a while, trying to make out any drops of Dieter's blood on the dirty pavement. Part of him, feeling a desire mixed with fear and thrill, wanted the attacker to appear again. He clutched the flowers, aware of how comic he looked stranded there holding them like a desperate lover, poised to run in either direction.

*

Gabriella and Balint lived across the river. The Danube glittered sweetly in the falling dusk and the tram car crossing the bridge was filled with tired commuters and schoolkids. An old lady sitting across from him smiled at the sight of the fidgety young man carrying a bouquet, and he tried to smile back but only managed a half-hearted grimace. He was afraid he was sweating through his nicest shirt, and was becoming terrified of the prospect of conversation and a celebratory dinner in honour of his performance. It took him the whole ride to decide to trust Gabriella's judgement all over again – she had, after all, proved to be a friend and a firm believer of his music.

The building itself was modern in a drab, bleak way, and Ferdi was glad to be bringing it flowers. When Ferdi knocked on the apartment door, Balint opened it in a colourless cardigan and an apron, and with a fixed faraway look of mild surprise, which had Ferdi momentarily in a panic that he had arrived on the wrong day. Balint then reached out to shake Ferdi's hand and Ferdi, confused, presented him with the flowers instead. Balint led him in and to the dining room.

'Gigi, your protégé is here!'

It was a comfortable room, overflowing with furniture made for a bigger house. Tapestries and small dark paintings crowded one wall and a marble-topped buffet leaned against the other, laden with trinkets and oddities, its liquor shelf entirely occupied by books. The apartment had a strong sense of texture and permanence and an earthy mood where, despite the jumble, someone could eat, drink and talk leisurely. The table, covered with an embroidered tablecloth that appeared handmade, was set for four people.

Gabriella surprised him with a hug. She looked more like her old pythoness self despite her plain clothes, and her short hair smelled of her usual cigarillos.

'You're in,' she announced, 'I just got word today. I'm so glad, Ferdi, so glad! It will be marvellous. Come here to talk – Natalia won't arrive for a little while. She still has the manners of a student.' She hurried to get him out of his coat. 'Something for an aperitif? There's walnut liqueur.'

She handed him a little gold-rimmed glass of a blackish spirit. It smelled of cinnamon and tasted thick and bittersweet, full-bodied like the polished old wood that surrounded them. They sat on the sofa while Balint could be heard fussing with pots and pans in the kitchen.

'Have you a piece in mind?'

He shook his head. 'I haven't had the time to prepare something.'

'It would be better if you performed something different than last time.'

'I think I can put something together, but it might not be perfect.'

'With your style, that might not be an issue.' She refilled his glass before he could stop her; his empty stomach was agitated enough, but he drank out of politeness. 'Balint, shall we have some music?'

Balint returned. 'Yes, there was something that I wanted...' He bent over the stereo and rummaged through its cabinets. He straightened up slowly, rubbing his back and holding up a record, its cover wrinkled and peeling. 'Found it.'

He slipped the disc out of the sleeve and handed the cover to Ferdi. 'What is this?'

'A rare piece. I was reminded of it when I first heard you play.'

He switched on the gramophone and it emitted a pleasant hum.

'I think the speakers are still connected to the CD player, darling, you must switch them,' Gabriella said, lighting a cigarillo, and Balint muttered in frustration as he fumbled behind the equipment, coughing in her cloud of smoke.

Ferdi looked at the track list, then turned the cover around. The front was a dark, blurry photo of a small man playing the piano. Only his hands were lit, caught mid-air, and his sweaty, egg-shaped head as it bent over the keys. The hair was thicker than the last time Ferdi had seen him and there was no hint of the pot belly of middle age, but there was no doubt as to who he was.

Salomon Esterhazy: Études.

The needle alighted on the edge of the record. There was a static-filled pause and then the sound of piano bloomed. It was as if someone had laid a hand on Ferdi's shoulder.

Balint picked up his glass and sipped, blinking in tune with the piece. 'Elegant,' he mused. 'Doesn't it remind you of Spain, Gigi?'

Ferdi had never heard such delicate lacing of the simplest clusters of notes. It came fast but unhurried, the breathless soliloquy of a sharp mind. He wiped his mouth. He wanted to tear the needle away and smash the record over his knee. He wanted to drop his glass and run out of the small apartment, out of the city. But he sat spellbound. Gabriella closed her eyes.

He excused himself and escaped to the tiny bathroom. He sat on the toilet lid, put his head between his knees. The music trickled in from the gap under the door, clung to his trouser hems, seeped into his clammy skin. He didn't want it – Salomon's music, his fingers on the keys; Salomon's hands passing the tray of salted butter, Salomon's glasses glinting over the top of a newspaper, Salomon's eyes watching him, examining his hair, his bruises, his red eyes, with the tiniest hint of an amused smile… Here was that smile again, it crept into the bathroom with the music, it made his knees give.

He recovered his breath, washed his face and stepped back into the living room. The record was still playing, on lower volume. Gabriella smiled at him.

'His style reminds me a little of you, Ferdi,' she said.

'Perhaps in execution,' said Balint. 'You put your weight on the keys in a similar way.'

Ferdi was silent. There was a story on the tip of his tongue of how that person on the record was familiar, the story of the genealogy of his technique. He wanted to share it with them, he wanted to speak about climbing into the piano room parched with the desire to play, of late-night wanderings in a house big enough to fit this entire apartment in its dining room.

They heard the front door open and close, and Gabriella rose from her seat.

'Always so quiet, Ferdi,' she chided him before disappearing into the hallway. Ferdi heard the shuffling of clothes and hushed conversation, then Gabriella returned. 'Natalia will be right along. Let's sit at the table.'

Ferdi stood up too quickly and swayed. The heavy drink sloshed around inside him, and for a moment he had to fight a wave of nausea. He sat where he was indicated at the table, while Gabriella went to help Balint in the kitchen. They re-emerged with platters of steaming pasta in a thick green sauce that smelled sharply of unknown herbs, and disappeared again bickering about the salad dressing.

He sat alone at the table marvelling at the beauty and care in everything that surrounded him, at the hum of messy jazz now coming from the record player, at the gloss that the items had acquired through generations of use. There were roots hidden in this graceless apartment building, roots that had been carefully removed and replanted into a new narrow container. Stocked memories of parents and grandparents and children of all ages, the carefully unwrapped comfort of an old family.

At the sound of footsteps he looked up to see the newcomer. Their eyes met, and both instinctively assumed a polite smile. Then the smiles disappeared. Standing in front of him was the curly-haired young woman from the café; Maggie's friend.

The walnut liqueur rose to choke him. He glanced around, expecting the woman in glasses to appear as well.

The curly-haired woman stared at him with narrowed eyes. He told himself there was no reason for her to remember him.

No reason at all. Of course he recognised her now: she had her father's sober face and long nose, her mother's widow's peak and prominent snake-green eyes...

Gabriella walked into the dining room and put a hand around her daughter's shoulders. They were exactly the same height and shape: long-limbed, angular and slender.

'I see that you've met my Natalia,' she said, beaming with pride.

Natalia tilted her head, frowning, and gave her a brief smile. 'We've met before, Mom. This is Sandor Esterhazy.'

Ferdi felt faint. Gabriella's smile shrank and she glanced from one to the other.

'No darling, this is Ferdi Molnar. The pianist I was telling you about.'

Both of them turned to Ferdi. He had to clear his throat.

'It's true, we've met before. I must look a lot like this person, then. He must be a good-looking man.' He attempted the shadow of a grin.

Gabriella burst out laughing. 'Aren't you wearing your contacts, Natalia? I'm sorry, Ferdi.'

'No need...'

Natalia's face hadn't softened. 'But Maggie Storm...'

'Oh, Maggie's in town? You didn't tell me, we could have had her over too!'

'We flew in together, of course. We met Sandor – Ferdi here – after the opera last week. Maggie swears—'

'It was a misunderstanding,' Ferdi hurried to reassure them. The girl's eyes were hard. 'I must have one of those faces,' he added. 'It keeps getting me into trouble.'

Ferdi could feel his shirt flutter with his racing pulse. Natalia sat across from him and he wondered whether his agitation was obvious. She looked uncertain and wary, watching him closely. Gabriella poured wine for everyone and Balint arrived with a big bowl of fragrant greens. They took their places, and Ferdi had to force himself to eat. The unexpected solidity of the food and its rich, foreign taste confused his senses.

'Sandor Esterhazy, did you say?' Balint scratched his chin, frowning. 'No relation to Salomon and Karolina Esterhazy then? Like the record we just heard?'

Ferdi was slowly drowning. He thanked his lucky stars that he'd decided to wear the signet ring around his neck that morning, but it burned against his skin at the mention of its rightful owner.

'Yes, Maggie mentioned these names. Their parents were friends when she was living here.'

'We met them a couple of times, Gigi, must be two decades ago now. At that New Year's concert right before my mother died. They were both performing, and we spoke afterwards. You were there, too, Natalia. Do you remember?'

'No, Dad, I was only a kid.'

'Such a pity, what happened,' Balint mumbled.

Natalia drew her gaze away from Ferdi. 'What do you mean?'

Balint took a thoughtful sip. 'We all knew they were grooming the boy for a musical career, but he never appeared at the Academy. Then suddenly the Esterhazys cancelled the rest of their season – this was some years ago. They disappeared from the public eye. It was a scandal. If they resurfaced, I didn't hear about it.'

'We lost touch with a lot of people after Balint retired,' sighed Gabriella.

Ferdi put down his fork with a shaking hand. 'And what happened to the boy?'

'There were rumours, bad ones. Mind you, many people were jealous of that family, it was too old, too rich. They said the boy was in trouble with the police – that he ran away, was disowned or something equally dreadful. I never believed them, to tell you the truth.' Balint slowly shook his head. 'The only thing everyone seemed to agree on was that the boy had disappeared.'

Silence fell. Balint reached for his daughter's hand and gave it a momentary squeeze.

'No parents should lose their child like that. It's not right.'

Natalia smiled and caressed his hand. 'Dad, I'm only a plane ride away. I keep telling you, you'd like New York! It's a whole new world. I'll take you to this jazz bar I know...'

'That's awful,' said Gabriella. 'Perhaps you shouldn't mention any of this to Maggie, it would only upset her.'

Ferdi recalled the young woman in the glasses and her letters to Sandor that kept being returned to her, and felt a surge of pity. It was just like Sandor to keep hurting people even in his absence.

Natalia planted an unforgiving stare on Ferdi.

'Perhaps he hasn't entirely disappeared.' She studied him for a weak spot. 'Perhaps we've accidentally unearthed him.'

Ferdi clutched his glass, making no move to drink. An unfamiliar sense of anger gnawed at the top of his throat. Gabriella and Balint turned their eyes on him, and Balint waved the tension away with a salad-laden fork.

'Nonsense. I've seen Ferdi play, Natalia: it's quite special. There isn't a chance for your conspiracy theories.'

'Why not?'

'Because it was common knowledge that the Esterhazy boy was sadly and utterly inept.'

And at the absurdity of the idea he laughed for the first time, a long, silent fit from the bottom of his stomach that shook the table and exposed a missing tooth in his upper jaw. Natalia sank back, tugged at a curl and watched Ferdi through her heavy lashes.

After Balint's shapeless panna cotta and more walnut liqueur, Gabriella agreed to pick up her violin and performed some jaunty solos. Ferdi once again marvelled at her speed and abandon, at the unselfconscious swaying of her right leg while the left stood firmly against the tide of the music. The nostalgic wailing that filled the room teased in him a deep-rooted sadness, one that tempted him to weep right there in the small sitting room. His chest tightened around the jumble of unwelcome thoughts flooding it. He pictured the hot dressing room at the concert Balint had mentioned, the Gedeons meeting the Esterhazys, the dim lights. Among the crowding adults the two children, primly dressed, shaking hands.

The mood was drowsy; even Natalia's head started to nod as if she was drifting off. Through half-closed eyes Ferdi thought he could see the snake dress wrapped around Gabriella, and the lithe green shape gently flexed its coils and watched him back through gold-sequinned eyes. It was trying to speak to him, struggling to move its stitched mouth; it was trying to say something very important. His eyelids drooped as he listened intently to make out the hissing words over the sound of the strings. But suddenly the music stopped and with it the room shrank and brightened. The snake was lost. He clapped along, trying to return to the present.

As he left Gabriella hugged him again, all elbows and shoulders, while mumbling advice for the concert that Ferdi was too tired to absorb. He stepped out into the dark corridor disturbed and perplexed, and fled home.

1980

Sandor was sitting in the warm living room by himself, drowsily doodling pictures of animals. Karolina appeared in the doorway. She hovered for a while, then approached him and gently wove her fingers into his hair. Sandor hated to be petted like this, but didn't have enough energy to protest so he let her.

'Why are you playing the piano during the night?' she whispered.

He glanced up at her. 'I don't. At nine I'm done playing.' It was only an hour ago that he had walked Ferdi back to the gun room, and his jeans were still muddy with melted snow.

'Two days ago I woke up in the middle of the night. You were playing soft pedal again and at first I thought I was dreaming, so I went downstairs and stood outside the door. I heard you. You were still playing when I went back to sleep.'

He returned to his sketches. 'It was probably Father.'

'No, I had just left him in bed snoring.'

Sandor's stomach gave a lurch. He looked up. His mother's expression was eager and curious. The tips of her fingers traced his ears, nostalgic for the time when he was still small and longed for her touch.

'I'm sorry if I'm hard on you, my darling.'

'It's all right, Mother.'

'You don't have to play at night, but it's fine if you want to. I won't bother you.'

'I won't do it again.' He leaned in and gave an absent-minded peck to her cool hand. 'I'm sorry I disturbed you.'

She nodded at his exposed wrist, noticing the burn mark. 'What happened?'

'Burned on the stove.' He tugged at his sleeve to cover it.

'I'll give you an ointment to help with the scar.'

She gave his hair one last ruffle and left. Sandor let his pencil fall and buried his face in his hands, taking long breaths. For a second his head swam, then anger erupted in him and he jumped and ran to the hallway, put his shoes on and stepped out.

The cold shook him back into his senses. He couldn't go to the gun room while his parents were still awake. He imagined them calling him and then, when he wouldn't answer, searching everywhere until they reached the unlikely basement – and the shock on their faces as they walked in and saw the two identical boys. He had to wait until it was safe. Shuddering in frustration, he stepped back inside.

When everyone was asleep he put his coat over his pyjamas and stole outside. These days he wore the key to the gun room around his neck, and the warm piece of metal was bouncing against his breastbone as he stomped on the snow. The night was inky and moonless, the air heavy. His anger amplified with every step, and by the time he climbed down the mossy steps and collided with the door his heart was kicking with fury.

Ferdi was lying on the table reading, wrapped in his blankets. His eyes widened when he saw Sandor, but he didn't have time to react. Sandor dragged him off the table, dug his fingers into his arms and shook him.

'What the hell are you doing? What the hell—?'

Ferdi struggled and pushed Sandor away, trying to free himself. His mouth opened in horror and he shook his head, unable to protest.

'You came into my house,' growled Sandor and his grip tightened, '*my* house! Anyone could have seen you! My mother was just outside the door!' He pushed Ferdi back against the table, where he stumbled. 'You did, didn't you? You were in the piano room at night, playing.'

Ferdi nodded once, and Sandor struck him in the face. Ferdi fell down and crawled backwards in horror. He touched his nose and saw the blood on his fingertips.

'I'm sorry, I'm sorry!' he gasped. 'I can't help it!'

'YOU DISOBEYED ME!'

Sandor took a step forward, raising his hand again, and the sight of Ferdi cowering on the ground with blood trickling sobered him. Disgusted and furious, he took a step back and tried to calm down. He rubbed his face.

'How did you get out?'

Ferdi nodded at the rusty door handle. 'The screws were loose. I took it out and then I put it back later and it was still locked. Nobody saw me!'

Sandor looked at the handle, turned the protruding screws with his nail, dug his finger under it and gave it a pull. The handle shook free and hung limp in its socket. All it needed was a screwdriver and the problem was solved. He turned back to Ferdi, who was still lying there watching him warily, the cuff of his sleeve held against his nosebleed.

'Pinch the bone of your nose,' Sandor told him, and Ferdi did. He looked scared and ridiculous, like a little boy.

'How long have you been doing this?'

Ferdi pulled himself up. 'Since that day you showed me the Chopin book. You said I wasn't ready. I wanted to try it.'

'*Chopin?* That was a week ago!'

'Yes.'

'Why?'

Ferdi looked down. He didn't reply. Sandor was hoarse with indignation.

'Where else in the house did you go?'

'Nowhere.'

'Not even to the kitchen for food?'

'No, I stayed in the piano room. I never even opened the door.'

'Why?' Sandor felt he was walking around in circles inside his own head.

'I wanted to practise a little more.'

'*Why?*'

'I don't know why, I just had to!' exclaimed Ferdi, and immediately seemed to regret it.

Sandor pointed a finger. 'No more of that, do you understand?'

Ferdi bit his bloody lip. A long moment of silence passed.

'Then let me play more,' he said at last.

The demand stunned Sandor into silence.

'I need more time at the piano,' Ferdi went on. 'You must find a way. Tell them you need to practise more. I don't know. You can think of something, surely?' His assurance faltered mid-sentence.

Sandor placed a cold hand on his forehead and let the chill pull his thoughts together. 'I don't feel very well.' His voice was a hiss. 'Damn you, Ferdi.'

With a mixture of guilt and vindictiveness he saw that his words had hit home. Ferdi lowered his gaze and the corners of his mouth dropped.

'I'm going to get a screwdriver to fix this. Don't – don't go anywhere.'

He stopped in his tracks and turned to look at Ferdi still standing there, bloody and dirty and pathetic.

'Why didn't you run away?'

Ferdi met his eyes. There was something in his look that made Sandor feel a profound, inexplicable shame. He turned back and left, and didn't bother to lock the door.

*

The screwdriver was brought, the lock was fixed. The key burned under Sandor's clothes that night, it tugged at his neck when he tried to sleep. He had a nightmare that the key had come alive and tried to throttle him, turning into cold hands that squeezed his neck until his face was blue, and then he woke up gasping with the chain stuck under the pillow and wrapped tight around his throat. It had left a throbbing red line. He yanked it off and tossed it away, then he got out of bed to feel around in the darkness until he found it again and tucked it safely in a drawer.

He woke up once more at dawn, sweating and hot. His shirt clung to his back. He kicked the covers away and drifted in and out of consciousness, shuddering and burning by turns, and gathering the blankets over him again. He could hear the wind blowing through crevices, and underneath that hushed mutterings, rippling around him like conversations by a deathbed. His teeth clattered until his skull was aching. The whole house was producing sounds: it creaked and rustled and groaned. The wind became so strong that the bed swayed and he hung onto it, while down in the kitchen the silverware rattled in its drawers and the plates danced in their cupboards. The water pipes clanged solemnly like bells, and naked branches scratched at the walls. A blast blew a window open downstairs, scattering dead leaves on the carpet. He pulled the covers over his face, shaking, wishing for the sleep that wouldn't come. He was freezing. A spasm shot up his spine and he twisted, curled up and sank back into unconsciousness.

When the fever broke he got out bed shakily and put on his dressing gown. His bones were aching and his throat dry, but his head was now clear. He stepped out into the dark corridor. Some of the night light stole in, illuminating the staircase and casting its shy blue flakes around the hallway. He walked quietly down the carpeted stairs and sat for a moment at the landing to recover his strength.

The house was still, as if everything was underwater. There was no trace of the gale. Sandor no longer trusted his own mind. He wandered around the hallways, peeking into the empty rooms: all windows were closed, the floors clean. In front of the double doors of the piano room he hesitated, then pushed them open and walked in. It was undisturbed. He approached the main window and saw that it was pushed into place, but not fully closed. Perhaps nobody had noticed all this time. He turned the handle until it latched. He tried to imagine Ferdi sitting alone at the piano in the gloom, surrounded by the echoing silence of the house and the wheezy plucking of the soft pedal. He left.

The first maid to enter the kitchen found him sleeping, draped over the cold marble bench next to a cup of oily black tea. It was the brown-haired girl, Dorika – his mother's favourite, her cheeks still blazing from her morning walk through the frost. She pushed his head back and put a rough palm that smelled of green soap against his burning forehead.

'Come on, Master Sandor.' Her strong arms pulled him upright and supported him as he swooned and nearly fell on her. 'Back to bed with you.'

He had a vague memory of being put to bed, of hearing the shuffling of slippers and the hushed voices of his parents in the hallway. The door creaked open and the side of the bed sank with someone's weight. It made him roll over. He recognised the smell of his mother: last night's perfume mingled with the heat of suppressed energy.

Karolina pushed back the sweaty strands of hair sticking to his forehead. 'I called your school. Go back to sleep, darling.'

He tried to nod, and sank back into sleep.

When he came to it was afternoon. Someone was knocking on the door softly. Dorika stepped in with a bowl of chicken soup, placed it on the bedside table and left. He ate a little and went back to sleep.

He was woken by the light touch of his mother's hand.

'It's dark already. Sit up a little, or you won't be able to sleep tonight. Finish your soup.'

He dragged himself into a sitting position, and Karolina lit the bedside lamp.

'Where's Father?'

'In the piano room. His concert is tomorrow.'

Sandor tensed, the fog clearing from his brain. He looked at his watch and felt his stomach drop. 'But it's my time to practise.'

'No practice until the fever breaks, darling.'

'I have to practise!'

'Sandor! We're killing ourselves trying to keep you interested, and you're making a scene to play now? You're not stepping into the piano room today. Now, finish your soup!'

'Let me just for a little—'

'Don't get agitated or your fever will worsen. Read a book. I'll have the television rolled in. I'll be down the hall if you need me.'

'Mother!'

She stood up and refused to look at him again while she fumbled with the soup, and left the room.

Sandor sprang up. In a fit of panic he considered climbing out of the window and down the wall, but even if he could manage to stand on the shallow ledge, the wall below was smooth down to the ground. He hadn't brought food to Ferdi in over a day. At least he had fixed the lock, and the tap was always working, but would he be all right? Had Ferdi followed his advice to always ration his food? Sandor had smuggled a couple of cans of meat a while ago for an emergency, but those could have gone long ago.

Fury boiled inside him. Let him starve then, that would teach him to obey! He could do with a couple of days of hunger. Let him sit there in the cold, stewing in misery and remorse, until he learned. He would wonder what had happened to Sandor. He would feel the minutes, the hours trickling away, he'd feel in his bones the luxury of the few hours in the piano room. That's what parents did with misbehaving children, they took away their toys. Ferdi should learn, even if it had to be beaten into him. If he persisted in disobeying orders, then Sandor had no use for him. *So let him starve, let him die—!*

Sandor sat back with a groan. He felt for the burn mark on his wrist, where the skin had settled thin and taut over his flesh. Let him die? It was foolish to give in to his anger like this. What would Ferdi's death accomplish? All this would be for nothing, the man in the tuxedo coming for him for nothing, the darkness hovering over his future for nothing. Ferdi was his only asset in the small, set world he was trapped in, a world rigid and patterned.

Sandor walked to the window and opened the curtains. It was a humid night and the moon shone feebly through the haze. For a brief moment the weakness of the illness overtook him and the world swung around him, and he was certain that none of this had actually happened – that it was in fact still last year and he had spent the evening in Maggie's room, and he was still light with laughter.

He sat on the bed, took out one of Maggie's books and resumed his struggle with it. But his eyelids were heavy, and the words too strange and foreign. The story refused to seep into his mind. He fell asleep with the book on his lap.

The next morning he woke up early, with the odd lightness that comes after a confinement. His fever had left him with aching bones and a deep hunger. Karolina let him stay home to recover fully and had Dorika stay at the house overtime to keep an eye on him, and by the time she too had left for her home, Sandor was consumed with anxiety. His parents had left strict orders for him to stay in bed with the hot water bottle, but as soon as he was certain the house was empty he picked up the key to the gun room, wrapped himself as warm as possible and made his way to the kitchen.

It was snowing when he stepped out, and a series of shivers struck him so powerfully that he had to pause to recover his breath. Snowflakes piled on his sweaty head and melted into water that ran down his hot scalp in icy rivulets. He rushed to the basement, his pockets heavy with gifts of remorse.

The gun room was so dark and still that when he stepped in he didn't dare speak, and stood in silence as he felt for the light switch. Then the dusty bulb flickered into life and he saw Ferdi lying in a small heap of blankets in the furthest corner, eyes squinting against the invasion of light. Sandor dropped the food he had brought on the table and ran to him.

Ferdi was unhappily pulled out from the depths of his slumber. As his consciousness surfaced he saw Sandor and his eyes widened. He struggled to pull himself up and clutched feebly at Sandor's arm.

'I won't do it again! I promise, I'll never do it again!'

Sandor paused in momentary horror at the sight of the boy's ashen face. Then he hauled him from the armpits to help him sit up and gave him a pear from his pocket. Ferdi ate it right out of Sandor's hand, smearing them both with juice. He took long gulps of air and some colour returned to his face.

'I thought – I thought you had left me for good,' he gasped.

Sandor was tempted to let him believe it, if only to make sure that Ferdi wouldn't defy his orders again.

'I was ill,' he said. 'I had a fever all day. They wouldn't let me out of their sight.'

Ferdi looked up at him and Sandor saw the purple hollows around his eyes.

'But this was as good as punishment as any,' he continued, mercilessly.

The thin body that he was still cradling in his arms tensed. Ferdi squirmed away from him and drew back.

'Don't eat all the food I brought you at once,' said Sandor. 'It will make you sick.'

But Ferdi was still weak. He pressed his knuckles to his eyes as tears welled up and ran down his dirty face. He stank, Sandor noticed. He had brought Ferdi a bar of soap and instructed him to bathe regularly by rubbing a wet towel over himself, but the boy had been wearing the same clothes for over a month. He had failed to notice it before, since Ferdi's natural smell was so like his own. Standing close to him was like breathing in the stale air of his bedroom in the morning.

Then he noticed Ferdi's hands. He took them in his own and examined them: the knuckles were raw, their skin torn and scarlet. On the back of his hands and around the wrists long red lines circled. He pulled up one sleeve and saw the scratches continue almost up to the elbow. Scabs had started forming here and there where blood had been drawn.

'What happened? Did you try to break open the door? I told you never to bang on the door or people will hear!' Ferdi tried to extract his hand from his grip, but Sandor wouldn't let him. 'Did you fall and hurt yourself?'

'No.'

Then Sandor understood. He let him go. Ferdi tugged down his sleeve in shame.

'Why did you do this?'

'I told you to let me play, I *told* you. Do you think I'm lying to you? I have to play, *let me play!*' There was no defiance in his voice, only despair. He broke into sobs, and miserably tried to stifle them.

Sandor sat back and remained silent for a long time. He was exhausted. A hint of nausea was circling him, but his body felt so utterly empty that he wasn't threatened by it. He looked at Ferdi's fingernails, caked underneath with dirt and dried blood.

'Your fingernails have grown too long,' he said, and his voice sounded flat. 'You can't play the piano like this. I'll clip them for you next time.'

Ferdi wiped his face with his sleeve. 'So you will take me back? I can play?'

'Yes, you can play.' Sandor got up. 'You *must* play.'

*

The echoes of the music breathed their last around the piano room.

'What do you plan to do with me?' Ferdi asked.

Sandor, in his usual seat next to him, let his gaze sweep the floor for a while. It had been many days since his illness, and he and Ferdi were on better terms now. He had taken care to bring him as much fresh food as he could find, many times hiding some of his own portions and going about hungry though there was never a shortage in the house. He even brought Ferdi books, which the boy devoured, always asking for more afterwards. Sandor would oblige him, choosing something a little more advanced each time.

Although Sandor went on locking the door to the gun room, Ferdi's agitation and urgent need to play lessened considerably when he could spend time with his books. Sandor even negotiated with his parents for an extra hour per day in the piano room. The claw marks on Ferdi's arms started fading away. Sandor was exhausted, barely getting enough sleep between school, homework and Ferdi's lessons. But it was worth it. He trained himself not to look directly at the distant glimmer of hope, in fear it would vanish, but its presence in the periphery of his mind gave him fresh strength.

Things were going well. Now, on the point of revealing his plans, Sandor was suddenly nervous of alienating Ferdi again and so organised his thoughts carefully before speaking. He reproached himself for this uneasiness. This was how things were supposed to unfold, this was Ferdi's reason for existing. This was how the man's sleight of hand was about to play out.

'I'm going to apply for a position in the Academy of Music this spring,' he said.

He saw Ferdi's eyebrows rise and his mouth open slightly, as if attempting to form a particularly complicated word. But he didn't say anything, and Sandor was glad for it.

'This is my last year of school. My parents' plans for me are set in stone: to support me through a higher musical education, like they attended. I wish things were different, I wish they would consider—' He stopped, feeling the familiar tide of anger, and pursed his lips. 'But there is no other option for me. I have to attend the Academy. That's all there is to it.'

'You do not enjoy playing the piano,' said Ferdi, and it wasn't even a question; but Sandor shook his head.

'No. I haven't in a very long time.'

Ferdi tilted his head and his eyes assumed an unhappy expression. It conveyed to Sandor such honest pity that blood rose to his face, and something in his chest convulsed. If only others had pitied him like this, if only they *understood*, as this wretched creature sitting next to him did...

'There will be an audition for the Academy,' he continued, 'probably early in the summer. I imagine I'll have a date for that by the end of spring.'

'An audition?'

'Yes. It's a kind of exam. In person.'

Ferdi's hands clasped the sides of the piano seat until his knuckles were white. He didn't speak. Smart boy, Sandor thought. He must have guessed. Still, Sandor felt the need to say everything, to set the facts on the table like unburdening himself of heavy things.

He leaned forward and looked evenly into Ferdi's eyes. 'Ferdi, I plan to send you in my place.'

This wasn't a question either. Ferdi blinked.

'You will take the audition as me, pass the exam, and attend the Academy as me.'

There was no response. Ferdi stared back at him. A few moments passed. Sandor reached out to put a hand on his shoulder and saw that Ferdi was shaking with feverish tremors like a tuning fork. He waited patiently until the boy had snapped out of it.

Ferdi's face softened. 'What will you do?'

'I'm going to leave for some time. I don't care where I go, as long as I'm my own man. But you will stay in the city and study: nobody will know you there. And – this is important, Ferdi – you will *never* contact my parents. I will take care of that. We will stay in touch for a while, so you can update me on your progress. I will call and visit home every now and then, so they won't suspect. In time you will graduate and I'll have the degree, this should make them happy... And after that... maybe then I can tell them that I put in my time. I don't know, then – perhaps I will come back, perhaps I'll move away – maybe the States...' He trailed off.

'And then, what do I do?'

Sandor glanced at him. 'I'll be grown up by then, I'll find you something. We could get you a ticket to the far side of the world where you can do whatever you want, and never come back. We'll never have to see each other again.'

Ferdi's eyes grew big. 'Sandor—'

Ferdi had never used his name before, and it cast a momentary spell over them. Sandor broke it, his voice almost shaking.

'Time for that later. In order to – listen to me, in order for you to pass the audition successfully, we have to work very hard. You will need to know many things by then. You'll have to perform, and we only have a few months to practise.' He waited for a reply, but there was none. 'But that is not all. There will be a written exam too, musical theory – you will have to know it perfectly: harmony, genre, form. It's a lot to study. These books I've been giving you are only a little of it.'

'Is all this even possible?' Ferdi gasped.

'Have you noticed the speed with which you learn? It's inhuman.'

The word must have stung, because Ferdi's face darkened and he drew back a little. Sandor sought to correct his blunder.

'What I'm saying is – if anyone can do this, Ferdi, it's you.'

Ferdi looked down at the piano keys, which were yellowed between their edges, like teeth.

'You can teach me all these things?'

'Yes. I know them, I'm just not good at them. You're so much better than me, Ferdi. You are a natural.'

Ferdi blushed, and Sandor saw it as a sign of imminent victory. The moment demanded diplomacy rather than commands. His pulse was racing and he closed his eyes, trying to calm down.

'I will do it,' said Ferdi, though he hadn't been asked. 'I want to do it. I want to talk to people. I want to know what the sun feels like. I want to be out in the daylight. I want to see many people together, hear their noise. I want to be able to play the piano as much as I can, whenever I want. I want to see the sea, or a lake, or to smell the rain. I want to—'

He stopped. His eyes welled up. He was looking past Sandor, focused on a point far beyond them. Sandor shifted uncomfortably. Ferdi clenched his jaw and didn't blink until his eyes were dry again. Then he lowered his vacant gaze onto Sandor.

'Who are you?' he asked. 'What are you, really? Are you my father? My brother? My god?'

Sandor opened his mouth slightly but no sound came. He was unable to move. Moments shuddered past them.

Ferdi slowly pulled his thoughts back together, and his head dropped. He looked dazed, like a moth that had hit the lamp too many times.

'And what am I? Am I a monster, am I a ghost? Can other people even see me? Am I even—'

Sandor reached forward and grabbed Ferdi's wrist. It was bony, cold and pulsating, with muscles and tendons grinding against each other under the skin.

'You are real enough.'

'Real enough,' echoed Ferdi, his palm lying open and limp in Sandor's grip.

He is such a child, thought Sandor. It didn't matter that when Ferdi was playing his neck was straining with the growing muscles of early adulthood, or that his fingers were set, angular and dexterous and hard. The hollow of the upper lip may have darkened with the ghost of a stubble, yet technically Ferdi was barely two months old. A child; a scared, indecisive child. Sandor wondered if he was up to the task.

Sandor then had the fleeting image of a memory, one so old he never even knew he had retained it: a warm summer day and himself small, so small that he stood at the front entrance of the house tugging at his clothes, too scared to walk down those three front steps that were almost half his height. And Salomon crouching on the gravel with arms outstretched and a smile, and Sandor stepping forward, tumbling down the steps and into his father's arms, sobbing and safe.

Pity surged in him – not a particularly tender sort of pity, but not a scornful one either; a crystallised sensation, a detached sadness in the face of emotional starvation. He pitied the orphan boy sitting there, living unloved and uncared for, having never been touched by sunlight or a mother's hand, having never smelled a girl's hair or returned home muddy from school.

He has only this, Sandor thought, wrapping his gaze around Ferdi's hands as they lay by the keys and twitched with anticipation over the next piece, their delicate bones anxiously sticking out like harp strings. *He has only this and it's still more than I ever had.*

1990

Erzsi, busy and moody, scarcely looked at Ferdi in the days following the attack on Dieter. Ferdi wrung mops and chewed on his nervousness, feeling desperately alone, deprived of the familiar bass of Dieter's voice. He recalled Dieter's dead weight against his legs, how he had stumbled out of the emergency room looking his age for the first time. On Sunday Ferdi followed a doggedly unresponsive Petar out to the truck and waited, shifting his weight from leg to leg. Eventually Petar finished unloading the packets and turned angrily towards him.

'What?'

Ferdi held his breath. 'I wanted to talk to you...'

Petar shot him a mean look. 'I thought you didn't like talking to little boys.'

Ferdi wore a pained expression. 'Dieter's been stabbed,' he said, pathetically.

'I heard.'

'Oh.'

'Don't worry, he's been stabbed before.'

'Yes, he mentioned that.'

'Well, what do you want me for? I didn't stab him. Sure, he drives me crazy. But he pays for my drinks.'

He reached for the door handle but Ferdi put his hand on it. Petar scowled. 'Are you trying to pick a fight?'

'I'm trying to talk to you.'

'Well then, talk.'

'Not here.'

Petar tensed and withdrew his hand. 'Where?'

'Somewhere quiet. Your home?'

'I have three roommates.'

'Mine, then.'

Petar drew back, sensing a trap.

'I'm not...' Ferdi began, but didn't know how to finish the sentence. 'Look, come for a drink. As a friend.'

'At your place?' Petar chewed on the ghost of his moustache. 'Tonight?'

'Yes.'

'Fine.' Petar climbed into the driver's seat. 'Get a few beers,' he said before driving away.

Ferdi picked up two four-packs on his way home, hoping they'd be enough. It would at least improve Petar's mood, he decided. It was almost ten o'clock and he was still contemplating whether or not he should have also got some food when the buzzer rang.

Petar stank of blood and grease. There was a smudge on his forehead that he appeared to be unaware of, and his nails and knuckles were lined with black grime.

'Came straight from work,' he said in response to Ferdi's gaze.

'The butcher's?'

'No, other shop. The garage. Is there somewhere I can wash up?'

Ferdi pointed at the bathroom at the end of the hall. Petar threw off his jacket and disappeared for a while. He returned with his neck flushed from scrubbing and his shirt wet and smelling faintly of oil, mingled with the scent of Miss Ilona's aloe soap around his bristly hair.

He accepted a beer, sat at the table and drank almost the whole can before looking at Ferdi. He graced him with a quick grin as he popped open a second can.

'I'm starting to get used to this place.'

Ferdi sat across the table. 'And I'm starting to get used to having you around.'

He received a sarcastic stare. The boy toyed with his hand in his jeans pocket, making a dull jingle. 'Go on, then. I came all this way and all.'

Ferdi reached for a beer just to have something to do with his hands.

'Remember that night you saw me at the abandoned building?'

The jingle stopped.

Ferdi concentrated on his can. 'I think,' he said laboriously, 'that the person who killed that man is the same one who stabbed Dieter. I think they've been following me.'

Petar squinted. 'What does this have to do with Dieter?'

'He was stabbed right here, on my front step. And he was with me when... I'd seen the man who died before. Once, in that same building. It was a few days before his death. Dieter was with me then, I believe that's why he was attacked. And there was something that Dieter's attacker said... I'm not sure. But these things feel connected. Somehow.'

'So it was your fault.'

'What?'

'Dieter.'

Ferdi glared at his beer. 'Yes, I think it was.'

'Don't get all weepy. Not much you can do about it.' Petar leaned in. 'About the attacker: you think it was the same person who gave you that scar?'

'I think so.'

'I'm guessing that he was trying to aim centre when he missed.'

'...Yes.'

'So, if it was them, why haven't they killed you already?'

Ferdi was taken aback. 'I don't know.'

Petar took a sip. 'Food for thought. What do you need me for?'

'For help.' Ferdi groped for words. 'Advice. You're the only one who knows. And you didn't – you didn't...'

'...Snitch?'

Ferdi nodded. Petar's cheeks darkened with the faintest blush.

'Told you I don't snitch,' he muttered, and drank.

'You never noticed anyone, then? When you were...?'

Petar looked at him. He offered no help this time.

'...Following me?'

The boy shook his head. 'You're a popular guy, aren't you?'

Ferdi squirmed. The beer was sour on his tongue.

'I don't do that anymore,' said Petar into the beer can. 'Outgrown it.' He threw a challenging look at him, but Ferdi was determined not to put his foot in his mouth this time. 'Why didn't you tell Dieter's girl, the head waitress? Erzsi? He says you two are close.'

Ferdi thought he detected some malice in that, but ignored it. He shook his head.

'Oh, I see.' Petar made dents in the can. 'I see. You thought she'd blame you, right? You thought she wouldn't like you anymore.' He made a strange sound. 'But you don't care what I think of you, do you? There's not enough beer in the world for this.'

He half rose to go. Then he saw Ferdi's face, shut and brooding and him refusing to talk back, and he seemed to change his mind. He sat back slowly, drank the rest of the beer and reached into his pocket. He withdrew his fist and banged it on the table, making Ferdi jump.

'If I gave you this, would you use it?'

He opened his fist to reveal a pocket knife with a wooden hilt and brass finish. The wood was faded and stained but the little thing shone like a jewel in the drab room. Ferdi picked it up and pried the blade open with a nail. It was curved. On the base of the blade were carved the initials *I. V.* He traced them.

'That was my father,' said Petar. 'Ivan Vukovic. It was his.'

'I can't accept this.'

'It's just a loan.'

'But…'

'Would you use it if you had to?'

'I don't know.'

He was fascinated by the absurd realness of the knife that demanded to be noticed, its beautiful compact form, smooth and uneven with age.

'Petar Vukovic,' Ferdi said slowly, turning the blade with horror and pleasure. He sensed a thrill in the boy upon saying his name, and let silence fall.

Petar opened another can and raised it in a toast, inclining his head but saying nothing. He drank, and Ferdi followed.

'They say,' Petar began, 'never give a child a new knife, because the blade shouldn't be as scared as the hand. This one's been bloodied, so you can trust it.'

'They also say that a knife should never pass from hand to hand.' The grey blade spun innocently around Ferdi's fingertip. 'I don't want to use it.'

'Maybe you won't need to. Or maybe you'll be glad to have it. Either way, take care of it. You're as safe as can be now.'

'Have *you* used it?'

Petar shrugged and made a noncommittal gesture. Ferdi tried to imagine Petar as a child: same close-cropped hair, same surly eyebrows. To picture him sunny and carefree was impossible. It was easier to assume Petar had come into the world troubled and wild.

'How old were you when your father gave this to you?'

'He didn't. I took it.'

Ferdi stifled a feeling of pity, pity that he hadn't dared feel for himself. Had Petar loved his father, or had he hated him? Or did he too feel that stunted emotion that was a mixture of both? Ferdi could barely imagine proper love and he was afraid he had never fully experienced hate, but life had taught him how likely it was to receive the second in exchange for the first. Flimsy, hate-imbued love was no more nourishing than salt water.

Petar took his time to finish his third beer and got up, reaching for his jacket. He picked up another can for the road.

'See you tomorrow, then,' he said.

Ferdi was still contemplating the knife. 'Yes, right after practice,' he said absent-mindedly.

'Practice?'

Ferdi bit his lip and glanced at Petar. His heart was beating erratically, and he couldn't understand why speaking suddenly came so hard.

'I have to practise. I play. The piano.' He cleared his throat. 'I play the piano.'

Petar watched him, stunned, then broke into laughter. Ferdi's face reddened. He had never seen Petar like this. Like Dieter he too was looking his age for the first time, but this was young and happy and beautiful. Then Ferdi knew the boy wasn't laughing at him, he was just surprised, glad and a little drunk.

'Maybe I'll hear you play some day.'

Ferdi blinked a few times. He nodded towards the knife. 'Thank you for this.'

'Don't lose it.'

He left. Ferdi walked to the window and saw him stride across the courtyard, but this time Petar looked back. Ferdi quickly retreated, but he was certain he had seen the boy smile.

*

Dieter had been stuck at home all week. When Ferdi visited, Dieter welcomed him by grabbing him with his good arm and dragging him inside a small, messy apartment, calling him vulgarities while squeezing until Ferdi felt his bones grind. He had brought cake and magazines, which Dieter received with disproportionate enthusiasm. He feebly insisted they shared the cake but Ferdi protested, and Dieter wolfed it down before Ferdi's coffee had time to cool. Then he sighed, sat back and lit one of his murderous cigarettes.

'You look well,' said Ferdi.

'I've been doing nothing but sleeping and healing for days. You, sir, are looking at a brand new man.' He flexed the fingers protruding from the sling. 'I'll be back to cooking by the end of the week, but someone else will have to carry the heavy pots for a bit. How's the temp? Holy Mother isn't thinking about replacing me, is she?'

'He doesn't use any garlic, and says salt is bad for you.'

'Now you're just trying to cheer me up.'

'Mrs Soltesz is disgusted. She's about to ask Erzsi to cook.'

'Oh, stop it.'

'So hurry up and get well.'

'And what about you? Did you miss me?'

'The pile of crates isn't nearly as good company.'

Dieter threw a pillow but Ferdi dodged it. He let Dieter smoke through his ill-concealed smugness and looked around him. The sitting room was flanked by a narrow kitchen and a curtained entrance to a bedroom. The walls were naked, the furniture and covers all dingy white, giving Ferdi the feeling they had been slowly stripped bare by time. The only personal touches in the room were a stack of classic literature in German, and a small potted plant still with a ribbon on it.

'So what was it that I felt in your right coat pocket?' asked Dieter.

Ferdi's hand flew to his side before he remembered he'd taken off his coat. Dieter was watching him through the smoke.

'Only a knife. You were hurt right on my doorstep' he replied, avoiding Dieter's eyes. 'Better be safe than sorry.'

Dieter thought for a while. 'It doesn't feel right, you carrying a knife around. Where did you get it?'

Ferdi was very uncomfortable. He put more sugar in his coffee. 'From a friend.'

'What friend goes around distributing knives?'

'I'm not that keen, either. I'm always aware of it, like it could jump out and start cutting people on its own.'

'Peel an apple with it, it will take the edge off.'

'I'm serious.'

'So am I.'

'I don't want to hurt anyone,' Ferdi said softly. 'I don't want anyone else to get hurt again, either. It's my fault you were attacked.'

Dieter's broad face coloured. 'Come on, Molnar. Don't tell me you're upset about this now! This is nothing, a scratch!'

Ferdi rubbed his bony knees that stuck up high from his seat on the deep sofa. 'It's just that I've been so confused lately...' He struggled for the right words but they wouldn't come. He rose. 'I'm sorry, I should be going.'

Dieter sat up. 'What's wrong? No, sit down, you don't look great. Are you ill?'

'No, just tired. I haven't been sleeping well.' He sat. His eyes were burning and suddenly he was terrified he was about to burst into tears again in front of Dieter. This felt different from when it had happened in that back alley after he'd chased Sandor; it felt irrational and childish, and he was too embarrassed. But his body was betraying him, and the pain in his ears became almost intolerable.

Dieter pushed himself up from the armchair and came to sit next to him. He patted him a couple of times on the shoulder and Ferdi recoiled a little from his touch, but didn't move away. Dieter put out his cigarette.

'We should go to the movies tomorrow, the three of us. That would be fun, wouldn't it?'

Ferdi nodded.

'Maybe see something trashy, cheer us up. Something with explosions. There's always one of those on. Come by after work tomorrow and we'll all go, all right?'

'All right.'

Dieter looked at him fondly. His bulk made the cushions sink and Ferdi had to work not to topple against him.

'Just get well fast,' Ferdi told him.

On his way back home, Ferdi pictured Erzsi and Dieter having a child: Erzsi's body swelling, then her with a wrinkled baby in her arms that would grow up to see things they could never imagine. Then he considered the Gedeon family and how Natalia's proud face was a peculiar mixture of the two people sharing the table, how she resembled them in an elusive way that Ferdi was forbidden to share with anyone. He had met Salomon and Karolina, and on them he had recognised Sandor's mouth – Ferdi's own mouth – Sandor's slanted eyes – his own eyes – Sandor's unyielding, lopsided jaw.

But here was Ferdi, kept out of the birth chain that connected every human to each other. He was arbitrary; a random, single thing. It was repulsive. He had never been an infant, never been carried inside the watery darkness of a woman's body. Never experienced birth – an experience, he had learned, that nobody ever remembered, but he was certain they still kept somewhere inside them. Sandor had had all these privileges. Sandor had been grown into life with patience and care, while Ferdi had been hastily brought into the world for the sake of an immature bet, and then shoved into existence. He was always unborn and, sometimes he feared, unalive. These were qualities he would never shake off.

He groaned. He did not want to die, but there was no way around it; if there really was some hidden connection between himself and that madman, then his death proved as much: even make-believe people like the two of them could die. Not that Ferdi had much doubt, after Sandor trying to shoot him – an experience that had left him acutely aware of his mortality. And yet it was a slight comfort to be no different in death.

The next morning Ferdi had the bar to himself, and he rushed through his chores to have more time to practise. He tried some classical pieces, then went back to his own work. He didn't know what he was practising for anymore, but calling it practice gave playing an unhurried quality that allowed him to tread instinctively through the music, as if wading through a river. Playing was liberating, bursting; but practice was discovering, wondering. Playing was gasping for air; practising was taking deep breaths on a crisp morning.

He found a brittle, surprising thread of happiness in the music that day, and he followed it breathlessly. He ducked under the swatting branches of the fearful parts, branches that were heavy and dark just as the load he suddenly seemed to be carrying was heavy and dark, and the body slipped from his sweaty hands, his foot catching on the thread like a root and snapping it—

There was a metallic jingle. Was it a ring falling on the pavement? Ferdi rubbed his eyes. He was in the dining room again, and the handle of the service door was rattling. He strode into the kitchen to unlock it and Petar tumbled past him down the steps with his arms full of bundles. The boy landed on his feet with a bark of laughter that he immediately pretended never happened, and hid his face in embarrassment. Ferdi, still dazed, saw but didn't notice.

Petar nodded towards the dining area. 'What was that music? You're blasting the radio when you're alone?'

'What? Oh... That was...' Ferdi realised he was blushing again and it maddened him. 'I was practising.' He bit his tongue, wishing the ground would swallow him, turned and began to put away the meat as fast as possible. Petar's silence changed.

'That was you?'

Ferdi nodded with burning ears. He heard Petar take a step but didn't dare look.

'That was you,' Petar repeated. He moved to the side of the kitchen bench, where Ferdi was cleaning with uncommon focus the watery bloodstains from where Petar had placed the meat.

Petar put a hand on his arm, and Ferdi's whole body paused. He allowed himself to be pulled away from the washcloth and looked up.

Petar seemed just as surprised but still he leaned in and kissed him, slowly, until Ferdi's knees weakened and he had to hold on to the boy to keep from falling.

The kiss went on and when it stopped Ferdi found himself disappointed and uncomfortable in a number of ways. Petar was vacantly staring at his mouth, and Ferdi's hand was still on Petar's shoulder, the thumb touching his neck. The boy radiated heat.

Not sure of what he ought to do and drunk with this new freedom, Ferdi pulled Petar into a hug. His face scratched against the bristly hair. Petar's hand moved hesitantly until it touched Ferdi's back, and clutched a handful of shirt. He lowered his head and fit the angles of his face against Ferdi's neck. They remained like that, breathing slowly.

When Petar stepped back the air was still warm between them. Ferdi wanted to soak in it but Petar was already retreating, collecting himself.

'The others will be here soon,' Petar said. And though Ferdi's heart crumpled at the words, and though the boy was walking away, Ferdi saw that his mouth was crooked with several kinds of happiness crowded together and his eyes sought Ferdi's own.

Ferdi closed the door behind Petar and when the sound of the truck faded away he collapsed on the step. How strange, he thought, that this fleeting contact could exist on its own and unmarred by memories. Until now he had only seen Sandor's revulsion whenever Ferdi had dared touch him, and it had made his blood run cold. How could he, a monstrosity, be allowed to touch and be touched like that? How could he allow the boy's lips to be exposed to his hideousness?

Ferdi recalled something of the madman's ramblings. *You are my brother, because neither of us was born...*

He thought about nothing but Petar for a long time.

That night he dreamt that he got out of bed and started rummaging in his drawers. A guest was sitting at his table, sighing with impatience. Ferdi was very anxious to please that person. He wanted to find whatever it was they had asked of him, but it was very dark and there were too many drawers, more than could possibly fit into that old wardrobe. He found what he was looking for in one of his gloves. The wedding ring was around one of the woollen fingers, and when he removed it he noticed that the glove was still warm. He gave it to the guest. The guest examined the ring with interest. His mouth made soft noises as his fingers ran over the shiny band and traced the inscription inside. He tried it on but it slid off; he tried it on again and it slid off again and he looked at Ferdi sadly. Ferdi took his hand in his own, and it was so cold that his pity burst through and his eyes filled with tears. He kissed the poor hand and it had no smell, no taste except that of his tears, no weight and no texture. *Take it back*, the guest said, *take it back*. But he refused. He was only keeping it for them, he said. But they shook their head and looked at him accusingly.

Ferdi woke up. There was a small repetitive sound in the gloom. Mice, he thought and turned over to resume his sleep. But the sound persisted, a little louder each time, and he forced his eyes to open. It was still dark, and when he looked out of the window he caught the glimpse of a star. Then he heard the sound again and realised that someone was knocking on his door.

Ferdi's first thought was to run, but it settled at once. There was a gap in his fear and he rushed to slip through it. Without asking who it was he opened the door, and Petar was there; and he came in without speaking either.

1980

It began with Dorika, the maid, championing an early spring cleaning as soon as frost ceased forming on the windowpanes. The rains would come soon and it would have to be completed fast, she insisted. She convinced Karolina and began her work with daunting energy.

For days on end Sandor didn't dare bring Ferdi to practice, in case he saw Dorika's hair bun peeking over the windowsill as she swept and scrubbed the stone pathways. He would sneak out late at night to bring Ferdi food and books on music theory, history, philosophy, art, and anything else he could find that he thought even remotely related to Ferdi's studies – even his old mathematics books from school. Ferdi spent this long confinement reading hungrily and absorbing everything, emerging from the pages glassy-eyed. Sandor had to remind him to pace around the room several times each day to keep his muscles from cramping. He found out that the boy did this with a book in hand.

Sandor watched and considered how all this reading was moulding Ferdi's mind. What was this young man made up of, now? A few dozen books: only science and a few fairy tales? These, along with the inside of the piano room, the sight of the cold night, and the finite range of vibrations produced by wood wrapped in felt hitting steel wires; these were Ferdi's inner world. It made a meagre map. But then again, he reminded himself, no more was required of him. So Ferdi would have to wait until the Academy to learn things such as words in a foreign language, how to tie a tie or how cars worked. Even so he wouldn't seem that much different than all the other wide-eyed, disoriented first-years.

Sandor realised that his fears were like those of an anxious parent sending their child off to school. When his eyes fell on the papers on his desk for Ferdi's next lesson, everything seemed morbidly funny all of a sudden.

Ferdi had asked Sandor for a pencil and at first he had refused, afraid that he might use it to hurt himself or even to pry the door open again. But the main force that kept Ferdi from doing all these was obedience, and not lack of tools. So Sandor brought him his old mechanical pencil and also an old notebook. He wondered if Ferdi had been created with the innate ability to write just as he could read, but didn't dare ask. The notebook was one of several unused New Year's gifts: it had musical staves printed on every other page, it was monogrammed and its soft leather cover was a warm burgundy colour. Ferdi had taken it in his trembling hands, unable to speak. The next day Sandor saw it lying open on the table, its first page black with small cramped writing.

Everything was beginning to run smoothly again when Dorika, red-faced at the end of a working day, suggested to Karolina that maybe it was time they aired and cleaned the old gun room again.

It was pure luck that Sandor was studying in the small living room downstairs and heard them. He froze, listening. Apparently Dorika had been cleaning its entrance all afternoon and the steps were finally *presentable*, but she couldn't get in as none of her keys would fit.

Sandor pictured Ferdi inside, bewildered and holding his breath at the foreign sounds, the scratch on the lock and Dorika's angry mumbling. He felt the key burn a hole through his chest and it took all his self-control to not reach for it and make sure it was still there. The two women left for the kitchen and he sprang up and ran after them. They were arguing, upturning drawers and peeking behind counters in search of the lost key.

'Mother…'

Karolina glanced up. 'Darling, have you seen the key to the small basement anywhere? It's that cellar around the side of the house. It's not on its hook.'

He shook his head and kept watching them, the blood pumping hard in his veins.

'Perhaps there is another key somewhere?' Dorika asked, but Karolina frowned and replied there had always been just one. His mother let out a frustrated sigh and walked right past Sandor to the piano room, where Salomon was leisurely arranging his notes. Sandor came into the room just in time to hear her convincing her husband to force the door open.

'No!' Sandor exclaimed before he could stop himself and his parents looked at him in surprise, unable to remember a time he had shown any interest in matters of the house.

'No,' he repeated, searching frantically for a good excuse. 'Father, there's no reason for you to hurt yourself. Let me do it when I have time during the holiday. We can fix the door, clean the place, and then we can close it up again.'

'Do you take me for an old man, Sandor?' Salomon replied. He patted his son's shoulder as he stepped into the hallway, put his shoes on and walked out.

Sandor ran outside after him. This short walk to the gun room had become something of a ritual for him: a few moments of solitude in the clear night, afraid to be seen with packets of food and books, anxious in anticipation of seeing Ferdi again. Now, taking the same path behind his father in the daylight felt unnatural. His world was tilting and threatening to collapse on itself.

He saw that the familiar stone steps were clean, glistening with a colour he never knew they had, and his stomach lurched. Salomon's heels fell loudly on them. He thought he should shout, fall on him, wrench his hand away – but he could only stand at the top of the stairs, frozen in terror.

Salomon tried the handle a few times with increasing strength, shaking it until it started rattling in its socket. Sandor watched, helpless, thanking his luck that he'd at least had the chance to fix it.

With a gesture much like his son's, Salomon dug his nail under the metal and tugged but with no success. He kicked the corner of the door and pressed his shoulder against it, his face reddening with effort. Salomon may have been round-bellied and short, but he was also sturdy, his arms lined with thin, strong muscle, and when he drew back and fell on the door again its hinges creaked and the lock let out an ominous groan.

'Father!'

Salomon looked up at his son, the gold-rimmed glasses sliding down his sweaty nose.

'You're going to hurt yourself! It's not worth it. Let's not bother with this anymore. Come, I've been meaning to talk to you about my audition.'

To his great relief Salomon stepped back and straightened his clothes. His father sighed with disappointment and wiped his brow.

'Ah, you are right. Maybe I am too old for this. I'll call a locksmith tomorrow, and have a new lock installed.'

He climbed up the steps and led his son back home.

Later that night, when Sandor walked into the gun room, he saw Ferdi standing upright and stiff. The young man struggled to stay still as Sandor strode up and down the room trying to collect himself.

'You have to leave,' he kept repeating, 'you have to leave,' and Ferdi flinched at every word. His eyes followed Sandor's pacing. 'You must leave, even if only for few days. But where? Nowhere is safe right now! And then,' he gasped, 'what about the future? My parents will keep a spare key now. I could steal one, but the second? I can't steal both without rousing suspicion. And you can't live here while a key hangs in the kitchen. Should I just give them the key, pretend I found it somewhere? Yes, that would be better, then there would be no reason to change the lock. Let the room be cleaned and then closed up again. Let the key hang on its hook for a while, and I can substitute it with a similar one, so that nobody will know the difference unless they try it... Nobody bothered with this room for years... But can we get through a few more months like this?'

As he ranted on he didn't notice the change coming over Ferdi, whose face relaxed as he stood there waiting for Sandor to reach the end of his monologue.

'Before anything we have to clean this room,' Sandor added. 'If it looks like somebody has been living here my parents will call the police. Everything has to go.'

His gaze swept around the place taking in the stacks of books, the piles of blankets and dirty clothes and musty towels, the little heaps of rubbish and rotting scraps of food filling the corners, the floor coated with dust and grime. The squalor he had Ferdi living in reached a small part of his distraught mind, and self-disgust wedged itself in.

Ferdi spoke for the first time.

'Where am I to go?'

Sandor looked at him and for a moment there was the faintest shift of power between them: Ferdi, standing upright and cool, and Sandor, who was hunched over with worry, his thoughts blurred with fear, his twitchy fingers running through his hair.

'I don't know,' Sandor whispered, and they both stood in silence for a while. 'In the forest?' He saw Ferdi's head tilt in curiosity. Of course he was interested. He would be interested in anything other than this damp cell he had been locked in through all his days. But the woods in the night were no place for anyone. It was only March, with winter still clinging on. The greenery was cocooned in frost every morning. It would be his death.

Ferdi must have seen the glint of doubt in his eyes because he took an eager step forward. 'I could live in the forest, couldn't I?'

'You can't,' said Sandor.

'Please, let me out, let me try, I will behave, I promise!'

'In the wild? You will be frozen to death by sunrise.'

And then it dawned on him; and it was so obvious that he wondered how he had never thought of it before.

The ambassador's estate. Of course. His parents had been complaining about how it had been abandoned now and how it had grown quiet and lonely with the estate, the only house neighbouring theirs, empty. The old manor had been left to itself.

Sandor felt a sudden warmth and turned to see Ferdi's hand clutching his arm. Ferdi was leaning forward as if stooping over the edge of a great precipice, and his act of bravery made his pupils blaze under the cheap electric bulb. Sandor knew then that this little prison would never be able to contain him again.

*

The journey to the ambassador's estate took ages. They walked haltingly in the deep night, not daring to lift the beam of the flashlight to look ahead, weighed down by bundles of Ferdi's things. Ferdi seemed to feel none of the exhaustion creeping up on Sandor. His large eyes took in everything: the creaky forest with its dripping pockets of snow, the yelps and shuffling of half-seen creatures, the stars peeking between the boughs. His face was lifted and his nostrils dilated at the scent of resin and damp soil.

When they finally arrived at the manor the building loomed over them, a patch of deep black. It had been built by the same architect as the Esterhazy mansion and, though more modern and smaller, its layout wasn't very different. Sandor had come to know it well and almost instinctively turned towards the front door, but then changed his mind and led Ferdi towards the kitchen entrance in the back.

The service key was still there where Maggie had shown him, in its secret place above the low marble doorframe. It was covered in grime and stuck with frost but he pried it away and cleaned it, and thankfully it turned and the door opened, releasing the heavy smell of mildew. The heavy silence made them pause on the doorstep. They let their baggage drop on the ground. Then Sandor stepped forward, walked through the kitchen and up the creaking steps to the hallway.

The familiar shapes of the furniture were all covered in white sheets, glowing in the dimness. The fabric billowed soundlessly as if by the breath of some unseen creature, and Sandor imagined he could feel the floorboards under his feet throbbing with its heartbeat.

Ferdi's whisper broke the silence. 'It is too big.'

'In the piano room, then?' mocked Sandor, but his words sounded mean even to himself. Ferdi's jaw clenched.

'Is there a piano?'

'There was, but it's been taken away. You have your books and they keep your mind off it, don't they? There is a gun room in this house as well.' He felt Ferdi tense. 'It will be safer there, and even if somebody came in you would still be hidden. It's in much better condition than ours, and it has another entrance from the inside of the house. I'll turn on the water supply as I leave now. I won't lock you in this time. You can go about the house to stretch your legs, but don't go outdoors, and don't use the flashlight at night in any other room, in case anyone sees it through a window. You'll stay here until I say otherwise, and you won't, under any circumstances, return home unless I come for you.'

He looked at Ferdi's pale face, all hollows and shadows.

'Can I trust you?' Sandor asked, and was surprised to hear the hoarseness in his voice.

The face turned silently towards him, and he had the uneasy feeling of walking past a mirror in the darkness.

*

Sandor barely slept that night. He had had to walk all the way to the ambassador's house again, carrying as much food as he could steal. Ferdi seemed a little more relaxed in his new lodgings. The gun room there was cleaner and better aired, so Sandor returned home somewhat reassured. He then spent hours scouring their own gun room for signs of Ferdi's presence, and afterwards could barely drag himself up the stairs to his bedroom. When his alarm clock rang it felt he had only slept for a second.

The locksmith came and went while he was still at school. As he walked up the gravel pathway afterwards he did not dare stop by to check. Karolina told him that it had been finally cleaned, 'filthy as it was', and they had put a new lock on the door. She mused that perhaps they could finally use that cellar for something, until Sandor calmly pointed out that already there were bigger and sunnier rooms in this house remaining shut and unused.

Still, he didn't dare steal the key again nor move Ferdi back. A few days passed in suspended anxiety as he struggled to figure out a solution without success. There was still no guarantee that the cellar would be safer in a week or a month's time.

He was unnerved to realise that he was missing Ferdi's company. He had grown used to seeing him every day, spending hours every evening in the piano room listening to him play and discussing their lessons. For all his meek silences Ferdi was decent company; he was bright, curious and laconic, a comforting presence. And even though Sandor would never admit it, Ferdi was able to produce such beautiful music that even he himself, with his complicated feelings towards it, found moments of pleasure in it. All this time he had thought of Ferdi as a pet but, he considered, perhaps he was closer to being a sibling – a monster sibling...

Then a familiar voice in his mind whispered, *who is really the monster?* And he found no answer to that.

It was days until Sandor had the chance to visit Ferdi again, on a rainy evening that left him sodden and cold after the long walk. When he stepped into the large, comfortable basement with its aging leather armchairs, he found it littered with Ferdi's paraphernalia but otherwise empty. For a second his heart leapt to his throat but then he sat and waited, until Ferdi appeared. Their eyes met and Ferdi stood very still for a moment, more surprised than afraid. Then his face lit up; he leapt down the steps and stopped at arm's length. Sandor had the uneasy suspicion that the young man had been about to fall into his arms.

'I brought more food. Have you been eating well?'

'Yes.' A blush. 'Thank you.'

'Have you been careful like I told you?'

'Yes.'

'Where did you sleep?'

Ferdi paused. 'I took the blankets to one of the bedrooms upstairs. But it was too big, too empty. I found these pillows and slept here.'

Sandor sat back in the armchair. It smelled of stale pipe tobacco.

'I don't know when you'll be able to return to your old room.' He saw Ferdi shifting his weight from one leg to the other. 'But you don't want to go back, do you?'

Ferdi shook his head.

Sandor clicked his tongue. 'I thought so.'

'I like being able to move around!' Ferdi blurted. 'I like it here. But I don't like it when you don't visit me, and it has been too long since I played something.'

'Show me your arms.'

Obediently, Ferdi rolled up his sleeves all the way to the elbows. The skin seemed intact.

'I'm trying,' he muttered.

'Show me your palms.'

Ferdi held up his hands for him. Sandor leaned forward and studied them. Three purple nail marks in the middle of each palm told of hours of clenched fists.

'Show me your neck.'

Ferdi pulled down his collar, exposing his neck and collarbone, which were crimson with fresh scratches.

Sandor sighed. 'I can't have you clawing yourself raw,' he said in a low voice.

'I'm sorry.'

'No, don't...'

In the brief silence they heard the soft sound of a door closing.

They stopped and exchanged a look. Sandor brought his finger to his lips and glared at Ferdi, who nodded and clamped his mouth shut with his hands.

Someone had followed him.

Sandor tried to remember if he had closed all the doors. There was only one light: the hurricane lamp in the gun room, its golden glow spilling out into the hallway from the door Ferdi had left open. He was about to jump forward and close it, but it was too late: they would be heard. The footsteps in the hallway came from the direction of the kitchens, hesitant but distinct on the stone floor, closing in on their patch of light. He held his breath. He turned and pushed Ferdi away, gesturing at him to hide in the bathroom, but in his nervousness Ferdi stumbled and fell, bringing down a chair with him in a dreadful clatter.

For a moment Sandor looked at him with his mind blank, and then he felt something move in the corner of his line of sight. He turned and saw Dorika standing at the top of the stairs. She was looking at them, her eyebrows raised. Her gaze fell on Ferdi, who was now trying to stand up behind Sandor, his face momentarily turned away. Ferdi turned to look at Sandor and, instinctively following his gaze, glanced back towards Dorika. They stood side by side, staring at her. Her mouth dropped open.

'Dorika,' Sandor began, but he didn't know how to go on and the sound of his voice died away.

She was clutching a shawl over her maid outfit, and her brown hair was dark with rain. Leaves and dirt from the forest path clung to her. It had never occurred to him how young she was. And beautiful too, with her flushed skin and those round, horrified dark eyes now staring at Ferdi, and darting between his and Sandor's face. She crossed herself twice.

Sandor reached out a hand. When he spoke he was thrilled to discover how calm and reassuring his voice was.

'Dorika, come here. It's all right.'

She went down a single step and stopped there. Ferdi was watching her too, not daring to move a muscle. Sandor had the fleeting realisation that this was the first time Ferdi had ever met a woman, or any other human.

'There is nothing to be afraid of,' he said, and knew right away that he had made a mistake. She pointed at Ferdi with a shaky finger.

'Master Sandor... What – what's *this*?'

He saw the heel of her foot still resting on the previous step, and her body leaning slightly backwards, ready to flee. His arm felt heavy as it stretched towards her. He took a step forward, never taking his eyes off her, and she watched him warily.

'Dorika,' he repeated. He had said her name three times already; and each time he thickened the sound with a layer of soft urgency.

Her heel slid down the step and planted itself next to the other, with a faint rustling sound that made his heart kick.

Dorika, Dorika, Dorika, Dorika, Sandor repeated inwardly, as if the name was a spell able to ward off the dark clouds gathering around the edges of his thoughts. His hand turned, facing the floor, now looking for something to grab. She had been looking at their faces and she missed the gesture.

Sandor had a moment to imagine it – the fingers digging into the soft flesh, pressing and tugging – and still the reality was very different. When he darted forward and grabbed her wrist he was startled by how hot it was, how terrifyingly real. Her pulse throbbed loudly against his thumb. Dorika twitched and tried to wrench her hand free but he wouldn't let her. He pulled her forward until she stumbled fully down the steps, still writhing and clawing at him until he got a grip on her other hand too.

It was a silent battle, all gasping and rustling. She was much stronger than he had assumed, and he felt her drawing free from his clutch bit by bit. There was still dignity to the fight, he thought, there was still reason – even if she ran he could still get away with it. A horrible, violent boy, they'd say; and it would be better than the alternative. Then helplessness flooded his chest and his muscles hardened. He pulled and crushed her into a steel hug, holding her against his chest until she could no longer move. They stood still for a while, panting, their faces red. He could smell the trees on her hair.

'I won't say anything,' she whispered. 'Please. I swear, I won't.' She glanced at Ferdi, winded. 'What is this – *what are you?*'

Sandor put his hand over her mouth. 'Hush.'

He didn't know what to do. His arms hurt and he struggled to maintain the strength needed to keep her still. Dorika sensed Ferdi approaching, and her eyes bulged in horror and she started to writhe. Sandor tightened his hold on her, sweat running down his face, but she bit his hand until he freed her mouth and she began to shout.

'Let me go, let me go!'

'Shh!' He clamped her mouth shut again and wrapped his arm around her neck while she kicked at both of them, her whole body convulsing.

'Stop!' said Ferdi, but Sandor didn't hear. In his tightening grip Dorika shook, her nails clawed at his clothes, her panicked eyes gleamed with tears.

'Sandor, stop!'

Ferdi began trying to wrench Dorika free. But at Ferdi's touch her arms abandoned the struggle with Sandor and flew up to fight him, scratching at Ferdi blindly. Sandor's grip around her throat hardened and her face turned crimson. Ferdi started pulling Sandor's arm with increasing panic, yelling at him to stop, and dug his fingers into Sandor until at last he managed to free her.

Dorika stumbled away, falling against a pile of Ferdi's books and gasping for breath.

'No!' Sandor exclaimed. He lunged at Dorika again, saw her fumble and pick up a book, and then something heavy collided hard with his head. He fell to the floor and the world turned black.

He lay there in shock waiting for the pain to subside. He blinked until his eyesight began to return, with bright blue spots dancing around.

A pair of hands took hold of his shoulders and helped him sit up. Ferdi's face came shakily into view.

'Where is Dorika?' Sandor said.

'She ran away.'

'What happened?'

'She hit you on the head with *Music in Western Civilisation*.'

Sandor groaned, his vision swaying when he moved. Ferdi pulled him to his feet and led him to a chair. Sandor collapsed on it, rubbing his sore skull.

'She left,' he muttered. 'My god, she left... What are we going to do? Look what you've done!'

Ferdi sat on the ground next to him and didn't speak.

'What if she tells someone? We have to get you out of here, and then where will you go? What if she tells my parents?'

I should have killed her, Sandor thought.

The thought came abrupt and uninvited, and left him with a vague feeling of nausea. His head was spinning. He took a few deep breaths.

'Perhaps they won't believe her. Perhaps they will think she's crazy. It *is* crazy.' Sandor wiped the sweat from his eyes. 'We should carry on. You'll move again, and we have to be careful for a while.'

'But I don't have anywhere to go.'

Sandor looked down at him. Ferdi was playing with the hem of his jeans, pulling at the dirty threads. He looked like a lost little boy.

'What if I never leave?' Ferdi went on. 'What if I stay here, in this house? I don't want to move again.' He looked up at Sandor. His jaw was set with comical determination.

'Don't be ridiculous. If Dorika tells anyone then they will find you, and then both our lives will be at stake.'

'I know how to hide. But I will not go away.'

Sandor leaned forward. 'You will do as I tell you.' He was met with a glare of defiance. 'You will never disobey me again.'

'You attacked her,' Ferdi went on. 'You told her there was nothing to be afraid of. She was your friend, but you lied to her. You scared her and you hurt her!'

Sandor hit him on the mouth. 'Don't you dare speak to me like that!'

Ferdi stood up, wiping the drop of blood from his torn lip, and gazed steadily into Sandor's eyes.

Sandor's voice was hoarse. 'There is only one reason you exist, you – you *creature*. And that is to obey me. That is to do as I tell you and never, *ever* step out of line again. You're not even human. Never again interfere with what I do, and *never* talk back to me like that.'

'*Not even human*,' echoed Ferdi, his mouth twisting into a grimace.

'That's right – you are not like me or Dorika, do you understand? Know your place. You are not *natural*, not one of us. You'll never be.'

'Stop saying that. We are the same – look, we are!'

'We were never the same.'

Ferdi's hands curled into fists. 'No!'

'Yes! You belong to me, and you are *nothing*.'

Ferdi covered his ears and shook his head. Sandor grabbed his wrists and forced his hands apart.

'You're a monster, Ferdi! Look at you! How can you ever be human? You wouldn't exist if it weren't for me!'

'STOP!'

Ferdi pushed Sandor away so forcefully that they both stumbled. Sandor landed back on the chair and leapt from it, aiming another blow at Ferdi, but this time the boy fought back. They began to wrestle each other on the dirty floor, kicking and elbowing like angry children.

And then their blows started landing with full force, crushing against bones, attacking exposed spots. Sandor clutched a fistful of Ferdi's hair and managed two brutal hits to his face, but then the air was knocked out of him – Ferdi struck blindly at his ribs with surprising strength and managed to shove Sandor away.

Ferdi staggered up but swayed for a moment, with a look of hesitation. Sandor saw the chance and lunged again, dragging him to the ground. Ferdi started thrashing so Sandor struck him once in the stomach and when the boy paused to gasp, he grabbed Ferdi's hand and pinned the other with his right knee. He gave Ferdi a loud slap.

Ferdi stopped. He shrank and looked away, trembling and heaving deep breaths. His cheeks were smeared with dust and blood was pouring from his nose; one eye was half closed and his hair was a sticky mess. There was a gash on his lip and the edges of his teeth showed red with blood. A tear slid down the side of his face, tracing a clear path through the grime.

Sandor lifted his arm one more time, his aching elbow creaking like the pull of a trigger. He was aware of the body underneath him pulsing with tension, of the ribs grinding under the clothes, the heart pumping with such ferocity that the neck and wrists convulsed. Another tear escaped. Ferdi's eyes swam, and slowly moved to meet Sandor's.

Sandor lowered his fist. He moved his knee to free Ferdi's hand. The fingers twitched in reflex but there was no other movement. Ferdi remained there, his chest rising and falling in deep, slow sobs.

Clio Velentza

Sandor pulled away, disentangling himself from Ferdi. His limbs were hot with pain and exhaustion. His left ribs were throbbing, and a corner of his jaw hurt when it moved. He wiped his mouth but there was no blood there: it was always Ferdi that ended up bloody. He eased himself onto the dirty stone floor with a groan. They lay side by side, two perfectly dishevelled copies of each other.

'I wish you never existed,' Sandor whispered.

'I know.'

Sandor turned on his side to look at him. Ferdi hadn't moved. His eyes were sweeping the ceiling.

'Ferdi.'

The eyes slowly shifted back towards him. Sandor saw his own hand move by itself and land lightly on Ferdi's cheek, which was sticky and warm.

His brain formed the simple words for an apology, but they got stuck in his mouth and dissolved. He saw Ferdi watch him, guessing his train of thought. The bruised mouth shut tight, and Ferdi's face moved once against Sandor's palm, pushing it away.

Ashamed, he took his hand off Ferdi and wiped the bloodied fingers on his sweater.

*

Sandor walked home in the darkness, kicking at the shrubs. A shapeless moon shone, sucking the colour from the greens. He changed his mind several times, doubled back twice and stewed until he decided all over again to give up. The forest around him took every chance to tear and stab at him, to hold him back with the resolve of an enemy. His trouser leg got tangled in thorns so impossibly thick that he fought to free himself until his eyes filled with tears, and long red gashes bloomed down his calf.

'I'm done,' he muttered. 'I'm done.'

As if in reply the thickets shook and something small and rat-shaped darted in front of him. He pushed forward through the darkest point of the path, where the ivy had wound itself around the trees into a short tunnel. He knew it was precisely fourteen steps to the other side and he counted them mechanically, with the mad hope that over there he would be met with the familiar sight of Maggie waiting for him.

He reached the garden tired and bloody. A lonely owl was hooting close to the garage, its cry echoing against the silent building. He was heading towards the service entrance when he heard a car screeching to a stop in the driveway, and then someone called his name.

The figure of a man was crossing the front garden in long, fast strides. His arm was raised and pointing steadily at him.

Sandor saw the glint of a wedding ring on the man's hand and immediately knew. 'I didn't harm Dorika', he hissed.

Sandor stepped back, but the man was advancing too fast and he found himself backing away into the trees like a cornered fox.

'I didn't do anything to her! Leave me alone!'

The man slipped in and out of pools of light, revealing a mess of brown curls over a round face distorted with fury. Sandor caught a glimpse of the flannel pyjamas under the man's coat.

'No! Go away!'

Sandor turned and ran back into the greenery, wet twigs swatting his face. For a moment he thought he was safe until a hand grabbed his coat, chocking him into a stop. Panic shot through him. He started thrashing about and in vain reached to get a hold on something, ripping fistfuls of leaves from their branches. Darkness started creeping around the world, a darkness that was blacker, emptier than that of the night.

*

It could have been hours afterwards – or perhaps a mere moment – when Sandor found himself stumbling back into the kitchen of the ambassador's house. He couldn't tell. The stench of blood was all over him. His body was numb, though his right hand shook, as if after some great strain. In his fist he was clutching something small and hard. He couldn't remember what it was.

He knocked on the gun room door. He couldn't recall how he had reached it; his vision was muddy. Slowly, as if through water, he opened the door and faltered down the steps, and stood blankly in the middle of the room.

Ferdi walked up to him with his dark eyes wide. Sandor then saw that his own clothes were torn and wet, that black dirt and crushed leaves clung to his skin.

'What happened to you?'

Sandor shook his head. His throat felt filled with lead. Ferdi took Sandor's clutched fist and tenderly pried the fingers open. He tilted his head in puzzlement.

'It's a wedding ring,' he said.

Sandor nodded. He began to shake. His stomach heaved.

'You're burning up. Sandor. Sandor.'

The world spun. The ring fell and clinked against the stone floor. Sandor fell forward and Ferdi caught him, easing him onto the armchair. Sandor felt his skin hot, and his whole body convulsed when Ferdi removed his coat.

Ferdi's presence shifted. Sandor grabbed him by the arm.

'Don't leave!'

In the haze he saw Ferdi smile.

'I'm going to get you some water. I'll be right back.'

He returned with a glass of water, from which Sandor could only down a few sips, and a wet towel. While Sandor kept shaking, Ferdi started cleaning the dirt from his face with smooth, gentle movements. The coolness on his temples was bliss. Sandor watched Ferdi as he worked: the side of his face was covered in blotches that would be livid tomorrow, his nose was crusted with blood, his lip torn. His expression was focused and calm, like when he played the piano.

Ferdi's careful hand washed Sandor's sticky neck, his chest, his grimy hands, cleaning each finger with caution. The rough cotton came off brown and black. Ferdi scrubbed his hair too, with gestures similar to Karolina's when she used to dry him after a bath. When he was done he wrapped Sandor in a blanket, still warm with Ferdi's residual body heat.

Ferdi pulled the other armchair close and sat quietly by him. He took Sandor's burning hand in his own and pressed it until the shivers began to die down.

'I didn't mean to...' Sandor tried to swallow. 'I never meant to kill him.'

Thick, hot tears started falling from Sandor's eyes and rained on in a steady stream until his head was left hollow. He leaned back, stifling the wave of nausea that crept up from some unfathomable depth in him. He closed his eyes, and exhaustion washed over him.

1990

When the first morning light appeared, Petar said he had to leave for work. They were lying still and quiet, pressed against each other in the narrow bed. Naked under the blankets, Ferdi was shivering. He felt acutely every bit of his skin that touched the foreign body. He looked around, aware of the presence of things: the cottonness of the sheet, the bedness of the bed, the airness of the air. The room was full of kindly, solid presences. He too could finally boast of his solidity, because he was conscious of his entire body and was utterly certain of this *here and now*, as if it had been cut off from the sponginess of Time and been set apart. He watched Petar's left ear as Petar was watching the ceiling with his right arm tucked under his head. Ferdi was sleepy and wide awake at the same time. The roof of his mouth was busy archiving all the brand-new scents and tastes, and at first he didn't register Petar's words.

'But it's my day off,' Ferdi caught himself saying, as if that should have determined the course of the world for the day.

Petar glanced at him and seemed embarrassed to have his face stared at from so closely in the dim light of day. He turned back towards the ceiling and stuck out his jaw, but his hand under the covers was still resting on Ferdi's leg.

'And I have to go to work,' said Petar, 'and then I have to go to work again.' He paused for a while. 'And then I could come back.'

It was a question, even if it hadn't been posed as one.

'Then come back,' said Ferdi.

*

Petar reinvented him: his fingers recalibrated every bit of skin they touched. Ferdi's body was slowly being rebuilt, painstakingly and with infinite precision. He was an invisible man being smeared with paint. Where Petar acted by touch, Ferdi reacted by becoming real. It was a stepping into the world, a coming into the light. And it was a loss, a great loss, an unstoppable leaking of heat and control.

Petar did not talk much but he laughed often, sometimes with no reason. Ferdi wondered if he was laughing at him and his clumsiness, the stumbling way his arms and legs moved, the ambiguity of his speech. These were hours when then boy got careless and laid himself bare, and Ferdi would jump to the chance to rain questions on him. Petar humoured his nervousness, but kept his mouth shut on his past when Ferdi asked for stories. They still knew nothing about each other. But, Ferdi thought, surely this didn't matter.

Ferdi discovered that Petar's body was riddled with scars of many kinds. There were wormlike lines on Petar's knees that could have been childhood souvenirs. There were small burns around his elbows and thumbs. There was a perfectly horizontal scar alongside his left ribs, which made Ferdi shudder to think of whatever sharpness had caused this, slicing so perilously close to the heart. There was the ram skull tattoo on the right forearm and something in Cyrillic letters tattooed above the left shoulder blade on a thorn-pierced band, wrapped around the image of a howling wolf. When Ferdi put his fingers on that, he discovered that the elaborate tattoo was covering another scar, wide and smooth like a misshapen star. Petar explained none of them. Sometimes he too would trace Ferdi's scar in silence, not with mockery but withdrawn in melancholy absent-mindedness.

One humid night the young man fell asleep in Ferdi's bed, his back widening with each breath as he lay on his side. Ferdi couldn't sleep. He was hyperaware of every little movement Petar made in his sleep, and was folded into an uncomfortable position he didn't dare change. Secretly he hoped the boy would turn in his sleep and put his arms around him, but it never happened. In the morning he was exhausted, and gladly submitted to Petar's wandering hands when they began to look for him again.

Petar left early. It was a sunny, glistening day, and Ferdi looked out of the window and wondered if the city had always been this beautiful. Not everything was despair, not all misery was deserved. There was a knock on the door and, thinking it was Petar come back for him, he rushed to open it.

The man in grey barged into Ferdi's room.

He looked thoroughly dishevelled; the black tie was missing and his shirt collar was unbuttoned. The colourless hair looked windswept. The man glanced sharply around and moved closer, making Ferdi recoil.

'The ring, boy, the *ring*! Where is it?'

Ferdi's eyes darted involuntarily towards the wardrobe drawers. The man turned to them, dragging them out one by one.

'Why are you here?'

The man overturned a drawer on the floor, spilling socks and underwear. 'Where is it? Give it to me!'

Ferdi hadn't moved. He slowly closed the door behind him. 'Why do you want it?'

The man crouched low, rifling through the dingy whites. 'It's none of your business. *I* sent it to you for safekeeping, and now I need it back.'

'What for?'

The man straightened up and glared at him. 'You're one to ask!' Spittle was flying from the flabby mouth. 'I'll teach him, oh, I will, I'll teach him to mess with things he shouldn't! Where's the ring?'

'Him? Are you talking about Sandor?'

The man swatted at the empty air and kicked the chair aside. 'Where! Is! It!' His face grew crimson. 'You have a nice life here, don't you? So you meet the girl at the café? Isn't she a darling? Oh, you're so blissfully ignorant, with your stupid piano and your filthy friends, while I have to break my back taking care of everything! But I'll show him, that piece of rat shit!'

Ferdi spoke quietly. 'No.'

'How dare you talk back to me?'

The words were uttered in a hiss that made Ferdi shrink. The man crossed the room in two strides and Ferdi backed away until he was pressed against the door, as if trying to fall through it. The man's face was close enough to touch, but his features remained vague, about to blur into each other.

Ferdi's body stiffened. 'I won't help.'

The man put a hand on Ferdi's shoulder and somehow it was worse than a blow.

'Did you forget everything already, you pathetic boy?'

Trembling, Ferdi shook his head.

'Who dragged you into this sorry world? Who fished you out of oblivion?' He rapped Ferdi's head with his knuckles. 'Who put you *in* there? Did you forget all that? Did you inhale too much kitchen steam? Better keep that in mind, because I could take it all away. Just like that.' And he gave Ferdi a little smack on his temple.

Again Ferdi shook his head. 'Leave us alone.'

The man kicked the door – it made a deafening sound. Ferdi realised that his eyes were full of tears, and he kept shaking his head. The man turned and went back to rifling through the drawers.

'I could tell you terrible things about yourself,' the man panted, separating Ferdi's socks and throwing them aside. 'Things that would make you wish you never had ears to hear them. I could tell you about all the things I stole from your memory, so that you wouldn't bring them with you into this world. Some people remember them, you know – some people who'd have loved to tell you given the chance… There are truths, and there are truths, and then there are truths that melt the flesh off your bones. I could tell you some and then you'd learn some manners. Like how – ah!'

The wedding ring tumbled out of a sock with a sound like a fairy bell that shook Ferdi to his senses. Ferdi lunged and caught it. The man stumbled and they fell on top of each other.

'I won't let you kill him!'

The man kicked Ferdi away viciously. 'I won't kill him, you idiot! I won't break the deal. I behave, you know – unlike *some people*.' He stood up with a groan and dusted himself down. A sock was hanging from his shoulder and he tossed it away in disgust. He began to rearrange his clothes and button up his crumpled shirt. 'Very well then, keep it – but keep it to yourself! Don't go giving it away!'

He exhaled and combed his thin hair with his fingers. He looked at Ferdi, who had crawled as far away from him as he could.

'Get a grip, boy,' he said with contempt. 'I don't give a damn about you.'

He left and closed the door behind him. Ferdi waited to hear his footsteps but there were none, as if the ground had swallowed him whole.

*

At work he shrank and shrank, keeping away from everyone. He felt tainted by the touch of the man in grey. He took his break alone, and shortly afterwards ran to the bathroom to throw up what he had eaten. The blood throbbed in his ears and his bones ached. He found that he had difficulty focusing. By the end of his shift he thought he would collapse.

Dieter failed to notice, but when Erzsi saw him she gave him some aspirin from the first aid cabinet and sent him home early. Ferdi's fever made it impossible to remember words, or whether he had told her anything. He kept trying to say that he just needed to sleep it off, but nothing came out of his mouth. He began to sweat, and walking from the tram stop and up the stairs to his room took all his strength. He fell asleep in his clothes, alternately freezing and burning, and woke up so many times that when daylight broke he thought many days had passed, and perhaps it was his day off again. He drank some water and drifted into a more peaceful sleep for a couple of hours.

A little later his doorbell rang. Afraid of who it might be, he hesitated for a moment. Then he pressed the button, unlocked the door, and returned to his bed. The door creaked open and closed. There was a rustling sound and Ferdi felt the mattress sink. He peeked out.

Petar was sitting there, yawning.

'I would have brought you soup,' Petar said, 'but I had no idea where to get soup.'

'At the bar,' Ferdi mumbled through the covers. 'Dieter always has a soup of the day.'

'He's the one who said that you'd left sick when I dropped by last night. He should have given me the soup himself. Move over.'

Ferdi shuffled closer to the wall and Petar stretched out next to him over the covers.

'Are you going to work today?' asked Petar.

'Yes, I don't have much choice.'

'When?'

'In an hour or so.'

'Good.' Petar leaned in and kissed him, but when he tried to pull down the blankets Ferdi wouldn't let him.

'What's wrong?'

'I'm tired from all the fever.'

'I'll just sit a bit, then.' Petar scoffed. 'Old man. I never get sick.'

Ferdi believed him. Why should he get sick? Petar was immortal. He watched as the boy kicked off his combat boots and crawled under the covers, but when he felt Petar's hands he flinched. Petar propped himself on one elbow and frowned.

'What now?'

'Nothing.'

Petar pulled the covers away. Ferdi was shirtless under them after a fit of fever. He winced under Petar's stare. In the daylight the bruises from the man in grey's kicks were livid spots, scattered across his chest and stomach.

Petar sat up. 'What's all this?'

Ferdi tried to cover himself but Petar was still holding the blanket. 'Accident.'

'Like hell it is! Did you get into a fight?'

'No. Give this back.'

Ferdi wrapped the bedsheet around his shoulders. Petar was furious.

'Why are you lying? Do you think I'm an idiot? You keep getting into this stupid trouble! Who did this to you?'

Ferdi bit his lip.

'Do I know them?'

A shake of the head. 'Just let it go.'

But the boy's hands were balled up into fists. 'Why didn't you use the knife?'

'I didn't think about it. Next time I will, all right? Now stop. I'm tired.'

'Next time? Are you still in danger? I'll kill them before there's a next time. I'll kill them!'

Ferdi's pained chest filled. 'Fine,' he said. 'Next time, you can kill them.'

'You'll tell me if there's a problem again?'

Ferdi nodded. They squeezed down in bed together, side by side. Petar reached out an arm and Ferdi laid his head on it.

'Promise?'

'Promise.'

*

The most frustrating thing turned out to be neither the physical aches nor the annihilation of any sense of security in his home, nor the violent horror of the intrusion – it was the fact that now Ferdi was worried about Sandor. Ferdi worked with effort, still drained from his illness, while his mind wandered. Where was Sandor? What was he up to? The idea that he could be attempting something dangerous enough to enrage the man in grey chilled him. What if he was trying to break his original deal? What would happen to Ferdi then? Would he drop dead, or would he vanish? But what if it meant freedom – true freedom, for the both of them…? Ferdi tried in vain to imagine such an untethered life. Yet the tip of his tongue tasted like storm: his instinct told him that now, after so many years of silence, Sandor couldn't be far. He knew he only had to wish for him, and there he would be.

Ferdi felt suddenly a deep longing for his basement at the Esterhazy mansion. He missed its peeling table and sputtering tap, the pitter-patter of the mice. It was a world where he had felt safe, sure of his mind and his purpose, and his path had been clear. But this nostalgia for his old prison didn't last long. Here and now were his friends, here and now was Petar, the chance for Ferdi to play his own music. Here was the dream of the sea and the warm south.

With a flash of absurd clarity, Ferdi understood why the curly-haired man had come for Dorika's sake in the middle of the night. He blinked in surprise, and smiled to himself. Something had been unlocked in him, since Petar had stormed so into his life – a bravery he had been unaware of. He would not falter.

*

'I'm going to tell you a story,' said Petar. 'You can choose which one.'

Ferdi put his finger on the long, trailing scar under the boy's left ribs. Petar grinned.

'I won that fight. I was thirteen. There were two of them and they were older. But I showed them.'

'Not much of a story,' mumbled Ferdi. He was falling asleep, his skin stuck to the damp bedsheets.

'All right. I was thirteen, I was helping at Dad's garage. He'd left me alone while he was out for a beer with his buddies, and these two kids came to rob us. One of them had a knife. I broke his arm against the counter. The other dragged me out to the empty lot and kicked me around; I fell on an iron bar and cut my side. Then I got up and gave him as good as I got.' He smirked. 'Saved the cash, too. Dad gave me a reward. And I had to get a tetanus shot.'

'What was your father like?'

Petar squirmed a little. 'Nothing exceptional. Wanted me to be a man.'

'But you are a man.'

'You know what I mean.'

Ferdi turned to face him. 'Not really.'

'A man. A tough man! A take-no-shit kind of guy.' He scoffed. 'Turned out all right, I'd say.'

'Did you ever tell him?'

'What, about myself? Don't be crazy!' He scowled. 'But I think he knew. Must have been *something* that he kept trying to beat out of me.'

'You don't know if he did?'

Petar shrugged. 'I don't want to talk about it anymore.'

Ferdi looked at his own hands, turning them over thoughtfully. 'I don't feel like a man,' he said at last. 'What's it like?'

Petar's scowl faded. He laughed and grabbed at Ferdi under the blanket. 'You feel like a man to me!'

Ferdi gasped, trying to free himself. 'No, I mean – I mean, not a proper one. Not like you. All these things you said, these things that men are supposed to be and to do, just because they are men...'

'What do you mean?'

'Look, I grew up very isolated...' Ferdi groped for the right words. 'I could have been anything, really. I could have been anyone. It was pure chance that I look like this.'

'Same goes for everyone.'

'No, that's not what I was trying to say… See, I have this body—'

'*Your* body.'

Ferdi's mouth twisted and he frowned. 'Sometimes it's like it doesn't belong to me, or I to it… Inside, I could be anything, anyone. Who knows who I really am? Who knows what I would actually look like…?'

'Well, I like it, anyway.'

'You like who you are?'

'Yes. I like who you are, too.'

Ferdi reddened. 'What if I looked different?'

'Oh, how the hell would I know? Hypothetical questions are stupid.' Petar made a grimace. 'I wouldn't change anything, all right? Would you?'

Ferdi brought the sheet up to his chin and stared at the ceiling. He tried to list all the choices he had made since that New Year's Eve when he had clambered into the piano room, and found himself surprisingly unaware of them all.

'Maybe I'd change some things,' he said at last.

There was a shuffle as Petar turned and lay on his stomach, facing away from him. Even his shoulders sulked.

'If you had, then we wouldn't be here,' came his indignant voice.

Ferdi smiled, and put his palm on the boy's back. Petar twitched, but didn't turn. Ferdi thought he could feel the shoulders smile. How long had this week been? At that moment, he had trouble recalling any time before it.

The next morning Ferdi found a letter slipped under his door. Late for work, he was already hurrying down the stairs when he opened it.

I don't know if this letter will reach you. Natalia disapproves of the whole thing. I understand that for your own reasons you had to begin afresh, but I hope you will forgive Natalia's mistrust. She's a good friend and only wants the best for everyone. I will make her promise that this will find you. It speaks volumes, I think, that Gigi and Balint like you. They are people with good judgement and that reassures her a little. She was kind enough to translate this letter for me, despite her protests.

I don't deserve such treatment, Sandor. Or whoever you want to be today. But for the sake of our old friendship I will say this: you broke your mother's heart. She still writes to my mother, did you know that? (Of course you don't.) She's afraid you've died, the way you dropped off the face of the earth. Am I supposed to keep her in this misery? Am I supposed to tell her nothing when I know that you're alive and well, and still in the country?

I find myself struggling to keep your secret. It's not my business to interfere and say, call them, let them hear your voice because Karolina got rid of the piano and Salomon has become a hermit. Do you think the living don't leave ghosts behind? Do you think we are born free of responsibility? If I hadn't left, would you have disappeared on me like that as well? I started doubting if I ever really knew you, because the Sandor who was my friend for years wouldn't have done that. This is a cruel feeling, and one that you're responsible for.

Soon I'll be back in the States. We will probably never see each other again, who knows.

(I don't know why I'm writing this, it doesn't seem to be of any consequence. You didn't look happy to see me, and I can't seem to find my lost friend.)

In case we never meet again – good luck.

Maggie

Miss Ilona was walking up the stairs, cigarette in hand. Ferdi realised he'd sat down on one of the cold marble steps, deep in thought.

'You'll catch your death, Mr Molnar,' she warned while bypassing him and the rough flannel of her dressing gown brushed his ear. Ferdi carefully folded the letter and hid it in his coat pocket.

On his way to work he paused at a phone booth with a wrinkled, water-stained volume of white pages. He leafed through it, unhurried. Many pages were missing. He found three Salomon Esterhazys. He jingled the coins in his pocket for a while, staring at the phone numbers. Eventually he closed the book and dialled the number Gabriella had given him. He thought he recognised the voice of the woman who answered, from the people he had met at the Academy. She knew his name, and when he said he had no access to a proper piano at the moment she reassured him that they would arrange one for him at the Opera House. Ferdi gave her his hours so that he could go and practise when it suited him, took down the details for the registration fee and hung up. Then he glanced at the phone book one last time, and went to work.

By the time Erzsi arrived the morning sleet had turned into wet clumps of snow, which fell against the frosted glass panel of the service door. Erzsi hummed as she cleaned, and Ferdi's hands soon became too numb for the knife. When the groceries and Petar arrived at the same time, Erzsi and Ferdi were already subdued, half-asleep over their coffee. The groceries were slowly packed away while Petar waited his turn, leaning against the counters, his eyes following Ferdi with a piercing look that made his ears burn. *Tonight*, the boy mouthed at Ferdi afterwards, as he was closing the door behind him.

'Ah, youth!' sighed Erzsi, making Ferdi blush.

But when tonight came, Ferdi waited in vain for Petar. He lay in his bed, listening avidly for the confident step and the knock on the door. For hours his whole body was tense with anticipation, and he fell into a fitful sleep with the lights on. That Petar hadn't even called or left a note caused him pain. He replayed in his mind the moment when the boy's lips – full, warm, nothing like his own, such a bliss to press himself against them – had formed the promising word that morning. Had he imagined it? Had Petar changed his mind, deciding never to set foot in this room again? Ferdi couldn't bear it.

Dawn found Ferdi wide awake and brooding, and when his alarm went off at six he simply glared at it. He had to be at the Opera House to start practising, before going to work at ten. He stepped out into the courtyard under a sky low and shut, and on a thin, slimy layer of snow that made his stomach turn. It always felt like that with the first snowfall of the year, and faint, unsettling memories threatened to surface. By the time the city was entirely covered with snow he would be used to it again. He was so preoccupied with picking his way along the slippery floor that he didn't notice Petar lurking in the shadows of the front entrance until he walked into him.

Ferdi started in surprise and grabbed Petar by the sleeve, and his hand tightened around the familiar arm. The night's desire was catching up to him in that short moment: he moved closer and leaned into the boy's hair that smelled of sweat. Then he remembered they were standing right outside Mr Polyak's door, and he took a step back.

Petar hadn't moved. He was watching Ferdi from under knitted eyebrows, as if still making his mind up about something. He jerked his jaw upwards.

'Where are you going?'

'I have to practise,' Ferdi whispered. 'Why didn't you come?'

'You have some nerve, you know that?'

'Let's not talk here. I have to go. Will you come tonight?'

'No!' Petar's voice dropped violently. 'What the hell was that, last night? If you want to end this just tell me. Just tell me, and I – I—'

Petar stood very still, but Ferdi knew the particular way his neck tensed, gathering momentum. Petar was about to move swiftly, do something reckless. Ferdi grabbed his arm again, and for the first time he truly felt like the older of them.

'I don't want to end anything. Of course I don't! What happened?'

The boy shook his arm free. 'As if you don't know! As if you weren't there!'

'I was here at home, waiting for you.'

Petar's eyes were brimming with tears. 'Why are you lying?'

'I'm not. Why didn't you come up and knock?'

Petar turned, stepped out into the street and stomped away, his breath leaving a trail of fog. Ferdi ran after him and caught his jacket.

'What are you talking about?'

He moved closer but Petar pushed him away. Ferdi saw tears running freely down his face.

'You're ashamed of me, aren't you? It's okay behind closed doors, but on the street I can't even speak to you. On the street you can ignore me freely, is that it? Don't touch me!'

Ferdi suddenly understood. *Sandor.* The world spun for a moment.

'Look, I – I was here the whole time. Listen to me, believe me, I would never...'

Ferdi took another step closer to him. He thought his chest would implode if he didn't do something big, something important, to erase all this unhappiness. To make Petar reach out and to touch him in forgiveness because it was his own fault; if he hadn't been a monster then none of this would have happened – no pursuers, no secrets, no distorted mirrors, no lies... He raised a hand towards the boy again, but didn't dare touch him.

'There are things I can't tell you,' Ferdi said. 'You know that. I'm sorry – I'm sorry, you must believe that if I could tell the truth...'

Petar retreated and wiped his nose with his sleeve. Crying enhanced Petar's beauty: the heavy lashes darkened and the dark eyes shone, the jaw protruded, his presence expanded.

'A secret is only as good as the man who keeps it, you said. So?'

He looked at Ferdi, expecting a reply. But Ferdi looked down and his fingers closed slowly around a fistful of air between them.

'Well,' Petar went on, 'looks like you're a great man, then.' He turned and left before Ferdi could think of what to say.

The white sky began to release snowflakes again. Ferdi looked up hoping to catch a glimpse of blue, but if there was any he couldn't see it through stinging eyes.

*

Without remembering how he had got there, he found himself in the front of the quiet, oppressive structure of the Opera House. Ferdi went mechanically around the building and in through the side entrance. Already there was a buzz of activity as the set design workshops were gearing up for the day's work. The scent of fresh timber wafted in the air. Ferdi was shown into a small room lined with dusty shelves laden with props, where a pristine piano stood half-covered, waiting for him.

Ferdi sat at the piano he had never dared dream about, lifted the lid and touched the lustrous keys. For a while it would be his, his alone, this elegant clump of wood with its mystical assortment of metal and wire. What else had he ever hoped for? What more could he possibly want? He should be happy – he should be grateful, ecstatic. He hid his face in his hands.

*

Ferdi walked towards the river through the Sunday lull, while transparent clumps of snow dripped and glinted until the whole city was a drooling mouth. The abandoned building stood unchanged. Ferdi sat on the ledge of its front windows and waited, until shivers began to cascade the length of his body.

Sandor arrived noiselessly.

They stared at each other from across the street. Sandor paused, then gestured at Ferdi to join him. Ferdi tried to stand up and found that his legs wouldn't obey, and it seemed to him that

Sandor smiled at that. He hesitated then sprang up, teetering on numb legs, and crossed the empty street.

Sandor set out walking parallel to the quay, heading downriver. They didn't speak, and their echoing footsteps were disproportionately loud. Ferdi followed as Sandor walked briskly to the junction, made a right towards the bridge and stepped onto its pavement. Below them, the river was so quiet it could have been frozen solid.

Traffic was sparse and Ferdi saw drivers looking at the two of them with curiosity as they stood there on such a night. The gigantic beams of metal around them radiated cold.

'Better here?' said Sandor. 'You won't have to worry I might lock the door.' He chuckled.

Ferdi felt anger rise in him and for a moment wanted to kill Sandor, to punch and to kick until blood gushed out – to hurt this person who dared to laugh at his pain, at the twisted, twisted way in which Ferdi had been nurtured – kept, like an animal, locked – caged – freezing – alone. He rushed at Sandor and grabbed his jacket, but as headlights from a passing car fell on them he let go at once and stepped back.

The corner of Sandor's mouth twitched. 'You've grown some nerve,' he said.

Sandor settled against the bridge's handrail, took out a pack of cigarillos and put one in his mouth. He patted his pockets, sighed, and hailed a passerby for a light. They exchanged a few words and the stranger laughed, then Sandor returned. The smoke smelled exactly like Gabriella's, and her memory came to Ferdi as a shock. He had forgotten that Sandor and Gabriella existed in the same world. He leaned against the handrail too, throwing Sandor sideways glances. He was tempted to take out Petar's knife for safety or comfort, but decided against it. At that moment he mistrusted himself more than he trusted Sandor.

Now that he could see him better in the low light of the bridge lamps, Sandor appeared to Ferdi much older than his years. Their once subtle differences, now, he thought, were more pronounced: Sandor's shoulders were hunched and his torso wider, the neck was thicker than Ferdi's, and the shape under the clothes gave the impression of a sturdier build. The unshaved face was heavy and the jaw seemed more protruding, as if from a lifetime of ill temper. Thin wrinkles gathered around the eyes, and there were tufts of grey on the temples.

How could Petar have been fooled? The thought sent a pang through Ferdi's chest.

Sandor was watching him back impassively, wreathed in smoke. Was all this so commonplace, so unimportant to him? Ferdi's entire body was taut, but those eyes returned his gaze lazily, half-closed. He tried to focus on the anchored ferries down below, which shifted sleepily against each other.

'How did you know where to find me?' Sandor asked.

Ferdi looked up. 'How did you know where to find *me*?'

'I've known that for a while.'

'Did *he* tell you?'

'No.'

'Why didn't you say anything all this time? Why haunt me like this, why not just come out and – and...'

Ferdi made a sharp gesture. Sandor's eyes followed it.

'I've a lot on my mind as it is,' he said. 'He came for that ring, didn't he?'

Ferdi's hand flew to his chest where the signet ring was hanging beneath the clothes, afraid he might mean that one, and then remembered. The wedding ring. 'Yes. What did you do to make him so mad?'

Sandor straightened up and leaned forward, making Ferdi draw back.

'What do you think I'm doing? I'm fighting for my life, inch by inch. Do you think that after that failure when I ended up with you – when I ended up with nothing! – I would sit quietly and wait for the end? I was torn away from my own people, I ended up a murderer, an outcast... If I can undo something – if I can at least undo *that*, then by hell I will!'

'Undo...?' Ferdi watched him in disbelief. 'And what about me?'

'What about you?'

'What will happen to me?'

'This has nothing to do with you.'

'Nothing? You're playing with my life – you're stealing my life!' All rose to drown him: Petar, Maggie, Natalia's face. That surge of helplessness, the knowledge of not being the master of his identity or his future was too much. He lunged and grabbed Sandor.

'Enough!' Ferdi gasped. 'Enough with this! I'm not your pet anymore, I don't belong to you! Go away and leave me alone!'

As he said this his whole body shook again with the desire to hurt Sandor, and at the same time rose the desire to touch him. Ferdi shoved him back with disgust, and Sandor swatted his hand away.

'What about *my* life? You stole it first!'

'You're one to talk! You abandoned everyone, you hurt every single person who ever cared for you.'

Silence fell and they looked around, but nobody paid much attention to the two hunched figures. Fog was already descending from the hill, dripping into the Danube. They drew back like injured animals, hobbling away from the fight. The two of them made a ridiculous sight, thought Ferdi, huddled against the rail like this. It was alarming how easy this was, how effortlessly they could be in each other's company again. It was familiar to talk and to fight in this way; this could be the piano room all over again, the gun room of the ambassador's house.

'I want you to stop,' said Ferdi. 'Go away and leave me be.'

Sandor didn't reply. He smoked for a while, then threw the cigarillo off the bridge and stared at the water. Bitter wind slammed against them.

'And what if I asked you to help me?' he said.

Ferdi was taken aback. 'Help you?'

'You have something that I need, for a start.'

'I can't.' Ferdi shook his head. 'I can't. You don't understand… He'll kill me. Or worse.' His friends' faces flashed before his eyes. 'You can't ask me that.'

'Do you *want* me to fail?'

They stared at each other.

'I get it,' Sandor went on. 'Whatever happens, it's a win-win for you. Why should you stick your head out for this?' He eyed him until Ferdi reddened and looked away. 'That wedding ring he sent you… What did you do with it?'

'I didn't give it to him.'

'Good boy. Always doing the right thing. Always trying to fit in.'

Ferdi straightened up, feeling his anger rise. Colourful dots began to dance around his field of vision. Sandor stepped closer to him, grabbed Ferdi's shoulders and for a moment his face was earnest.

'Ferdi, what if both of us could be free?'

At these words, Ferdi's body softened. He let his head hang and he reached for that familiar body, but Sandor let him go. The sudden loss made him sway.

'I could use your help with more than that,' said Sandor.

'Like what?'

Sandor paused and looked at him. 'Bringing someone back to life.'

A laugh escaped Ferdi. 'You're mad.'

'Yes. Perhaps.'

'That's impossible!'

'You were impossible too, once.'

Ferdi looked away. The far side of the bridge was already being gobbled up by the fog. 'Who is it?'

'Abel.'

Ferdi's heart skipped a beat. 'The man you killed?' He stared at Sandor. 'What do you need *me* for?'

'I'll need the ring that *he* gave you, for now.'

'But that's just a plain wedding ring.'

'It is,' Sandor replied, 'and it also isn't. Depends what you use it for. See, I had to use my father's wedding ring once...' He stopped for a minute, as if he had stumbled upon an unpleasant memory. 'Abel's wedding ring alone won't be powerful enough for my plan, though. I'll need its pair, to act as an anchor to us.'

'Dorika's ring?'

'Yes, they're strong together.' He smiled. 'They bridge life and death.'

'But—' Ferdi groped for words. 'It's not real, is it? It's just... symbols.'

'What do you mean, *just symbols*? Once, a long time ago, I went into the woods and carved symbols on the ground – and that was how you came to be.'

Ferdi ran a hand through his hair and realised that it was wet with cooling sweat. Sandor had never spoken to him before about that night. His heart was racing – he was desperate to know about this, it was his conception, his beginning – and at the same time he wished he would forget what he'd just heard.

'Why would you want to bring him back?'

Sandor looked away. 'If I bring him back then I'm not a killer anymore.'

Silence fell. Sandor's eyes were sweeping the north.

'Murder sets a human apart. My contract – it was a disgrace how I was duped and ended up with you, but it is unbreakable and I'm not a weakling – I'd do it all over if I had to.' He tossed his head defiantly. 'But if I can undo this mistake, my worst one... Then I could meet my fate a free man.'

Ferdi stared at him, and for a second he saw the boy Sandor had been, and pitied him. But it didn't last long. He thought of all the nights spent in the gun room, nights frozen like this one, and the blood rushed to his head.

'Your worst mistake?' he asked hoarsely. 'And would that make up for everything?'

Sandor ignored that and tightened his scarf. 'I'm going away for a while. Here.' He gave Ferdi a piece of paper: it was a phone number scribbled on the torn page of a book. 'If you want to get in touch, call this number and leave a message for me. I won't be hiding around anymore.'

Seeing him turn to leave, Ferdi didn't move.

'My friend, Dieter. Was it you that hurt him?'

'Ah. Yes. The big fellow. I had to.'

'Why?'

'He's all right, isn't he?'

Ferdi's hands were balled up into fists. 'And that poor man I'd found dying?'

'I had to, or he would tell you... There are some things that you are better off not knowing, Ferdi.' Sandor's jaw was set. 'There was no other way for him. That is all.'

Ferdi's mouth was a thin line. 'And so – he had to die – just like that...'

'It's over now, Ferdi. That's all that matters.'

Sandor straightened up and began to walk towards the main street, reached the end of the bridge, then stopped. He turned back towards Ferdi, who had remained behind, unable to make himself think or move. Cars rushed by, dipping them in light.

'That boy, the foreign one.' His voice carried through the still night. 'I walked into him the other day. It was dark, and he must have thought I was you.'

Ferdi's insides turned to ice. 'Yes.'

'You know he kissed me?'

Ferdi put a hand on the freezing rail to steady himself. 'And what did you do?'

Sandor turned and began to walk away. The echoes hammered on.

'I pushed him away, of course.'

1980

Sandor blinked awake and found himself in the gun room of the ambassador's house. It was morning, and Ferdi was gone.

His body was stiff after having spent the night in the armchair. He squinted at the grey light slipping in from the corridor, and swept the silent room with his tired gaze. Outside the birds were frantic.

He kept hearing the same thing, a memory carrying on from his dreams: a ring clinking against the stones. A ring clinking against the stones. A ring clinking against the stones and rattling to a stop.

He wrapped the blankets tighter around himself.

Another dwindling echo: a mossy stone against a man's skull. A mossy stone against a man's skull. The sound a little softer and wetter each time.

His body was hurting at the oddest places. Patches of his skin burned and his ribs complained every time he drew breath.

He went back to sleep.

*

He opened his eyes and took in the feeble sunlight. The man in the tuxedo was sitting on the steps of the gun room, looking at him.

Sandor gazed at him numbly. He tried to sit up but his body was so heavy it felt paralysed, confined to the stiff armchair. He closed his eyes and realised that he could still see the dimly lit room and the man with his elegantly combed hair, with his face half submerged in shadow. The impeccable dinner jacket was so freshly black it looked as if he was wearing the void.

The man was shaking his head and laughing. 'You fool,' he said.

Sandor waited for the fear but it didn't come. Just a persistent numbness that sucked exhaustion deep into himself.

'I give you an opportunity and this is what you do with it!'

The man's left hand was busy playing with something small and shiny, which kept appearing and disappearing between his fingers like a coin trick.

'You squander, Sandor Esterhazy. It's what you do best. Anything you've ever been given, you have misused it and tossed it aside.'

He clicked his tongue in disapproval. The glinting thing slipped and stood between the tips of his index and middle finger: it was the curly-haired man's wedding ring that Sandor had been clutching. He held it up and squinted to see the inscription inside the band.

'*Abel and Dorika. Until Death*,' he read. He sighed. 'Children,' he added under his breath, and shook his head again. The ring disappeared back into the darkness of his hand. 'Fool!' He turned back to Sandor, who could barely control his breathing. 'Yet you didn't do so badly. A girl who barely escaped with her life, and a dead man in a shallow grave. I knew I saw great talent in you, Sandor; you haven't disappointed.'

The man got up and crossed the room with light steps. The crisp heels of his shoes echoed around the room. He took Sandor's limp hand in his own and turned it, running his thumb over the burn mark: a dead patch of pink on the transparent skin. It was less obvious now but still there, haloed by green veins. Sandor had used Karolina's ointment but it had made no difference.

The man exhaled. 'I should just let you rot away in prison, you know. That would teach you. But teaching people is such a bore.'

Sandor felt as if he were still sleeping but knew that the man's frog-like eyes had met his own and were sizing up what they had found there.

'But I'm an old softie.' The man rubbed the burn mark. 'Go home, you foolish boy. Don't worry about the girl, she won't remember a thing. Go, as if nothing happened.' His thumb kept tracing the mark, in smooth, hypnotic movements. 'But it's not my job to step in for you, remember that. Next time, you're on your own.' The man let Sandor's hand go and it fell lifeless on his lap. 'Give my regards to your little pet, and don't forget his leash. He's being very impertinent even as we speak. Tell him, I know what he's made of.'

Then he straightened up, winked and smiled his inhuman smile.

Sandor's heart was lurching and his lungs screamed for air. When he opened his eyes the room was exactly the same, grey and dim, impervious to the weak morning sun.

Only the man was gone.

*

Sandor didn't know how long he remained sitting there. The numbness kept spreading, settling inside him like a layer of dust. The hunger that tugged at his stomach was something detached, irrelevant. He didn't trust himself not to throw up anything he would eat.

Around noon he left the gun room and wandered around the echoing mansion. The windows were shut and the sheet-covered furniture glared at him. In a drawing room there was nothing left except a long row of mounted deer antlers. The once spotless walls were now stained with the ghosts of paintings, where ovals and rectangles of dirt disfigured the mute hallways. His feet moved of their own accord, and he found himself in Maggie's old bedroom upstairs.

The bed frame was still there, sturdy and bare like the washed-up bones of a sea creature. The desk where her books were usually scattered was covered, and the wardrobe door was gaping. He closed it. He pulled the sheet off the desk and opened every drawer hoping to find something that proved she had once existed in this airless room, but there was nothing, not even an ink stain.

He curled down on his usual spot on the floor and sat hugging his knees, his back against the bed. In his mind he put a record on the invisible gramophone that stood in the corner. The Maggie of his memory was sprawled on the desk chair, ranting about how she *had* to get him headphones for his next birthday. It had turned out to be the birthday she would miss.

*

When Ferdi finally appeared it was late in the afternoon. He stepped into the gun room wearing Sandor's school uniform, prim, clean and well combed, with a purple bruise by his eye that gave him a menacing look.

Sandor stared at him in shock until the boy trotted down the steps and his face eased into the sober softness that was so distinctively Ferdi's own.

'Where have you been?'

'I filled in for you.' Ferdi sat on the chair and started taking off his shoes and socks.

'What do you mean?'

'I went to your home last night.'

'*What?*'

'After you came here, you fell asleep and you weren't... You weren't right. You talked, you were sweating. When I tried to rouse you, you wouldn't wake up. I didn't know what to do, so I went back to the house. It was night, but in the garden there was a woman standing: tall, with long bright hair. She was calling your name. I thought I might climb in through the piano room, but when I stepped into the garden she saw me.'

Sandor's heart kicked. 'My mother saw you?'

'Yes. She called to me, and I had no choice.'

'What happened?'

'I washed, I slept. I was woken up. I dressed, had breakfast with your parents...' A sheepish smile tweaked the corner of Ferdi's mouth. 'I didn't know their names. I still don't.' He hesitated. 'I never had cheese like that before. And the jam. It was so sweet.'

'They didn't notice – they didn't realise anything was wrong?'

'They didn't say anything.'

Sandor sat, and for a moment felt like a small child who had lost his parents in a crowd. His shoulders sagged.

'You need to change,' Ferdi reminded him. He handed over the shoes and socks, and went on to take off the sweater and the shirt. Sandor started taking off his clothes, mechanically putting on the ones Ferdi passed him.

'What did you tell my parents about the bruises?'

'School fight. You got grounded for this, I'm sorry. Your mother was so angry. How was your day here?'

Sandor's jaw clenched. 'Quiet. How did you manage school?'

'I took your schoolbag and walked down the lane until I saw children wearing the same clothes and I followed them. I avoided people, pretended I was sick. One teacher suggested someone should come and pick me up but I refused. Another teacher was appalled by your attempts at Russian and gave you double homework. I'm sorry for that too.'

'Homework,' echoed Sandor, and the word was foreign, hollow.

When he was back in his hand-me-down clothes, Ferdi paused, biting his lip. 'I hid him, last night. In the forest.'

Sandor glanced up. He noticed now that Ferdi's fingernails were broken and scratched.

'I hid him well. The animals will take care of the rest.'

Sandor slowly buttoned up his shirt. He put on the sweater, straightened the cuffs with care, and combed his hair with his fingers. 'Good.'

Ferdi's eyes followed him as Sandor brushed the dirt off his coat and put it on with crisp, purposeful movements, just like he'd seen his father do so many times. Sandor avoided looking at him until the expectant look had faded off Ferdi's face.

He started to leave, then hesitated.

'Salomon and Karolina,' he said. Two more foreign words, as familiar as they were unused. 'My parents' names are Salomon and Karolina Esterhazy.'

*

Sandor stepped into the house and hung the wet coat in the hallway. The mercilessly lit rooms made him uncomfortable after all the time he had spent in the basement. He put on his slippers and left his shoes next to his father's. His own shoes were larger than his father's now; he was surprised he hadn't noticed that before. The worn slippers were there too, and from the depths of the house came the echoes of the piano.

Karolina appeared in the middle of the foyer. Her lush hair was drawn up into a tight ponytail that exposed the wrinkles around her eyes and the stringy muscles of her neck. She looked older, fearsome. Age became her; time would make her awe-inspiring onstage. Her face was stern. Sandor saw the fragility of her anger and pitied her.

'You're supposed to be grounded.'

He nodded. His mouth was dry. 'Did Dorika come in today?'

'Yes, but she's gone now. Why?'

'No reason. Did she say anything?'

She watched him, one eyebrow raised. 'Did something happen? Is that where you got these bruises?'

'No! I mean – no, of course not. And she's—' He was about to add *she's married*, but stopped.

'All right then, nothing more to discuss. Go to your room. I'll call you when it's time for dinner.'

'Mother...'

She held up a hand. 'It is embarrassing to look at you. Is this how we raised you? To get into fights like a drunk? Look at the state of your face! Didn't you treat that like I told you?'

The piano paused and Sandor caught himself hoping his father wouldn't walk in. Then the music began again. He walked towards her, stopping at arm's length. She moved in, raising her hand to touch his bruises, and then changed her mind, crossed her arms and straightened her back. He was glad she didn't touch him. He was sullied, unworthy of any affection.

'Do you think they would tolerate this at the Academy, that they would even consider you if you showed up for the interview with a black eye? Don't you *care* about your future at all?'

'Mother...'

Karolina shook her head impatiently. 'No, no. Don't start. Do you think your father and I will sit back and watch you *squander* your potential like this?'

The word, flung with the same contempt as by the man earlier, stung him.

'Or,' she went on, 'do you believe that you're accomplishing something, acting out just months before you graduate, before the audition, when everything—'

'Mother. *Mother.*'

He reached out and took her hand. Her words failed her, and she shot him a suspicious look.

'I'm not going to the Academy, Mother.'

Her eyes widened.

Sandor hadn't known he was going to say it until he did. He had been walking to his death, and against all reason, he had been given a reprieve. But the mixture of guilt and relief evaporated quickly. Now the displaced tension had left him tired, resigned to the truth; the only levels of truth he could communicate.

'They wouldn't take me anyway. I am no good.' He chuckled. 'I am worthless. I know it. You know it, Father knows it. Everyone who has ever heard me play knows it.'

'Sandor...!'

'No. I have been... I've tried, Mother. I really have. There's nothing I can do about it. It's not in me. It never was. I know

I'm not good enough. I know what a disappointment I've been. I shouldn't be your son. I'm sorry.'

Karolina slapped him.

Sandor staggered. Neither of his parents had ever laid a hand on him all his life.

His mother's eyes were brimming with tears, her face growing red. Sandor had never seen her cry. The sight made him faintly sick.

'Do you have *any* idea...?' she began, and paused to collect herself. 'How *dare* you say this? How dare you talk like this, in this house! You were born here – your father was born here – do you think that you can...'

At a loss for words, she pinned him with the force of her stare, heedless of the tears running freely down her cheeks. She put her hands on her waist.

'If you believe that, Sandor, then you really do disappoint me.'

He shook his head. He was no longer the little boy who marvelled at her, following her everywhere. Things like this no longer mattered. Whatever she still saw in him – it didn't matter.

'I'm sorry,' he said, and left.

*

Sandor returned to his room. Nobody called him, nobody bothered him about dinner. He slept very little, sweating and thrashing, and woke up in the small hours.

I don't want to be a murderer.

There was nothing he could do, no way to reverse this. He was lost, forever set apart from the rest of the world now.

He heard it again, the mossy stone against the man's skull. *I knew I saw talent in you, Sandor.*

Fix it, he said to himself. *Fight, do not succumb! Fix this!*

There was only one thing left he could do. Only one loose end to tie up. It was nothing – nothing compared to what he'd already done.

He stumbled out of the bed, put his clothes back on, went downstairs to his father's desk and started digging through the bottom drawers. He found what he was looking for and hid it in his coat. Whispering to himself the same thing over and over, he stepped out into the night.

*

'I don't want to be a murderer.'

Ferdi woke up at the sound of Sandor's voice. He was curled up on top of the oaken table, surrounded by his books. He yawned and turned to resume his sleep. Sandor placed a hand on his shoulder and shook him. The young man moved about groggily. The room was dark, lit only by the stray beam of Sandor's flashlight, which he had left on the floor.

Sandor pulled the blankets away. 'Wake up.'

The cold made Ferdi shiver and groan. 'I'm thirsty,' he mumbled.

Something metallic glinted between them. Ferdi sat up and rubbed his eyes. He looked at the metallic thing, then back at Sandor.

'Do you know what this is?'

Ferdi remained still, staring at the gun. 'Someone might hear,' he said.

Sandor's mouth twitched. 'There's nobody. And when they come, it will be my body that they'll find.'

Ferdi drew back.

'It will be a tragedy,' Sandor went on shakily. 'People will say, "what a waste" and "he was so young". And then I'll be free. Nobody searches for dead people.'

'Free?' spat Ferdi. His face was twisted in disbelief.

'Yes! Free from you, free from everything. There's no other way!'

Ferdi searched Sandor's face like someone trying to find their road on a map. 'You want me to die for you.'

'I want you to stop existing. I want you to… If it wasn't for you, none of this would have happened – and I wouldn't have to be a murderer!'

The gun was trembling. Sandor held it with both hands to steady himself.

'But – you brought me here!'

'I never should have!' The ground beneath Sandor was swaying. He saw Ferdi's expression, and something kicked inside him. 'No, stop! Stop crying!'

He pushed the gun forward and pressed it against Ferdi's convulsing chest. Ferdi made no move to protect himself.

'I have to do this, I have to… Stop crying! It's too late!'

It was no use; Ferdi was sobbing like his heart was breaking. Sandor fumbled for the safety catch. The effort it took sucked too much of his will. He pointed the barrel at Ferdi's forehead and the boy recoiled, his crying stopping abruptly. Sandor saw the betrayal in his eyes and it was worse than the tears. It made him feel dirty.

'It doesn't matter. Don't you see? You are not real. You aren't even human!'

He tried to pull the trigger, he really did – but his finger was frozen and it suddenly hurt.

'I'll be free,' Sandor muttered in despair. The pain spread to his wrist.

'Please,' Ferdi whispered.

The pain crept up Sandor's arm.

'Please.'

And then, suddenly, the pain was gone. His hand relaxed. Sandor looked at the gun in surprise. Ferdi followed his gaze, opened his mouth to speak, and Sandor fired.

*

His ears were ringing. The recoil had left his arm sore, and he rubbed his wrist. Sandor let the gun fall on the ground and the sound was as deafening as the shot. He felt oddly light without that chunk of metal consuming his strength.

Sandor picked up the flashlight and looked around. Ferdi had fallen off the table and was lying on the floor. Next to him was a spatter of thin black drops.

He lifted the beam to the walls. The glass of an empty gun cabinet was in pieces, and there was a black spot on the wood inside where the bullet was lodged. A shard of glass dangled and fell, shattering in gleaming bits. The sound was oddly musical.

There was a long, muffled groan in the dark.

He waited.

The groan was repeated, louder.

'You flinched,' Sandor said. He heard his own voice, flat and unimportant in the wake of the gun shot.

He found Ferdi with the flashlight. The young man was slowly coming to, groaning and gasping for air. There was a red streak on the right side of his face, where the bullet had grazed the cheekbone and carried off a small part of his ear. Ferdi's eyes blinked open, foggy and unfocused. He tried to sit up and then swayed, turned, and vomited on the floor.

Sandor didn't move.

'You disobeyed me again.'

Ferdi didn't seem to hear. He rolled on the floor and rubbed his head, moaning in pain. His back arched, his heels dug into the stone.

Sandor stood there, watching him writhe. His mind was numb, his chest empty. There was no anger, no pity, no misery to be found, as if all his emotions had been birds that had scattered with the sound of the gun. He pointed the flashlight at the open door, then at Ferdi's thrashing body, then back at the exit again.

Sandor paused for a moment. Then he turned his back on Ferdi, and walked away.

Interlude

The soil was an uncomfortable place for Ferdi. It belonged to Sandor: the soil, the roots, the hanging branches, the cool, squelching mud, the wriggling things that shifted the bristles of moss. Ferdi was never at ease in softness. His world was flat bricks radiating cold, that slab of mottled marble littered with blankets and books, the shelter of inviting pavement nooks.

Now, pressed from all sides by this yielding thing that filled his nostrils and mouth with rot-sweetness and digested bits of bark, it was hard to breathe. The darkness was dissolving, he could see the little dormant bulbs emitting the pulsating glow of a secret, the hair-thin ends of roots above his head, the forked, slimy wormholes. His arms were pinned to his sides. Something was nibbling at his sock.

He was calm. Not in the least put out, except for the breathing. All dreams must end. All nights must be suffered.

The curly-haired man was lying next to him, like a husband does. On his blackened, decomposing face the eyes were a striking, child-like blue. He was blinking lazily and humming a song to himself. With every move, his eyelashes swept crumbles of wet soil. When he turned his neck to look at Ferdi, there was a snapping sound.

Ferdi's legs were trapped under the load of the earth. His arms were pinned to his sides. Something was nibbling at his sock and was moving on to his skin.

When he spoke, the man's voice was Petar's.
'Ferdi, what if both of us could be free?'

PART III

1990

Winter fell abruptly that December, like a bedsheet sliding off a clothes line. One morning Ferdi stepped into the atrium and the snow was up to his ankles, the delicate points of the flakes gleaming. It was a slow walk to the Opera House, where, insulated in his practice room from the sounds of the city, he had begun to try all kinds of experiments until the music left him dazed and hung-over.

Ferdi had discovered that nobody else used this room apart from himself. In his absence it remained empty and mute while carpenters, seamstresses and harassed-looking assistants hurried by. It was small but comfortable and he had grown attached to it in the past few weeks, as it became part of his daily routine. Yet he felt none of the exhilaration of someone who was supposed to be fulfilling his life's purpose. No great exultation washed all other aches away, and if music was still his home it was now a lonely one, full of shadows. Ferdi was wary of the guilty contentment this home brought him, of the compulsion to give up on the rest of the world, step into the music and dissolve. What had he ever had, other than this?

He studied, edited and reshuffled his piece to exhaustion. He saw his compositions as the only thing that truly belonged to him. Ferdi couldn't count the minute physical differences that set him apart from Sandor, the expressions or the sound of his voice, his own character and mannerisms – but his compositions were unequivocally his own, coming unspoiled from a part that he felt was *his*; and if that part lay dormant in Sandor too, it no longer mattered.

Melancholy tenderness underlined everything. At home, he had left Petar's knife stuck in the table like in a slab of cheese. Ferdi liked its cold presence, how it reminded him of the dead Ivan, the departed Petar. It glinted softly, cutting the darkness. The boy had disappeared, in his own way. Their paths rarely crossed now, and when they did Ferdi was faced with an empty gaze. This, in such contrast to his previous burning looks, made Ferdi miss Petar the most when he was right there within his grasp.

Ferdi paused his playing and looked out from the narrow window while his mind wandered. He hadn't gone looking for Petar when they met; he hadn't sought love or attention. He wouldn't have known these things well enough to look for them. But the boy had rushed into his life like a gust of wind blowing open a window, and warm light had been cast on the darkness inside him to reveal a vast unimagined landscape. And now the light was gone, leaving behind the terrible awareness. There could be no more looking away from it, pretending that such a place did not exist.

Perhaps he should help Sandor, for all his arrogance and selfishness, if it meant that at least one other person would have a chance at what Ferdi had lost. Perhaps the story of Abel and Dorika didn't have to end like it had. And he was complicit, after all. With a shiver he imagined the woods, wet and stiff with cold, and himself digging bare-handed to unearth what he had buried. He rooted around his pockets for the paper and looked at the number Sandor had left him. *Call today*, he urged himself – *call and be brave*.

There had been no news of Sandor, and Ferdi wondered if he had made any progress on his great experiment, or whether it had already failed. It had been an impossible idea to begin with. Sandor always had a propensity for grand dreams: the ambition to defy evil was no crazier than the attempt to harness it. In his heart he might still be a boy. Ferdi caught himself envying his faith and determination, the talent for defiant tenacity that Ferdi hadn't inherited. Sandor was truly alone now, left with nothing but his mission. Ferdi was tempted to feel sorry for him. Even sanity seemed to be ebbing away from Sandor, and the strange gleam of his eyes still haunted Ferdi. It revealed a desolation of a man; and this peculiar inner loss, so hard to pinpoint, had evidently made him stronger. But in Ferdi, always plagued by baffling emotional responses, it elicited a deep sadness that he was unsure to whom it should belong.

Ferdi realised that he had been sitting in front of the shut piano for a while now, and his fingers were numb with cold. The heating in his practice room needed a while to start in the mornings, but usually playing kept him warm enough not to notice. Now his nose was beginning to run. He wiped it on his sleeve, put on his coat, scarf and gloves and headed back into the snow to look for a phone.

*

On Christmas morning he woke up to the feeling of a foreign hand on his forehead. The dream he had been pulled away from was gentle and hazy and left him predisposed to tenderness, and, without opening his eyes, he kissed the unfamiliar, rough hand, which smelled sourly of nicotine.

'Good morning.' There was a low, deep-throated scoff.

Ferdi blinked the sleep off his eyes. Sandor sat on the bed by him, still enveloped in the night's cold.

'Are you here to take me back?' Ferdi asked groggily.

'Too late for that. Do you have anything to drink?' Sandor got up and rummaged in the cabinets under the sink until he found the bottle of vodka, sniffed at it and poured some into a mug. He sipped while Ferdi put on a sweater and sat up, yawning stupidly into the gloom.

'It's Monday morning,' said Sandor, 'so we have one week.' He fished in his pocket for smokes and lit one. The momentary flame cast its shaky shadow on a monstrous face.

'Why a week?' Then Ferdi remembered. 'Oh. New Year's Eve.'

'That's right. We're throwing you a birthday party.'

Sandor put down the mug and moved towards the bed again. Ferdi drew back, but Sandor only lit the bedside lamp. Then his eyes fell on the burgundy notebook. He picked it up and opened it. Its brittle, water-stained pages stuck together.

'You've kept it, all this time,' he muttered.

He leafed through it. Musical notes cluttered the pages like crushed ant lines. Faded bus tickets with smudged writing and the leak of cheap ballpoint pens slipped against his fingers. Sandor squinted myopically, leaned closer and examined it. He put a callused finger on the soft leather of the back cover where the initials *S. E.* could still be traced, though Ferdi had scratched the gilt paint off. He drew a long, soft breath, and at last he put it back. Then his eyes fell on something else on the nightstand.

It was Salomon Esterhazy's signet ring, its stamped octagonal bloodstone as sober and elegant as its former owner, refracting the light into red and green gleams. Sandor picked it up, straightening slowly. He slid his index finger into the smooth gold band and flexed his fist until the veins on the back of his hand bulged.

Sandor's expression showed no change, but suddenly Ferdi felt him emit the pulsing heat of that rage he had come to know so well. He pressed himself against the wall on the far corner of the bed, horror rising in him unchecked. He looked into Sandor's face and for a moment the grey hairs and scruff were gone, and there was that boy again, staring Ferdi down, putting all his willpower into trying not to hit him.

'You little thief,' Sandor spat. He took off the ring and clutched it. Then he seemed to change his mind, and threw it back at him. 'Keep it, then. I don't care.'

Ferdi caught it and closed his fist around it, embarrassed by his fear, and glanced up at the stranger who used to be Sandor Esterhazy. Night shifted around them as dawn began to dilute the darkness. He tried to imagine what Dieter would say if he knew that the man who stabbed him was now sitting on Ferdi's bed, and then Ferdi felt a burst of jealousy, remembering that Sandor was the last person Petar had kissed. Why had Ferdi called him? Why was he suffering his presence in this home, on this bed where Petar once slept?

He jumped off the bed and began going through his socks. He found the one with Abel's ring and after a moment's hesitation he tipped it into his open hand. Sandor followed his movements like a cat watching a bird.

'There,' said Ferdi. He felt an aversion for this thing that had first brought the man in grey, then Sandor. 'Take it, then.'

But Sandor made no move.

'Take it!'

Ferdi burst forward and pushed it into Sandor's hand, but Sandor jumped as if it had burned him. The ring fell and Ferdi caught it again.

'What's wrong?'

Sandor grew pale. He took a breath, which erupted into a nasty, wet cough, going on until he had to collapse on the bed, clutch at his side and wait, gasping, for his chest to settle.

'I don't want to – I can't – *you* take it...'

'You need it, don't you? You said so.'

'I do. It's the only way.' He looked blankly at Ferdi's clutching hand and gave a slow shake of the head. 'You don't know... Don't ask this of me.'

'I didn't ask anything of you.'

'I can't.'

'But – you said... Abel...'

Sandor gave him a haunted look. 'Abel?'

'Yes.'

'You dragged him into the forest, you dug a hole for him.'

'Yes.'

'I had a stone, a wet stone…'

'Yes.' Ferdi's heart was thumping now too. He wished Sandor away, far away into a strange country; he wished him well into the ground. Ferdi moved closer to him and Sandor made a spasmodic gesture, but stayed put. He opened Sandor's hand and placed the ring in his palm in one careful, deliberate move. Sandor's fingers closed around the small cold object.

Slowly his back straightened and his face cleared, calm and detached as before. Ferdi thought he could hear Sandor's heart snap shut again.

'Dorika,' Sandor said quietly, and stopped.

Ferdi waited.

'I found her,' he went on. 'She's in the city. We need her.'

'She's here?' Ferdi felt that familiar gnaw of panic.

Sandor shoved a hand into his coat and dropped the ring in an unseen pocket. 'She doesn't remember anything. *He* made it so then. But she'll remember when she sees me. She'll know.'

'But then she'll tell someone!'

'I've watched her for a while now. She has a quiet life, a good life… A job, a baby: a little girl – and a good man to come home to. Even if she remembered, do you really think she would talk to anyone about us, about what had happened that night?' He paused, looking grim. 'I don't believe so. Her time at home – at my home – must be a sealed and painful memory. She thinks her husband left her, that's what she told people. An empty bed, a goodbye note, and Abel gone. Then she abandoned the post at the big house, and sought the city just like you did.'

Ferdi remembered the terrified girl, her leaf-strewn hair. 'So what now?'

'I'm going to meet her, and I need you there.'

Ferdi sat on the far side of the bed. He began rubbing his temples. 'No,' he said softly.

'She needs to see you or she won't believe me.'

'No.'

'You said you would help. You owe this to me.'

'*I* do? I don't owe you anything, nothing at all – it's *you*—!'

'You were the secret, Ferdi. You're the reason that man is dead. You're the reason she's a widow.'

'It was you who did this – I helped *you*!'

Sandor's eyes flashed. 'Then help me again! Help me do this, and you will never have to see me again – never have to be in the same room with me, the same country!'

Ferdi got up. His head was heavy and his body slow, as if all oxygen was being sucked out of the room. He wanted to open a window and let the clear air in. He put some water on to boil and went through the motions of preparing coffee for two people, as he was used to doing when Petar was there.

The nicotine-stained hand was on his shoulder again. 'Come with me.'

'Not today. I have to practise, I have to work.'

'No, you don't.'

Ferdi had completely forgotten about today's holiday. A perfect occasion to drag a woman out of her warm home and back into a nightmare, he thought bitterly. He pushed the coffee away.

Sandor took one scalding mug with no word of thanks, drank the thick, sweet contents and heaved a contented sigh. He tossed the dregs in Ferdi's sink. 'Let's go.'

They stepped out as the steel-grey morning was trickling down into the city, while on the icy pavements darkness still clung. There were few signs of festivity apart from the tourist spots. Shop windows were shut and barred, the streets desolate. The usual hum of cars and trams was sparse and faint. Ferdi, wrapped in his warmest clothes, face hidden in his scarf, thought he could feel

Earth's suspension in the Milky Way at last; and that any glance upwards was a long fall into the cold stillness of space.

Sandor walked on for nearly an hour in the fading twilight, leading him towards the eastern neighbourhoods of the city that Ferdi didn't know well. By the time Sandor's bulky shape finally stopped, gathering its shadowy folds into a gesture of silence, Ferdi was as lost as a rat in a maze. The buildings here were low and the white sky seemed wider, yet the facades were discoloured and damaged, covered in rusty metalwork. The stumpy apartment building they had stopped at was patchy and bare, with a single balcony jutting out above them like a broken tooth.

Sandor led Ferdi further back a bit, and they stood to wait by a forlorn patch of shrubbery. Sandor put a cigarette in his mouth and looked at his watch.

'Night shift has been over a while now. I hope we're on time.'

As if in response, the sound of footsteps broke the silence. Ferdi recognised the dull, heavy sound of steel-toe boots. A small, thick figure appeared, clad in in a factory uniform under a bright parka. She was too far away for Ferdi to see her face clearly, but something about her made his heart clench. She approached without noticing them and headed for the sunken, peeling front entrance of the building.

Sandor stepped abruptly forward between her and the door, damp cigarette dangling from his lip, and hailed her.

'Morning, miss, do you have a light?'

She paused warily, and pulled down her puffy hood. Her hair was held back with a headband, revealing an open, ruddy-cheeked face. She squinted at the men: the one calling her and the other hanging further back, observing her timidly. Ferdi saw her size them up, and tightened the scarf around his face.

Dorika pulled a lighter out of a pocket and held it up to Sandor, who stepped closer and leaned in towards the flame. Ferdi held his breath.

Dorika showed no sign of recognition. Then slowly her eyes narrowed as she took in Sandor's face. She extinguished the light. Sandor nodded politely and smiled at her. Ferdi couldn't see his eyes, but sensed the impish tension of Sandor's body as he made no move to leave.

'Pleasure, miss. Thank you.'

'You're welcome, Master Sandor.'

Dorika glanced at him and brought a hand to her mouth, surprised by her own words. Sandor's smile broadened. Somewhere above them a radio was switched on.

'I'm sorry,' she said, 'I thought I knew you.'

Sandor took her hand softly. 'Look at me.'

She did, reluctantly at first and then with increasing intensity. Ferdi watched her as understanding slowly dawned: her eyes grew large and the blood drained from her bright skin. Her mouth parted in unutterable emotion.

'*You!*'

'Me.'

'No,' she whispered. 'No, it was a dream.'

He held her hand tighter. 'It wasn't.'

Dorika stepped back, blinking furiously as the memories shoved and crowded through her. She grabbed Sandor's coat, patting and pushing to make sure he was real.

'I had forgotten – how could I forget – Abel – he went looking for you, that night! But – but – he left me – there was a note, I read it, I remember – I know that I read it…!'

'There was no note. He's dead. I'm sorry, I truly am; he's dead and buried.'

'That's crazy – he isn't, it's not true – let me go – he left! He left me!'

'He didn't, he wanted to protect you. He had come looking for me that night, remember? You know that he did.'

'No!' She struggled to pull herself free. 'Liar!'

'Don't shout,' he said, 'the baby's sleeping.'

Dorika stopped as if struck, and her eyes darted up to one of the quiet windows.

'Ferdi,' said Sandor. He gestured at him. 'Come, come here.'

Ferdi looked at the two of them, twisted together once again as they had been when they were a boy and a girl, just as scared and as desperate. Fighting the urge to withdraw and leave, he abandoned his corner and joined them. Up close now, he saw the tears running down Dorika's cheeks while she stared in surprise, quite unaware of them. So young, Ferdi thought, surprised by the treachery of his memory, where she had cut a formidable figure – could it be that Abel was just as young back then, as bright, frail and alive as she was?

Ferdi, feeling slightly nauseous, pulled the scarf off his face and scowled at the empty street while she stared at him. Dorika went limp at the sight and she would have folded if Sandor hadn't been holding her tight already. He propped her up and she stood leaning against him, gazing into Ferdi's face until his ears burned.

'But there was only one son,' she whispered.

She paused and rubbed her face, suddenly looking very old.

'I see now, yes... I remember... Monsters...'

'I'm sorry,' Sandor said, and Ferdi winced at the coolness of his voice.

'Where is Abel? What happened to him?'

'He's dead, that's all you need to know.'

Dorika shoved him away. 'You dare tell me what I need to know!'

'Shh!'

She began to writhe in his grasp. '*You* know – *you* know what happened to him!'

'Yes, but—'

'Tell me!'

'I know, but he's gone – listen! He's gone. But I know how to bring him back.'

She went still. 'Bring him back? Abel?' The tears kept falling. She looked wildly around at the quiet neighbourhood. 'But you said that he's dead. He didn't leave me, he's dead... Nobody could...'

'I can. If anyone can, it's me.'

'You would do this?'

'Yes.' A pause. 'I want to make amends.'

Ferdi couldn't suppress a wave of bitterness. Amends? Here they were, two among so many people Sandor had left damaged, and he was recruiting them to ease his own conscience.

Dorika clutched at him. 'Please,' she said. 'Please bring him back.'

Sandor gently extracted himself from her grasp. 'I need your help. I need you to be there when I attempt it. And you must bring your wedding ring, the one from ten years ago. Do you still have it?'

'Yes, of course I do. Just that? My old wedding ring? How...?'

'Will you do this? I will be at 9 B— Embankment, before midnight on New Year's Eve. That's Monday next. I will wait for you. Will you be there? It's vital that you'll be. I can't do this without you, Dorika.'

She pressed her lips together, as if about to scold them. Her dark eyes paused on Ferdi again and he opened his mouth, looking in vain for something to say, maybe a warning, but she quickly looked away as if ashamed. What was it about Sandor that held such sway over them? Hope – perhaps that was it; he kept tempting them with some wild, improbable hope. A part of Ferdi momentarily wished that Dorika would refuse to help.

But her broad, clever face was resolute and tense and, turning away from both of them, she nodded. She stepped away, pushed through the heavy front door and let it shut behind her.

*

As the rest of the week oozed by, Ferdi began to feel that something was truly dying away with this year, that something precious that had only now begun to form was already fading. Dorika's face haunted him. On that Sunday, the day before New Year's Eve, thin rain was floating as Ferdi made his way to work, taking no notice of time, and when he stepped out again for break it was already nightfall. He paused before returning to the kitchen and took a deep breath, letting his mind clear, when he noticed a strange, repetitive sound. It had a wet and smacking quality that eerily reminded Ferdi of the flapping of fish. He followed it.

Around the corner was Petar. His back was turned and he was hunched up, stomping his dirty sneakers on the wet pavestones to keep warm. For a second Ferdi completely forgot all the bad blood between them, and he bit down on a sudden urge to laugh at this hilarious, wonderful sight. Petar's awkward dance turned him enough to catch a glimpse of Ferdi and he froze, embarrassed. They exchanged a shy smile.

'What are you doing here?' Ferdi asked.

Petar had obviously not decided what he had meant to say, and Ferdi felt bad for catching him unprepared. He backed away a little so as not to spook him.

'Were you waiting for me?' Ferdi's heart leapt. 'Did you want to talk?'

Petar nodded and looked away, biting on the zipper of his jacket. Ferdi waited while panic began to take hold of him.

'Look, I have to go back in,' Ferdi said, although that was not what he meant to say. 'Shall we…? You can come in if you want. Have you eaten? I can make you something.'

Ferdi watched the boy's face fall and began to despair. One false step and he would lose him, he knew. Then an insane inspiration seized him. Ferdi had never been a risk-taker, but perhaps the encounter with Sandor and Dorika had left something wild in him.

'Listen,' he began, then lost courage and had to force himself to go on. 'There is something I'd like to share with you – something I'd like to show you. Will you let me? Just meet me here, when I get off work tonight. It won't be long. Will you?'

Petar looked at him curiously. 'All right.'

Ferdi nodded and, afraid he might change his mind, rushed back to the bar without a goodbye. When at last he wondered what it could be that Petar had wanted to tell him, he was already back at his sinks.

*

Ferdi didn't find the nerve to ask later as they walked, Petar following him silently one step behind. The usually quiet streets were brightly speckled with people queuing by street vendors and basking in the glow of festive shop windows. They found the riverfront abruptly, where the amblers paused to gaze at the golden reflections on the water and the stage-like beauty of the illuminated hills beyond. Petar must have guessed where Ferdi was taking him, but didn't speak. They stopped outside the familiar abandoned art-nouveau building.

Ferdi unlocked the door with a key Sandor had left him. It had been oiled and mended so it didn't scrape on the old, uneven marble step anymore, but the hallway was as gloomy and musty as before. He let Petar in and closed the door, and they paused while their eyes got accustomed to the dark. Petar's breathing came even and low beside him, just as when he was asleep. Ferdi's body tensed. He should have been terrified by what he was about to do but now, as he stood beside Petar, there was only the overwhelming desire to kiss him. Maybe in the dark it could be a secret, and they could pretend it never happened.

The boy moved and brushed past him. Ferdi's chest was empty for a moment, as if his entire existence was hollowness. If Petar sensed it he showed no sign, and moved forward. Ferdi could make out his shape on the dimly lit staircase, and hurried to follow.

They climbed carefully. Ferdi had the urge to shout something, make himself known, but the house had the oppressiveness of a cathedral. When they reached the top floor he didn't knock. He put a hand on the bronze handle, which was carved so that the door's metalwork looked as if it had been grown from a tree, turned it softly and went in.

At first the place seemed unoccupied. They blinked against the light stealing in, a glare after the darkness of the stairwell. Last time Ferdi was here the place had been empty, but now it was littered with clothes, books and empty packets of food. Surrounded by all this debris, Sandor was sleeping soundly on a narrow camp bed, with one arm hung over a book dropped on the floor, and the other draped across his eyes. Only his recent, patchy beard was visible over the blanket, but it was clear he was sleeping in his clothes and coat.

Ferdi had come this far, but now he was afraid. He glanced up at Petar by the doorway, staring at the sleeper, looking like a little boy, vulnerable and small. What had been going through Ferdi's mind, dragging Petar here when all he wanted was to protect him? He felt ancient and weary, misshapen with miserable years.

Sandor shifted in his sleep. Ferdi noticed how young he seemed like this, peaceful and boyish. He was reminded of an illustrated book, showing a pagan priest holding his knife over a fawn draped over the stone altar. He put a hand on Sandor's shoulder.

In a flash Sandor was awake and his hand darted at Ferdi's neck and into a grip. Then he groggily looked around, taking in his surroundings, and loosened his hold. He rubbed his eyes while Ferdi coughed and rubbed his sore skin.

'What the hell are you doing, sneaking up on me?' He yawned and scratched his cheek. 'What day is it?'

For a moment Ferdi thought that anger would get the better of him – anger at Sandor and at himself for giving in to fear like this – and he fought back the visceral terror coming straight from that first night in the piano room. Then he remembered Petar. The boy had taken a step forward to help him, but had stopped midway. He gazed at them strangely.

Sandor noticed him too. He frowned, then a slight grin appeared on his dry lips.

'You brought the kid to the zoo?' he chuckled. He fumbled by the bed, fishing a battery-operated camping lantern. 'Can't see the beasts with no light,' he said, and turned it on.

The light blinded them. Ferdi was unprepared for the shadows they cast on the stained walls, and turned away. Sandor, owl-like, barely blinked; but Petar backed away outside the spotlight.

It must have been an underwhelming reveal. It was plain in Petar's face: what could Ferdi mean by bringing him to this man's dirty kip? At first glance there was nothing remarkable about Sandor, who was wrapped in several thick layers, unwashed and unshaven. Sandor must have thought the same. He leaned into the light and stared at Petar.

Slowly, the boy's eyes grew wider. Ferdi couldn't bear to watch and sat by Sandor, his gaze fixed on the floor. The silence was unbearable.

'You have a twin,' Petar said at last.

'No.'

It was Sandor who had spoken. His eyes shone and he was deriving some devilish pleasure from this, but Ferdi could not bring himself to resent him for it. He was relieved to have their secret dragged into the light: first with Dorika and then, of all the people who should have known – Karolina, Maggie or Erzsi – here was the butcher's boy, in whose chest was already bubbling the laughter of disbelief.

Petar's glance darted between the two of them, and the corner of his mouth was drawn into a half smile.

'Stop screwing with me.' He let out a nervous chuckle. 'Come on, Ferdi. Let's go.'

Ferdi's heart kicked at the call and he half obeyed. Petar's eyes were on him, but he returned the gaze helplessly.

'Come on,' Petar repeated.

Petar had nobody and this was what Ferdi was doing to him. He hated himself.

Sandor grabbed Ferdi's arm and hauled him up to stand next to him. Sandor's usual stoop was gone and he stood in the manner of his mother, back perfectly straight and chin up, matching Ferdi's height to a hair. He held up the lantern.

'What do you see, kid?'

Petar brought a hand to his neck where his gold cross hung, which Ferdi had often felt against his skin. He mumbled something in his mother tongue. Sandor's grin was gone, and he pinned poor Petar with his unbearable gaze.

'What do you see?' he repeated. 'Look closer.'

Petar stepped forward, mesmerised. Ferdi could smell him now, that familiar mixture of blood and grease. Petar was looking intently at Sandor, like someone transfixed by some great and terrible sight.

'It was you,' he whispered. Ferdi followed his eyes as they paused on the spot on Sandor's cheek where Ferdi's scar was.

The three of them stood close in the shaky circle of light. Ferdi's palms were sweating and he felt oddly superfluous. What if Petar preferred Sandor over him? What if he now detested Ferdi even more?

Petar let out a breath and stepped back, looking dazed. His lip was curled upwards and he was frowning. He glanced at them both, turned slowly and left the room. They heard his unsteady walk down the stairs, and then the front door shut behind him with a soft reverberating thud.

Ferdi rushed to follow, but Sandor caught him.

'He'll need time,' he said.

Ferdi collapsed on the camp bed. A painful shudder went through him. Had this place always been this cold? He felt dry and empty, a useless, thoughtless thing. What use was a petty thing like longing or jealousy, in the face of their horrible truth?

Sandor was smoking, and flakes of ash landed on their shoes. When Ferdi looked, he offered it to him and Ferdi took a shallow, absent-minded drag. It was still wet from Sandor's mouth.

'I'm not coming tomorrow,' said Ferdi.

'What?'

Ferdi's heart was pounding. 'You have Dorika now, she'll help.'

'Don't be an idiot. I need you there, I told you.'

'You didn't need me last time.'

'This is far more difficult, far more dangerous! Ferdi, you're connected to this man's death as much as I am – we have to finish this!'

'*You* started this, *you* finish it. I wish you wouldn't even try it – if you can't do it without me, then don't do it at all. And you're a fool if you think *he* will let you get away with it. You've angered him already – he'll be furious, and then—' Ferdi clenched his fists.

'You know best, don't you?' said Sandor, moving closer. 'I suppose that you'd be fine going back to where you came from, wouldn't you?'

Ferdi pushed him away and Sandor staggered, anger shooting through his eyes in intermittent bursts like a dying flashlight. Then the wry smile returned. He combed his hair with his fingers and picked up the cigarette from where it had fallen, scorching the cover of the book he'd been reading. He licked a finger and pressed it against the smouldering spot. 'I thought you wanted to be free,' he said.

'I don't believe that I'm not free. Not anymore.'

Sandor watched him. 'Time to know for sure, Ferdi. You're a grown man.'

'Except that I'm not a man, am I? Not really – just like my hair isn't *really* black, or my eyes aren't *really* brown. These are *your* eyes and this is *your* body, isn't it? So if I'm not a man – if this body is not my body – then there is no way I'll ever know what I am, is there?'

Sandor paused, looking at him strangely. 'No, there isn't. This will have to be enough.'

'Enough?'

'Yes.'

Ferdi groaned. His heart was heavy, and he wondered whether he should had caught up with Petar before Sandor stopped him leaving, before it was too late...

Sandor glanced at his watch. 'Let's go and grab something to eat, while the shops are open. I have to be up early tomorrow.'

'You're not going through with this without me – you said it's dangerous!'

'Of course I am.' Sandor's jaw was set, his face ominous. He unearthed a scarf and a hat from a pile on the floor, and was soon out in the hall and heading down the stairs with Ferdi at his heels. At the foyer, Ferdi stopped.

'You can't mean for us to go outside together, with so many people about,' Ferdi said.

Sandor turned back towards him, but his face was hidden in the dark. He had his hand on the handle. 'You think anyone will notice?'

Ferdi didn't reply.

'Nobody sees,' Sandor said quietly. 'Nobody cares.'

He pulled the door open and stepped out. Ferdi remained where he stood until Sandor's footsteps faded. Then he walked outside, locked up, and left in the opposite direction.

1990

New Year's Eve dawned in a puff of mist. Ferdi woke up before the sun was out. He watched the slow fade of night into an uncertain blueness, then into the familiar pulsating grey. Condensation dripped and fogged between the windowpanes, and he followed the paths of the drops from his warm bed. His body was drowsy and still but his mind was awake, oblivious to the passing of time. Briefly he considered calling Gabriella to withdraw his participation in the concert. How could *he* stand in front of a crowd again – and such a crowd, too – in a matter of three weeks, and play? It was a fool's errand.

He took his time practising that morning, in the bleak, quiet bowels of the Opera House, and then took the tram to work instead of walking. The wind blew south-west, tempering the cold with pungent gusts coming from the heaving river. Ferdi paused to feel the wind through his hair, but approaching footsteps made him hurry on.

Few people showed up at the bar that day and there was plenty of leftover food, so Mrs Soltesz had tables pushed together in the dining room and the food was brought out in big platters for everyone to share. Ferdi was squeezed between Dieter and another cook, and had to wrestle their hands away as they fought to soak their bread in gravy. Mrs Soltesz sat with her cheeks growing pink, dipping bread crusts into her wine glass and chain-smoking.

Ferdi failed to notice how many times his glass was refilled with the house red, until he drifted slowly off in his chair. He woke up with a jolt. His head was resting on Dieter's shoulder, which was shaking as the big man laughed. Ferdi groaned and stretched.

'Back from the dead, Molnar?'

'What time is it?'

'Time to go home.'

When they walked outside together Ferdi's head began to clear and he thought he could sense the city holding its breath. Dieter followed him home, made coffee thick with milk and smoked until the room grew dim. He fell asleep on Ferdi's bed, and the sound of fireworks at midnight failed to wake him.

Ferdi threw a blanket over Dieter and sat at the table, feeling wide awake. He leafed through his notes listlessly, while echoes of passing revelries came from the street. He kept expecting Sandor to walk in, triumphant, glorying in his success. When the front door below creaked open he glanced out eagerly but it was only a middle-aged couple who stumbled in, paused in the atrium to kiss, and moved giggling up the stairwell. A door opened and closed. Silence fell.

He turned off the light and squeezed next to Dieter, who muttered in complaint and shifted against the wall. Ferdi felt the tide of Dieter's breathing next to him, lifting and letting him sink again. His body refused to relax and he peered into the gloom, chewing his lip until he tasted blood.

Quietly Ferdi sat up and put his shoes on, grabbed his coat and stole out.

The eerie silence amplified his uneasiness. He picked his way carefully: frost had formed in the atrium and the pavements beyond were treacherous. He hadn't been out at an hour like this in ages; it was the forgotten side of the world, the side of perpetual cold and hunger. His teeth began to chatter and he quickened his pace. From somewhere far away came the diffused sound of sirens and music.

He broke into a run until, panting and with side-splitting pains, he found himself in front of the familiar abandoned building at the riverfront.

He glanced upwards. From the topmost floor trickled a faint, flickering light. Ferdi wiped an involuntary tear of anxiety and tried with frantic movements to open the front door, which was stuck again. Its heaviness maddened him. He pushed his body through it and heard fabric tearing. He dashed up the stairs, heart threatening to kick its way out of his chest.

Ferdi was aware of an unnatural silence as he reached the topmost landing. He stopped, gasping for air.

The same uncertain light came through the frosted glass, and within it something large and dark was moving.

Ferdi stood paralysed. He grasped the handrail but his feet refused to move. The shadows shifted. He remembered the man who had died there, the warm blood on his hands, the reek of piss.

Shaking all the while and with enormous effort, he pulled himself forward and walked up the last steps. The door was ajar. Softly he pushed it and stepped inside.

The strange light came from a horde of mismatched candles, lit and placed haphazardly on the floor close to the windows. Hypnotised by their trembling flames, Ferdi took a step closer. Among them he saw crude shapes and scribbles upon the hardwood floor, like children's pavement drawings.

He squinted to get a better look, and suddenly Ferdi's knees gave. It was as if someone had struck his tendons. The room spun and the floor began to tilt towards those drawings, sucking him in. He shut his eyes and grabbed the door handle until his hand hurt. Slowly he turned away from the drawings, and gravity restored itself. Avoiding the lights, he opened his eyes again and looked.

Sandor was at the far end of the room, lying crumpled on the floor like a toy that had been cast aside. Next to him stood a passive, hazy figure, looking down at Sandor with an expression of mild interest. The figure was standing in a circle that had been burned into the peeling hardwood floor.

The curly-haired man stood in his striped, powder-blue pyjamas, which were clean and well-worn in a pleasant, intimate way. Ferdi knew him at once.

Abel was close enough for Ferdi to see his neck, which shivered prettily through the collar. His eyes really were blue, bright-hued even in the soft light, with pupils wide as coins.

Fear hit Ferdi like water from a broken dam. *It's not him, it can't be.* He was dead – he had buried him – this couldn't be real.

But who was he to call someone not real?

Ferdi started as Dorika stepped out from the shadows behind him. Her face was drawn and damp, her cheeks lined with nail marks, and she seemed out of breath. Indifferent to Sandor's limp body, she fixed her eyes on the luminous, misty figure.

'Abel,' she called.

There was a groan from the far end of the room. Sandor moved and was still again. Ferdi ran to him, kneeled and held Sandor up, searching for injuries. Sandor moaned and his lids fluttered until the whites gleamed.

Dorika moved closer, ignoring them.

'Abel!'

The curly-haired man looked up and gazed around, and Ferdi saw that he was missing a finger. His stomach turned. Abel's detached stare fell on Dorika.

'My poor Teja!' he said. His voice came hollow and distant. 'Don't cry! Go to bed and rest. I'll go there right away and I'll show him!'

Ferdi felt Sandor convulse as his chest heaved with a gurgling sound, and he came alive with a spasm. He sucked in air and spat out a viscous mixture of mucus and blood, then blinked awake, dragging bloodshot eyes over his surroundings.

'Ferdi,' he rasped. 'Something went wrong. The man... he was so angry, he wouldn't let him go... He wouldn't let me have him... You should have been here, Ferdi, why didn't you come?' His fist was clutching something unseen.

'I'll show him!' Abel repeated in a flat tone like a tape recorder. Then his body began to vibrate as if the ground he was standing on was shaking. Though the quiet room was still, there was a sound like a gust of wind.

'My love, my little bear.' Dorika began to cry. 'Is it you?'

'It's all right, my little Teja, my little woman. It's all right. Come here.'

'No, no,' Sandor said.

Ferdi pried Sandor's fist open. It was empty, but on the hot, clammy skin were burned two small circular outlines. Dorika stepped closer, reaching out a hand.

Abel held out his own and gestured at her. 'Come, I'll show him.'

Sandor struggled to get up but his limbs failed him. He began to crawl towards Dorika. 'No!'

Abel's round, boyish face looked eagerly at his wife. He smiled and stepped one foot outside the circle.

Immediately the strange intangible wind picked up, beating at Abel's soft brown hair and billowing the flannel pyjamas. Abel stumbled out completely and floundered to meet Dorika's arms, and the wind began to howl. His flimsy body shook violently, and began to dissolve like sand against the wind. Abel glanced down at himself and then at Dorika with startled eyes.

'My little Teja,' he said, and he was gone.

*

Silence fell. Dorika stared at the spot Abel had been standing on, with an expression of disbelief.

'Where is he?' She turned to Sandor. 'Where is he?'

Sandor did not look at her. 'I failed,' he said in a low voice.

Dorika blinked a few times. 'Bring him back, then.'

'I can't.' He shut his eyes and fell against Ferdi, who tried to help him sit up.

Dorika then looked hard into Ferdi's eyes. 'Can *you*?'

Ferdi tried to reply but couldn't speak. He shook his head, burning with shame. *I'm sorry*, he mouthed.

Dorika swayed, staggered towards the door and paused to lean against the frame. She ran her hand through her hair: again and again and again and again.

She turned and stared at the both of them for a long while without speaking, her face inscrutable. Then she pulled herself forward and walked shakily downstairs.

Ferdi waited for something to happen, someone to tell him what to do. Minute after minute passed, stretched thin and silent. He began to shake Sandor, whose head lolled.

'Come on. Come on, before *he* arrives. Let's go.'

Hot tears landed on Sandor. Ferdi wiped his eyes and, with joints creaking and teeth clenched, he hauled him up. Sandor wobbled and pressed his legs firmly against the floor.

'The candles,' Sandor said.

Ferdi couldn't move without letting Sandor fall. He glanced towards the candles and got woozy again. He couldn't trust himself not to collapse midway if he tried to approach them, so he held Sandor up and walked him laboriously away.

They had reached the doorway when Sandor writhed out of his stupor, set his feet firmly and brought them both to a halt. He shook his head. Even in the half-light Ferdi could see the awful pallor of his face, the sweat drenching the grey temples.

'Let me go, I'll try again.'

Ferdi pushed him forward but Sandor put a hand against the doorframe and wouldn't budge.

'I'll try again, I have to.'

'Don't be crazy, come on.'

Sandor shook his head again, shivering all over. He coughed

and spat. 'I have to,' he stammered. 'Let me go!'

Sandor pushed him and turned back, but it proved too much effort and he reeled. Ferdi caught him, dragged him out of the room and onto the landing. His stomach sank at the sight of all the stairs, at the complete darkness of the corridor. He began to haul him down the staircase and cursed loudly.

'Whoa! Language, Molnar!'

Ferdi's heart lifted before he could place the voice. He squinted until he saw the gleam of a silver-blonde head in the gloom, and nearly wept.

'Dieter!'

'You're a terrible date.' Dieter covered the distance between them two steps at a time. 'Imagine my indignation when I woke up to an empty bed…'

His voice died when he caught sight of the limp body hanging from Ferdi's side.

'What's going on?'

'Help me get him downstairs. I'll explain later.'

Dieter grabbed Sandor from the other side, throwing Sandor's lifeless arm around his neck and all but lifting him altogether. Ferdi drew a deep breath as his load lessened. They began to make their way down.

'Can you help me carry him to my place?'

'We can't go out now like this,' said Dieter.

'We can say he's drunk.'

'The police might stop us.'

'Then I'll find a taxi.'

'At this hour on New Year's? No chance. What's wrong with him? Is he injured?'

'I don't know, I don't think so.'

'Maybe we should go to the hospital. Did he take something?'

'I don't know.'

Ferdi was panicking. What if Sandor had some serious internal injury? It was hard to tell what had caused this state. And how could he know if Sandor hadn't overdosed on something or other in the course of his strange rituals? Ferdi couldn't see well enough in the dark, but he could feel Sandor's burning skin through their clothes.

'Dieter, hold him up. I need to search for his ID if we're taking him to the hospital.'

'Is he in trouble?'

Ferdi didn't reply.

Dieter exhaled. 'Right. You don't know.'

Ferdi patted Sandor's pockets until he found a wallet, but it was too dark to see its contents. Then it struck him. He couldn't walk into any hospital with Sandor, and with the two of them having different last names, too.

And – Dieter. How could Ferdi have been such a fool? They were moments away from stepping into the light and Dieter seeing Sandor's face. The memory of how Petar had ran away yesterday flashed before him.

'What's wrong?'

Ferdi had frozen. He couldn't carry him home on his own. Perhaps they could leave Sandor behind, and call an ambulance to find him. As he held Sandor's lapel, Ferdi squeezed it until the rough fabric hurt his palm. Wouldn't his life be much easier, much less complicated, if he let Sandor die? If he was so keen on carrying on with his suicidal mission then Ferdi had no reason to stop him.

He looked at Sandor's shaggy head, which nodded faintly as he slipped in and out of consciousness.

'Let's get him downstairs for now,' he said.

It was a slow descent. The three of them struggled to move blindly as one, keeping Sandor's faltering steps from making them all stumble. When they finally made it to the ground floor they sat down on the bottom step to catch their breath. Ferdi eyed apprehensively the hallway before them, bright compared to the slippery stairwell.

'*Before you go, Ferdi, my boy...*'

Ferdi jumped. He knew that voice: it was the man in grey. It had come clear and strong, but there was nobody around but the three of them. Sandor, who was slumped against Ferdi's shoulder, moved suddenly as if he'd heard it too. He raised a hand to rub his face, and groaned.

'What was that?' Ferdi whispered.

'What was what?' Dieter glanced up.

'That voice.'

'What voice?'

'*...For you, a parting gift.*'

Ferdi tensed. 'There. Did you hear it?'

'No, it's all quiet.'

Ferdi was seized with the wild urge to leave this place. 'Come on, let's go.'

They reached for Sandor but he fought their hands away and shook his head madly. Ferdi tried to hold him down.

'Calm down, we're almost outside...'

'No!' Sandor grabbed Ferdi's arm until it hurt. 'Don't listen to him!' He looked into Ferdi's face, struggling to focus.

The voice came into Ferdi's head again. '*Shall I tell you a secret?*'

'Don't listen!'

'Easy, now.' Dieter's voice dropped to a low, soothing tone and he tightened his hold on Sandor, but that just made him struggle harder. With surprising strength he pushed Dieter away, grabbed Ferdi and shook him.

'Leave, Ferdi! Go, now! Shut your ears!'

Ferdi drew back and covered his ears, but that made no difference. The voice came unimpeded, burrowing loud and clear into his mind.

'*Shall I tell you a secret?*'

Sandor put his own hands over Ferdi's and the world was muffled. Ferdi could hear blood pumping. Sandor's palms were sweaty and hot. Ferdi stared back at him in horror.

Sandor tried to sound calm. His face was close, watching him. 'Don't listen to him, Ferdi, he lies.'

'*Clever Sandor, he found out all about you. And he tried so hard to hide it from you, boy. Why do you think your madman had to die? This one here didn't want him or me telling you, boy.*'

'It's all right. It's not true, I promise.'

'*You've been here before. Isn't life a lark?*'

Sandor tore his hands away and frantically began to go through his pockets. Dieter, who had been watching the last moments in confusion, dove again to stop him but he fought him off. Sandor got out a formidable pocket knife and fumbled to open it.

'I'll kill him!'

Ferdi drew back, but Sandor was looking behind them and he began to crawl up the stairs on all fours, slipping and stumbling on the way.

'You swore!' he shouted. 'I'll kill you!'

Ferdi rushed after him. He scrambled up, having to grasp at the floor and the handrail to pull himself forward. In this burst of unexpected strength Sandor was moving fast, and Ferdi's muscles were unyielding and stiff. They went up a full floor before he could reach him, and when he managed to grab Sandor he fought and cursed, his body tense and convulsing. Sandor didn't seem to notice anything else, his entire being was pointing towards the unseen enemy upstairs, and Ferdi was out of breath. He fought to subdue Sandor's arm and retrieve the knife, which was slicing blindly at the air.

Sandor escaped once more, throwing Ferdi down. He was up the second flight of stairs, hands and feet to the ground, when Dieter rushed by Ferdi and with unlikely agility caught up with Sandor. Dieter fell on him, pinning him down, and twisted his hand until the knife fell. Sandor shouted and squirmed underneath Dieter, kicking and punching at him.

Ferdi saw them and, fearing that Dieter might do Sandor serious harm in this deranged state, he began to shout desperately and scrambled towards them.

'Dieter!'

Dieter looked back at the sound of his name, and Sandor took advantage. With merciless blows he fought Dieter off and drew away, wheezing and panting. Ferdi was almost upon them and dove to catch Sandor, but he slipped away.

Dieter lunged at Sandor again. They wrestled in the dark until Dieter was pinned against the handrail, leaning precariously over the emptiness. Sandor, struggling to break free, shoved as hard as he could and Dieter lost his balance, made a frantic grab for the smooth, slippery handrail which escaped him, then toppled and fell.

*

Sandor was shaking Ferdi's shoulder.

'Come on, let's go.'

Ferdi glanced up. There was the noxious smell of smoke. A blaze coming from upstairs heated the air on the ground floor where they stood. Warm flickering light illuminated them. There were creaking, snapping sounds, and the high-pitched echo of glass splintering.

Ferdi frowned at the sight of the fire. 'How...?'

'Didn't you...?' Sandor frowned. 'I was upstairs. You saw me go.' He paused. 'Better if nothing's left.'

Ferdi shook his head. He had no memory of that. He had no memory of going back down the stairs. He was sitting by Dieter's misshapen body, keeping watch.

'Come on.'

'We can't leave him.'

The hand was on his shoulder again. He shook it away.

'Ferdi.'

'I won't leave him.'

'Come on.'

'It wasn't too high up.'

'It was high enough.'

Ferdi turned a blank face to Sandor. All madness seemed gone and Sandor's face was gaunt and sober. He wore an exhausted expression. Ferdi had the impression he had never met this man before.

'You don't know that,' said Ferdi.

Sandor pressed his lips together. He bent over Dieter and carefully lifted his hand, put two fingers on the wrist, and waited. He shook his head. Dieter's visible eye gazed at them lazily, and Ferdi thought of the gutted fish.

'The fire is getting stronger. We have to go.' Sandor reached out to shake him again, but Ferdi drew away.

'Don't touch me.'

He got up unsteadily. For a moment his head swam, silver dots danced before his eyes and he swayed. He grabbed something to steady himself and it was warm. The handrail, leading down straight from the fire, had the temperature of a living, feverish thing. He let it go.

They stepped out into the shocking cold. Ferdi looked up. The flickering light coming from the loft was now menacing, uninhibited. He expected to see faces by the windows but there were none. The street was silent. The river was low, opaque and still.

He stumbled back home, with Sandor following.

Around daybreak he woke up. Sandor was fast asleep on the floor by the bed, wrapped in a tight bundle of Ferdi's clothes. His face was serene and pale blue in the dusk, and he was breathing heavily.

Ferdi felt something intrusive and awful rise up inside him like vomit. He dug his face into the pillow that still smelled of Dieter, and wept for a long time until consciousness ebbed away from him again.

*

A few days later, Ferdi read about the fire in the paper. It hadn't managed to spread, didn't even bring down the top floor properly. The body was soon found. Ferdi couldn't get that word out of his head. *Charred.*

Police inquired at Dieter's workplace and it was no secret that he and Ferdi had left together on New Year's Eve. Ferdi stated that they had gone their separate ways, knowing from past experience how to make himself entirely uninteresting to the authorities. They didn't bother with him again.

Charred.

Ferdi had thrown the paper away.

It was as if a soundproof wall was put up between him and the world. Sadness and despair were nowhere to be found. Erzsi too was pale and remote after the news, forgetful and quiet in a way unlike her usual sharp self. Much like Ferdi, she seemed to have gone utterly numb.

One night, as he was finishing his shift, Erzsi waded through the kitchen to say goodbye to him: she had resigned from the bar. Ferdi would have liked to tell her to stay, perhaps to keep each other afloat, but couldn't find the words. How could he be of help to anyone? He stepped heavily out into the street, and when he glanced back he could still see Erzsi. She stood looking at him, one leg down the steps of the service door, her face calm and impenetrable.

The bar closed down for the funeral. Ferdi couldn't remember any sign of religious faith in Dieter and was surprised by the spiritual nature of the service. He could almost hear Dieter's voice, gossiping and laughing at them. Petar stood on the far side of the small crowd in a black suit that hung baggy on him, and didn't seem to notice the sleet. Ferdi hid under his umbrella. They hadn't met in almost a week, since the night he had brought the boy to meet Sandor.

Petar's gaze fell on him. There was none of the usual anger, only an involuntary twitch of distress. They boy's eyelids were red and puffy, and the dark circles made him seem older. They watched each other across the stiff bit of land that was burned with cold, while Dieter's coffin was lowered. Ferdi tried to muster the strength for an apology but failed. Petar looked away.

*

Ferdi went through empty days mechanically; reading nothing, sleeping endlessly and waking up tired. He had been cut adrift. He began to suspect that his friends were tricks his mind had played on him. Time had been eerily stretched out, and it was peculiar how a day could feel like twice the amount of time.

But now he had little more than a week left until the concert, which was taking place on the Sunday after the next. It took an absurd amount of energy to begin to focus again, to return to his piano at the Opera House every morning and find some solace in his routine. It was incredible that someone could feel this drained of life, Ferdi thought. The world he was returning to seemed uglier than ever.

One day he looked up from his sinks and realised that it was time to look for work elsewhere. He gave his notice to Mrs Soltesz, who simply nodded gravely and offered him a small laminated icon of the Virgin Mary. With its bright colours and dazzling shapes it seemed the most alive thing Ferdi had set eyes on in a long time, and he regularly patted his pocket to make sure it was still there.

That night he woke up softly and saw two large figures sitting quietly at his table. Dieter and Abel were staring at him reproachfully. In the strange clarity of the moment Ferdi wasn't afraid, and stared back. Dieter shook his head and Abel shut his eyes. *I'm sorry*, said Ferdi. *What do I do?*

Their faded faces were sad. Ferdi's eyes were heavy with sleep and he lay back on his pillow. When he opened them again they were gone.

A letter from Sandor was waiting for him the next day. It came in an unstamped envelope with no return address, in a neat yet shaky hand, where words shot out unevenly and letters sprouted odd angles. The content was just as disjointed.

You have no idea what you've done. All my work now has been for nothing because of you. Do you remember that first night at the piano room? I should have killed you then, but you were my only hope, so I thought... Now there is nothing left: not my past, my future, my family.

You did not come. Now he has taken this last thing from me and I've lost everything. I'll be an outcast for as long as I live. And after that?

I thought I could trust you. I thought you were loyal, but you betrayed me worse than anybody else. If I could unmake you, I would.

If I could then I would unmake everything, even myself, and then I would rest happily in nothingness and everything would finally be all right, and maybe we were in the forest all along – and I was always the stag and I died a nameless death near a body of water.

Once when I was a child my father took me hunting. I have no memory of that. But I think something got into me that day, and I was infected.

I tried, but I wasn't enough.

*

Goodbye to the pots and pans that Dieter had sweated over. Goodbye to the dreary dining room where he once shared bread and coffee with Erzsi, to the forlorn piano that had rekindled his hope. Goodbye to the kitchen bench against which Petar first kissed him. Ferdi left the bar for the last time that Wednesday night with the Virgin Mary in his back pocket, his insides full of Mrs Soltesz's wine, and a gift of apricot brandy. He sat by the Danube and drank from the small bottle, watching the lights on the far bank blink sluggishly. To hell with it all, he had thought when he passed the blackened front of the art-nouveau building. He stretched on the bench, the heaviness of his thoughts being a welcome change to them being absent altogether.

To hell with it! This January he had lost all sense of the seasons. Even the winter cold was something abstract and the world was reduced to a rigid greyness. This was no way to live. Petar would know what to do, he always knew what to do; that boy went about life with a painful awareness of it. But Petar was gone, and here Ferdi was now, or what was left of him: the bare bones of a questionable soul.

Ferdi gazed at the water where the ill-omened fish had lived. A toast to soul-bones, then, he nodded, discreetly spilling some brandy onto the pavement. He recalled that autumn night when he had fallen asleep on this same bench, and a stranger's hand had shaken him awake. So many pairs of eyes were on him then, so many feet traced his steps. All this was over. He was now utterly alone. He made his way home northwards by the river, throwing wistful glances over his shoulder. Perhaps if he kept following it due south, he would find a new home, a new country, and he could start his life afresh. The futility of the thought was amusing, and he carried it to bed with him.

But soon after he started from his sleep with a throbbing head. He knew that something important was still clinging to him, but it dissolved as he tried to recall it. What was it that the man's voice had said?

You've been here before.

Painstakingly he drew out each word from his shaky memory until the coherent sentence formed. He reached for the pen and, lacking paper, wrote it on the palm of his hand. Still sleep-dazed, he sat and stared at the words in confusion.

Then he sprang up, ran to the bathroom and scrubbed his hand clean until it was raw. Nausea rose in him, worse than ever before, and he barely had time to lift the toilet lid. He vomited until tears ran from his eyes, and collapsed by the bowl. His heart was hammering and his hands shook. Slowly he pulled himself up and washed. He didn't want to remember that voice, he didn't want to know. He crept back into bed, shivering, and pulled the covers over his head.

*

On Saturday, the eve of the concert, Ferdi woke up before daybreak and made his way to a less familiar part of the city. Everything was still. The air smelled of mildew and gasoline.

The butcher's shop had not yet opened, but the shutters were rolled up. Ferdi stopped at a distance. A bright shape moved about inside, appearing and disappearing from view. Then the lights were turned on and Petar appeared in his apron. He rolled up his sleeves and stifled a yawn. Petar's usually cropped hair had grown out a bit and was revealed to be a pale, dusty sort of brown. Ferdi sank back, watching the small stage that shone its blue light out into the morning gloom.

Holding his breath, he covered the distance in a few long strides. His chest was suddenly too weak to contain him, and was terrified his courage would fail. He knocked on the glass.

Petar, bent over the display, glanced up and froze. He straightened up slowly and they looked at each other while the neon lamps buzzed and sputtered. Then he turned his back and Ferdi's stomach sank, but Petar unhooked a bunch of keys from the wall and came to unlock the door. He let him in without speaking.

The smell of stale blood brought Ferdi's barely contained memories to the surface, and he was suddenly afraid. He was a fool; he'd always been a fool.

Ferdi fished the pocket knife from his jeans and held it out.

'I came to return this.'

Petar blinked. He took it, opened it and examined the blade. 'Did you use it?'

'No.'

Again the expressionless stare. 'Did you have to?'

'Yes.'

It was odd to see no sign of Petar's scowl, yet still sense the anger radiating from him, deep and purposeless. His brow was free of the vertical creases of disapproval, and the small gap that used to form in his mouth was gone. His lips were firmly pressed, and there was an air of detachment about him. He looked Ferdi straight in the eye.

'So you don't need this anymore?'

Ferdi felt suddenly very small. 'I'm returning a loan.'

Petar's fist closed around the knife. They stood awkwardly.

'I can't explain,' Ferdi suddenly blurted out. He brought a hand over his mouth, surprised by its betrayal. 'Forgive me. There's nothing I can explain. I barely understand myself.'

'What happened at that house?'

Ferdi shook his head. One of the creases reappeared. Petar's voice came low. 'Did you kill Dieter?'

'No.' Ferdi's heart kicked. 'Never.'

'Did *he* do it?'

Ferdi hesitated. 'No. It was an accident.'

Petar tilted his head slightly. He looked at the knife, and then back at him. Ferdi thought he caught in that glance a fleeting gentleness.

'Look—' Petar began, but then he seemed to change his mind and didn't finish the sentence. A cloud settled over his face and Ferdi knew he wouldn't get anything more out of him.

'I have to open up the shop,' Petar said at last.

'I understand.'

Ferdi let himself out. Before he turned the corner he glanced back at the illuminated shop window, but Petar was nowhere to be seen.

1991

On the day of the concert a brilliant sun rose, turning the snow-covered pavement into mirror shards. Ice melted from eaves and windowsills to land on the sweaty heads of unsuspecting pedestrians, and the sky was the improbable blue of a travel brochure. All details were magnified in the glossy winter light: the steam rising from the grates, the headlines of crumpled newspapers, the peeling posters advertising bus tours. Ferdi, too agitated to eat, had tea on his feet leaning against his window and watched the comings and goings in the atrium below. The perpetual puddle in the middle had frozen solid and children skidded across it with arms outstretched.

There wasn't much left to do: his suit had been picked up from the rental shop, the piece he would be performing was ready, even his hair was tamed at last. He looked back into his room as the fragile sunbeams pierced it, and found it desperately quiet. It was strange to remember all these people who had paused here while passing through his life.

Ferdi walked to the Opera House to get his blood moving. By the front entrance of the building, glowing pink and gold in the blue hour, there was already a small crowd smoking and chatting. He made his way around the back and stepped into a medley of perfumes and nervousness. One of the performers – still in school by the look of her – sat green-faced, gazing into her patent leather shoes. The string quartet were sharing a flask between them and the harp player asked Ferdi if he had a cigarette she could bum, and when he shook his head she stormed off, irate. Though the room was cold, Ferdi began to sweat. He retreated to an empty seat next to the young girl and both of them sat grim, the whites of their knuckles glowing.

It seemed an eternity later when a supervisor walked in, followed by Gabriella wrapped in her sequinned snake. As the door opened and closed behind them, there came the brief noise of a crowd herded into the foyer and up the wide stairwell, the voices amplified by the marble and the vaulted ceilings. The supervisor read out some last-minute changes to the programme and the sound of each name brought a sense of dreary finality. Ferdi was placed between the quartet and a flute solo.

Pausing to exchange greetings, Gabriella made her way to him.

'It's a good spot,' she assured Ferdi. 'Right before the finale. Don't be nervous.'

Ferdi nodded, too busy trying to keep the room from spinning to speak.

'Can I have a word outside?' Without waiting for an answer, Gabriella led him out into the quiet corridor. When they were alone she put a hand on his arm and Ferdi felt her fingers, calloused and permanently ridged from the violin strings, dig into his flesh.

'What's wrong?'

'Ferdi, Karolina Esterhazy is here.'

'Karolina Esterhazy?' His throat tightened. 'Why would she…?'

'Natalia and Maggie, they decided to find her. I'm sorry, Ferdi, I didn't know. I told Natalia to stay out of it, that people's lives are their own. I did! But I saw Karolina walk in just now: she's in the audience, alone.'

Ferdi looked at the snake, which held his gaze darkly. 'You don't believe that I'm… I'm not – I'm really not—'

'Gigi!' Someone was calling unseen from the underbelly of the Opera. 'Gigi, it's time!'

Gabriella squeezed his arm again. 'No matter now. I believe in you, Ferdi, I really do – so don't be a fool. Don't run. Go play and forget about us. It doesn't matter, Ferdi, nothing matters when you're up there.'

She gathered up her dress and walked briskly away. Silence fell. Ferdi found that he had trouble breathing. He fought to undo his bowtie, which proved impossible. A chime sounded, the door to the anteroom was flung open and the harpist stormed past him, white-faced, and disappeared around the corner.

Ferdi walked back in to wait along with the rest. One by one, some cheerful, some glum, they rose in a slow procession and exited the room.

*

When at last it was Ferdi's turn he stepped onto the stage and it seemed to him a wholly alien experience. There was the elastic feeling of the floor propelling him forward, the instruments resting like play-fatigued children, the dizzying frescoed ceiling, and the cavernous, solemn room where flakes of golden light shifted and hid.

A sea of faces was watching him. He breathed in the dust from the curtains, and faint wafts of hairspray came from the auditorium to cling to his throat like rank butter. Ferdi glanced into the gap of the empty orchestra pit. He should be down there, he thought, sheltered and unseen. What was he doing up here, so exposed?

There was movement in one of the side boxes and Ferdi had the fleeting impression he had glimpsed Dorika, with a thick, grey-clad figure sitting beside her, its hand on her shoulder. But perhaps it was nervousness – Ferdi squinted to get a better look, and then the spotlight swept and caught him.

He paused, stunned, while the audience gave him an encouraging round of applause. A low voice came from the folds of darkness behind him.

'Move into the light.'

He stepped forward. The piano was inexplicably warm and gladness swelled in him, as if seeing a loved one from long ago. The people hushed.

Ferdi sat. It was delicious how time stretched, accommodating. Just him and the music. In this sweet-smelling softness, light, darkness, wood, polish, soil. The memory of closeness. His body, usually a cumbersome thing, now fit him: it knew what to do, how to move. The world was falling into place. Gabriella was right after all: nothing mattered but this.

My boy, you are always alone.

And the man in grey was wrong. How could Ferdi have been so fooled? People would come and go; they would leave him broken and hollow, they would forget him or revoke their short-lived affection.

But he had never been alone.

No, he didn't even need a piano, not even ears or hands. He didn't need to utter this language to know it. This music had always been a part of him, it coursed every nook and cranny of his being.

Ferdi pressed a single key: a solitary, questioning note like a bird calling its mate. Someone in the audience laughed. He glanced up, remembering briefly that he should be afraid.

Come on, Mozart, be a man.

Ferdi felt the familiar weight of Dieter's hand push him forward, gently but resolutely.

Except that I'm not a man, am I? Not really.

From somewhere a cold, menacing draught came, stroking the back of his neck in warning. He tossed his head. *I do not care*, he told it in defiance.

He flicked his wrists to be free of his cuffs and cast about for truth in him. And then it was as if a vast body of water suddenly swelled, surging and washing over him, and he began to play.

*

Light-headed, Ferdi stumbled behind the partition and unseen hands pushed him back onstage where he bowed again and again,

while the applause still soared. He retreated backstage once again
and put a hand on his stomach. The heady song was still lodged in
him, coiled into a spiral.

Standing there alone in the dark, he had the irresistible urge
to kiss someone. For the first time since Petar had left, Ferdi felt
his own purposeless desire like a broken compass. He made his
way back to the anteroom. The string quartet's flask did a full
round, passing every name on the roster, and whatever was in it
burned and evaporated in Ferdi's throat. There was a wildness
inside him as they all returned to the stage, stepped out together
and bowed, clutching each other's sweaty hands. Ferdi tried to
focus on the faces in the audience, but they all appeared as the
same one.

Back into the anteroom he fumbled for his coat and scarf,
and stepping out into the corridor he collided with Gabriella. She
kissed him bumpily on the cheek.

'Ferdi!' The tender tone sat strangely on her raspy, gruff voice.
'Well done, very well done!'

'Thank you – for everything, Gabriella – if it weren't for you—!'

'Oh, time enough for that later. Now go give them a smile.'

She pushed him into the tide of people making their way out to
the main hall and he was carried off with it, while every now and
then a stranger hailed him to shake his hand or pat his back.

Ferdi was sweating and grinning, his hair stood on end, he was
terrified that any moment he might burst out laughing and he had
a desperate need for another swig from that flask. More laughter,
more joy, people tugging him about. As the crowd slowly thinned
he tottered down the marble steps with his loose bowtie flapping
about, and stepped outside into the narrow square.

Cold and silence embraced him. Clumps of snow that had
melted earlier were now frozen, reflecting the sporadic light.
Most of the audience had dispersed but small groups still dotted
the pavement while waiting for the musicians, holding flower

bouquets slowly freezing to death in satin ribbons. The schoolgirl clambered down the steps at an odd angle against the weight of her cello case, and disappeared into the embraces of a company of middle-aged people.

'Ferdi.'

He turned, and Erzsi hugged him without any warning. She smelled different and at first he couldn't place it, until he realised: there was no smell of food on her, no hint of frying oil or cooking wine. She now had the odd, foreign scent of someone wearing new clothes. Her hair was shorter, and her bright hazel eyes were shining.

'I promised you I'd be here, didn't I?'

Ferdi didn't want to let go, but did. He had forgotten how happy the sight of her made him.

'Oh Ferdi, how wild, how splendid!'

He smiled sheepishly.

'Happy?'

The question took him by surprise. 'Yes, perhaps. In a way – for now – yes.'

'That's all any of us can hope for.' They exchanged a smile. 'How are things with Petar?' Feeling him tense, Erzsi turned to look at him. 'No change?'

'No. It's over.'

'I'm sorry... But I don't understand, he was so – so smitten.'

Silence fell again. The city was falling fast asleep.

'Ferdi,' she said, 'I'm leaving.'

'Shall I find you a taxi?'

She squeezed him. 'Leaving Budapest.'

'When? Why?' Then he paused and said quietly, 'Dieter.'

She avoided his gaze. Neither had spoken his name since the funeral.

'It hasn't been right, since... The city sucks the life out of me. I was only thinking... I was thinking about vineyards, and orchards.

I want to see hills again, like those at home.' She fell quiet. 'I'm afraid that if I stay any longer I'll never leave.'

'I understand,' Ferdi said, although he didn't.

'I have a few minutes before I have to grab a taxi to the bus station. I've left my things there.'

'You're leaving tonight?'

'I only stayed this long for the concert.' She linked her arm with his, and they looked around at the festive square, the diamond-harsh stars. Ferdi thought he was in a dream.

'Will I ever see you again?'

She considered it. 'Not soon.' They moved closer, drawn to each other's body heat. The traffic in the main street was languid. 'I will send you my new address when I'm settled, so that you can visit.'

He decided to believe her. After all, truth had a way of shifting around him. She ruffled his hair, and Ferdi offered his freshly shaven cheek to be kissed.

'Your piece tonight was a gift. Thank you.'

Erzsi hailed a taxi, and Ferdi realised that he would never get used to people leaving him. She had one foot in the car when she stopped and looked at him.

'Petar was here tonight, wearing a smart shirt and everything. I thought that I'd find you together now. I'd given him Dieter's ticket, I thought you knew. You didn't, did you?' She paused. 'Maybe it's not over, Ferdi. Sometimes it never really is.'

Ferdi took a step closer, looking in vain for something to say. His throat burned. He held the door for her, and she blew him a kiss.

'Safe trip,' he said at last, and the car was gone. He watched it disappear and turned to walk away.

A woman was standing alone, staring at him.

'A friend?' the woman asked.

'Yes,' replied Ferdi.

At first he didn't recognise her. He was so transfixed by the intensity of her gaze that all other details eluded him, and instinctively he took a step back.

Karolina had changed little in a decade. She maintained her regal bearing and blonde mane, and her skin was drowned in freckles. She showed more bone now, but it only made her more elegant. Her clothes were dark and fine and her eyebrows were starkly painted. Her wrinkles, thin and spidery, appeared only when she spoke.

'Sandor—'

'Ferdi,' he corrected her before he could stop himself.

The colour rose in her cheeks and the conflicting emotions showed plainly on her: he knew she would refuse to utter the name if she could.

She clenched her powerful jaw. 'You missed the funeral.'

Ferdi clutched at the signet ring hanging under his shirt. 'The funeral?'

She averted her eyes and Ferdi had the fleeting image of Salomon's glasses again. His grasp tightened. It couldn't be; people like Salomon Esterhazy didn't die. People like Salomon Esterhazy were meant to be a cornerstone, a foundation.

'Gabriella is an old friend,' she went on. 'You can imagine my shock when I read her daughter's letter... Natalia wrote to me about your new name, your new life... She told me about this concert.' She paused. 'You didn't know? No, of course you didn't.'

Ferdi reddened. She looked down at him.

'Well, don't you have anything to say?'

He finally met her eyes. The irises were storm-blue, spattered with golden fissures like lightning. He was done – *done* – and would never allow himself to be Sandor's stand-in again if he could help it.

'Why did you come tonight?'

He watched the last remnants of hope drain from her face.

'Because you are my son,' she said.

Ferdi would have taken her hand then, had they been strangers. He was struck by the memory of her fingers on his face, that day when she had examined his bruise. Perhaps he had dreamt it, it was so long ago.

Karolina reached out and held his face again, in the same gesture. She touched the pale scar on his right cheek, and gave it a faint rub.

'What happened to you?'

He looked away until Karolina retrieved her hand. He felt her gaze again, examining him just like Maggie's had done. It paused over the thin face and stringy limbs, the callused, cracked skin on his hands, and he knew she was comparing him to the wilful child she had loved.

She pressed her lips and gathered herself. 'The house has been sold. I wanted you to know, I signed the final papers this week.'

This news stunned Ferdi. The Esterhazy mansion – his birthplace – his jail. To have it passed on to strangers, as if nothing remarkable had taken place there... Karolina pulled from her handbag a thick, sealed envelope and a pencil, and scribbled something on it.

'It didn't go for much, but it's enough. This is your share. Do with it as you wish. No,' she added, seeing his expression, 'don't try to give it back. I won't have it.' She pushed the parcel into his hands until he had no choice but to take it. 'My new address is on it, if you'd like to...'

Ferdi wished he could disappear. It was obvious, surely, that he was not her son – if anyone could tell them apart it must have been her, who carried Sandor in her body, fed him and kept vigil during his childhood fevers. But the years apart had done their insidious work, and Karolina wavered. She would never be able to account for the long, merciless days and their obscure lessons, and was suffering a cruel defeat. And that quick temper, that which her son had inherited, was losing purpose in the face of the inevitable. Ferdi sensed her sudden hatred of him, of herself and of the meanness of life, as if it was something only now revealed to her. Thin, icy raindrops began to drift down on them.

'You are composing, then,' she said quietly. 'Just like your father.'

Ferdi clenched his fists, blushing. She waited for a response and, finding none, she wrapped her scarf tighter and turned to leave.

Ferdi dug into his clothes and took Salomon's signet ring off its chain. He gave it a turn, swiftly noting its weight and feel, and thought that this was all right, that it was due.

'Wait – please.' He caught up with her. 'This belongs to you.'

Karolina took the ring in her gaunt, gloved hand and looked at it for a long moment. Then she wrapped her fingers around it and lifted her eyes to meet his.

'I don't care what name you choose.' She took his hand. 'Won't you come home? Won't you?'

They looked at each other. Ferdi wiped the rain off his face and tried to smile, flooded with pity. He knew this wasn't what she longed for and he was ashamed for it; but the tender, quiet feeling persisted nonetheless. Karolina sensed it. She let go of him, nodded, and walked slowly away.

Ferdi rubbed his eyes and tugged at his hair, and let go of the breath he had been holding. He looked back into the vacant foyer, hoping that Petar would emerge, that this night wouldn't have to end this way. Why had Petar come if he didn't want to talk, if he despised him? Why, when Ferdi hadn't even dared to invite him himself?

He crossed the quiet street towards the metro station entrance and, as he paused halfway for one last glimpse of the Opera House behind him, he saw Sandor.

Ferdi hadn't lain eyes on him since the night of Dieter's death. He froze.

Sandor was stood right where Ferdi and Karolina had been talking. His gaze was turned towards the street where the thick, damp night had swallowed her.

'Sandor!'

Sandor looked at him. Even in the dim orange light of the street lamps Ferdi could see the awful, twisted expression on his face.

Ferdi touched the pocket of his dinner jacket where the envelope bulged under the coat. Time to get rid of it all, he thought, time to cast that borrowed name off. He began to walk back towards Sandor in long, quick strides. When Sandor saw him he retreated and walked quickly away.

'Wait!'

Sandor quickened his pace and then, seeing Ferdi wouldn't stop, he began to run.

For a second Ferdi stood, aghast. The sight of Sandor running away from him was the most astonishing thing in a night already replete with extraordinary occurrences, and he had the fleeting urge to laugh. But then something in him kicked in foreboding. Sandor had seen him speak with Karolina. Ferdi suddenly remembered that horrible letter Sandor had sent: there was no telling his state of mind now. Ferdi hesitated a moment, then rushed after him.

He followed Sandor westwards down the empty main street, darting under the naked trees, the crisp rented shoes digging into his feet, slowing him down. Their footsteps echoed in the Sunday lull. Sandor kept throwing glances over his shoulder, running faster every time until Ferdi could hear his loud, ragged breathing.

And in the shut, still night, disrupted only by themselves as the city lay dormant and hidden from the January cold, Ferdi heard another sound, so indistinct that at first he wasn't sure: a third set of footsteps, following at a distance yet steady and purposeful. He turned to see, but there was nobody there.

It couldn't have been more than ten minutes later when Ferdi smelled the river ahead and came abruptly to the waterside park by the Chain Bridge, yet his whole body was aching. He paused to clutch his straining ribs and saw Sandor, too weary to run now, crossing the square in slow, arduous steps. He cut such a forlorn, pitiful figure that Ferdi could have been looking at an old man, bent and wheezing.

Sandor made his way towards the bridge, which rose hulking and eerie in the night mist, like a crossing into the underworld.

'Sandor—' Ferdi panted. Then, louder: 'Sandor!'

He got up and went after him. Sandor had dragged himself onto the pedestrian crossing of the deck and had managed to reach the first tower before collapsing at its root. Ferdi walked up to him and leaned against the stone parapet, winded. The river flowed stealthily underneath. Cars passed behind them, crossing the bridge while muted under the river's reverberating growl, but the two of them were sheltered behind the high stone wall of the tower separating them from the street. They stayed silent, catching their breaths.

'I have your money from the sale of the house,' Ferdi said at last. 'Your mother thinks I'm you.'

Sandor glanced up at him, trying to discern Ferdi's face. He drew pained breaths and took a long time to reply.

'She wouldn't know me if she saw me. Give it back to her.'

'She won't take it,' Ferdi replied, massaging his side stitch.

'So?'

'It's yours.'

Sandor coughed and spat. 'I don't want it.'

'And what should I do with it, then?'

'Throw it in the river.' Sandor got to his feet, his chest heaving.

Ferdi shivered. All of a sudden he fell on Sandor with a choking hold, and pinned him against the wall. But then he let go; this pathetic creature could offer him no release. He dug his fingers into his own face, pulling at the hateful skin, and let out a frustrated snarl. Sandor glowered at him, and something of the boy Ferdi had known returned in those cloudy eyes. He noticed for the first time how much Sandor was like his father. In almost all aspects Sandor resembled Karolina: height, bones, temper; but now Ferdi could see the familiarity with Salomon. In the right light, their insides could be full of mirrors. They were opaque souls. And behind that something moved, powerful and unseen.

'Look at you.' Sandor advanced until Ferdi stepped back. 'Look at you, with your friends and your boyfriend and your shitty job and your shitty little room. And what do I have? Nothing and nobody. I saw how my mother spoke to you – it's what you wanted, isn't it? You wanted it all for your own.' He reached out to hold onto the stone. 'You have everything – and I nothing. I'm no longer human, it has been stripped away from me. Abel never came back. I failed.'

Ferdi's pulse was beating wildly, his mouth was dry. 'Do you really think it made any difference whether he came back or not? When the blood had been spilled already?'

'No difference? No difference whether he lived or died? I was innocent until that night—'

'Stop it!' Ferdi's face grew hot and the blood thumped in his ears in synch with the river, the traffic, the city that smothered them. 'You, innocent? You brought me into this world, you locked me up, and then you abandoned me! You attacked Dorika and then you brought her back to this, you made her remember – and for what? So she could see that – that *thing*!' He was feeling dizzy again, as if he were back onstage. The tight shirt was choking him. 'Would bringing him back make all that disappear? This was not making amends – it was all for *you*, for your own selfish reasons!'

Sandor looked as if Ferdi had punched him. 'Don't you dare—' he began, but Ferdi cut him off.

'You fool! Whether you brought him back or not, would that undo a murder? Would that make everything all right? And what about that poor man you killed only a few weeks ago? You were never innocent, *never*! Here – take this money and leave, there's nothing keeping you here. Leave! You've done it before.'

Sandor shook his head. 'Leave?' he mumbled.

'Or,' Ferdi went on, 'confess.'

'Confess? *Confess?*' Sandor pushed Ferdi back until he stumbled. 'How about *you* confess? How about *you* tell everyone what you are?'

Ferdi slapped his hand away. 'I didn't kill anyone!'

'And does that make you anything less than an abomination?'

'You should pay for what you've done!'

'You think I haven't?' He grabbed Ferdi's coat. 'Come on then, if you're so eager. Kill me if you want it so much. Then you can go and confess to your heart's content!'

Ferdi struggled to wrench him off, and glanced at Sandor's face. Tears were running down his cadaverous cheeks. Ferdi realised, with a dreadful wave of weariness, that he could no longer blame him for his own existence. Sandor was culpable for many things but not for everything, and Ferdi couldn't go on blindly like he was used to, faltering in the dark. Wouldn't it be better to move forward with eyes open?

They stumbled back from each other, and Ferdi wiped his brow.

'Why did you try to stop him from speaking to me? What was it you didn't you want me to hear?'

Sandor was fighting to breathe again. His expression was strange. 'Do you really want to know?'

Ferdi blinked in surprise. Perhaps it was a trick of the passing headlights, but Sandor's eyes looked at him with gentleness. Ferdi's stomach fluttered; Sandor had never looked at him like this. If he had, their lives might have been different.

'I'm human though – I am – aren't I?'

Sandor met his eyes. 'If you're human, Ferdi, what does that make me?'

Ferdi opened his mouth, looking for words – but then he saw Sandor stiffen up and his eyes widen, looking past Ferdi into the dark.

Ferdi turned back following his eyes and saw whose footsteps had haunted their pursuit. And strangely, as though he had been expecting her all along, he wasn't startled.

Dorika approached them, pinning Sandor with her cool gaze. 'What does that make you, indeed?' she said.

She walked past Ferdi, paying him no attention, and took Sandor's unresisting hand in her own. The tenderness of the gesture baffled Ferdi, until he saw that Dorika was staring at the shapes of the twin rings burned into Sandor's palm.

Sandor's haggard face bent eagerly towards her.

'One more try,' he pleaded. 'We could do it, together we could bring him back...'

Dorika shook her head. She put a hand in her pocket and took it out again and, before Ferdi had time to react, she made one rapid move.

Sandor staggered.

'No!' gasped Ferdi.

Dorika pulled out the bloodstained knife, and with a quick gauging glance below she tossed it into the river, which ate it up soundlessly.

Sandor leaned heavily against the tower and Ferdi rushed to him. Dorika walked away without sparing them another look, and before she reached the bank she had been swallowed by the mist.

Ferdi frantically undid the weather-stained coat and scarf to check the damage. Sandor began to laugh.

'Nicely done,' he panted.

'Quiet,' said Ferdi. Sandor's clothes were drenched and hot. He looked madly about for a stranded passerby, a car, a tram.

Sandor nodded, straightened and then fell against the parapet. He gazed over the rail into the dark, swift water beneath, a long drop below them.

'Ferdi,' he said, groaned and grabbed his stomach. Ferdi caught his arm; Sandor shook him off and began to climb onto the parapet and over the rail in fury. Ferdi hauled him back with all his might, but Sandor mulishly held on.

'Why won't you stop fighting for once?' Ferdi exclaimed, and Sandor laughed again. In the faint lamplight his face was ashen.

'Ferdi,' he repeated, then the last of his strength ebbed away. He fell limp against him.

Ferdi collapsed under his weight. He sat up, raised Sandor and carefully laid his shaggy head in his lap. Then Ferdi saw the slack mouth, the sagging, dark lids, the empty eyes.

Here was the gutted fish again, and Ferdi's hands all wet and bloody. He leaned against the stone.

In Ferdi's mind music began to play: the song with no name, the song that had always been there. And as he sat and his fingers began to pluck the tune on the cooling, damp coat they held on to, the river kept flowing heedlessly on.

Epilogue

Natalia's childhood room was in need of fresh air. The shelves above the bed were heavy with books, dusty souvenirs and photos: Natalia as a toddler, playing in the snow. Balint carrying her on his shoulders at a picnic. A family portrait taken in a foreign city. Natalia holding up a diploma, beaming. Snake-green eyes everywhere, looking down at him as he lay groggily on the unfamiliar bed. The pillowcase was embroidered and made the back of Ferdi's neck itch.

There was a knock on the door.

'We're leaving,' came Gabriella's muffled voice. 'There's stuffed peppers in the fridge for you.'

'Thank you.' Ferdi heard the shuffle of coats and shoes, then the front door opening and closing. He sat up heavily, rubbed his burning eyes and yawned.

Gabriella hadn't asked many questions when he had called her to say he was giving up his room. When she learned that his departure date and his train ticket to Trieste were a few days apart, she offered to put him up. The money from the envelope had taken care of his bills, the rent, a quick passport and a train ticket. It would pay for the ferry south to the Mediterranean, for food and comfort for a while; Ferdi felt no trace of guilt. It had also paid for the express delivery of a long letter to the butcher's shop, to which there had been no reply.

All of Ferdi's possessions now fit in a backpack: some clothes, the notebook, the book of fairy tales and the concert programme with his name on it. Perhaps, he mused, someday he'd play again, but not for a while. And there was something he needed to do first.

He ate a quick breakfast, got dressed and set out. At the sight of the bus terminal his insides clenched: the familiar mixture of oily smells brought back shunned memories of aimless drifting, of awe and loss. The journey seemed much shorter than a decade ago. Back then it had been broken down into erratic, miserable chunks, days when he didn't know where he was going or whether he would get to eat. Ferdi scratched his scar.

When he arrived he noticed new houses around the neighbourhood. The roads were wider, the greenery was trim and the edges of the forest thinned down. Perhaps the place had never been ominous or wild – perhaps it was all the ominous and wild things that had taken place there. Ferdi saw details that he remembered with alarming clarity. Here was the broken lamp post, the small crossroads, the bent front gate. As the landscape grew more familiar, his heart beat louder.

It was a pleasant morning for a brisk walk, despite the frost. There would be snow in March, Ferdi thought. The breeze came clear and fragrant from the hills. It was a good place to live, a good place to raise your children. The sun fell kindly on the prosperous neighbourhood. *Come, this is a safe place*, said the trimmed gardens, the gleaming cars, the neat alleyways. He passed an unkempt estate hidden behind overgrown shrubberies and dishevelled trees, and recognised the place Sandor had called the ambassador's house. The villa, deep into the grounds, was dark and lifeless.

The gate of the Esterhazy manor was propped open. A large sign hung off it, which advertised a construction company. The gravel driveway was upturned by tyre marks. Further in by the toolshed was a damp pile of cement sacks. Ferdi stood in front of the gate, unable to make his body move. He took in the ruffled greenery that had once been the flower beds. The trees were grown so wild that they almost scratched at the shut windows. His eyes fell on the south side of the house, where the stairs to the gun room were just visible.

Ferdi forced himself to walk towards the front door, stumbling on the uneven pathway. Had he ever used this path before? There had been that day when he played the part of Sandor Esterhazy, and he could step in and out of the house as he pleased. But he had never done this as Ferdi Molnar. Only when he mustered the courage to put his hand on the doorknob did he realise his stupidity.

He gave it a slow turn: of course it was locked. He looked at the heavy door for a minute and then retreated and sat on the front step. He had the contradictory impression that everything was simultaneously smaller and less intimidating than he remembered, and at the same time absurdly large. Who would need such a huge house to live in? What would anyone do with all these rooms, all this space? Sandor, Salomon and Karolina must have gone through their days here like ships passing each other at sea.

Ferdi got up and began to make his way around the building. He passed the gun room, keeping his distance. Seeing how tiny and miserable it was sickened him, and he didn't try to see if it was locked. He didn't want to know. He moved on towards the eastern side of the house, which overlooked the back yard where trees hugged the walls from all sides. The large window of the piano room reflected the weak sunlight and momentarily blinded him. He walked up to it and pressed his palm against the warm glass.

It was unlatched. It yielded under his hand and creaked open, releasing flecks of chipped paint. Ferdi blinked, uncertain, and then climbed inside.

The piano room was completely bare. As his eyes adjusted to the dimness, with sunlight diffusing through the dirty glass, he noticed that the grand piano was gone. So was the small writing desk at the far side of the room. The built-in bookshelves were empty, even the curtains were missing. Where the piano had stood, the hardwood floor was a shade lighter and there was a cigarette burn on the varnish, but otherwise this room might have never been occupied. He opened the double doors as quietly as possible, and stepped into the hallway.

It was just as bare. The walls were dotted with dusty shapes where paintings and mirrors used to hang, and wooden floors that had spent decades shielded by lush carpets now shone. The house was now an ugly, skinned creature. Dead-eyed, something embalmed and mounted. The hairs on the back of his neck rose. Poor Karolina, to be left alone in here. No wonder she had left as soon as she could.

Ferdi found it impossible to stop. He checked every room he passed: all were silent and empty. He went down to the cold kitchens, where the heavy marble sinks sat desolate. It was like those nights when he would steal into the house to play, and he would imagine himself in the belly of a giant sleeping beast. Faint creaking sounds surrounded him, as if the structure had lost its balance after having all its furniture removed.

Eventually he made his way upstairs. The staircase, stripped of its carpeting, seemed to be floating and holding onto the ground by sheer habit. Ferdi climbed, conscious of every step and creak. His hand slid along the smooth, mottled varnish of the rail. Of all the rooms only the door to the master bedroom was open, and Ferdi peeked inside. Dust mites floated into the light stealing in. His eyes fell on the spot where the small desk used to sit, from which he had once stolen the signet ring.

Outside Sandor's room Ferdi stopped before the closed door, his knees suddenly weak. *Come on, Mozart.* He grasped the handle, squeezing it for some time until the bronze grew warm, and turned it.

The door was locked.

Ferdi rested his forehead against the polished wood, and softly banged his head against it. He recalled Erzsi's words.

How wild, how splendid!

He laughed then, quite unaware of himself.

*

When he got back to the Gedeons', the apartment was empty. Ferdi had lunch, cleaned up, and then saw Balint's glasses left on top of the fridge. He smiled; Balint would regularly forget them, popping back at odd hours to squint around for them.

Had they guessed that Ferdi would never be coming back? Did Gabriella know that tomorrow would be the last time they saw each other? Maybe she did. Or maybe, having seen more of life, she had a different concept of time. Maybe she knew that sometimes people collided again unexpectedly. He couldn't say; he was glad not to know certain things.

The doorbell rang. Ferdi picked up Balint's glasses and hurried to the front door.

'Got them!' he shouted.

He threw the door open, and his heart leapt. There was Petar, with the letter crumpled in his hand. And on the boy's face a slight, ambiguous smile was beginning to form.

Acknowledgements

Thank you to:

My family, for their manifold support throughout years of writing; the Fairlight Books team for their valuable editing advice and dedicated work; Jason, for his keen eye for detail and unending support; Ipek, for being the first reader and for providing me with all the pencil lead I could wish for; Éireann, for running the cosiest writing residency where part of this was written; Gianna, for her advice; Myrto, for giving me a place to stay in Budapest; and Anthony, for believing in me from the start, and who was gone before he could see this book.